RAVEN

BIRDS OF FLIGHT - BOOK TWO

J. M. ERICKSON

Raven: Birds of Flight—Book Two (2nd Revision)

Editor: Suzanne M. Owen

Cover design: Cathy Helms
Avalon Graphics, LLC
http://www.avalongraphics.org

Layout and eBook conversion done by eB Format
http://www.ebformat.com

Publisher: J. M. Erickson
Blog - https://www.jmeindieblog.com
Publisher website - http://www.jmericksonindiewriter.net

ISBN (MOBI Format): 978-1-942708-33-9
ISBN (ePub Format): 978-1-942708-34-6
ISBN (Softcover): 978-1-942708-35-3

Printed in the United States of America

Praise for *Raven: Birds of Flight*

"J.M. Erickson's writing style is exact and linguistically flawless...In addition, he subtly builds the suspense to a breaking point, creating a climactic scene that is both aesthetically rewarding and realistic." – *Independent Professional Book Reviewers*

"The writer refers to true-to-life events, contributing to the realism of the story in its descriptions of Military Intelligence strategies, ambushes and the realities of intellectual terrorism. – *Readers' Favorite Reviews*

"An ambitious thriller that looks at the gray areas between vengeance and justice, law and morality." - *Blue Ink Review*

"Erickson has created a taunt suspenseful thriller sure to entice fans of Clancy, Flynn, and Ludlum. Intertwining current events from across the globe brings a sense of realism to the plot." - *US Review of Books*

"As with "Raven," the author uses his extensive knowledge of psychology to create characters that are complex and multi-dimensional." – *Readers' View*

"...*Raven: Birds of Flight* proved to be an exhilarating thrill-ride filled with exciting action scenes and dramatic plot developments." – *Independent Professional Book Reviewers*

"Erickson depicts government agents, spies and rogue operatives as well-rounded characters with discernible inner lives." – *Kirkus Review*

"...This book is full of unpredictable twists and turns, and I particularly appreciated the sense of realism in this story..." – *Palmetto Review*

Other Works by J. M. Erickson

Action/Adventure Thrillers

Albatross: Birds of Flight—Book One
Raven: Birds of Flight—Book Two
Eagle: Birds of Flight—Book Three
Falcon: Birds of Flight—Book Four
Flight of the Black Swan

Action/Adventure Science Fiction

Future Prometheus I: Emergence & Evolution—Novellas I & II
Future Prometheus II: Revolution, Successions & Resurrections—Novellas III, IV & V
Intelligent Design: Revelations
Intelligent Design: Apocalypse
The Prince: Lucifer's Origins
Future Prometheus: The Series
Intelligent Design: Revelations to Apocalypse
Rogue Event: Novella
To See Behind Walls
Time is for Dragonflies and Angels

"...And he sent forth a raven, which went forth to and fro, until the waters were dried up from off the earth.

Also he sent forth a dove from him, to see if the waters were abated from off the face of the ground;

But the dove found no rest for the sole of her foot, and she returned unto him into the ark, for the waters were on the face of the whole earth: then he put forth his hand, and took her, and pulled her in unto him into the ark.

And he stayed yet other seven days; and again he sent forth the dove out of the ark;

And the dove came in to him in the evening; and, lo, in her mouth was an olive leaf pluckt off..."

Genesis 8:7-11; King James Version

Prologue

"Forsan miseros meliora sequentur" - "For those in misery, perhaps better things will follow" Virgil

"DAMN IT! DAMN IT! DAMN IT!" Foreign Intelligence Agent Alexander J. Burns said repeatedly as he ran down the final set of steps onto the street. Burns was having difficulty firmly holding onto his semi-automatic weapon and pushing another ammo clip home as he bolted through the front door. His neck snapped left and then right, looking for his target until a dark van came to life and roared away.

He pursued it, stopped and steadied his aim, but didn't shoot. He knew he would never hit the driver at that distance. Frustrated, he frantically looked around for a car, unaware of the onlookers' fearful expressions as they watched him—a man covered with blood and holding a gun, obviously in a rush.

Ignoring the civilians' screams, he looked ten feet ahead of him and saw a man getting into a car, oblivious to his surroundings and the commotion behind him. As he came up from behind, he pushed the man onto his own car. The forceful thud was just as surprising to Burns as it was to the man who was reacting not only to the push and crash, but to the burn of his coffee on his chest.

"Federal agent! I need your car! Keys! Give me your keys, damn it!"

"What? What do you want?" the man yelled.

The man was in shock as his briefcase contents and coffee spilled all over him, car hood, and ground. Burns snatched the keys from the dazed man's extended hand above his head.

"Federal agent! Get out of the way, now!" he yelled. With the keys in his possession he pulled the man away from his own car and jumped in. Burns gave no time for the car to idle. His foot pressed to the car floor as he threw the car into gear to pursue his target. With sounds of other cars honking and brakes screeching, he focused ahead to spot where the van had sped off to. As he felt the car respond to his driving, he tried to wipe the blood off on his pants so he could better handle the steering wheel. His target's two bodyguards did not give up easily. While using one man as a shield, he had to shoot both men at close range, leaving their blood on his hands, arms and chest. Burns didn't even have to think in that situation. They were going to kill him. He focused back on the road and saw his target weaving in and out several car lengths ahead of him. Burns nearly crashed into a car going the actual speed limit.

"Move. Move. Move!" he yelled at the senior driver.

Pains in the asses! Damn civilians, he thought.

Burns's mind was whirring along as he calculated how far he was from the Golden Gate Bridge, the target's van, and how the hell he was going to stop them before they completed their mission. He felt his chest and grip tighten as he pushed down harder on the accelerator, a surge of anger flooded him at the thought of them getting away.

"No way! Not today! Not with me on your ass!"

Burns became conscious of someone calling his code name, *Falcon 5*, in his ear. He shook his head to clear his thoughts. Finally, he was closing in on his prey. With his heart skipping beats, he saw he was within twenty feet of his goal as they both closed in rapidly on the famous bridge. As the voice in his ear receded, he felt his pulse racing even faster and his eyes darting left and right, looking for something, anything, he could use as a weapon in addition to his car and gun to stop the target's van.

Suddenly, his plan became clear as he now moved slightly ahead of the target's van with a minivan between them. On impulse, he steered right in front of the minivan, forcing it to collide in front of the target's van. The target's van crashed into the minivan. Burns slowed his car to drop behind the van and then he accelerated into the van's rear, causing it to spin as the minivan flipped over to its side. He heard a cacophony of braking vehicles, horns, and yells as he felt his own car lurch toward the now spinning van. With eyes blinking from the sting of salty sweat, he focused on the van as it finally crashed into two other cars against the guide rail before tipping on its side.

The surge of victory passed when he felt his body lurch sharply to the left after hearing crunching car metal from behind his own car. While centripetal force pressed him against the driver's door, he felt his entire left side press even harder into the car door as his own car's spinning was stopped by hitting a huge SUV.

Dizzy, dazed and slightly nauseous, Burns reoriented himself. *Van... explosives... yeah. Kill the bad guys. Defuse the bomb.*

He looked around and finally found his gun, and pulled himself through the passenger car door. He was confused for just a second.

Where the hell did the door go?

He lifted himself off all fours as his dizziness subsided. He spotted the target's van amid the smells of burnt tire tracks, oil, and scraped metal. He turned to look behind him to see misshapen cars in various stages of destruction littering the road. There were civilians slowly evacuating the area. Burns focused on his target's van, now lying on its side. There was some movement near the shattered windshield.

"Not for long."

He checked his gun to make sure a bullet was in the tube as he walked silently toward the target. He could see the target slowly kicking out the shards of remaining windshield as he tried to get through it without further injury. By the time the target was fully aware, Burns had his weapon leveled at his chest. He felt some satisfaction as the target's eyes widened, clearly not expecting anyone, especially someone with a gun trained on him, to be there watching. Burns immediately thought of Debbie Foley, an analyst whom he had been just getting to know, and whom he would never see again. A pixie of a woman with blonde hair, sharp as a tack, and funnier than anyone he knew. They were both supposed to be in New York, but intelligence separated them in different places. He was sure he could have saved her if they were together. He felt chills and his blood run cold as his finger slowly depressed the trigger.

She's gone because of you and your friends.

"No!" the target yelled as he sprung toward him before he was shot. Burns felt the corners of his mouth curl up as he pulled the trigger repeatedly, hitting the target dead on in the chest. Once the gunshots cleared, the noise of civilians' screams started to trickle into Burns's consciousness. He felt his breathing slow and his pulse dropping to normal as he made sure his target was dead. Convinced that his prey was defeated, he surveyed the destruction all around him until his attention honed in on a very unfamiliar sound. Typically, he would point his gun in the direction of a strange noise, but this one sounded like an infant crying. Lowering his gun, he felt almost paralyzed as he followed the sound's source to the demolished minivan he had used in a pincer maneuver to crash the target's van. The cold chills returned and poured out of every skin pore as he felt his pulse jump and his breathing grow shallow. Still unable to move, his thoughts raced to an obvious question.

If that's a baby, where's the mother?

~

Operations Director Eric I. Daniels leaned back in his chair, stroked the sharp stubble on his face, and forced himself to appear calm. His sitting still was in sharp contrast to the frenzied yet deliberate activities of his team members. They were multitasking different theaters of war through their monitors. He looked at the clock. Only a minute had passed since last he looked. To distract himself from obsessing about the time, he reviewed the last ninety-six hours as a way of focusing on something constructive rather than the anger that welled inside him.

He felt his eyes narrow and his heart fall heavy as his mind went from silence to darkness in a flash. While *Falcon 2*, Ron Shaffer, had effectively coordinated with local authorities and stopped a group of terrorists from attacking the Eiffel Tower, *Falcon 7* had been killed in a firefight with terrorists attempting to take over a plane in Heathrow. *Falcon 7*, Debbie Foley, was an excellent counter-terrorist analyst, but she was not a field operative like Maxwell and Burns.

Every time he thought of her, his jaw clenched and his heart sank more. If he could do anything over again, he never would have sent her. While spirited, feisty and smart, she was not trained to handle volatile, hostile situations. He had planned to put Burns and Foley together in New York, but the intelligence gathered required him to spread resources. Daniels, Alexander Burns, and Anthony Maxwell had spent months tracking chatter and leads of what seemed to be disconnected intelligence at first. Deb Foley and Ron Shaffer had joined the team just a couple of months prior and helped piece together the puzzle that pointed to coordinated attacks at London's Heathrow Airport, Paris's Eiffel Tower, and the U.S.'s Golden Gate Bridge and Hoover Dam. Webber had been working on what seemed to be a third part of the attacks, but he was bogged down with more disconnected data pointing to something about airport security and airplane maintenance.

But what? Daniels obsessed. *Was it all Heathrow? Is it a bomb of some sort?*

The attacks in London and Paris occurred around dinnertime— when a great deal of people were either on their way home or out for the evening on a Thursday night. Daniels found himself shaking his head.

"How many civilians would they have killed? The whole world is just spinning out of control," he had said repeatedly throughout the day. As September seventh had been the day for the European attacks, today, September ninth, was clearly the day for the American attacks. Earlier that day, Shaffer and Burns did generate a possible theory that the next wave of attacks after today were coordinated to strike civilian targets at the height of congestion, such as civilians at lunch, commuting, heading home, dinnertime or any time when a lot of people would be in one place. Additionally, the attacks were moving from west to east, which was confirmed when Maxwell completed a late night, preemptive strike on the terrorists' apartment on September eighth where intelligence found at the scene indicated that the launch date and time was set for 12 p.m. on September ninth—the time when a large number of tourists would be at the Hoover Dam. It was up to Burns to locate and eliminate his target before 12 p.m. on September ninth.

Daniels pulled his thoughts to the present. Convinced that the ten minutes he experienced had transpired, he sighed when the clock indicated only two had passed. He turned his sights back to his middle manager, Thomas Webber, who was adjusting his headset's volume control to get a clean signal from *Falcon 5*. He fought the urge to jump up and snatch the microphone away from Webber. Instead, he sat, stroking his hairy chin, wondering whether this assault on American soil would end well. He felt more moisture on his hand from his chin. He then became aware that he was sweating from his hairline, forearms, and the sides of his torso. As he leaned forward, he also noticed his shirt was sticking to his back as he felt new sweat droplets stream down his sides. Perspiration was the norm in the small Operations Center, which had never been designed to hold the twenty analysts at the same time. He looked slowly around the room. Daniels could smell fresh human perspiration as his team watched for any new intelligence across its particular field of analysis. He was uncomfortable with hair on his chin magnified by stress and heat. Still, there was no time for shaving, or anything for that matter, as every second counted to get ahead of the terrorists' plans. Webber was being trained for field operations, but teaching him to exude calm and authority was difficult.

How do you teach "acting" in the battlefield with live fire?

After looking at the clock again, Daniels knew he had kept his pulse normal by concentrating on his breathing and monitoring his body. He also knew he would continue to check the clock every sixty seconds until *Falcon 5* either answered or until he took over from Webber. With that in mind, Daniels decided if *Falcon 5* didn't contact Webber, he would make contact himself. While his picking up where Webber left off would change nothing, at least he would be doing something and get Webber out of the hot seat. Nobody liked him. Under normal circumstances, Daniels would have let his middle manager run his course, but these were far from normal circumstances.

After rapid deployment of resources the night before, *Falcon 4*, Tony Maxwell, had effectively stopped a small team of Muslim fundamentalists from taking two trucks rigged to explode across the

Hoover Dam. While the damage to the dam would have been minimal, the number of tourist deaths would have been well into the triple digits. More importantly, it would have been a significant blow to America's safety within its own borders. His attention returned to listening to Webber's attempt to make contact with *Falcon 5*.

"Falcon 5! Are you there?" Webber asked more urgently than Daniels wanted.

Calm down. Relax. Everyone is looking to you for strength.

There was silence. He could feel the tension increase exponentially as his team members started to drown in their own sweat.

Of course, they're sweating. It's a thousand degrees in here. We need better air conditioning, he thought. The Operations Center's modified computers' electricity produced both heat and fused circuit smells that stayed well ahead of all the fans and the air conditioner's capacity.

In addition to the smell was constant background noise from engines and processors of every shape, size and power, all producing a discernible rhythm. Whenever the background noise shifted, Daniels could easily tell.

Someday, we'll have more money to do it right. Bigger air conditioning. Air filters. Larger screens with multiple feeds. Sound insulation. Yes... someday... Daniels thought as he looked back at the clock.

Sixty seconds again. Just like the last twenty-eight "sixty seconds."

Without saying a word, Daniels stood up from his chair, walked up to Webber and put a reassuring hand on his shoulder to indicate that he would take over. Startled, Webber jumped at first but then relaxed after realizing it was his boss. It took a moment, but he saw that Webber picked up on the non-verbals and turned off his microphone as Daniels turned his on.

"Falcon 5? This is Falconer. Do you copy?"

Daniels knew his voice was soothing and regal.

There was continued silence. Daniels's immediate thought went to Deb Foley.

If you're dead, you won't pick up. Don't let me down, Burns, he thought to himself. His mind fell back into silence and then a voice crackled to life.

"Falconer. This is Falcon 5. Target eliminated. Threat being disarmed by hazmat and bomb squad. Over," Burns responded.

Air seemed to fill Daniels's lungs. He breathed for what seemed to be the first time in thirty minutes.

"Thank God this went right," he said to himself. So many things could have gone wrong. Some things did, he regretted.

One disaster at a time.

"Falcon 5. Status report," he requested.

Instead of a rapid report, there was a disturbing silence. Daniels couldn't figure out what bothered him most about Falcon 5. Was it the long pause and his subdued voice when he eventually spoke? And when he spoke there was a lack of the detached, curt reporting that Burns was known for. With both of these happening simultaneously, Daniels could tell something was wrong.

"Target is dead. A van with TNT, nails, and a dirty bomb were discovered and both are being diffused."

The tension jumped again in the cramped room, and Daniels swore he could no longer hear anyone breathe. Even as he contained his own emotion, he felt his muscles tighten along his back and at the corners of his mouth and eyes while his hands clamped down on his hips.

Shit. A dirty, nuclear bomb. This is pretty serious.

"Do we need to evacuate the bridge?" Daniels calmly asked.

Not that that would do anything.

The pause seemed shorter this time, but Burns still sounded subdued.

"No. Both teams believe the threat is averted. Perez and Martinez secured the terrorist's apartment with the local police. More Intel. All is well."

Daniels looked to his left and saw two official screen shots of Jose Perez and Marie Martinez, Burns's hand-picked support team on one of many banks of computers. Ruthless, skilled and experienced, Daniels didn't like them one bit; he didn't know them. Burns recruited and kept them off the books.

His eyes narrowed as he took in each of their relatively blurred images. The pictures were official as in they were the only ones they could get from surveillance. Again, Daniels was drawn back to Burns's voice. It was subdued. It was different. It was wrong.

"But there was a civilian casualty. In order to stop the van, I involved a smaller vehicle that killed the driver," Burns said.

Daniels felt a sea of eyes fall on him as the last sentence reverberated through the speakers. He felt his teeth gnash and his fists tighten in anger.

Goddamn it! Two deaths in Lansing two years ago. One in Chicago before that. Jesus Christ, Burns! We're here to protect civilians, not kill them.

Silence filled the crowded room as he turned away from the monitor to think. His jaw, back, and fists clenched up. Even with his anger he still heard more in Burns's voice: is that regret in his voice? Burns responded before Daniels could say anything more.

"The child in the backseat is alive, Director. I... I'm sorry about the woman..." Burns's voice trailed off.

Daniels felt his jaw and fist release as he thought about what changed in his number one field operative.

So there it is. It's not the fact that the bad guys got their hands on a sophisticated weapon and nearly detonated it on U.S. soil. He killed a child's mother. Maybe there's hope for you, after all. Come to think of it, he was upset with Foley's death, too. That's unusual for Burns. Maybe...

Daniels pulled back and focused on the present.

"Are first responders on scene?"

"Yes," was Burns's short response.

"All right. Make sure the area is secured, and we'll coordinate with Maxwell to get you home. And I take it your support team will simply disappear?"

"Yes," he said.

That was one of many things he did not like about Perez and Martinez, too; they could appear and disappear without a trace. Daniels had tried for three years to find them. No go.

I don't like that at all.

Daniels was about to sign off when Burns asked an important question.

"Director? Is the CIA and Bureau aware of the potential threat on the East Coast and the timeline?"

Daniels felt a sudden rise in his blood pressure and was certain he felt one of his famous bloody noses coming on at the mere mention of his sister intelligence agencies.

While the Foreign Intelligence Agency was the brain child of the Department of Defense and relatively new to the intelligence game, its track record for data collection and analysis were remarkable. Four terrorist attacks thwarted in two days with all operations documented via live audio-visual feed to confirm the center's effectiveness to the non-believers, and yet he was positive that both the CIA and Bureau were not taking his team seriously. Daniels was plagued with the absurd vision of comparing himself to Galileo trying to convince the church bishops to look through the telescope to see the other planets.

With a deep, cleansing breath, Daniels spoke with as little enmity as he could muster.

They are more than aware of our projections, Falcon 5," Daniels answered.

Burns's response was rapid.

"They don't believe that the next attacks will probably be on the east coast in two days, do they, sir?"

Daniels had to admit that Burns could read the situation pretty well.

Assholes! All this data and they want to keep it all quiet and to themselves. God, I hate that!

While breathing in through his nose he made sure a blood vessel didn't burst. Daniels put on his best stoic face, and with regal voice responded to Burns and his entire team. *Acting.*

"Falcon 5, we all have our orders. You did a good job today. You and the others. You kept this day from being a national tragedy. You kept America safe. Come home so we can continue to keep it safe. I need you rested and in the Operations Center early Sunday. If the pattern of attacks is accurate, and all this started in London, that means the next wave of attacks will occur on the U.S.'s east coast and probably in the early morning. That said, I need everyone back here to narrow the field. Webber thinks it's going to be launched from D.C. I'm betting New York—"

"Boston," Burns blurted out.

Daniels was caught off-guard. It was an unusual and unsettling feeling to be surprised. He did not like the feeling at all, especially when he couldn't understand it. Daniels rapidly reviewed everyone's assessment.

Maxwell thought it would be from there, too. Less security, high concentration of people. Shaffer wasn't sure, but he didn't rule out Boston.

He had alerted his superiors to concentrate their focus on Boston and New York, but he knew his warnings were not being seriously considered.

"Either way. I need you all back for re-deployment."

"Acknowledged," Burns answered.

Finally, a classic Burns response. Short. Sweet. To the point.

Daniels closed his microphone and took his headset off as he returned to his elevated chair and cold coffee. He saw that Webber was dutifully pulling in the recorded audio-visual feeds to be filed for review, evidence, and storage. It was easy to see that Webber was under a lot of stress to pinpoint the next wave of attacks. His specialized area was terrorist cells in Afghanistan and Pakistan, and it was still unclear who was behind the attacks. Data seemed to indicate at least two separate groups were coordinating efforts and resources. One was led by an unknown player named Oman Sharif Sudani. The other terrorist leader was still in the shadows. Personally, he was of the opinion that Sudani was orchestrating all this drama as subterfuge for a large attack.

That's why I need Maxwell, Shaffer, and Burns back here, he pondered as he returned to stroke his chin. *Webber has skills, but he's not an analyst like the others.*

Daniels also noticed that his teams were taking brief moments to stretch back in their seats, breathe, and wipe more sweat from their brows. For the first time in weeks, he could feel a smile pulling at his mouth. It felt so different to have his jaw relax from the tightly clamped position he'd experienced for months now.

What a group. They've been glued to their posts for days with barely a break. What a team.

Daniels allowed himself to enjoy the moment before his mind shifted back to the next possible target date, September eleventh.

"Where are you going to attack next, you bastards?"

He looked at a projected, magnified section of the U.S. East Coast. His thoughts also drifted back to Foley.

What sacrifice. What dedication. What a damn shame.

He looked closely again at Boston and wondered whether the attacks were really going to happen there. *Where are you going to attack next?*

"God, I hope I'm wrong," Daniels said to himself.

Chapter 1

"Forest fortuna adiuvat" – "Fortune favors the brave" Terence

OF LATE, WARRANT OFFICER Diane Welch found herself thinking more about her past when in the field. After fourteen years in the Marine Corps, she was tired and hated the mission she was executing. Earlier that morning, she emerged from an unusually pleasant dream where she was back home listening to her husband's singing while the kids played games and the smell of chili permeated the air. When she awoke, she found herself more depressed than usual because the dream was so real and faded so quickly. As she lay awake before dawn, she found herself wishing she could at least hear the familiar background noise of battle, but there was nothing but wind. Even during "peaceful" times, some battlefield sounds were always in the distance in Afghanistan.

But here, well within the borders of Pakistan, there were only quiet murmurings above the noise of shifting winds and sands. Welch hated the lack of familiar noise, and she hated the small group of counterintelligence specialists who were tagging along on her mission. She was having more vivid dreams that attacked all her senses as she slept. All the dreams shared two opposing themes. They were either crystal clear images of being home with her husband, kids, mom and friends or they were cold, dark sights, sounds and smells of dead and dying soldiers. Falling asleep of late had been a crapshoot of either being sad upon waking from a pleasant dream or being depressed when waking up from one of her dark, death dreams. Fearing she might fall asleep again, she got up from her rumination to face the day.

God, I hate this place.

She felt her muscles resisting her attempts to stretch them out.

"You know... after fourteen years, you can retire. No one's pushing you to stay," she said to herself.

Welch pulled her gear together and after surveying her immediate surroundings, she found herself conducting a headcount of her troops as well as keeping track of "the other guys" as she called them. She knew she was running an "off the books" black operation when she needed to run nearly every operational decision by a short, balding arrogant man. Welch was truly baffled by the dichotomy of how this man's shadow sported a round middle as the sun reflected off his sweating, bald head, and yet he carried himself as if he were American royalty.

He really thinks he's someone important. Even his name, Thomas "Steel" Webber screams of arrogance and idiocy. What the hell?

Welch knew it was her nature to be consistent and level-headed; she was a creature of discipline and duty. Her troops were loyal to her because she respected them and made it her personal business to keep them safe. She was proud that she had one of the lower casualty rates in her unit and still completed every mission thrown at her. Still, the young men and women lost under her command were not taken lightly—she hated writing the letters home to the fallen soldiers' parents, spouses, and loved ones. The worst moments were when she would sit and think about what to write the next of kin about their son or daughter or spouse's special quality or talent and how the person would be missed. She always felt it. After having her own kids, the deaths were somehow worse as she felt a piece of herself slipping away every time there was a casualty.

She had a particularly bad feeling about this mission because it was a wild card at best. And while she insisted on professional courtesy and discipline, she allowed her men some latitude in regard to Webber and his crew. While the "other guys" were referred to as "assholes," Webber's group called him "sir" or "Steel." His undisclosed rank was confusing, but it was clear her superiors wanted critical orders to be cleared by him. He also kept his entourage, three similarly mysterious, counter-terrorist specialists, near him at all times.

Who are these people? NSA? CIA? British Secret Service?

Welch could see that paranoia filled many of the gaps in his life. Unlike other counter-terrorist specialists, one of his specialists was a very attractive woman whose military occupational specialty was unknown.

And what the hell do you do?

Welch was continually assessing his team and their mission. While Marine Air Ground Task Force operations always involved Marines with various elements of their own branch, it was very unusual to have a command group from the Department of Defense Foreign Intelligence Agency's Operations Center so directly involved. Another key giveaway that the mission was off the books was its conducting human intelligence and counterintelligence in the Swat Valley, Pakistan. Far from the borders of Afghanistan, miles away from the designated "battlefield," she found this mission's location, allies, targets and timing less than favorable.

Her dreams, paranoia, and her own edginess along with her men's were clear signs that the operation didn't feel right. Yet, she was a soldier, and she knew that many of the enemies' weapons originated from this very valley. If she could stop the flow of weapons coming into Afghanistan, it would keep her people from dying. She also knew that she was stubborn.

Maybe my dreams of death might stop if I close this leak.

At times like these, Welch believed the end justified the means. She quietly hoped this mission would not haunt her later.

Well, at least I didn't volunteer for this mission.

She often recalled her father's advice before she joined the service. Being a Marine himself, he was supportive but always worried about her career choice, and he had plenty of advice to keep her safe. Never volunteer. As part of her own immediate intelligence team, she had elements of a sniper/surveillance group and combat support service making up a full squad of fourteen soldiers. All the while, Welch watched as Webber and his minions constantly listened, watched and reported into command.

Which command? Is it ours or your "Operations Center?"

Every interaction between Webber and her group was always tense since she saw his team as nothing short of parasites—they took everything and offered little in way of information, tactical, strategic or otherwise. They depleted limited supplies and seemed to think they knew every damn thing.

Going against her better judgment, Welch kept her eye on the objective: find the weapons suppliers' cache and shut it down at all costs. She kept thinking of the soldiers who could be saved if she just shut the weapon flow down. Still, her gut kept saying to pass on the objective, report she could find the group and get out of Dodge.

But after nearly five days of searching, ducking, evading, and stretching the lines of communication to its limits, Welch and her team were finally near their objective. It took two additional days and two nights to confirm that the small hamlet she was observing at a distance held supplies of weapons smuggled in from Iran later to be transported by truck to Afghanistan. There was an additional bonus: two terrorist assets and three "persons of interest" came in on the second day.

This is a great day for freedom, she thought as she peered through her binoculars. Welch found herself smiling her "stressful smile" as thoughts of finishing this mission and a vision of returning home fluttered in her head.

Was that idealism? That's something I haven't thought of in a long time.

Then, like her dreams of late, pleasant thoughts shifted to darkness; she peered through her glasses again and saw an all too familiar sight. Typical of many terrorists operations, these terrorists had human shields—women and children—in the same town. Further, these human shields looked exhausted and malnourished as evidenced by their disheveled, gaunt appearances.

Just as Welch could see the patterns and rhythms of the days' shadows and winds, she could easily see that the hostages went back and forth from one building to the next every couple of hours until they were sent en masse to the other side of town, all while under constant guard.

She found herself angry and saddened by the hostages. If they weren't there, she could call in an airstrike, be done with Webber, and go home. But there were hostages, and wishing there weren't didn't make them go away.

Resigned to oath and duty, Welch did what she did best.

Time to become creative.

Welch knew Webber's view on the captives' lives was that they were more "bothersome" than worth protecting.

While on one level she could understand his thinking, she found herself feeling disgusted with herself that she had originally had the same fleeting thought that he kept articulating. She spent a couple of hours trying to figure out who was worse—Webber for his lack of concern for civilians or the terrorists for the same reasons.

Too close to call, she ultimately concluded.

Viewing the hostages in the town and talking to Webber was difficult. For days, Welch watched him constantly consuming liquids, fanning himself and complaining about the sun and sand. She had to suppress a laugh when one of her very young recruits, PFC Parks, a nice kid with a short trigger, lost it after one of his rants of it being too hot.

"We're in a fucking desert! It's usually hot and sandy!" Parks blurted out.

Welch had to take Parks aside and reprimand him. It was the usual speech she often gave him: "Damnit, Parks! Think before you speak!"

After the "incident," she observed Webber watching the young man with hate in his eyes. It didn't take a degree in psychology to see that Parks bruised his ego.

Not good, Welch thought.

She kept an eye on Parks from that moment on. She also asked Sgt. Thomas "Nine" Williams and Lance Corporal Daniel "Ice" Maddox to watch Parks just to insure the boy's safety. Welch knew why she liked Parks; he reminded her of her eldest son back home. While he was eight years older than her son, he had the same bright but impulsive attitude that she thoroughly enjoyed. Seeing Parks always reminded her of home.

Webber's plan of attack was simple. He wanted to call in an airstrike and destroy the entire town.

Nuke the town. Kill everyone. Women and children included. Have a soda and go home to play video games. Good plan, she sarcastically thought.

Welch spent more time than she wanted arguing for her plan, which called for destroying the weapons and capturing or killing the terrorists after they got the civilians to safety. It was easy to see that getting the civilians to safety clearly bothered him. Still, her plan was also real simple. All she needed to do was send in elements of her combat support team when the civilians were being moved, have the sniper teams take out the guards watching them, move them to a minimum safety distance, and, finally, drop predator missiles from above to soften up the surviving terrorists for capture.

"Easier than brain surgery," she explained to her men.

Parks laughed out loud at that one as Ice and Nine suppressed rolling their eyes. Still, if they could save the civilians and also get prisoners for intelligence in addition to destroying enemy weapons, lives would be saved. While Webber reluctantly agreed to the plan, he was clear that he still favored leveling the site and going home.

We all want to go home... and where the hell is "home" for a creature like you? Welch kept thinking as she obsessed about every detail to keep her men and civilians safe.

With very little sleep and continued tweaking of her plan, she was both grateful yet worried that she couldn't remember having any dreams. She wasn't necessarily superstitious, but she didn't like the change of going from having dreams to suddenly not.

I worry, but it's about the big things.

Welch didn't even bother to attempt sleeping. Sitting quietly as she went over the plan again in her head. Nine quietly approached her with his usual serious presentation and eyes scanning everywhere.

"Ma'am. Thought you should know that Ice woke up from one of his power naps. He had one of his dreams," he said, making eye contact at the last part.

Welch felt her chest tighten as she wanted to know what the dream was, but she still needed to proceed with the mission. She was truly ambivalent about Ice's Ojibwe background. While she admired his talents and skills, his belief that his dreams could foretell the future, good or bad, had an effect on her team.

Sighing, she decided to hear what the dream was all about.

Maybe it's good news, she hopefully thought.

"Fire and ruins, ma'am. Wolves packed together against bears with two ravens watching. Smoke, ashes, and sorrow," Nine said. He spoke as he continued his scanning. It's what he and Ice always did, never relaxed and always prepared.

Just great.

Nine continued before she asked her next question.

"Ice only told me, and we're not planning on sharing with anyone. Thought you should know."

Nodding, Welch gave him permission to continue his patrol.

"Thank you, Nine."

Sitting once again quietly, she sighed as she knew the dawn couldn't come fast enough.

Sleep is definitely off the table.

Before dawn broke, Welch dispatched eight of her men to enter the town and hide in the building along the route they expected the civilians to walk. She then placed four snipers at key points to insure the guards were neutralized and to keep the other combatants bottled up at the town's other end until the civilians were escorted out of danger. Once the civilians and her men were at a safe distance, she would call in predator missiles to rain down death. From Welch's vantage point, she could take in the entire fire zone, assess, improvise and alter the plan as needed.

A lot of moving parts, she had to admit. *Still, how many times have I done this?*

Pvt. Parks was the communication specialist who would call in the grid numbers for the targets; two of her snipers, Nine and Ice, would acquire additional targets to make sure the zone was obliterated. The other snipers would insure her men and civilians weren't pursued. Welch made sure all her snipers were armed with .338 Lapua Magnum, which had enough penetration in skilled hands to stop anyone and anything mechanized. Everything was in place and ready to go. Once things got moving, Parks and she would be critical in coordinating all aspects of the mission. Welch usually had her medic, Bobby "Red Cross" Calandra, with her on the radio, but she wanted to keep an eye on Parks and she needed R.C. close to her fire teams in case of wounded. With some final touches, the plan was good to go, she thought. Fortunately, it was not her team's first day on the job. They had been a tight group for nearly seven years. Longer than some marriages she knew.

As Welch found herself driven to completing this mission at all costs, she had a hard time understanding why this mission seemed more important than all her other ones.

Maybe it's the weight of losing a lot of good men and women from 2001 on, she thought. Hopefully, today's mission would save more. She did have one major reservation. Webber and his people, who typically acted as if they were playing a video game, were unusually quiet. Like her dreams, she didn't like this change either.

Welch didn't have long to focus on this behavioral change.

"Okay. It starts," she said more to herself, watching from her vantage point.

Parks picked up the first transmission from her squad.

"Nine to base; train is leaving the station. Seven women, twelve children, and four guards."

"Ice confirms."

Sweat started to fog up Welch's binoculars as a full minute later, more chatter finally came in:

"Ice has solid visual on train, and they're approaching the three quarter mark." Welch's grip tightened on her binoculars as she felt sweat dripping in her armpits. This always happened; she always got nervous once the mission started.

Welch: "Grimm? Your people ready to move."

Grimm: "We're green. Just give the word."

"Nine to base; activity is brewing. Looks like assets are getting ready to move."

Welch turned her attention to the other end of the town. There was definite movement. It looked like the entire band of bad guys was mobilizing to move everything out. This was going to be tough.

Webber had been watching and decided his input was necessary: "We gotta target those terrorists and weapons now."

Welch continued watching the activity in the town and was calculating distances and time to see whether all the moving parts were adding up. They were.

"We can do it all; we just need a minute to take out the guards and then we can move the civilians."

"There's no time to get them out. By the time you get them to minimum safety distance, the key assets will be gone," he complained.

Welch turned to look at him to reassure him that things were going to go according to plan.

"Webber, this plan will work!"

She turned her attention back to the fire zone. She knew it would be close, but killing innocents was not part of the plan, especially with her men in harm's way as well. She was about to update her teams and give the green light when she heard a shot from behind her. A sharp pain that felt like hundreds of separate thin shards of small glass suddenly pierced her side. Not needing to look, she knew her wound was in her leg and part of her torso. With teeth gnashed together, she inhaled a sharp breath and exhaled out one word in a low tone: "Shit!"

But it was the sound, the lone gunshot that echoed down the small rise to the hamlet that jumped to Welch's mind first.

Damn it... they must have heard it... she thought, fighting through the pain.

Welch rolled on her good side and saw that the radio had exploded and sprayed plastic and metal pieces everywhere. She next heard Parks cry out, "What the fuck!"

That's weird, she thought. *I'm feeling pain, and Parks is crying out.*

She turned her focus from the shattered radio to Webber holding a gun on her and Parks. Touching her side with her hand, she felt warm blood, cloth and dirt mixing. There was no question she needed help.

All her men—sniper teams and ground forces—were deployed, leaving her and Parks stranded with Webber and his team. With her team and the bad guys alerted by the gunshot, and no radio communication, she knew that Nine and Ice would support her combat teams and carry on with the mission. Once the battle was engaged, it would only be after the mission was completed that she could expect any support with the caveat they too survived. Even as she was weighing the options, she heard sporadic gunfire in the distance.

Welch turned to see whether Parks was all right, and with the exception of some superficial cuts, the boy seemed to be. Even though their situation appeared dire, she ran through various scenarios in her head to determine whether her own fire teams could protect her ground team and civilians, and maybe kill all the terrorists. Feeling suddenly dizzy, Welch realized that without the radio, there would be no air strike, no extraction, and no supplies—all were gone. As she continued her planning and pulled pieces of radio debris out of her leg, she watched Webber's female "assistant" talking into her own radio that seemed to have a direct feed into their Operations Center.

"Those bastards," she muttered. It became too clear how she and her team had been used.

Hoping that Webber was too distracted by his own voice and feeling in control, Welch slowly inched her way to her sidearm. Unfortunately, while Webber might not have any field experience, his team's watchful eyes noticed everything and moved quickly to seize her and Parks's weapons. She hoped Webber now felt confident enough that Parks and she were no threat and that he finally could do what he wanted, that his swaggering would lead to another of his self-indulgent rants. The more he talked and the longer he stayed, the greater the chance he would not focus on his objectives, allowing her team to do its job and help her and Parks out. As she surveyed her own situation, it took her milliseconds to deduce that she was partially correct; Webber would rant and carry on, but his team would stay focused, complete its own agenda and then get the hell out.

Damn it! I underestimated his team! I concentrated too much on him!

Welch looked out toward the battlefield while Webber dried the sweat from his forehead. That's when he started his proclamation.

"Diane, sometimes sacrifice is needed to obtain a greater good.

Today is one of those days. The greater good will prevail." Webber was preparing for a longer soliloquy, Welch suspected. It was always about staging for Webber, she cursed.

I don't have time for this! Welch's mind was screaming.

"Grids 304, 305, 306 are inputted, sir. Ops Center has control of two predators and will be here in thirty seconds... extraction is two minutes out," the assistant reported.

Welch felt Parks jump beside her and a wild look come over him. She knew Parks had been obsessing about the exact grid numbers of the fire zone so he could make sure there would be no "friendly fire." His reaction spoke volumes, and she instantly knew Webber planned on going back to his original plan: destroy everything in the town— terrorists, weapon caches, innocent women and children, and her ground forces.

My ground forces. The men I put there to protect the civilians. Damn him!

Welch attempted to get up to confront Webber, but the needle-like pain in her side and leg kept her at bay.

"Fuck... that's the entire town," Parks said. Welch then noticed that Parks's superficial cuts were deeper on the side of his arm and face, indicating he was close to the radio when it was hit and probably more injured than she originally thought.

Thinking of her boys at home when she reprimanded them, she squinted her eyes and jabbed her index finger toward Parks to stand down. He must have seen that look before from an angry mother because he immediately stopped his behavior.

Welch had no time for drama. She reasoned that because Webber was egotistical, she had to make him believe he had a stake in not screwing up the operation.

"Webber... this is crazy... we can hit the town, save civilians, and still all get out of here."

To her own surprise she spoke calmly as she could under the circumstances.

Webber continued to look off toward the town's horizon, seemingly disengaged from all that was happening around him.

As the pain seemed to subside, Welch shifted strategies to give up on the civilians and focus on American soldiers.

"Please. At the very least, let my men get out. We're on the same team."

Guilt filled her heart as she gladly became willing to sacrifice the civilians now to save her men, the same men she had put there. It was clear that he was mesmerized by the ensuing battle below and was unmoved by her pleas and made no eye contact with her.

"Diane... I said, 'sacrifice.' All those brave soldiers' service will be honored..."

Welch felt the pit of her stomach drop and her blood run cold as she realized he was planning to kill her men. Forcing the pain away, she looked away from Webber and returned to the operation. Grabbing her discarded binoculars, she saw that the guards had already been taken out and that her ground forces had already rounded the women and children to get them out of the fire zone. She watched her snipers keep the terrorists pinned down, but they appeared to be regrouping either to counterattack or retreat.

"Ten seconds," Welch heard the female voice again.

Welch turned back to watch Webber standing over the crest, watching the events unfold as if it were a video game.

"Webber! That's murder!" she yelled. *So much for using logic or tactics.*

"No... those men are heroes, and the civilians are collateral damage. You should be proud..." he went on.

He sure loves his own voice.

Welch turned back to the town. She felt someone beside her watching and knew it was Parks counting down the same ten seconds she was. As ten seconds turned into eleven, twelve and thirteen, Welch had a moment of elation as nothing happened.

Maybe the predator's damaged?

She looked at her ground forces and the train of civilians was moving; *maybe they can make it,* she hoped. Her stomach felt like lead as she helplessly watched her ground team miraculously move everyone within thirty yards from the town's walls.

"Come on, Grimm. You can make it. Move," Parks said quietly.

Even though she knew the town would be hit by a series of high-yield missiles, her heart jumped, startled by a series of flashes bursting along the town's horizon from east to west. In rapid succession, she watched the earth explode in nearly perfect intervals every twenty feet as the corresponding explosions ripped through the buildings, terrorists, and weapons. Against all reason and hope, Welch prayed that the explosions would stop halfway through the town. Instead, the explosions relentlessly marched along the entire length of the town and consumed everything in its path a hundred yards beyond the west end limits. Unable to watch the carnage any more, she dropped her binoculars and covered her face in her bloody hands. As she lay on the ground, absorbing the full weight of all those people's lives violently ending, she had an overwhelming, heartfelt vision of ripping Webber's face off and vomiting down his neck.

"Sixty seconds until extraction," a calm, feminine voice announced. Forgetting that Parks had been watching the entire nightmare without binoculars, Welch felt him suddenly jump up. He was only eighteen, and he had nearly dropped out of the corps until he transferred to her expeditionary force. She knew that if she felt like killing Webber, Parks would try it.

"You bastard!" Parks yelled as he turned toward Webber.

"Stand down, Parks!" Welch ordered. Her hand shot out to grab him, but Parks moved too quickly for her to get a good grip and Webber's men were well-trained enough to keep their distance and to keep guns leveled on them.

While gunshots, death and battlefield wounds were no mystery to Welch, the gunshot that hit Parks sounded unusually loud to her.

"Forty-five seconds, sir," Webber's assistant continued.

Forgetting her own pain, Welch was beside Parks as he dropped to his knees. He was holding his chest in disbelief that he was shot. Having seen fatal wounds before, she knew her role now was to provide comfort for his final moments. She was able to grab Parks when he fell from his knees onto his back. With her own leg and sides aching, she held him close and watched blood spider-web through his fatigues. She put her hands on his chest to apply some pressure, but there were too many wounds. She had a mixed feeling of wanting to take care of Parks and to kill Webber. With the town obliterated below, she calculated that the remainder of her squad would be there in two to three minutes. By then, Webber and his team would be gone and Parks dead. While she kept her eyes on Parks, she listened to Webber's team. With her ground troops killed, and Parks about to die, Welch figured that Webber would prefer no witnesses and would kill her next.

"Sir... our ride is almost here," the assistant said to Webber.

Clearly having summoned up some courage, he shortened the distance to get closer as she felt the sun blotted out by his portly shadow. Not wanting to give him the satisfaction of making it easier for him to kill her, Welch looked straight up at Webber's face. To her surprise, no gun pointed at her head. As he stood over her and her dying soldier, he issued one word: "Sacrifice." With that, Webber made his exit, leaving the female assistant to keep a watchful eye on her and Parks until he retreated.

How Webber got a helicopter into Pakistan was beyond her.

He had to have a secondary group in the same area with a number of assets to pull this off.

While it was too late, the ugly truth was that anything was possible with Webber and his team. This "operation center" was resourced.

Welch held on to Parks. She experienced the surreal feeling of emptiness as she seemed to watch everything unfold as if she were watching someone else.

How could I have underestimated him? How could I have screwed up so much? How did this mission get away from me?

But then, the whole operation was covert and off the books. There were no rules of engagement; there was no code of conduct. It was so painfully clear that her ambition to end the flow of arms made her team the perfect "search and destroy tool" that was also expendable.

From the distant, outside perspective of Welch's inner eye, she watched the female assistant talking as she was backing away toward her extraction site: "Mr. Webber wants you to know that if you and your team make it out, this mission is to remain classified. You will also

receive promotions, medals for valor, and any choice of assignments..."
As the woman kept talking, Welch pulled herself back and refocused on
Parks. It took two minutes for the helicopter to leave them behind. Glad
that she could finally talk to Parks without yelling, she wanted him to
hear a kinder voice than she typically gave him. He was fading fast.

"Parks, I've told you a thousand times to think before you act." It
was easy for Welch to slip into her maternal voice as memories flooded
back to her own children and her husband back home.

"Sorry, ma'am... I just get pissed sometimes."

God, I know.

"Me too, son..." she answered.

Welch felt a shiver run through her body as Parks's body shook a
moment. He looked up to say something... *was it "Mom?"* She could
have sworn Parks called her "Mom." Suddenly, Parks's eyes rolled
back and he was gone. She felt tension in his body release and go limp.

Conscious of her own breathing and warm blood on her hands, she
lost track of time. Memories of growing up in the projects of South
Boston flooded her. While many would say she was poor and the town
rough, everyone had seemed happy. The Marine Corps saved her from
crime and pregnancy. Her whole life was the service. She looked at
Parks. *This is someone's boy. Gone.*

Welch was roused out of her trance when she saw the last six
surviving squad members surrounding her as she continued to hold
Parks's body. She shifted her gaze to see that Ice and Nine were
surveying the horizon as R.C. closed in to talk to her.

She said nothing, leaving R.C. to talk first.

"Fuck me. Sir? Are you all right?" the medic asked. Her response
was to look at Parks one more time before she had to be a commander
again.

Welch looked up and saw that Nine glanced back at her but then
he silently returned to scanning the area. She knew he was a religious
man, but he was all about making sure no one else was killed. He was
looking for a target.

*You want a target? I'll give him a target! A fat, short, arrogant
son of a bitch target,* her mind seethed.

"Ma'am? Your orders?" Ice asked in an unusually soft tone.

"Orders?" Welch took a moment as she laid Parks on the ground, closed his eyes and stood up.

With blood on her hands, and her jaw and fists clenched, Welch discovered a new purpose in life.

"Orders," she said as she unclenched her hands to form an even tighter fist than before. Barely containing the vehemence in her low voice, she finally said something she was positive she could do.

"Here are your orders. Order number one—kill Webber. Oorah?"

Without hesitation, a resounding response rang out, "Oorah!"

There was a moment of silence. Welch composed her thoughts into words.

"If we plan to kill that slack-jawed, poor excuse for a miserable son of a bitch some day, I need everyone of you to stay alive, today," she continued as her voice gained strength with every "Oorah" she got from her men.

Standing to her full height of five-feet-nine, she felt anger and passion guide her words.

"We need to find weapons, communication, supplies, anything to stay alive. It may take days or years, but as long as I'm alive I will not let one day go by without taking another step closer to killing Webber. Oorah!"

"Oorah!"

Welch had never been a vengeful person until now. The search for weapons, communication and survival was on for one purpose: kill Webber.

He killed my people. Women and children. That son of bitch must pay.

How she got down to the still charred, smoldering ruins was a blur. As she explored the near moon-like landscape that was once a town, Welch entertained visions of escaping the desert, hunting that fat, balding bastard down, and burying her knife in his skull.

In addition to securing supplies, the most difficult detail for Welch and her team was retrieving the fallen soldiers' tags and bodies. Men and women she had worked with for years. And while she was still feeling raw from witnessing her team members and innocents be killed, she had to focus so she could find a working cell phone or shortwave radio, contact friendly NATO forces she knew were in the area, dig in deep, and kill any non-friendlies who came within two thousand yards of their perimeter.

And then kill Webber at some point in my life. Sounds like a great, new plan. Screw court and justice—kill that fat cow!

While her surviving team was in search mode she was not surprised they didn't ask what happened. She never reported to her team what happened, but it didn't take a rocket science to figure it out.

She tried to focus on the present. While the predators' bombing run killed all human targets and made impressive hits on the key buildings, it did not destroy everything. The landscape of the smoking, partially burning ruins made for an eerie background as her team searched for supplies.

There was a brief moment when she began to believe she might be lucky or that God might be watching as her team located a radio that was not completely obliterated. Feeling as if there might be light at the end of the tunnel, her hope skyrocketed when she discovered that her intelligence was right about NATO forces being in the area, just four hours away. As quickly as her hope for the future surged, it crashed within seconds of learning from NATO that it saw enemy forces heading toward Welch's location. The bad guys were about an hour away, drawn to her location as a result of the bombing.

You really fucked us over, didn't you, Webber!

While memories of innocent civilians and her soldiers perishing in flames at the whim of a small minded ego-maniac burned in her brain, she had no plans of dying no matter what. Welch dug in deep and prepared for battle.

You had your chance to kill me, Webber, and you missed. They're not going to do your dirty work for you. I won't be just another MIA or KIA. None of us will.

She looked at the horizon. She knew her team had fifty minutes at best to set up a defensive perimeter within the hamlet's ruins, and retrieve as many workable weapons as possible. Welch figured she had the element of surprise since the enemy had no idea how small and pissed her team was.

Well, if we can't kill Webber today, these poor bastards will have to do. Talk about victims of bad timing... I almost feel bad for them. Almost.

To ruin Webber's plan further, she was not going to be so close to rescue after he marooned them just to die an hour or two before the cavalry came over the hill. With their fallen brothers' dog tags in her pocket, and a small supply of workable assault weapons, grenades and rocket-propelled grenade launchers, she arranged her men to use all sniping first to keep the enemy at a distance. Every step the enemy took toward them, she wanted one bad guy dead. Welch knew this plan might work for about two hours, but after that their sniper ammunition would be gone and her team would have to fend off being overrun by a superior force. She planned to fall back in pairs deeper into the ruins when the time came. She made sure everyone was dug in deep.

In the pre-battle silence that preceded every desperate conflict, Welch typically found herself thinking of home. But this time, she thought of Parks calling her "Mom" and Webber saying, "Sacrifice."

As she took in her immediate team's position, she found herself smiling.

Baffled, R.C. asked, "Ma'am? Something funny?"

For the first time in months, Welch truly found her situation just too crazy to overlook. The irony of the last two hours were about to unfold in yet another turn of events.

How crazy is this? I mean really? How is this even possible?

Abandoned in the desert with dried blood on her hands, and untreated injuries along her entire body, she found herself feeling sorry for the incoming enemy.

She tilted her head in the enemy's direction as she responded.

"They have no idea what they're dealing with. We're a pack of hungry wolves waiting to strike. They picked the wrong Marines to screw with and the right place to die!"

From R.C.'s expression, she knew he had to be wondering whether she was fit for command.

She shifted gears and gave two standing orders: "No one else here dies! Live to kill Webber! Oorah!"

"Oorah!"

As the battle progressed, the hours seemed to tick by slowly. Welch and her squad held off hostile forces for nearly three hours. They were getting close to the end of their supplies, and everyone was hit to some degree. Welch knew her team would follow orders, though. They would not die. *Not today. That time has passed.*

She was sure they could hold out for maybe a half-hour more since the sniping was more effective than anticipated and they had good luck with the rocket-propelled grenades. Finally, she started to believe in God since she and her team had made it this far, considering all they had lost in the last five hours. NATO was still about an hour away when the terrorists and their allies decided that following an unknown force into a collapsed, burnt-out town was suicide and opted to cut their own losses and retreat. After three hours, the desert was quiet with a strong breeze blowing in from the west.

Once she was convinced they were safe, she sat quietly and said the "Lord's Prayer" while her men quietly listened, scanning the area for movement. R.C. sat and teared up. He always did when there were casualties. He was the "sensitive one," and an unspoken rule evolved that allowed the medic to cry in their group. Regardless of how it started, she just knew it was important that it happened. She had always assumed he cried so the other guys wouldn't have to. Looking at her chaotic surroundings with her bruised and bloodied men still alive, she watched with renewed anger how Ice and Nine never took their eyes off the battlefield.

Yeah. You want to kill Webber almost as much as I do.

Welch sighed after her prayer but then she saw Ice and Nine looking skyward as if something were falling. She and the others looked in the same direction. She caught sight of two dark birds receding into the horizon. Looking first back down to the ground and then to Ice, she saw that to a large degree, his dream had meaning.

Un-fucking believable, she thought. Sitting quietly, she prayed again.

As the hour passed, Welch could only imagine what it must have looked like when NATO ground forces arrived at the smoldering, leveled town. With three thousand yards of sand still littered with bodies and wrecked vehicles, it had to be a strange sight to find a shot up, filthy band of soldiers holding every kind of handheld weapon possible.

Because they were NATO forces, they included an embedded foreign journalist who saw the carnage and valor firsthand, and broke the news to the world via the Internet.

As Welch and her team were being transported back to friendly lines, she was already seeing Internet reports of "U.S. Soldiers Survive Modern Day Little Big Horn" and "Pakistan's Alamo Remembered" and "Yankee Allies Destroy Terrorist Camp." It was easy for her to see there was more bullshit to come.

It took only three hours for all the news headlines to speak of courage, loyalty to fallen comrades, and the noble fight against terrorists. Because the news agencies and major networks picked up this "positive" story, Pakistan's Militia Government confirmed the mission was sanctioned by it to allow its U.S. Allies to assist in locating and destroying terrorist camps. That she was a woman, mother of two young boys, and her husband a schoolteacher, just made the story sound perfect.

Once back at Command, wounds treated and families contacted, she gave her debriefing. She made sure to put in every ugly detail about the mission. But before she even started, she knew there was a problem. The mission "didn't exist." The briefings were classified, the real story buried, and the cover story was upheld: her team went to find terrorists and lost a good many of their own so more would live.

Next day, after checking in on her men, Welch was thrust into a meeting with her boss, reviewing the commendations, medals, and promotions coming for her and her surviving team. Recalling in vivid detail Webber's assistant telling her that "if they survived," they would all have their choices of commendations, medals, and postings, Welch decided she was done. She loved the corps, but she was done with it.

After she was dismissed, she returned to her bunk, looked at her family's picture, and made her decision to resign her post. She scanned the image of her husband's smiling, soft eyes. She was deviating from their long-standing practice of discussing big decisions before making them. As she smiled at her boys' faces, she realized that Joe never disagreed with her when it came to her career. "Professional courtesy," he would say. Welch placed the family picture down and squeezed fourteen years of blood, loss, sacrifice and memories into four sentences, resigning from the corps effective immediately following her tour of duty. She knew a firestorm of politics and shit would come her way.

While her boss initially asked her not to resign, he did very little to pressure her to stay. Since the look on his face indicated that he was truly puzzled, she was sure he would dig into the facts of the story, especially the cover-up. They had only worked together for a month, and eight days of that time he was off-base and she was in the field.

Several hours later, he came back to her with an explanation for his actions.

"I just got some insight as to the true nature of your last mission and your actual situation. I'm sorry, Welch. If I had known, I wouldn't have carried on like I did about medals, promotions, and shit."

With that, he turned around and left. She liked her C.O. While he was an older guy and by the book, she had to respect the man's integrity to admit when he was wrong.

Wish I'd gotten to know you better, Helms.

A full-bird colonel, the Pentagon, the entire Armed Forces Public Relations Department and two senators all applied pressure for her to lead the ceremonies, accept promotion, medals and everything. At first, Welch respectfully declined, and she might have gotten away with it but then her entire team declined as well. The mass refusal to accept recognition for valor could not be overlooked. She finally got pissed when a Pentagon attaché implied that her decision not to be forthcoming and positive about the publicity was "self-centered."

She had one response to that, "Make me." It was not her most elegant response, but her old South Boston, "D Street" neighborhood attitude reared its ugly head. Secretly, though, she knew her dad would've been proud of her if he were alive to see it.

Maybe he did see it all, she hoped.

When the Pentagon backed off and reported that it would not push her into public relations and would keep the award ceremonies short, Welch had to reiterate that she had no intentions of ever accepting the medals and would refuse any promotion.

Finally, she was called to her boss's office where she met Eric Daniels, Chief Operating Officer of the DOD Foreign Intelligence Agency. Upon entering the room, she first looked for Webber and then focused on Webber's boss. He might have been the nicest man on the planet, but Welch was too intent on burying her concealed combat knife into Webber's throat to notice.

Barely paying attention, she did finally hear that Webber would be "reprimanded," and that "America needs heroes."

Her focus honed in on Daniels like a heat-seeking missile as she nearly spat her words out at him.

"'Reprimanded?' He killed my men and innocent women and children! What does he have to do to get fired? Nuke an American city?"

She only remembered Daniels objecting to her sarcasm and then she tuned him out since an opportunity to kill Webber was not to be.

Not today. Some day. But not this day.

Welch felt her resolve solidify as she gave her best smile and declined to participate. When Daniels threatened court-martial and a dishonorable discharge, her response was "go ahead" as she enjoyed the look of genuine shock on his face.

That also got her attention.

Was this the first time someone had said, "No" to this asshole? Welch pondered. Helms stepped in and gave her permission to return to her bunk. Upon exiting, she could hear Daniels's voice yelling at her CO. She knew that career-wise, he took a bullet for her.

He definitely is old school.

Welch also knew that many of her peers, subordinates and commanding officers knew something more was afoot, but she prided herself on following orders no matter how tough.

I'm a Marine.

Based on her interaction with Daniels, she was waiting patiently for her court martial papers to be processed when Nine, Ice, and R.C. brought her a bunch of newspapers instead.

They were all smiles, yet they refused to tell her what was in the papers until she read it herself.

And for Ice and Nine to smile, it had to be big

Welch was not only right, but she was amazed. Once again, it was the press that saved her and the Internet that sent the message worldwide. The captions discussed how America's sweetheart, the ideal of a "courageous hero, wounded in battle" was now being picked on by the Marine Corps and "some covert agency." She knew that while this publicity would save her ass, it was a public relations nightmare unfolding for the corps.

Ice asked the question everyone wanted to know: "How did this get leaked?"

Welch sat down before she fell over as she guessed who had to be behind all this.

Helm? Really? Wow... he is an "old school" Marine. We don't leave anyone behind and we never die. We just regroup in hell...

She knew it had to be her boss who got the word out. With laptops and radios turned on as the first reports were starting to hit the air waves, the Internet was the first to compare her to the great Roman leader Cincinnatus. Every American and many U.S. allies were siding with her.

This is going to piss off that Daniels guy... and Webber... when I find you I'll kill you.

Twenty-four hours later, her boss, on "behalf of the corps," offered to release her early from her commitment. She had mixed feelings as the thing that had saved her life once so many years from the streets of Southie and made her whom she was, now was letting her go.

Five hours later, Welch avoided her going away party and took an earlier transport out. It was night when she arrived on a commercial flight at Logan Airport nearly fourteen hours later. With no parades, crowds or loved ones waiting for her at the airport, she had hours to reflect on her time in the corps. She was startled by her thoughts when the cab driver announced she was at her home address.

I'm home, she thought. *Is this one of those dreams? Am I going to wake up in Swat Valley?*

She hesitated before starting up her walkway as if to allow time for the dream to reveal itself so she could awake with sounds of shifting sands and distant battle. But as she approached the house and carefully put her hand on the door to give it a gentle push, she didn't wake.

I'm really home.

When she entered her home, she could hear her husband finishing up laundry in the basement. Joe had a thing about clean laundry. She felt a genuine, easy smile emerge from her mouth when she heard him talking to the family dog as it howled in unison with his voice. The next foreign thing she experienced was that her smile was devoid of both force and stress, and seemed to be naturally produced by relaxed muscles. In addition to smelling fresh spaghetti sauce, she could hear both boys arguing upstairs about whose turn it was to choose the video game. Welch took a moment just to breathe and feel the warmth of the home fill her lungs.

Her eyes filled with joy for the first time in months. Maybe she could do what Lucius Cincinnatus had done when he returned from war—plow the fields and prepare for harvest—Welch thought as she stood in full uniform. She knew someone would eventually notice she was home, so she waited and casually picked up a stack of mail as she considered different options. She thought it might be better to get a job in law enforcement rather than farming.

I hate gardening, she concluded.

She suddenly remembered that her old friend from Southie, Steve Andersen, might have connections with the state troopers. He had returned from Guantanamo three years prior as an interrogator for Army intelligence. He always had connections, she reminded herself.

Jesus! I gotta call Mom and Darlene too, she realized.

Suddenly, she heard her dog's collar jingling louder as if it were coming up from the basement.

It's great to be home, she thought. Tears erupted from her eyes as she remembered speaking to Parks's mother earlier that week. She had an overwhelming feeling of just how unfair it was that she was home while he was not.

He was so young. His whole life in front of him, snatched away because of my need to get a mission done... at all costs.

As she sat down and started to cry, she felt the dog leap into her lap and heard her husband's feet climbing the stairs.

Chapter 2

"Fluctuat nec mergitur" - *"It is tossed by the waves but it does not sink" Unknown*

I've definitely had better days, Denise Cratty thought. She took her time to take in the size of the room before she dropped her bag to the floor and pulled out her semi-automatic handgun for storage. Her last several months at the Department of Defense Foreign Intelligence Agency's Operations Center, Bravo Team, had been fraught with a series of ups and downs but more downs than ups. Prior to the Merrimack Valley Crisis, she remembered being described as open, approachable, and even "fun" to be around. Her leadership style was often seen as even, fair, and just. If you made a mistake, you always had a second chance to redeem yourself with her. Cratty pondered the old image of herself—long hair, nice perfume to lure her girlfriend closer, an easy smile. That was before her mother died, her partner left her, and her chances of adoption melted away. That was the good news; *that was just my personal life.*

Without thinking any particular thought, she smiled to herself while rearranging her locker. Shoving her bag and belongings in her locker, she thought back on how an ex-agent-gone-rogue had returned from the dead and set the Merrimack Valley in Massachusetts on fire. *Burns.*

Actually, that would have been better. Those were the "good old days."

When Burns did his Lazarus trick her operation was compromised and classified data was stolen under her watch. While she was exonerated for this significant breach, she knew it would never be forgotten.

Her smile mutated into a scowl. For reasons beyond her intellect, rearranging her bag to fill the narrow space was taking too much effort. It always did when she reviewed for the millionth time whether she had missed something back on that miserable May second. Because she had followed protocol to the letter and demonstrated leadership under fire, and "almost" apprehended the terrorist, she was allowed to hold onto her clearance and have a shot at continuing her command once the Operations Center was relocated. But her promotion vanished and her boss, Webber, was demoted. Cratty was no fool, though, for she knew that if Jillian Davis were not made the scapegoat, it would have definitely been her.

Once it was clear there would be a primary "Alpha" Operations Center and a secondary, backup "Bravo" Operations Center, she knew that if she were assigned to Bravo team, she would probably have a year at best before being pushed out. It was no surprise that Webber blamed her for his demotion.

"Taking vacation when the world is burning up is not a good plan!" Cratty said to herself. To her relief she slammed her locker door after finally finding her aspirin. If anyone were in the changing room at that time, she did not see her.

Cratty knew she talked to herself often, but it helped her think.

"Screw them. I can talk to myself if I want. My psych-evaluation said I was sane."

There was no response in the changing room. Cratty took a seat on the elongated bench and took her aspirin dry. Whenever she had a quiet moment, she rehashed obsessively how she got to her present point. Once she relocated to New York, she was hoping for a new beginning and to salvage her career. But with Webber assigned to Operations Center, Alpha in Virginia, that fantasy died a quick death.

Complicating Cratty's career was her coming under the scrutiny of Chairman Eric I. Daniels, the man who had made the Foreign Intelligence Agency what it was today.

What is Daniels's middle name? Ichabod? What does the "I" stand for, anyway? Who uses middle initials?

Cratty stood up to stretch her legs and cracked her spine for some relief. While there were many critics outside the agency, Daniels was the most vocal about "cleaning house" and having anyone "who let those terrorists go" be brought up on charges. Cratty knew the final nail in her coffin was when she declined to be on the team to apprehend Burns. She just could not bring herself to be part of a plan for going after not only Burns but his "entire crew."

"Burns's 'crew,'" she sneered in disbelief. She had access to the classified data on Burns's unlikely civilian crew now labeled terrorists.

Unbelievable! One of the more powerful counter-terrorist agencies was now targeting a prostitute turned nurse, a psychologist, and a mother and her baby girl. These people are the new faces of evil?

She might have believed it, but she found out how they were all targeted for elimination when Burns went of grid the second time. How they were victims of poor timing and place. How they did nothing wrong.

Cratty rolled her shoulders, shook off some of the anger and walked with heavy steps to her office. She was still flabbergasted by the thought that a baby was now the equivalent of evil. Head down, she focused on all she read.

Burns's official support group, Perez and Martinez, she could understand apprehending them; they were professionals and focused on their own agenda. But even they vanished with no desire to be involved.

But a baby? A mother? A blind therapist?

Before she knew it, Cratty had passed her office door. She oriented herself, sneered, and retraced her steps.

Maybe Daniels was right about something, she reluctantly thought. She didn't want to piss off Burns. Even though Davis explained her own shock that Burns could have used lethal force in their confrontation and had chosen not to, it did not minimize the level of dangerousness he could be driven to if he were so motivated.

Experiencing the damage Burns and these civilians inflicted firsthand was sobering.

They were just people with no training. And they did all this shit without civilian casualties. That's just not his MO. If this was the "old" Burns and he ever went back to his old ways, what havoc could he wreak? What if he decided to take lives next time around? I can't be the only one that sees this?

As a result, she was more interested in bargaining back critical and potentially embarrassing classified files in exchange for these civilians to get back their lives—the same lives her agency took away.

She pushed her office door open and moved right across the short, Spartan space and stood by the transparent glass overlooking the newly configured Bravo Operations Center. She left her office light off as there was enough light from below to dimly illuminate her small space. Her mind wandered as it often did of late.

Cratty knew both from personal and professional experience that there were things you could never be given back. Cutting a dark, motionless silhouette as she peered through the Plexiglas, she remembered reading the reports of Dr. Caulfield's wife's death. While never confirmed to be an Operations Center mission, it had all the telltale signs. That kind of thinking put an expiration date on her career, and her involvement in "the Burns case" was restricted.

Still, she thought, *if I'm pissed at what this place cost me personally, I wonder what I would be like if I were Burns.*

As Cratty finally felt the corners of her mouth curl inward, she still remained motionless as she watched her team below. Thinking about Burns always made her smile these days. But when it happened, she always felt it melt away as she remembered how her partner would come into the room or when she would hold an infant or when she would cook with her mother. With her hands clamping down behind her back, she felt an all too familiar frown emerge. With the sole exception of knowing that Burns had screwed Daniels and Webber, there wasn't anything for her to smile about.

Pretty sad... my only joy is knowing he's more pissed than me.

She knew anyone watching her from below would see a still, slim, dark, frowning figure and know it was her.

Wow. That would be unnerving. I gotta lot of hate going on. I should probably see someone about it.

Before leaving Massachusetts, she had said goodbye to a number of friends and colleagues. One person in particular was a social worker she and her partner had been working with to prepare for adoption.

Feeling both a bond and respect for the woman, Cratty just wanted to talk briefly with her to make sure her mental health was sound before leaving. Expecting a ten-minute meeting, she was surprised when it became a thirty-minute session.

Good thing she doesn't have another appointment, she remembered thinking.

Cratty never forgot the total surprise on the woman's face and how she professionally recovered in seconds. It became clear to her that her former therapist thought a lot more clinical work needed to be done and a ten-minute evaluation and "You're good to go" was not where the therapist was going.

Sitting back, her former therapist took on a more direct approach than Cratty had yet seen.

"Denise, we've worked together for a while. When you and Renee first came in about adoption, it was clear you were more invested in the relationship and a family than she was."

Cratty remembered all too well the sessions leading up to that realization. She felt her grip on her hands and her frown deepen even at the thought of Renee's name.

"At the same time," the therapist continued, "your last surviving parent, your mother, dies. The same woman you took care of toward the end of her life. The one who always supported you, including when you came out and in your pursuit of your profession and field."

Cratty began to re-experience the same clammy feel of perspiration under her armpits even as she recalled the last session.

Ma and Renee never liked my job. But Ma always supported me.

"And now your only place of success has been taken away—like everything else precious to you. Everything is beyond your control right now, and you want me to say, 'Happy trails; you'll be fine'? Denise, I would strongly urge you to stay here and find something more meaningful in your life. Find a way to heal."

She remembered her own flatness of emotions. It felt much the same as it did here in New York.

"If you must go, you have my number and can call me anytime. I have your contact information, so I will forward you two possible people I think might be a good match for you. Please use them," the therapist had urged.

Cratty hadn't. And worse, she knew she was depressed. It came out as controlling, sarcasm, and anger. It was so tiring to have all of these emotions eating at you.

So tiring.

"But at least I'm not stupid," she said to herself as she thought immediately of Webber.

It was easy to see that Webber's plan was to terminate her role as manager as soon as he showed the world that "terrorists like Burns can't expect to do what they do and live." She couldn't help but note the irony. When Burns was authorized by the government to destroy, kill and injure, it was patriotism, but when he was helping innocent people escape false persecution, sanctioned murder and bargain back their lives, he was a terrorist.

Again, she felt a sharp upward pull on her mouth as her frown evolved back into a smile.

"That kind of thinking might make you a collaborator," she said aloud to an empty room. She felt a smile grow at the thought of someone angrier than her. While she accepted that talking to herself helped her think, she also knew that few people wanted to talk to her. She knew she was radioactive.

Yeah... I need to see someone. This mood is killing me.

Cratty turned away from the Plexiglas and noticed her black blouse was more wrinkled than she liked. She had taken to wearing dark clothes. She remembered Jillian Davis would wear black clothes and would spend an inordinate amount of time pacing the Operations Center's control and observation rooms.

What would you think of me now, Davis, if you saw me, she mused.

With the irony not lost on her, Cratty arrived early to duty just as Davis used to.

"Where else am I going to go? Empty apartment? See my mom?" Cratty asked a bit louder than maybe she wanted. Even as the words came out of her mouth, she knew she was second guessing her decision to move to New York.

After a short time in New York, Cratty made decisions to keep busy to clear her head. She started with her hair by cutting it from shoulder-length to a short, cruel cut. An unexpected result was that it made her light blue eyes more piercing than normal. When she wasn't working, she would be swimming, running, weight training and spending an inordinate amount of time on the gun range. Cratty channeled her anger into shooting as she buried her sadness in work. While she was very much aware that her salary went mostly to her apartment and ammunition for the range, she found solace in her "quiet time" of either cleaning and maintaining her empty apartment, her weapons or researching any data she could access about Burns. The most constructive thing she did was stay away from alcohol. Alcoholism ran in her family, and she liked hard alcohol in particular. With strong motivation to drink, she made deliberate efforts to stay away from the stuff. Keeping busy and being distracted helped.

Cratty knew that other managers referred to her as "The Dark One." Back in Massachusetts, everyone wanted to work for Cratty. Now only sub-par performers were under her command for her either to fix or terminate. She remembered her old team had been very bright, articulate civilians.

Yes. That was a time when I smiled more at work too... the "nice" smile

Now, with little energy to expend on others, she knew she would need less energy managing people if she slipped back to her earlier career managing style of being a "hard ass, code confirming," military officer.

Bitch—yes. I wasn't happy then, either.

Hence, her dark clothes tended to be of paramilitary design. When one of her peers attempted to make conversation about her clothes, her response was, "I don't have time for matching." That ended the conversation. She smiled again at the thought of that last attempt to make small talk as she checked her emails. There were none. No personal ones like those she used to look forward to from her mother or Renee. Cratty felt her heart sink a bit and her fist clamped shut into a fist.

There's that loss again. Mom. Renee. Family.

Rather than use the two names her therapist in Massachusetts gave her, Cratty did go to the agency's employee assistance program for "support." The young, attractive female counselor meant well, but she had difficulty understanding why she was so "well-defended" and not open to new things. That was the last session she went to, but she still kept the two names on her bureau at home.

Since that time, it was not unusual for Cratty to be armed. While she kept her .45 automatic handgun in her assigned bin, she kept the holster and extra magazines on her person all the time. She also carried a fixed-blade knife and a concealable, collapsible baton. The spring-assisted knife that was a gift from Davis she kept at home.

If Davis could see me now...

With no interesting email and nothing to distract herself, Cratty got bored of her negative thoughts. She left her office and walked to the Operations Room. Her thoughts fluttered back to the young counselor's psychological use of "well defended" to her literally being well armed; she laughed at the irony.

Two ironies in five minutes, she thought. *Maybe today will be busy at least.*

By the time Cratty was at the center's locked door, her smile, even the dark one, was gone. As she entered the Operations Center, she took her time looking at raw intelligence and reports coming in over the monitors. While glancing at the larger monitors, she noticed all sections in the pit were operational except for Boston, Massachusetts, which was running "dark."

Without taking her eyes off the black monitor, Cratty asked, with a voice that was unmistakably pissed off, "What's going on in Massachusetts? Why is it running dark?"

She knew that even if Gandhi or Mother Teresa responded, she would find fault with any answer provided.

Unaware that Cratty was behind her, the unfortunate operator of that monitor bank nearly jumped out of her chair. Her victim was flustered but regrouped quickly.

"Sorry, ma'am... it looks like Alpha Team is running an operation and has restricted our access," the young analyst reported. As Cratty made eye contact with the analyst, she could see a burst of perspiration form on the young woman's forehead.

That was another thing about this team that annoyed her; *there are too many women working here.*

For every one male, there were three females. She liked working with men because there was typically no drama.

Cratty refocused on the monitor.

"Ahhh... the ultimate 'fuck you...'" she said more to herself.

"Yes, ma'am..." the analyst said.

Cratty closed her eyes at the analyst's response. She allowed an uncomfortable five seconds of silence to pass before she spoke next. Her delay was more out of frustration than to set a dramatic pause. Without even looking at the analyst, Cratty knew the speaker was Dillon. Everyone in the immediate area realized the speaker's mistake in responding as all of them did their best to focus on the most infinitesimal data that might stream across their monitors.

Taking a sharp intake of air, she spoke in a low and even voice as her hands clamped again behind her back. Even with her light skin, blue eyes and blonde hair, Cratty could feel herself becoming darker.

"Dillon, did I ask you to respond?" she hissed out.

Cratty knew Dillon's problem before Dillon knew it herself. That was part of the problem. The young analyst had a history of offering her opinion when not asked. To extinguish this behavior, Cratty generated a very simple performance measure to correct it. Dillon was only to offer an opinion when specifically asked, and if she offered it without being asked, like today, she would add thirty minutes to her shift. Every opinion, another thirty minutes. Comply or resign.

How simple can I make this? I'm doing you a favor.

The analyst turned in her chair, stood to attention, and answered:

"No, ma'am. You did not ask me a question."

"Did I ask you anything after my first question of why Massachusetts was dark?"

"No, ma'am. I mistakenly gave you my opinion when you did not ask me, ma'am," the analyst said, eyes forward, back ramrod straight.

Cratty took a moment to see who might be watching this exchange. If it were humanly possible, all of her staff continued to be fully "engrossed" in their work as if their very homes were under foreign attack.

Cratty walked around the analyst. *How can I get through to you?* she thought.

"Do you like working for the Foreign Intelligence Agency?"

"Yes, ma'am" was the short response.

"See, that surprises me, Dillon. Your former manager found your opinions annoying and hoped that a transfer here might break you of that. He's hoping you learn better and can return to the morning shift. I am not sure you will return at all. Does that surprise you?"

Cratty watched and waited for a response. The struggle was clearly visible on the analyst's face as she did her best to think of the right answer. All seemed lost to Cratty until she saw Dillon's expressions suggest that she may have fallen into a "correct" answer:

"I hope to learn that skill, ma'am."

Cratty waited a moment. There seemed to be a shadow of a smile. This time, it might have been a remnant of the "nice" smile—*from when I used to care about my staff's growth.* The smile faded quickly.

"An answer that demonstrates your intelligence. Are we done here, Dillon?"

"Only if you say we are, ma'am."

"Hmm... another good answer. The additional thirty minutes you earned with your loose lips is now rescinded as a result of your demonstrating your intelligence and insight," Cratty concluded.

The analyst remained at attention and did not respond.

She looked closely at Dillon and had a moment of compassion.

Maybe the "old Cratty" is still in there? Maybe I still care a little bit.

She closed the gap so she could talk directly to Dillon in a low, even tone:

"Dillon, you have skills. You have the capacity and the gray matter to excel. Believe it or not, I want you to. But you have to watch your mouth. Watch. Review. Think. Then talk. There are worse assholes than me here who won't be as forgiving."

Dillon's eyes seemed confused and softer, but she did not talk.

Cratty stepped back from her and started to walk away with her hands still folded behind her back. She stopped halfway and turned back to the analyst, who did not dare move until she was given permission.

"Get back to work, Dillon."

"Yes, ma'am."

As Cratty ascended the stairs that led just above the pit of monitors, she scanned the darkened floor-to-ceiling screen sections that indicated Boston, Massachusetts. Cratty noted the time and date: 4:50 p.m. Eastern Standard Time, March fifteenth. She stood still, looking at that blackened screen, as hands moved from her back to grip firmly the handrail.

"Fuck you, Webber," was all she could say. She was sure the majority of her staff heard it, but she didn't care.

Then Cratty's thoughts unexpectedly jumped back to Burns... *He really gave the bosses the ultimate "Fuck you!"* Cratty smiled.

Chapter 3

"Malum consilium quod mutari non potest" - "It's a bad plan that can't be changed" Publilius Syrus

It's time already?

It was 9:05 a.m., and John Helms was arguing with himself. He was going back and forth on a plan he devised, implemented and ready to engage. He checked his automatic handgun before placing it in his holster.

Why do you want to help Burns and his people?

He knew plenty of law enforcement agencies were after these "domestic terrorists," so it wasn't an issue of helping "the good guys."

"Maybe I'm just pissed at the fact that this group of people walked into my region and made a mess of everything and then walked away unscathed.

Rechecking the length of his jacket to insure his hip holster was properly concealed, Helms found himself rethinking the "unscathed" part of his thinking: a psychologist loses his vision and his wife, two women and a baby are marked for death, and a rogue agent, whom they helped, is trying to save their lives from a U.S. agency.

Maybe "unscathed" is not the best word.

Either way, Helms reflected on today's meeting.

March fifteenth was the day Burns scheduled to make an in-person contact with the Federal Bureau of Investigation. At least that was the plan. After much debating, arguing and plotting, the actual plan was finally agreed upon and then put in place. After ten months following the "terrorist attacks" that were reported by all news accounts as foiled by local, state and federal agencies during the "Merrimack Valley Crisis," Deputy Director Helms of the Bureau in Boston, Lieutenant Steve Andersen of the North Reading Police, and Jillian Davis, former Foreign Intelligence Agency's Operations Center manager and now "private contractor" for Helms's team, were about to make face-to-face contact with one of the principals of Burns's crew.

Finally, we can put this chapter behind us, he hoped.

He turned and picked up the thick, color-coded file he had been rereading an hour earlier and that Davis and Andersen had put together on this group. Thumbing through the file's well-worn edges, he reviewed the firsthand witnesses' accounts and spattering of data they put together including an in-depth briefing with behavioral profiles and personality traits for each person. Nearly a year ago, Alexander J. Burns had returned from nowhere after being missing in action for four years. Somehow, he and three civilians were able to create a large-scale diversion in Massachusetts' Merrimack Valley for the sole purpose of stealing classified information to broker their lives back. Within six hours, they had disrupted all law enforcement agencies and shut down communication and the entire Northeast US corridor.

All this just so they could be left alone.

During the process, they were able to compromise three federal Operations Centers, obtain five years of classified Department of Defense special and "black" operations files in addition to genuine, official blank passports and birth certificates, and a cache of cash. This was all done with no civilian casualties being directly attributed to Burns and his crew. While the death of Senior Field Agent Anthony Maxwell occurred at the hands of his own private contractors, it was debatable whether, if Burns had not used him in the setup, he'd be alive today. If Helms didn't live through the experience, he would never have believed this report was real.

It would have made a great movie though, he thought. *I'd definitely see this one on the big screen. A little farfetched but entertaining.*

Helms leaned back in his char and indulged himself, thinking of who might play him. After mere seconds, he looked at his watch and picked up his cell phone with wireless ear transceiver that would tie him into Janeson and the control room while he was in the field. Placing the transceiver in his ear, he waited patiently for Davis and Andersen to arrive at his office prior to their meeting.

Months ago, Andersen and he had hatched an idea to retrieve the majority of classified data to insure it was never leaked into the wrong hands. Insuring national security was the goal.

The less data out there, the safer the United States will be, he reasoned.

He knew that in addition to being an FBI agent and marine, he was a law enforcement officer sworn to deter, defend and protect. This was a big job—a sensitive, volatile operation. From the very beginning he knew he needed his own task force to find and pull Burns back in.

The list was pretty short in his mind. Jillian Davis was recruited for her intelligence and field experience, and also because she had met and dealt with Burns firsthand. Steve Andersen made obvious sense since he had one of Burns's principals in custody for hours and got to know a lot about the group. That kind of insight was priceless. Also, he genuinely liked Andersen. Andersen also pulled in a colleague, Diane Welch, whom he believed brought an important skill set of direct field tactics and intelligence gathering that would only enhance their team. Of the four, Welch was the only one who had not been involved months ago when Burns's team hit. As Helms started his routine of pacing in his office while we waited for his team to show up, he remembered his short tour of duty with Welch at the end of her career. She was a Warrant Officer in the corps, who had spent more time in the field than most at her rank. He had heard a lot about her and he knew from firsthand experience that her troops respected her and she respected them. Back then, it took time for him to find out what had happened in her last assignment in Swat Valley, and he was sure there was a lot more about that mission he would never know. While the operation's success was critical, and the loss of life relatively low, he had to respect her decision not to accept her commendation and resign from the corps. He did everything possible to minimize her contact with the head of the agency that had killed her men and civilians. And when it looked like Daniels was going to box Welch in, Helms "accidentally" left a reporter in his office with memos from command about pressuring Welch.

What kind of idiot does that? Oh, to be young and stupid, again.

At the time, he was able to convince others that releasing her before her end of tour would be wise. In a rare moment of logic and the absence of FUBAR (Fucked Up Beyond All Recognition), everyone agreed and she was home thirty-six hours later.

I wonder what that homecoming must have been like? America's hero. No parades. No notice. Just, "Honey, I'm home!"

Helms knew that Andersen and Welch went way back to growing up in the same neighborhood. Still, Andersen told him that Welch never spoke of her experience in Afghanistan. He knew her husband very well too, and he considered himself close to her. Helms was surprised to know that Andersen was able to get her interviewed with a friend of his, which eventually led her to the position as the State Troopers' Commandant in his region. He took a moment to wonder whether Andersen could get him a job at the State House.

For a North Reading detective, he has some clout in Boston. How does he do that?

Another reason for pulling Welch on the team was because Burns had made it clear he was glad she wasn't around during the crisis last May second. For Helms, that was a ringing endorsement of her skill set.

For today's meeting, however, Helms wanted Welch to watch everything from the FBI Control Room that monitored critical "real time" missions. Even as he was reviewing the time and location in his head, he couldn't understand why Burns picked this place to meet. Since he had five years of classified data, he had more leverage than anyone to pick and choose time, players, and location. Helms figured he would let Burns do what he wanted since he could anyway.

Still his parameters were quite confusing to all parties on Helms's team. Burns insisted that the meeting would be in the middle of Boston's Plaza Center, which was typically very busy with commuters, patrons, business people and tourists, all taking in the sights or heading to work. The plaza itself gradually dropped below street level in an open area that was literally in the shadow of the FBI's Regional Office. Why he was having this meeting occur in the Bureau's backyard when he could pick anywhere on the globe was confusing. But Helms had come to understand that Burns was not your average specialist. He was positive that if Burns picked the place, you knew he had all angles covered and his reasons would be for his benefit and his opponent's detriment.

The plan, as articulated to him by Andersen via Burns, was simple: during Boston's rush hour time, 5:30 p.m., Jill Davis was to walk toward the middle of the plaza. She was to be unarmed and carry an open mike to monitor the communication while Helms was allowed to have three clearly identified FBI agents to maintain the perimeter. Burns allowed for both Helms and Andersen to be on the perimeter as well, in addition to Davis and the other three agents. All could be armed, but they needed to remain at a distance from Davis for her to have contact.

It's brilliant, Helms admitted after he thought about it longer.

At that time of day, the entire plaza would be flooded with people. In this way, a firefight was not likely to occur, especially from a law enforcement perspective where public safety and risk to civilians were tantamount. After careful review of the situation and to demonstrate good faith, Helms decided not to use the three additional agents but rather to have his Control Room monitor the meeting. Burns was agreeable to this change. Helms did plan to have more than fifteen of his agents on station to move on-site within three minutes if something went wrong.

Semper paratus, "always ready."

For Burns's part, he would have one of his crew meet in the middle of the plaza and give a flash drive to Davis of more samples of classified information. Once completed, everyone would walk away to review. At the time, he found it amusing that for a former Army intelligence guy, Andersen did not understand why the quick meet. Helms understood the reason for the meeting as did Davis and Welch. Welch was kind enough to articulate what the plan was about—"Burns is testing his opponents' genuineness and to see whether we follow directions."

Even as Helms waited, he still had to suppress a laugh, thinking back to when Davis had asked whether she needed to draw stick figures and use monosyllabic words to help Andersen "get the picture." As always, Andersen demonstrated restraint and simply smiled. That was an indicator to him that Andersen was worried about this drop. While Helms could appreciate Burns's test to see whether he could be trusted, the fact that he was doing it in the Bureau's own backyard and having a civilian make the drop demonstrated both confidence and coldness. If anything went wrong, Burns would not be there. Helms didn't like it, but he had to appreciate his planning.

After obsessing over some minor details, Helms concluded that he and his team were ready; his troops were on standby, and his control room was commanded by his top team. The only thing not cooperating was the weather since there were more clouds than sun. But since it was March in Boston, when the sun did cut through, it was bright and beautiful. Helms looked around his office and decided he needed a change in his environment. He decided he would wait in the lobby for Davis and Andersen to show up. As he walked absentmindedly through the corridors to the elevator, he hoped all went well today. In eight hours, he would know.

~

Unable to sleep, Burns awoke earlier than usual, but he remained in bed since Samantha's arms were draped over him. He had noticed she had taken to holding onto him pretty tightly in the morning, making it difficult for him to leave her. He looked at her as he always did. Rather than endure the physical pain of leaving her in bed, he opted simply to stay in bed with her.

Not a bad solution, he thought. *I've had to do much worse in my life.*

The only drawback was that it gave him time to obsess and ruminate about things and plans he needed to put in place. He found himself focusing on things that could go wrong. This focus was different from the way he used to operate years ago. When he thought of the plan to which he had reluctantly agreed, he found himself frustrated and angry that he could not come up with a better idea. Burns knew that it made sense to negotiate with Andersen and Helms, and that's why he responded to the communiqué that Andersen had sent weeks ago about trying to work out a deal. If it were just Burns, he never would have agreed to meeting and would have lived in the shadows for the rest of his life.

He felt Samantha loosen her grip for just a moment until he realized she was only readjusting her grip to pull her torso and legs to envelop him.

Yup. It could be worse.

He watched her nearly angelic face continue to sleep. Even though he knew there was no blood relation between Samantha and her niece Emma, he swore they both looked identical as they slept.

He looked at the green illuminated clock and saw it was 9:20 a.m. before looking back at the ceiling. He attempted another round of seeing whether they all could live in the shadows, staying underground in hiding forever. He knew the answer already. They were talented and had done next to the impossible. They literally "held the wolf by the ears," and survived. But they were still civilians. Even the best covert operatives, he knew, made mistakes. How could he expect them to remain undercover indefinitely?

So how can I use them in this drop?

When the time came to make the meeting with Andersen, he had originally planned on doing it himself. Much to his chagrin, Samantha Littleton, love of his life, used cold, calculating logic to convince him that his showing up was a tactical mistake that would be the death of them all. Without him as the "boogie man" everyone feared, no protection would exist for any of them.

He turned to listen to her breathing and shook his head.

You've changed so much. I hate it when you're right.

Looking back to the ceiling, he knew then, as he did now, that she was right all along. Still, he was impressed by the earlier discussions about the meet. They had to have a video conference link to engage fully in the discussion, much as he did years ago when he used to be an asset for the U.S. Government. It was encrypted and secure with David and Rebecca in Kea and Samantha sitting on the bed. Like any mission, he found himself weighing all the arguments.

David and Samantha were the most articulate in telling him not to go. David, however, insisted he should be the one to make the drop because he had spent hours with Andersen. Additionally, David thought he presented himself as the least threatening since he was blind. Without saying it, Burns knew David thought he was the most expendable if something went wrong.

Logical, Burns had thought at the time. *But we're not doing that. You have no idea how really important you are to all of us.*

But before he could respond, the idea was ripped off the table.

David had just countered with his final point of "I'm the philosophical, long-winded blind guy... who's going to shoot me?"

"They will for those very reasons," Samantha responded without hesitation.

While Burns knew a long relationship between David and her allowed for this kind of banter, he was positive she was protecting him and her sister, Rebecca, who clearly loved him. There was universal agreement with that point. Even through a blurry, pirated satellite link, Burns could see that David tried not to take it personally. The unstated reason was clear to David at some level since he dropped his argument altogether. Further, he wouldn't let him be used because he wouldn't do that to his friend.

The thought of David as a friend was also something he had come to value greatly.

Just as Samantha had moved to protect David and Rebecca, Rebecca was next to volunteer since she didn't want her "baby sister" in danger. David knew Rebecca had done a lot of things over the years to protect Samantha, so she was not about to let her walk into harm's way now. Burns also saw firsthand how, over the course of nearly five years, Rebecca had physically and mentally prepared herself for her newfound athletic body and acquired skills in handguns, long-range shooting, and the use of edged weapons, all of which did make her a viable candidate. However, like David, Rebecca was needed to be Emma's parent.

"David, Becky, don't even start. Emma needs her parents. There's is no discussion," he said more softly than expected.

Feeling both movement behind him and a smile, Burns turned from the video conference to see Samantha sitting cross-legged on the bed with a smug look of victory on her face. He felt his jaw line tighten, eyes narrow and body tense up.

"Maybe I could get Perez or Martinez here in time?" he said quickly.

His former support team was good and perfect for such a task but he already knew the answer—they were both in deep cover and off-grid. It would take months to find them. That was time they didn't have. And Samantha's response was telling—cool, calm and dripping with 'I win, you lose.'

"Really? The dynamic duo left you a forwarding address? Didn't it take you like half a year to find them last time?"

Burns remained silent.

I hate it when she's right, he thought then as he did now. *Screw logic and reason!*

Burns did not like the plan of having his lover, friend, companion, his "Sam" putting herself at risk. Logically, she was the natural choice. She had known danger, violence, and had risked her entire life on a daily basis as a prostitute. She was also logical and articulate when it came to planning and obtaining goals. Of all of them, barring Burns, everyone knew she was the most capable to handle herself in a dangerous situation. And if she had to kill, she could.

Fortunately, it remains to be seen under what circumstance David or Rebecca could take a life. Hopefully, never.

Burns heard a sudden, long intake of air as Samantha seemed to stir a little bit and was now pushing her nose and chin into his chest as her legs more firmly trapped his under the covers.

How does she manage to twist herself all over me without waking up?

Sighing, he returned to his staring at the ceiling as he found himself fully embracing the absolutely illogical idea of him conducting the meeting himself. His being captured could not be risked. Shortly after the video conference, Burns still wanted to explore every other venue before giving up. It took Samantha two solid weeks of wearing him down.

Years ago, before his head injury and treatment, he wouldn't have cared whether Samantha went, just as he would have been fine sending David to the meeting. But he had changed. While there was still logic, reason, tactics, and strategies, there were also emotions—strong emotions of love, fear, compassion, anger, and the need to protect others. Turning back to look at her sleeping face with her mouth slightly open, he felt panic—even though she was so clearly at peace.

All illogical. All emotional. I don't want you to go, Sam. Simple. No logic. Don't leave. Don't go. Please, don't go... no.

He turned away so he might be able to banish the panic. He still felt the defeat he always felt when he acquiesced. He set the date, time, and location.

That day was today, March fifteenth, and it came sooner than he wanted.

Burns found himself sighing again before he turned to look at Samantha. Feeling a smile come over his face, he pulled her even closer so he could feel her.

"Don't leave me," he said to her as she slept.

~

By the time 11 p.m. was closing in, David had been puttering around the house for hours while Emma was sound asleep in bed. He knew he was distracting himself from worrying about Rebecca being in Paris and Samantha making her exchange in Boston. While being left out of the operation's loop was nerve-racking, he knew that if he were pulled into the mission that would mean something had gone terribly wrong. As a result, he felt relieved not to be pulled into the operation but anxious because he had no role but to wait.

So this is how first responders feel, he thought. *But they're not halfway around the world in Greece waiting for trouble in Boston.*

He rearranged a basket of fruit on the counter for the hundredth time. He then felt the time on his watch.

"3:30 p.m. Boston time," he said to himself.

He was pacing as he always did when he was thinking. He checked the basement door just to make sure it was unlocked on the unlikely chance he would have to "descend into the chamber," as Rebecca had often joked.

For months, David had been on edge about what was going to happen after they had escaped last May. Back then, he had been so focused on executing the plan that he had never thought about what would happen if they made it. Over the past couple of weeks following their video conference, he had been pleased to hear more from Burns than less. His uptick in phone calls and talking was the clearest indicator that he was very anxious about Samantha's role in meeting Andersen.

I still think it should have been me, he had continued to thing.

While the actual calls from Burns increased, he never spoke about the mission as much as he just spoke about day-to-day events. He was hoping that after the drop, those conversations would continue.

As David focused on slowing his pacing, he also found himself smiling as he remembered how Burns had spoken about his morning routine and why Samantha's putting on her makeup and "getting ready" was an hour-long process. He had also spoken about the changes Samantha had made in her life, including more exercise, less provocative dressing, and her hair color changing from dark brunette to bleached blonde and then back to raven black. Fortunately, David had warned him never to provide commentary on Samantha's wardrobe, makeup, and hair. He was fine with everything she did... except maybe the hair. Based on Burns's description, it was evident she had tried to find the right balance herself, but she had consistently overshot her goal and gone darker than necessary.

Burns had to have been an only child, David had often thought, because he always seemed baffled at the exchange Samantha would have with her sister.

"It's a shame I'm not deaf," David remembered telling him as Burns recounted in detail the black hair issue.

Rebecca had commented that Samantha had "crow color hair to match the feet on her eyes." David knew the remark had been in jest, but Burns had realized Samantha was hurt when she asked him whether her hair was too dark. Smiling, David was amazed at his response. While he might have years of experience in the field of counter-terrorism and intelligence, he was a novice in the battlefield of relationships.

"So I said, 'Crow? As in the bird? God, no! Becky has always been jealous of you. Why do you even listen to her?'"

"Brilliant," David had said.

"David, you have no idea. Samantha can sniff out bullshit from miles away. She just stared at me with her eyes and watched for anything to give me away."

At the time, David was curious how Samantha reframed her thoughts about her sister making such a harsh jab.

"What did she say?"

Even on a long distance, cell phone call, David could hear Burns trying to give David the verbatim response.

"She said something like, 'Yeah... she does get jealous. Anyway, I would call it raven black. Crow is so mundane,' she said. You know David, I dodged a lot of bullets, but the ones I encounter with Samantha always seem to be closest. You know what I mean?"

"Sure do," David kindly said.

Shaking his head, David didn't have the heart to tell him that he should try living with them for a couple of years as he had to.

You haven't seen sibling rivalry up close and personal until you live with them both for a couple of years alone. You do that; then come and see me about dodging bullets. Being deaf at that time would have been a blessing.

As the days drew closer to March fifteenth, so did the frequency of phone calls from Burns. Little by little, he discussed small, irrelevant aspects of the operation such as how he thought that Samantha didn't require a great deal of makeup for the drop off and how she needed to blend in with a "business casual" look. During the last call the day before, Burns had gone on about how important it was that she not stand out in the throng of humanity heading home after a long day in the office. He seemed to obsess about how simple clothes, dark slacks, and a blouse with an all-season waist business jacket made the most sense. The only time Burns seemed exasperated was when Samantha needed to get "sensible shoes" that matched and could be stylish yet functional should she have to run. Having been married before to a woman who had two closets full of shoes, David had firsthand empathy for Burns.

Smiling at the last phone conversation with Burns, David found himself getting tired, so he navigated to the kitchen to sit down again. As he approached the table, he listened to the house's silence. With Becky in France and Emma asleep, the house just seemed too quiet and empty.

David sighed and felt his watch for the time again.

"3:40, Boston time," he announced to himself.

Not bothering to sit down, he returned to the bowl of fruit and decided its original place four hours ago was a better location. After seconds of moving the fruit again he rubbed his hands together and wondered how he was going to get through the next two hours.

~

Burns had to admit that he felt he stuck out like a sore thumb. As Samantha was leaning against him to check the length between her shoe and the bottom of her slacks, he was able to steal a glance at his watch.

5:05... Do we have to be late for this meeting?

Normally, he would have been pushy, but since he didn't want her to go, he was fine taking his time. But he couldn't help picking up on the odd looks passersby were giving him.

Is it Sam or is it my gym bag?

Since he knew what was in his bag and they could not, he reasoned it had to be Sam's attractiveness that drew the stares—mostly from men, he noticed. Just to be safe, he glanced at his bag to make sure the zipper was not open, revealing the sniper barrel or gunstock.

"We should go," Burns said gently.

"Oh, yeah. Let's go." Why she was so cheerful was beyond him; she finished re-fitting herself into her shoe and straightened out her slacks. As they started walking, Burns returned to reviewing—in the most obsessive, detailed fashion—every aspect of every part of a "simply say 'hi,' drop off, and walk away."

While he did not like the plan of using Samantha, he had a better feel for the drop site. Nearly two years prior, Burns had placed four high definition cameras tied into public lighting and overlooking the plaza where the drop was going to happen. It had been done then to prepare for the May second "attacks" that would have a "suspicious backpack" left in the middle of the plaza that would be belching smoke. Perez and Martinez were to make that magic happen. While it was a good plan at the time and City Hall Plaza perfectly fit the bill, there was no need for it when the Operations Center site was discovered in Waltham. Busy with other things, Burns decided to leave the equipment in the field. The one major drawback with the site was that the "drop zone" was only one block away from the FBI Regional Office. That meant that a flood of federal agents could be in the area in less than four or five minutes if they were on standby—bad for Burns and his team if they were double-crossed.

Regardless, he decided long ago to leave the cameras in place in case they could be of use later. Now was the time. Three weeks before, he had tested all four briefly to see whether they worked. Three did. Since today's weather would mostly be overcast with short periods of sunlight, the use of black-and-white was better suited to have clarity with limited glare. Burns was cognizant of the radio frequency waves, so he also tested the cameras for a short time two hours prior and turned them off in case their video/radio frequency was picked up by a third party. He obsessed for weeks about the meeting site, the cameras, and his own observation post he had chosen so he could keep an eye on her drop.

Also weeks before, Burns decided that he wanted another set of eyes on Samantha—remotely through the cameras—so he was free to be close by and attend to "real-time" events. If a third party were monitoring, he needed to have the signal transmitted to a laptop, which would redirect it to an email account that could be either copied or retransmitted elsewhere. To make sure the person making the copy on the email's other side could not be traced and caught, the plan called for Rebecca to go to France and use a public cafe to obtain images and monitor. He figured it would take a minimum of thirty minutes to mobilize local assets if the signal were traced to its destination.

Burns knew that while Rebecca understood why he could not make the drop, she was not happy at all that her sister was in the line of fire. She had argued with Samantha about it many times and never given up. He empathized with Becky—once Samantha made up her mind, no one stood a chance to change it.

Maybe David or Emma could have changed her mind. But only those two stood a chance, and he noticed she had been ducking David and Emma's calls to talk to her. He knew she didn't want to be convinced to drop out of the mission. Rebecca continued her efforts right up to the day before.

Neither one of you is going to admit defeat.

Burns knew Rebecca was happy to be part of the plan and to have the role of literally watching over her sister. Samantha would keep an open cell phone link to Burns and Rebecca via bridge so both could listen in and provide tactical information from multiple vantage points.

While Burns knew it was both his nature and profession to obsess about details, he recognized he was being particularly fastidious about this mission. As they walked, he focused on trying not to scratch his itchy scalp. He had noticed that as the days got closer, all his scars started to itch, but especially on his scalp. While he knew that spontaneous itching was quite rare for scarring from years ago, he experienced the itching when his stress increased; for him, it was a classic symptom of his anxiety taking bodily form.

He walked quietly with Samantha to the staging area while he continued to process all possible angles. He took a moment to watch her as she made a pouty face at the sky. He could tell that she preferred to have a completely sunny day. But even as she caught him smiling at her, he continued to review the plan of how she would enter the plaza from the east and walk to the middle where she should see the woman named "Davis." Samantha kept using Davis's old code "Cougar," from when they had first seen her months prior to finding the auxiliary control center.

Burns did appreciate that while he had allowed the Bureau to have six people on site, Andersen had said they would use the FBI Control Room to watch everything and that he should expect Deputy Director Helms and himself to be there as backup to Davis. He was positive they had no idea that another set of eyes would be Rebecca. He looked at his watch as the appointed time closed in.

Digging in his pocket, he found the transmitter that would activate his own cameras and give Rebecca time to sweep the area for anything out of the ordinary. Burns had already coached her in detail on what to look out for since anything could be construed as unusual when stressed.

He stopped short of banging into Samantha as he realized she had stopped at their designated point, where she was to go ahead to the meeting and he was to head to his own lookout.

With a nervous smile, he firmly embraced Samantha and gave her a heartfelt kiss. As she pulled away, he still hung on longer.

"You know Rebecca never lets go either," Samantha commented.

I don't want you to go, he found himself thinking.

"Then I'm in good company."

Samantha started to walk away and then turned back; she said quite proudly in Latin "*Aut vincere aut mori.*" She had picked up some phrases and parts of Burns's prayers. She seemed to like both Latin and German. She also enjoyed springing such phrases on him, and he typically loved it.

Burns's stomach fell. His throat felt as is if it were closing from anaphylactic shock. His eyes narrowed and stung as he peered into her eyes. His scalp flared as if his skin was made of sand and it was on fire. Gone were the days of being emotionless for he knew his expression must not have been what she expected.

"Did I say it wrong?"

Burns remained still and then relaxed his muscles. He was able to regain his composure as he followed up with his own question.

"I'm sorry, Sam. What were you saying? I think I must have heard it wrong," he said quickly before his mouth dried up.

She had a way that made Burns melt when she got something wrong.

"I thought I said, 'Fortune favors the bold.'"

Burns fell right into his acting mode.

"Oh yeah...'*Audaces fortuna iuvit*.'" Burns smiled as he recognized the saying almost immediately.

Samantha smiled too, shrugged her shoulders about the mistake, and did her best to walk without strutting.

Burns watched her leave.

His smile immediately evaporated as he watched her go. He almost ran to stop her. He envisioned himself chasing her and pulling her aside and telling her, *"Forget it. We're leaving."*

"Don't go," he said softly.

He was not a superstitious man, not by a long shot. But he was disturbed that she had mistakenly pulled the Latin phrase "Either conquer or die" as a motto to embark on. If she were trained in counterinsurgency and heavily armed, with years of field experience as a special operations soldier, he would have appreciated the saying. But she was not a soldier, and he loved her. He knew what she had meant, but it was not what she had said. She turned the corner, out of eyeshot.

What would I do without her?

Burns felt ill at ease but then shook the feeling off as "pre-mission jitters"—something he never experienced. He turned and went in the opposite direction. It would take him eight minutes to get to his pre-designated site where he would rapidly set up his partially assembled .338 caliber, long-range sniper rifle with scope and laser target. He had located his sniper nest weeks prior when he thought he might have Rebecca cover him from this very location when he planned to make the drop. The building was under major renovation, but it had a few empty offices partially set up with minimal security. From inside an empty office, he would lie prone on a conference room desk by an open window above the plaza where Samantha would be. With his breathing trained, a chin/cheek support with strap, and a solid biped for stability, he was positive he could hit a human target nine hundred yards away with everything close to just right in regard to weather, wind and bullet drop. While initially he had planned on using the .50 caliber rifle, he opted for the lighter weight of this rifle and a custom-made, twenty-round detachable magazine instead. He also considered that he was interested in protecting Samantha; he did not want collateral damage or to take out vehicles. As the penetration capacity of the .338 Lapua in the right hands would be enough, he reasoned that the .50 was simply overkill for the job. Now he had to wait. Looking to the west, he could see the clouds were thinning more than he would like, allowing more sun to come through than desired. The sun was low in the horizon and could pose a glare problem on his scope that might give his location away. He would have to be careful.

Even with these mild logistics problems, Burns still kept replaying Samantha's phrase of "Either conquer or die" when she had meant to say, "Fortune favors the bold." He tried to shake off his negative thinking again and convinced himself it meant nothing. He decided to focus on things he could control and went back to reconnoitering the drop site.

The die has been cast, he thought. *But then why do I feel like shit?*

Chapter 4

"Alea iacta est" - "The dice has been cast" Caesar

Once she entered the dimly lit cavernous room, it was easy for Diane Welch to feel the heightened energy on "live mission status." She was escorted into the FBI Control Room by an agent that looked five years younger than her son, which made her feel far older than she wanted to be. It was evident by the number of young analysts and operators moving around in a clear determined fashion, that even though their boss, John Helms, was in a field operation, a great deal of work needed to get done. In fact, as Welch was standing in the sea of bodies and computers, she saw that nearly all monitors and screens were either on or around Boston's City Hall Plaza where her friend, Steve Andersen, a private contractor named Davis, and Helms were patiently waiting.

Welch got a closer look at Helms. She had seen him weeks earlier when she was brought onto "the team."

Jesus. Seventeen years later you haven't changed a bit, she thought.

Next, Welch took in all three and one thought jumped to mind: *Forget covert operations. If they're trying to blend in, they're doing a really bad job.*

It was obvious to Welch that they wanted to be very conspicuous.

It didn't take long to adjust to the control room's noise, energy, and lighting. She looked around for the person in charge. Andersen had briefed her on who would be in charge and that she should not be "put off by her lack of social skills."

Welch looked around for the manager. Andersen also said she

would be easy to spot: "She's a very attractive young woman, tall with pale skin, deep blue eyes, and constantly surrounded by two of her staff—Gilmore and Johnson."

She remembered looking at him like he was crazy.

"What do you mean she's constantly surrounded by two of her staff?"

At the time, Andersen was cooking dinner on the grill as they both had a beer. She remembered he had been reluctant to give a briefing while barbecuing, but he must have decided to give her the heads-up about the scene she would be walking into when she arrived at the control room. He was flipping the chicken and gave his best effort to summarize.

"For this operation, Helms had to choose between three people in the control room to be the interim director while he is in the field. Rachael Janeson has both intelligence and military experience, but her brilliance is only matched by her lack of interpersonal skills. Gilmore and Johnson, the two guys who will undoubtedly be close to her, are very skilled civilian analysts and have very good intuitive skills. I wish I could tell you which one is which and their first names but they're almost interchangeable. Anyway, both guys have significantly better social skills than Janeson. Since all three emerged as leaders during the Merrimack Valley Crisis, Helms focused on developing their abilities as a team and had them run missions together. Apparently, their teamwork and success rate were excellent, and they were being considered as a model for future control room management for high profile and dangerous operations. Since Janeson has five years of military experience, she was put as team leader. Gilmore and Johnson could probably have been assigned the leadership role, but for some reason they declined the role. They work best with Janeson."

Welch remembered her face scrunching up in confusion.

Andersen shrugged and said, "I don't know how or why it works. I just know they all work well as a team."

She was reflecting on the impromptu briefing a couple of days earlier when she spotted Janeson. She was exactly as Andersen had described; and no more than five feet away, manning the bank of monitors right in front of her, were two men engrossed in conversation and then they turned to continue the conversation with Janeson.

Welch knew that her presence alone had to complicate today's mission, so her plan was to remain as quiet and as unobtrusive as possible. Anyway, the whole operation should take five minutes at the most, she speculated. As she approached the team, Janeson spotted her and waved her to join the group. Brief introductions were followed by uncomfortable silence, so Welch thought it made sense to lighten the moment.

"So I am guessing you did a background check on me?" she asked in a playful manner as she smiled. She got the smiles she expected from Gilmore and Johnson, but Janeson had taken the question literally.

Janeson turned directly to face her and seemed to force herself to make eye contact before she began a briefing on who she was.

"Yes. You do have clearance for this operation. Our research indicates that you are Diane Welch, a former Warrant Officer in the Marines. You are now involved in this ongoing investigation that Deputy Director Helms and his team are conducting. Mr. Gilmore and Mr. Johnson were able to find the most data from unusual channels: you made national news several years ago over finding a terrorist camp, and somehow, against desperate odds, you engaged the enemy and survived. Still, though, there are gaps in the information. Based on the circumstance of your leaving the corps, I am guessing you were so deeply disturbed by whatever happened that accepting a promotion, citations, and fame was repulsive."

It was apparent to her that Janeson was so deep in thought as she recited the vast information from her record that she had digested that she was missing the clear, non-verbal cues by Gilmore and Johnson to stop. Unfazed and unaware of the social etiquette, she went on.

Well... you were right, Steve.

"Both official and unofficial reports suggest that your experience in gathering innate intelligence, battlefield and law enforcement is more likely at an "expert" level. You have nearly thirty years' experience of combined military and law enforcement. You entered the Marine Corps at age twenty-one, right after college. You and Detective Andersen come from the same neighborhood, South Boston, that was significantly below poverty level with an inordinate amount of crime at the time of your youth. You have two grown sons, and you are recently widowed..."

Welch's jaw now tightened and her fists balled up at the mention of Joe's death. Worse, she couldn't tell whether the reason she was hot was because of her anger or a hot flash coming on menopause. The hot flashed had been a real pain in the ass lately.

Remembering that had been warned her about Janeson Welch collected herself and started to fully grasp what Steve Andersen was telling her about Janeson.

The two men beside her took a very direct approach with their boss. Johnson was the first to respond pretty bluntly and with urgency, but somehow he did it in a respectful fashion.

"Boss? Mrs. Welch was joking when she asked about the background check. I am guessing she also knows a great deal about her personal and professional record."

Gilmore chimed in next by turning to confirm Welch's earlier question.

"You're overstating the obvious, boss. Not necessary here. I'm guessing, Mrs. Welch, that you were making small talk when you asked about the background check?"

It took Welch a moment to respond.

Now I get why you warned me, Steve. What the hell did I sign up to? Is she for real?

It was very wise of Andersen to warn her about Janeson; otherwise, she would have taken great offense. It took a conscious moment, but she was able to relax her jaw and fists; unfortunately, the hot flash would have to run its course.

Jesus, I hate these hot flashes.

After Welch regained her bearings, she responded to Gilmore's question.

"Yes. I was just joking. I'm sorry," she added.

Janeson looked at all three of them as if she were calculating their expressions.

"I am very sorry for my lack of sensitivity and overstatement of the obvious."

Janeson glanced back down at a tablet as if something had flashed on.

Welch noticed that Janeson's use of language was formal and precise. And while she apologized, she was evidently sure of the intellectual reason why she should apologize, but not necessarily the emotional reason.

"Boss, I think you took the 'background check' question as literal. I also think you're anxious about today's mission, and when you are tense you screw up on social cues," Gilmore summed up.

Welch was impressed with his articulation and his balls to say that to his boss.

Janeson looked up from her tablet and looked as if she had figured out something.

"Ahh. That makes perfect sense."

It was clear this type of interaction was common. Janeson seemed almost appreciative of the interpretation.

"Is that why the boss seemed angry with us today?" Janeson queried.

"Oh yeah, Boss. He's nervous as hell," Gilmore said.

"Thanks, guys. Again, I am very sorry, Mrs. Welch."

This time, Welch noticed, there was positive, actual feeling behind her words. Now that Janeson understood how she had made the *faux pas* and she was aware of all the other social cues, it seemed as if she could feel sorry for the mistake

Welch felt she had seen this situation before, but she was having trouble remembering why Janeson seemed familiar to her. Nonetheless, she decided she would keep her questions concrete and to the point and leave subtlety and joking aside.

"So how does it work here?" she asked. She had a maternal voice.

Janeson took lead on the answer.

"Typically, we will have about three or four assignments going at the same time, but because of the nature of this operation all eyes and ears are engaged on this assignment only."

"So I noticed there are no uniformed or active military staffs involved."

"Yes. This control room is staffed with all civilians, though a few of us have military experience," Janeson answered.

Welch looked around, giving the appearance of being impressed, which was easy. She was impressed especially with the youth of the room. The average age had to be late twenties or early thirties. Not that age was important in all things. She could still run three miles a day without *totally* exhausting herself.

A figment of my former self.

While her doctor was impressed with her blood pressure, cholesterol, and overall health "for a woman of fifty-two," her medical degree provided her with very few suggestions to control the hot flashes that were driving her crazy now.

If menopause was a guy's disease, it would have been cured already! Men or young people can't understand, not even close to understanding.

Distracted by her thoughts, she found she was having a hard time reading Janeson's non-verbals.

"So, Ms. Janeson, did I come at a bad time or were you expecting me?" Welch asked.

Damn it! Welch thought. *I was being sarcastic there.*

"Yes. You were scheduled to be here per request of Deputy Director Helms, and your role is to observe, and, if necessary, provide any assistance. Is there another reason, Mrs. Welch?" Janeson asked.

The beautiful young manager looked confused. She regretted that she had stated the obvious with a joke buried in it.

While Gilmore and Johnson had been directing other staff to complete preparation for the operation, they were clearly keeping within earshot of their boss to provide her support if necessary.

"I think what Mrs. Welch is asking is why are you so socially stiff and incapable of small talk," Gilmore chimed in from just below them. It was obvious he was multi-tasking and was running preliminary diagnostics of his own tablet.

No, not really, but that would greatly help me deal with her.

"Oh. I am sorry. My psychological testing indicates that I have a number of symptoms consistent with over-myelinization of my right hemisphere, which makes reading social cues and social situations more difficult for me. Apparently, this condition does not detract from my brain's frontal lobe and left hemisphere. There is some question as to whether I may have enhanced cognitive abilities in various analytical and logic areas. Deputy Director Helms says I'm 'the smart one' and likes that I utilize my team for deficits in my skill set."

Welch felt cooler but she was confused at the detailed anatomical description of Janeson's neuroscience.

How do you respond to something like that? She's not being arrogant or an asshole, and she sure as shit would fail miserably at a social mixer.

Welch was trying to form some kind of response, but fortunately, she did not have to as another analyst, Johnson, interrupted. His look was serious, and he was all business.

"Janeson, I am picking up on a separate visual radio frequency of third-party surveillance cameras... about three that are slaved to a remote access point and being bounced to an Internet address. They have to be tied into streetlamps for power."

Janeson put on her headset and stood in front of the floor-to-ceiling monitors. The control room cameras were showing images on the plaza while images just outside of the plaza were divided up into teams to observe.

"Minimize our camera sights to half the screen and tap into the other cameras' views, and put it on the other side. Do not interrupt it. I want to see what it's seeing," she said.

Welch next saw twenty people swiftly and silently move into designated positions in front of various banks of monitors and CPUs. It was clear they had moved from "pre-mission" to live mission in less than ten seconds. She decided she would not ask questions and just watch the situation develop.

While the control room's cameras had more wide angles and could move, the other "mystery" cameras were on a fixed mount with normal angle. In addition, they lacked color and were black-and-white images with high definition vision that provided very clear pictures of the majority of the plaza. From a military and law enforcement perspective, Welch noted for the future that high definition, black-and-white cameras might be more effective for field operations because glare was significantly reduced. Because there was overcast weather with periods of sun, glare at a particular moment might be a problem.

"I bet there is another one that is either not operating or shielded. It looks like three quarters of the plaza is covered," Janeson said.

"Confirmed. Three cameras are tied into three streetlights that are at each corner of the plaza. Looks like whoever did this tied into the light's own electricity to pull some juice to operate it," Johnson said.

"That means they could have been there for a while but turned off so as not to attract attention," Janeson said.

As Johnson was about to say something more, Welch noticed that she was seeing something in the view, and it was evident she did not like it. Welch looked and just saw a large number of people seemingly going along with their business. Maybe something was wrong with both the control room's visuals and the other group of cameras' visuals?

"Is something wrong with the cameras?" she asked quietly.

It was a solid minute of silence before Janeson responded to her question. Without taking her eyes off all the images, Janeson identified what she was seeing.

"No. It's not the cameras, but something's wrong with some of the pockets of people in the plaza. Something about the flow of people. The control room's cameras that have color did not pick up the pattern, but with the contrast of black-and-white images at nearly the same angles, it was actually more apparent. I see Helms, Andersen, and Davis in one place but then there are four or five groups of three or more individuals moving back and forth as a group equidistant from each other. At times, these groups are going with the flow of people toward the subway and train station or garage and then going against the flow of people in the opposite direction."

Just as she was explaining the pattern, Welch saw Davis heading to the place where the brief meeting was to be held.

Welch watched the screen as she sensed Janeson moving her microphone down from her headset to inform Helms of this situation. All the pieces were in motion.

"Deputy Director Helms, this is Janeson. Are you there...?"

"Where else would I be? I put you in charge, right? And call me 'boss'; it will be faster than the full title."

Welch couldn't help but suppress a smile. Janeson looked at Gilmore with the "What-did-I-say-wrong?" look.

"He's nervous about the drop and he's grumpy," Gilmore conjectured.

"Too true," was Johnson's confirmation.

Janeson nodded her head to acknowledge she understood.

In this very brief interaction, Welch now understood the dynamic between the three. Janeson had a huge aptitude, but she needed support in social etiquette. Gilmore and Johnson filled the gap.

"Boss, we have a third party's set of three fixed surveillance cameras covering the same area as us. Further, we identify at least four groups of four to five individuals who do not fit in with the regular commuters. There's another mission going down here. It's too large to be Burns, and it certainly is not us. I recommend you abort mission."

Welch turned to see three analysts on the lower level focusing and isolating the groups Janeson had identified as they searched for more anomalies. She had the same thought about aborting as soon as the cameras and ground forces were discovered.

Another operation going on in the same place and same time? What are the odds of that?

"Can't do it. No way to communicate with Burns directly... hold on," Helms said.

The conversation was on public speaker for all in the control room to hear. Next, they all heard Helms through his microphone as he talked to Davis.

Janeson covered the mike and directed her next order to Johnson: "Have the support teams in their cars, loaded and engines on. If this gets hot, I want our team extracted immediately."

He acknowledged with a nod and then was on his direct line to the support teams in the garage.

Maybe a bit paranoid, but better to be prepared than not, she concluded. Welch's attention was glued to the monitors and the verbal exchange.

"Davis, there is a problem. There's another set of eyes on us," she heard Helms tell Davis. At that point Davis was walking to the drop zone.

"Maybe it's Burns?" she said.

"The cameras might be, but unless his crew grew to ten-plus people, I think there is another thing going down. Abort the plan; wave off the contact."

"Will do," Davis responded.

Janeson came back online with Helms.

"Boss. It's 5:30 p.m., and we have no visuals of the contact. Will advise when spotted. Janeson out." But she wasn't done yet.

"Gilmore, have Thompson and Peters set up and implement a trace. I want to see if we can hack into the Internet feeds and trace it to an endpoint. We need to have Jackson monitoring the radio frequency at the higher end of the spectrum in case there is chatter that goes along with these unauthorized images."

Without taking a breath of air and with urgency in her voice, she continued giving her staff direction.

Hmm... very clear direction and well configured, Welch thought, impressed.

Janeson turned back to Johnson with his task.

Johnson, make sure all computers and online servers have been thoroughly checked for bugs and monitor them for anything that looks suspicious. Have Jakes and Davenport keep two of the servers and monitor groups 'Delta' unplugged and off-line in case Burns sends us another virus. Let's move people."

As the team split into three distinct groups, four more personnel appeared with more tablets and immediately took over some of the vacated seats to fill in the positions.

Team work, good communication, solid speculation, smart and a good sense of humor—all good qualities of a solid team. Maybe I made the right decision to help Steve out on his investigation, after all.

Seamless interactions, and they do all the heavy lifting. How does he find these gigs?

Welch shifted hear gaze back to the pockets of people, Davis and the varied viewpoints and images. She was not happy with the complications that came up with this simple "drop meeting." Focusing intently on the black and white screen, she felt a sudden dread as she watched Davis walking slowly to the plaza center to warn her contact and abort the mission.

Yeah... something is very wrong here.

Chapter 5

"Si vis pacem, para bellum" – *"If you want peace, prepare for war"* Vegetius

It had taken about three days of travel and reconnaissance to find the right public, all-night cafe with free access to computers in the middle of Paris. They were becoming extinct. She needed a minimum of at least three possible computers partially hidden from prying eyes so she could set up remote surveillance. It was strange to be about to watch her little sister from across the Atlantic.

If you have the money and contacts like Burns, anything is possible.

Becky was at the cafe an hour early to stake out her computer and to set up and run diagnostics. Since it was closing in on 10:30 p.m. when she arrived, she accurately guessed fewer people would be around at that time. There were people there and more than expected, but it was nothing compared to when she had been there at lunchtime. She was fifteen minutes out before she made phone contact with Burns and Samantha together. Ten minutes after that, she would go online to the email to pick up a real time broadcast via Burns's laptop within a three block radius of the cameras. The minutes passed slowly as she watched the time count down. Her mind wandered to what David and Emma might be doing right now. She was sure Emma would be sound asleep and David would be pacing.

Poor thing... he worries so much.

Then her mind wandered to how she finally was able to calculate wind velocity and elevation and how it might affect a long shot target at a thousand yards. Somehow, Burns had been able to obtain reconditioned .338 and .308 caliber sniper rifles with all the accessories back in the United

States and then he had coordinated the purchase of the latest successor to the .50 caliber from a contact in Libya. She had been practicing on it at home in Kea. For her "regular shooting," she liked the AR-15, but it had to have the flash muzzle, scope and collapsible arm for her to use it effectively.

The smell of strong coffee and recently baked croissants filled the air, dragging Becky's attention to the counter. She felt hungry all of a sudden. As she pulled herself out of her olfactory trance, she noted it was finally time to make phone contact.

"Well, hello, big sister, or should I say, 'Tiny,'" Samantha answered playfully.

God, it's great to hear your voice. You sound so happy.

"Hey, Sam. Ready for your date with 'Cougar'? I hear she's pretty good with men, though I also hear she likes it a bit rough," Becky responded, trying to make a crack at Burns. He didn't bite. She recalled the impromptu nickname for the person they had watched for a period of time, which turned out to be the same person Burns had to fight with to get his cache of money, documents, and hard drives.

"Just so you know, my name is 'Raven.'" Becky turned her thoughts back to what Samantha said.

"Oh... the hair. Why not 'crow'? Makes more sense. Or was that something Falcon picked out?" she bated again. She continued to run diagnostics while she was hunched over, looking at her screen as she talked to sister on her microphone.

"Forget it, Tiny. He's all business and not in the mood... you know... I have to tell you about these shoes though. Slick, sexy, and comfortable at the same time..."

Becky's hands went to her mouth to suppress a laugh at the obvious attempt to push Burns into some kind of repartee or at least to get him to focus on something less serious for a moment.

Talking about shoes? She'll say anything to provoke him.

"All right, you two. You're killing me. Becky, are you green to go?" Burns pressed. His voice was firm with a slightest touch of nervousness. That was unusual. Becky could see what Samantha was doing and how Burns was more serious than normal.

He's gotta be worried about Sam, too.

"Sir! Good to go, sir!" Becky mimicked.

"Great... Tiny? No talking from you until I say so; Raven, I love you and be careful. Out," Burns said.

Becky felt her mouth slacken and eyes narrow in surprise. More awe and wonderment than surprise. She was nothing short of shocked at what Burns had said and the circumstance around it.

Wow... that's out of character. He must be worried and stressed.

Suddenly worried, she wondered whether Burns knew something she didn't.

Is something wrong? Something specific or just in general?

Becky heard Samantha's silence. It reminded her of listening to snow hitting the ground on a cold, windless night in the forest.

She has to be stunned.

She had never heard Burns say in public, with witnesses no less, that he cared for someone, let alone that he "loved" someone.

"I love you, too," Samantha responded.

Becky could tell her sister was moved close to tears: the tone, volume and intonation of each syllable. Even her nose sounded blocked up the way she did when she was younger and she was on the verge of crying. Her mind drifted to David and Emma. David said he loved her once in a while, but his behaviors spoke volumes. His tender moments and the times he would hold her and Emma made her feel more loved than she ever had before she met both Burns and David. Becky felt odd and had to say something.

"I will open the email account in four minutes and run silent. See you all on the other side.

Somehow using a Burns's military, technical phrase helped her focus. The cold vernacular pulled her from her emotional spot and worry to the present.

"I can't wait for this shit to be over," she said.

~

Welch turned back to see that Janeson was watching the screen closely as her team focused on their individual bank of monitors and assignments.

Davis was getting close to the plaza's center and still no sign of her contact. If Janeson were affected by the waiting, Welch did not see it.

Maybe part of Janeson's condition is that she doesn't experience anxiety or nervousness.

She would have continued more speculation, but a voice now drew attention.

"Boss... I got some chatter at a very high frequency. Military bandwidth; cryptic. Sounds operational," Johnson summarized.

"Put it on audio," Janeson ordered.

Welch found herself tilting her ears up to hear even though it was unnecessary. *Just habit,* she thought.

"Red Team turning back."

"Blue Team in place and holding."

"Green Team moving forward."

Gold Leader to Eagles, what do you see?"

"Eagle One clear."

"Eagle Two clear."

"Eagle Three... may have target..."

Having heard similar chatter before, Welch experienced a burst of perspiration in her armpits and neck. It was not a hot flash. She immediately turned back to the video feeds to see Davis in the center; she was now waving at her contact with the universal sign to back away. Then the audio picked up again, confirming Welch's worst fears. Someone with a tactical force was watching the same events she was:

"Eagle Three to Gold Leader. I have confirmation of target. Contact is waving target off. Have acquired target. Green to go."

"Eagle Two, eyes on target and contact. Target acquired."

Welch turned to tell Janeson to warn Davis and her team, but she was already speaking rapidly into the microphone.

"Boss? We have chatter from a second team. Much larger group with snipers. They have eyes on Davis and have acquired the target from two vantage points. It's not Burns. It's someone else's operation. Abort."

Welch and Janeson had independently come to the same conclusion about the situation. The "teams" were the groups on the ground while the "Group Leader" was obviously in charge and probably watching from the cameras. The "Eagles" had to be high up and could see in real-time both Davis and whom she was looking at. This was either a paramilitary operation such as S.W.A.T. or a military operation altogether.

Everyone in the control room simultaneously watched everything play itself out as they monitored their own individual screens. Welch turned back to the screen and watched Helms and Andersen break from position, guns drawn to protect Davis.

Janeson covered her microphone and called to Johnson: "Mobilize support teams now!" Johnson, who had kept his line open to the mobile team with eye contact on Janeson throughout, gave the order: "Go in hot; expect resistance, establish a perimeter, and wait for instruction."

Back on the monitor, Helms was yelling at Davis, "Davis! Get everyone down! Snipers!"

Welch saw Davis immediately stand up as tall as possible, waving her hands frantically, yelling, "Get down! He's got a gun!" Welch knew what Davis was doing was an unusual tactic for a soldier in a fire zone. Normally, law enforcement officers and military trained personnel would drop low and make themselves a small target to avoid being hit. A bodyguard is more likely to do the opposite to draw fire at herself rather than the intended target. Davis was trying to draw fire rather than her contact.

Very dangerous maneuver, Welch thought.

Pandemonium broke out. All the civilians started a wave of screaming and dropping to the ground except for Davis and a dark-haired woman, dressed in business casual—dark slacks, a blouse, and an all-season waist business jacket—who was saying something but to no one.

It has to be her. She's talking into a microphone and the range can't be too far with such heavy cell volume. Burns must be close by. Suddenly, the woman turned and ran in the other direction. Beyond the woman, Welch made out at least three groups still standing, but they quickly went to a crouched position with hands moving toward their hips. Welch focused back to Davis, who turned toward Andersen and Helms to get their attention.

More chatter burst over the speaker, providing an eerie narration of events on the screen. It was frustrating to see one mission being compromised by another. It was painfully familiar. Swat Valley flooded her thoughts. She pushed those memories out.

No time for that!

"Eagle Two, losing acquisition."

"Eagle Three, about to lose acquisition..."

"Eagle Two, wing contact..."

Welch heard Janeson yell out to Helms: "They're shooting!"

A distant shot could be heard. Not a loud one, but a definite shot from a large caliber. From the control room's grand view, Davis was sent spinning a few steps back, and he fell hard to the ground. Welch could tell it was a high caliber with good penetration and accuracy. Having spent years with snipers, she could see that the shot was meant to clip and not kill.

Skilled shooter. They're professionals with experience in urban areas. Not good.

Welch's hands were clenched and her breath went shallow as she helplessly watched Helms and Andersen's guns turn upward to a building out of view of the cameras.

From the way Davis went down, Welch started mental gymnastics to guess where the shot originated from. Janeson was faster and guessed that the shot came from right in front of her, which would put the other shooter who had the target in his sight, right behind Helms and Andersen.

"Boss, second shooter is behind you. Either at roof level or window."

Andersen drew their guns at the building behind them, looking for a silhouette. Welch could see frustration on both men's faces as it became evident they saw nothing.

"Eagle Three... take the shot."

Janeson yelled into the microphone, "They're shooting again! Damn it!"

There was a lot of emotion in that warning. Fear, frustration, anger, everything? Welch felt it all to. It was too familiar.

A muffled shot—distinct and clear seemingly erupted in the confines of the center. A collective inhale of air was made by everyone in the control room, except Welch. She kept her breathing level. She could tell everyone was hoping their boss got the warning out fast enough to make a difference.

But it was too late. The target looked as if she were hit square in the back. Welch felt her own back wince as she watched the dark-haired woman skid to a stop and reach for her back as if she had been stabbed. As she tried to turn around, she lost strength in her legs and fell hard to a sitting position. Welch knew the woman's injury was severe, having been shot a couple of times herself in battle, but the adrenaline was often able to keep the person moving when injured. However, when the reaction was that sudden, that meant the caliber had high penetration and inflicted a severe or fatal wound for which the adrenaline could not compensate. After a short moment, the dark-haired woman fell onto her back, and again, Welch felt her pain as she fell on the entry wound.

"Son of a bitch," Welch said.

She saw Andersen and Helms shooting toward something.

Maybe they saw? Maybe a hint of a muzzle flash.

Welch went back to the shot woman and returned to see that Andersen and Helms stopped and dropped their sites to turn back to cover Davis. Then, through the microphone's speaker, there was another shot, but from an entirely different source. With no previous order to shoot coming over the speakers, Welch and the team heard an unexpected cry instead.

The chatter suddenly picked up in urgency and intensity.

"My shooter is down! Did these guys set up their own snipers?" asked the disembodied voice. The disbelief and surprise from the speaker was palpable.

Everyone in the control room froze. Welch turned to Janeson. Janeson read her non-verbal question well.

"We have no snipers in place and victim was on their side," she said as she scrutinized the screen.

"The hunters are now the hunted," Welch added. With little in the way of logic, she couldn't understand why she was happy" a civilian and a sniper were down, her friend was in the fire zone and civilians were all over the place.

It's a Goddamn nightmare.

"How long till our guys get there?" Janeson requested.

"Three minutes. The streets are jammed with civilians," Johnson responded.

Welch watched Janeson scanning the screens as she spoke aloud.

"The sniper who shot Davis and the contact is now dead, and it wasn't from either of us, and I am sure their own side did not shoot one of their own." Janeson was logically deducing the events.

Welch had to agree it made sense. Micro-seconds passed.

"Fuck... it's Burns..." Gilmore said.

"This just got messed up bad," Johnson added.

"All groups. Secure the perimeter!" the voice from the speakers called out.

The control room's screens came alive with six separate groups of men and a few women with fully automatic guns moving in from all angles to secure the kill zone with minimal crossfire. Welch saw that Helms and Andersen had guns trained on various targets, but they did not shoot. There were yells everywhere of "Drop your gun" and "Federal Agents." Her team did not drop their weapons but kept them trained on the groups closing in as they both backed their way toward Davis to cover her. The advance of the ground forces stopped as rapidly as it began. While a number of citizens lay on the ground screaming and crying, the advancing group of armed men and women sent to maintain the perimeter came under fire themselves.

The assault group closest to Davis's contact started to swarm around the downed target. More shots could be heard. They were more muted, like the backfire of an old-style car, but still a loud, ominous popping sound. Suddenly, two of the four men seemed to stop, sputter, and fall down while feeling for and finding they had been hit with bullets. The two surviving members of the group backed off suddenly, looking for cover.

The speakers were blaring with chatter and single gunshots.

"Green Team is down! Eagle Three? Do you have the source of the sniper fire? Eagle Three?"

More muted shots.

"Team Leader, Eagle Three and her spotter are down; Green Team is pinned down; advise your ground teams to hold position; change satellite visual to infrared search. Start at five hundred yards and move out. Search for elevated positions."

"Eagle One? Do you have a target?"

"Negative Team Leader."

"All teams, hold position."

Magically, all movement stopped with the exception of Davis.

The teams on the ground stopped their advance. As a soldier, it was evident to Welch they had no cover, so half of each team was looking skyward for muzzle flashes while the others kept eyes on Davis, Helms and Andersen.

This is just unbelievable. This is the very definition of FUBAR!

Welch took in all the visuals to see if there was some place her team could successfully retreat and find cover. There was nothing. Boston City Hall was a death trap. It's probably why Burns had picked it as a drop off site.

Though the shootings and the advance of the other forces were now halted, Davis had managed to get to her knees; she stood up as well as she could and ran to the dark-haired woman. Welch and the entire control room personnel watched as she carefully came to the woman's side and got very close to check for vitals. It was evident that Davis's left arm was working but with great effort and pain. From the angle, it seemed as if the woman were alive and saying something. The control room cameras moved in and saw some discussion between Davis and the contact.

The conversation is going to be brief, Welch thought.

She experienced a sudden flashback to PFC Parks, but forced herself to stay focused in the present. The dark-haired woman seemed to be looking away but then she reached toward Davis's throat.

Was she trying to hurt her or grab onto something? A hallucination or something tangible.

The woman seemed to grow paler by the second as she had to be losing blood rapidly. Davis caught her hand and held it above the woman's chest. Then, the woman used her other hand to hold onto Davis. She looked like she was saying something again and then Welch could clearly see her eyes begin to drift away while Davis kept holding her close. Sirens were filling the air as Davis stayed with the woman and then she looked around in front of her and then to the side. Davis went back to hold the woman quietly while Helms and Andersen kneeled above them both with guns trained outward toward the armed teams of men and women. As the sun broke through the clouds briefly, the black-and-white cameras maintained clarity while the color cameras pixilated slightly with the glare.

Silence pervaded the control room with the exception of sirens and breathing.

Welch was truly drained of emotions. A simple exchange of flash drives had turned into a shooting gallery within minutes. Already there were five or more bodies, and her team, with her close friend, was pinned. She was still strategizing an exit strategy when she found herself seeing something unusual on the black-and-white video feeds and was trying to focus on Davis.

At that moment, from Welch's perspective, Davis looked straight up toward a set of FBI cameras or rather above the cameras. She wasn't the only one who noticed Davis seemingly zeroing in on something important. *Burns, maybe*, she wondered.

"What is she seeing?" Johnson asked.

It was clear to all in the control room that something had caught and held Davis's focus. As the armed sea of men and women held ground and kept the perimeter closed, citizens got up and scurried away. Davis looked down at the dark-haired woman and then back up; she looked around in the area she had honed in on just moments ago, but she must have lost sight of what she had originally spotted. She returned her focus to the woman, folded her hands, and stayed close to her on the ground. Even though Davis was in a sitting position, Welch thought she saw her physically tilt to her side and then attempt to control her own collapse beside the woman. Andersen moved closer to Davis, who appeared to have passed out. He checked vitals while keeping his gun trained on his own targets. After some facial exchanges between him and Helms, Andersen dropped his gun, and he took off his jacket to use pressure to slow the bleeding in Davis's arm.

"Jesus Steve… how to hell did all of this happened?" Welch said to herself quietly. She had a visceral response to hit something. Watching helplessly, the scene was near exact to her past: death happening around her, innocent civilians killed, soldiers in danger, and the whole simple plan thrown in the shitter. The more she watched the colder and angrier she felt. Welch was not aware of how quiet the control room had become until she heard a familiar voice.

"Fuck me," was Gilmore's response.

Janeson's voice shook everyone out of a shocked state.

"Snap out of it, people!"

Wow… Janeson's voice can carry. Okay—call it Janeson!

"I want that trace on the endpoint of that transmission secured; confirm all audio-visuals are recorded and run them through all the servers to obtain faces for recognition. Track for more hostile communication and make sure we are recording all cell phone activity within a three-thousand-yard area for review. Johnson, make sure our people get back to our shop. Nowhere else. This is an extraction. Do not focus on holding onto the crime scene or the body; let them have it. I want you to send in Martin as lead field agent. Have him do it exactly like we saw him last time."

Welch saw a sudden shift in Johnson's response to Janeson.

Johnson froze and uttered, "You can't send him!"

Gilmore jumped in: "Boss! That's crazy!

What the hell?

Janeson shook her head in disagreement.

"He's the only one who can be bigger than anyone they got down there. If anyone can exude authority and make it clear he owns a fire zone, it's him. He's done it a bunch of times. Tell him now so he can get his head in the game and pull it off. Get it done and get 911 there, now!" Janeson shot back.

"But, boss… the circumstances are very different. I only put him on the extraction team as a sign of force. Observation only," Johnson continued.

Janeson shook her head, indicating to Welch that her mind was made up.

"Guys, look! Our team is outnumbered and down. Burns is out there and might kill our people. I am not leaving them behind. He can do it. Time for faith."

Johnson's response was slow but decisive: "Yes, boss."

Shoulders visibly dropped as Gilmore approached Janeson and gave her a tablet of information.

If this doesn't work, we're all fucked," Gilmore added out of earshot of the other staffers.

"If we do nothing, we're fucked anyway. Act of omission or commission? Which would you choose?" Janeson asked.

No. You're right, boss. It's just really outside-the box thinking," Gilmore articulated.

Welch started to wonder who this Martin maverick was to inspire confidence and fear at the same time. Nipping at her memories Welch found herself thinking back to her own firefights in Afghanistan—Kabul, Jellalabad, Malakand, Khost—and Swat Valley, Pakistan.

We leave no one behind. No one dies; not today.

Welch turned back to the monitors and then she looked around the pit and banks of monitors. Janeson's team burst into overdrive; phone calls were being made; a couple of spare agents who were helping with data analysis ran off to get their tactical gear. It was evident to Welch that this rapid, well-practiced response must have been a response to the last crisis to occur for this office on May second. Andersen had told Welch that Burns's team had created so much chaos and then nuked the control room that it had made an indelible impression on this group of analysts and field agents. It had made an impression on everyone. The FBI was not prepared then and since then it had been prepared for war per the deputy director's mandate.

By the time she turned her attention back on the monitors, she could see the extraction team was already in place. The color video feeds pulled back to show that the FBI agents were above the camped groups of armed men and women. It also looked like the Boston Police were backing up the FBI in force.

If this Martin guy doesn't pull this off, this could get worse.

~

In the past, Samantha couldn't help but wonder what it would be like to be "normal" as she watched the "normal" people heading home to see their families. When she was a prostitute, she had wondered how normal people had intimate relationships. That is until she met Burns. Smiling as she walked, she felt as if she were now like the other people who surrounded her.

He loves me, she thought.

She was on time and had turned the corner that led into the plaza. A bunch of commuters were walking toward her, so she had to edge her way through. She was now trying to clear her head from her last voice contact with Burns. This was the first time he had ever said he loved her. It was the first time anyone had said it to her, and she felt it.

Her eyes were still filled. *He loves me,* she kept thinking to herself.

She knew he cared for her by the way he embraced her, talked to her, waited for her in bed or for breakfast. While his behaviors spoke volumes, it was the first time she heard him use the phrase "I love you." He never had to say it, and she had never believed men when they had said it to her in the past. They never treated her the way he did. Maybe because Burns never said it, it now had a powerful feel to it. She continued to walk, but she was still feeling weepy.

It's not my period, she thought. *Maybe the stress of the mission.*

Samantha stopped for a moment, almost to catch her breath. Maybe she was weepy because he loved her, he had said it, and she knew it was real. She loved him, and that really scared her. Becky, Tony, Emma, David... they were family. Burns... Alex... he was foreign to her.

A man who loves me without obligation to or wanting something. What the hell?

She started to walk again as tears formed in her eyes. She was happy, but it was frightening to love and to be loved, she admitted to herself.

Jesus Christ! This is so complicated.

She kept going as she became aware that voices were coming over her earpiece.

"Raven... I see our contact is beginning to wave in your direction. She's waving her hands... something is up? Tiny? What do you see?" Burns asked.

Samantha heard something in his voice. More tension than usual.

"I see it, too. Place looks busy. I don't think she sees Raven yet, though. Who is she waving to?" Becky asked.

Samantha could tell that Becky felt tense and confused as well.

It's gotta be hard for her to watch everything but not be able to do anything.

She felt sad that they were worlds apart with her in Boston City Hall Plaza and Becky in a Parisian Cafe.

Man... what time is it in Paris? It's gotta be close to midnight or something.

"Tiny, focus on Andersen and Helms. I got the contact. If they move or do anything, shout it out. Raven... slow your pace down."

"Kinda hard to do that without stopping," Samantha said, now in full view of a crowded throng of people trying to head home. She did eventually stop, but she was in plain view; plenty of people were between her and her contact. Her thoughts of love and Burns had vanished as she returned totally to the present.

Becky was the first to say something next.

"Raven! Andersen and Helms are running to the contact... Guns are out!"

"Sam! Stop and crouch. Get ready to run!" Burns blurted out. Samantha felt panic. Burns had used her real name.

He broke protocol. This is bad, real bad. Shit!

Samantha heard a woman yell out, "Get down! He's got a gun!" In response, a wave of people started dropping to the ground and screams radiated out from the center of the plaza where her contact was supposed to be. As everyone dropped, Samantha had clear view of her contact who was standing as tall as possible, waving her off. Then the contact turned toward the guys with guns.

"Wait a minute… is she telling me to get out of here?" Samantha asked.

"Get out of there," Burns hissed out. She heard Becky's inhale of air as if her hands were to her mouth, suppressing a scream from nearly thirty-five hundred miles away. *Helpless.*

"I'm gone," Samantha said, and with that she felt her legs spring to life as she bolted in the direction she had come from. Then there was a shot. She looked back and was positive she saw the woman who was waving at her before falling to the ground.

"Fuck," she said out loud.

She figured she was about twenty feet from cover as a wall loomed in front of her all the while Burns was talking in her ear: "Sam, don't look back! Just run straight."

Things gotta be bad for Burns to drop protocol, she thought as she concentrated on running.

Sam took a quick look before she was about to pick up speed.

I'm so happy I picked up these sensible shoes.

Without ever hearing the shot that hit her in the back, Samantha's first thought was that some monster hornet had stung her. It felt like a sharp knife or a massive bee stinger was imbedded between her shoulder blades. Stunned, she caught herself slowing down her pace and stopping as she tried to reach back to see whether she could feel what was sticking in her. She heard more shots, but the burning sensation was increasing and she was feeling suddenly tired and needed to sit down. She thought she had controlled her rate of trying to sit on the ground, but the ground came up too fast and she hit it hard. She was suddenly very tired and dizzy so she lay down. While now feeling a burning sensation traveling below her shoulder blades, she heard more shots and yelling, but she honed in on her sister's voice first.

"Sam! Sam!" Becky pleaded.

"Becky! Shut up... Sam... talk to me..." Alex's voice was soft.

It's gotta be bad, she thought, *for him to get all upset while in an operation. He dropped Becky's code name, too. Everything must be really fucked up.*

Her mouth felt dry and she had to swallow before she spoke next.

She started to feel cold.

"Fuck... that really hurt..." Samantha responded.

What do you feel, babe?" Alex asked.

"Stabbing, burning feel. I... feel kind of weak and cold... I can't feel my legs... I think I might be going into shock..."She felt woozy as she spoke. At the same time, she felt like she used to when she was a young child, overtired and very sleepy with the only desire to fall asleep in her sister's warm bed where she felt safe and secure. It was an extremely rare feeling that she experienced only with Burns of late.

"No way, Sam. Just rest. Cougar is there; she's coming up beside you right now. I don't think it's going to hurt."

Samantha felt pressure from someone by her side. It was the contact she was to meet. She looked like shit, though, she thought, and she had blood on her left arm.

"You should get that looked at... looks like a flesh wound, though..." Samantha said to the woman.

"Will do. Can you hang on? You have to hold on," she said.

"No..." was Samantha's response before she knew it. She was still a nurse after all. Then, she heard something unusual.

"Becky?" Burns started. "Could you just talk to Sam for a moment...?"

Why was he letting Becky talk during an operation? she wondered.

There were more shots. Burns was quiet.

"Hey, honey. Kind of stupid to get yourself shot. That wasn't part of the plan you know," Becky was saying through a sniffling nose.

Bad cold? Crying? That's it, Samantha concluded, *Becky is trying not to cry. Oh, fuck! I'm not going to make it. I got shit to say...*

Panic set in as she felt time was slipping away too fast.

"Becky... I love you. I love Emma. Say goodbye to David and Emma for me, will ya, honey?" Samantha was feeling herself slip. *It's too fast,* she thought.

"I expect you to do that, Sammy. I love you, Pumpkin..." Becky stopped suddenly as if she couldn't go on. Her sister had not called her "Pumpkin" in years.

There were more shots. Then silence except for Burns's voice:

"Sam... is that a cross hanging off Cougar's neck?" Burns asked softly.

"Yes... you can see it?" she asked.

"Yes. I'm watching you from across the street to your left. Don't look, though. Look at the cross and see if you can hold it," Burns coached her through.

Samantha reached out and grabbed it. The woman held her hand there. Then, Samantha's other hand went around both their hands.

"I got it Alex... Alex... could you pray for me? The short one... do it in Latin... please... I've done some bad things and need forgiveness..."

"Absolutely, babe. For you I'd give the world..."

'Ave Maria, gratia plena, Dominus tecum.

Benedicta tu in mulieribus,

et benedictus fructus ventris tui, Jesus.

Sancta Maria, Mater Dei,

ora pro nobis peccatoribus,

nunc et in hora mortis nostrae. Amen.'

I love you..." Samantha could hear that Alex was barely holding on. His voice was struggling to stay with her.

Poor thing. This has to be hard. If it were him, I don't think I could watch.

"I love you, Alex... I am glad you are here with me... Alex..."

Samantha felt lightheaded. Her vision was trailing off. She heard his voice again.

"Don't leave me, Sam. Please... no."

She wanted to respond, she did but it took too much energy. Her stomach felt empty, and her body felt weightless. She was happy she didn't die alone. This woman, Cougar, was with her, and Alex was safe, but somehow he was right there with her.

Thank God he prayed for her.

She felt tension leaving her face as she felt herself passing... *maybe with that last prayer, I might be forgiven and steal my way into heaven... like that thief when Christ was crucified... was it at Calvary?*

She always felt safest when she slept. She could make out that sirens were getting closer, but somehow everything got quiet for her. She didn't care anymore. For a moment, it looked like the sun was streaming through but then her sight was tunneling from brightness, solid lines and shapes to soft, fading gray.

Chapter 6

"Carpe noctrem" – "Seize the night."

Becky was frozen in fear as her hands clutched her mouth and a sense of stillness descended on her. Completely helpless, she watched her baby sister die from three thousand miles away, and she couldn't do a damn thing. Her intake of air was sharp, and her eyes were filled with tears. With her nose completely blocked up, her thoughts kept racing, saying the same thing over and over again: *No! No! No!*

She knew Burns gave her the first turn to talk to Sam before she died. Samantha was probably the most lucid at that point. She appreciated that. She had no idea whether she made any sense, but at least Samantha heard her say that she loved her.

How will I live without you? How am I going to tell Emma? How will David react? Why? Why did you have to go? Why? Tony... no. Not both of you...

She wanted to hate Burns for everything, but she couldn't. At the end of the day, she had never seen Samantha so happy as when she was with him. They seemed like soul mates. But Becky wanted to make someone pay, and she wanted it to be Burns... *but what would Samantha say?*

Becky heard the shots prominently from Burns's microphone. He had made at least five people pay for Samantha's death.

That's not enough! That's not even close!

Then, within seconds of pulling a trigger that probably killed people, Becky heard Burns's voice softer than she had ever heard him. Even softer than when he would play with Emma. He gave Samantha love and meaning in the end. And when Samantha asked him to pray for her in Latin, he did without hesitation. Becky couldn't even talk.

Becky felt as if her own life, her own soul, was slipping before her eyes as Samantha lay down on the ground. Darkness, empty, pitch-black night fell upon her, seized her. She felt her own life ebb away leaving reflections of memories. She immediately saw the little girl whom social services had brought to live with her and her family as if it were yesterday.

When Tony was alive. Before Emma was born. Before she had met David. Before everything changed.

"No..." Becky said to herself.

She listened and watched her sister die, holding a cross while being held closely by a stranger who was trying to warn her of danger. All this with her soul mate praying for her.

I should be there. I should be holding her. Why did it have to be you, Pumpkin? You're not supposed to be there.

And then, her hot tears flowed over her cheeks and hands, burning her, and she felt her own breath become shallow like her dying sister as she heard Burns talk next:

"Don't leave me, Sam. Please... no."

The pain, she thought. *My pain. Almost as much pain as me. Tony... Sam... no.*

Becky watched in harsh black-and-white, high definition as two men, Helms and Andersen, were protecting their own friend and her dying sister while holding off many more people with guns. She had no idea how much more time passed before she heard Burns's voice. Soft and croaking a bit, but he was back.

"Becky... Becky... are you there?" Burns asked. Becky noticed Burns had dropped all protocols and used real names.

"Yes," was her short response. She felt empty and breathless.

Emptiness. Hollow. Nothing. I feel nothing.

She felt almost nothing. Darkness gripped her. Emptiness filled her.

"Shut down the connection. Turn off your computer and hang up. Get out of there. I will call you within two hours."

"Burns?" she asked.

She had lost her brother and now her sister. *Who's next? David? Emma?*

"How do we end this? How do we keep Emma and David safe and kill the bastards who killed my sister?" she asked. Anger welled in her stomach as only vengeance filled her mind.

"I'll tell you in two hours," Burns said. Then he added, "Tell David what happened and have him call Andersen in an hour to let him know that the 'dead man switch' has been pulled. Tell him 'The flood is coming.' And Becky? Please... don't tell Emma until you're back home safe with her, all right?"

"Acknowledged," Becky said blankly. She felt empty.

So that's how Burns is keeping it all together. He's formulating a plan to save everyone before killing the bastards who did this, she concluded.

The others. The three contacts. They looked surprised by everything too, Becky thought. She slowly arranged to pack to everything up to leave the cafe. She saw herself moving and acting as if she were watching a movie of herself act. Her thoughts were racing as she tried to figure out what happened. Who was on her side; who was against her?

One thing for sure, Cougar, Helms and Andersen were not the ones who had killed her. It looked like they were trying to save her. At least, they were with her so she didn't die alone. A sudden intake of air and a moan came from her throat.

Becky wasn't sure she could ever forgive herself for not being with Sam in the end. She couldn't protect Sam from her cousin so many years ago, and she couldn't do it again. Feeling unreal and disconnected, she felt alone and robotic in the City of Love. With no idea how she was going to live without her sister, she absently closed down her Internet connection and collected her cases together to leave. Without even noticing the young patrons talking and laughing around her, she walked toward the tallest structure she could see with deep-seated hate building in her veins. Smoldering, burning, no outlet for enmity. No target. No one to hit, strike at. No one. Nothing.

Samantha and Tony... gone forever.

It was a long time before Becky broke out of her haze and noticed people were staring at her. Unsure why, she touched her face and saw that her makeup was all over her hand, indicating that it must be completely smeared, and her eyes and nose probably red.

She turned around and looked for a public bathroom she could use. She went two blocks and came across one that went underground. There were not many left in the city. She was still whirling from the images in her head of her sister dying as she placed her cases on the floor beside the sink to wash her face. She got the water running, but there was very little soap. Her attention suddenly shifted from her pain to why there was no soap in the dispenser. She hit the dispenser harder, and she got a little more soap on her hands. As she started to rub them together, the water stopped. Becky smacked it and the water started again. She went back to the soap dispenser, but this time no soap was released. She hit it again and there was still none. She was about to hit it again when the water stopped.

"I said stay on!" she yelled at the water spout as it started again. Then, it stopped suddenly. In a more rational moment, Becky might have figured out that the water was timed to shorter intervals when repeatedly hit. She knew she was losing it, so she took in a deep breath and went to the sink right next to it. She hit the water knob, but there was no water. She stopped as she was about to smack it really hard and then she controlled her breathing and decided simply to dry her hands and leave.

They're gone... both of them... why?

She managed to walk over to the paper towel dispenser. As she turned the lever to release the paper, the paper jammed up and was stuck in the feed. She looked at it for a moment and then she attempted to dig out pieces of the paper towels so she might get a hold of a bigger piece. But the paper kept ripping and the paper jam was getting bigger.

Why won't this work?

Becky felt a physical pulling at her heart as a wave of feelings surged.

"Because nothing ever works for you! Nothing's ever easy!

Everyone you love dies! You live and they leave you!" Becky's voice exploded as she stared at the dispenser.

A ball of anger and pain completely filled her stomach and chest. She became aware of her breathing getting heavier and then she put both her hands on the plastic paper holder, and with all her strength she wrenched the paper dispenser off the wall and hurled it at the toilet stall with a guttural, primal scream erupting:

"Goddamn it! Why? Why? Why the fuck did you have to take both of them? Who's next? Why?! What kind of God fucks with people who have nothing? Who the fuck are you? What do you want from me? What did I do to you?!"

The roll of paper towels was now everywhere in the bathroom. She suddenly turned on the soap dispenser and raised her leg up and kicked it off the wall with her foot. The container of soap released easily from the wall and sent pink liquid soap splattering everywhere. As Becky saw that the mirror was dirty, she picked up her hard computer case and wound up for a wide arc swing, yelling at the mirror before it shattered, "Oh, you want some of this too! You want to leave, too?"

Shards of glass were still sailing in the air when she saw two young women, who must have been in the stall, run out of the lavatory as her rage crescendoed with her breaking the mirror.

Becky caught her breath as she saw in the mirror, which was still intact, that her makeup was worse and she looked completely insane. Becky got her head together and realized she had to go.

"Why?" Becky asked more softly. She felt her chest sag, shoulders droop, and her rage fall into anguish and sadness.

Minutes or seconds passed. She couldn't tell. Then a cogent thought struck her: the two women who witnessed her madness might be going to get the police. Becky suddenly collected her belongings and ran up the short flight of stairs. She made a sharp right and walked with determination down the street to avoid being seen by the police. She began to control her breathing... *They're both gone... Tony and Sam...* She wondered what she was going to do without them. The tears continued to flow down her cheeks as she kept walking.

How am I going to tell Emma and David?

~

Burns felt hollowed out. He had been shadowing Samantha from eight hundred yards in a renovated office complex that overlooked the meeting site. He had scoped the area of ground forces, but he focused more on Sam and the contacts. He had missed the teams on the ground entirely. He was sick to his stomach that he could be so blind as to miss the obvious. He felt like things were going to work until he saw his contact, the woman he confronted months ago, waving Samantha away from the scene. His scars on his scalp and arms burned when he scoped back and took in the full view from near the plaza's center. He saw quickly that in each building looking out over the center was at least one window open with no blinds, no light emitting from it. By the time he had told Sam to stop, the contact took matters into her own hands by yelling, "Get down! He's got a gun!"

Chaos ensued. Burns watched as she stood up tall and made herself a bigger target, rather than hitting the ground for protection. This was the closest to panicking he had ever experienced as he readily recognized this standard procedure to protect a potential target by taking the shot yourself. This would also give the clear message that the area was compromised.

With venom in his throat, he repeated, "Damn it! Damn it! Damn it!"

Suddenly, he saw a suppressed muzzle flash from the window that caught his contact in the arm. From the force she was struck with by the shot, he could tell that Cougar was deliberately winged. Her left arm was probably torn up a bit and could lose blood, but no permanent damage had been done.

Burns felt as if he had broken into two personalities. One was screaming about Samantha—*I gotta get her out of there!*—and the other was the professional field agent noting fields of fire. To save her, he shifted to assess the enemy before his emotions for her overwhelmed him. He had to do this fast to act. His thoughts leaped to the enemy's caliber, which was on par with his since it could penetrate at least eighteen inches into a person, causing him to stop in midstride. Burns's calculations put the shooter at least seven hundred yards closer to the target, allowing the shot to be more accurately placed to kill immediately with either a head shot or to the torso. If it were a torso shot, it would be a fast two minutes for the person to bleed out. That meant his target was the third building to the left.

"Get out of there!" Burns hissed out as he zeroed in on the dark window.

Run for cover and don't look back, he thought as he had a vague outline of two people.

A spotter and shooter... but which one is which? Damn it!

He knew the second report would hit her if she were not behind the wall. With both the shooter's spotter and the building angle obscuring his shot, he began to depress the trigger, unsure whether he could even hit his hidden target. When the second shot from the shooter came, the spotter moved and Burns took the shot. He hit his target, but it was too late. He turned his focus back on Sam; he had seen her stop, clutch her back and then fall to the ground, hard.

No!

Burns felt his brain split in two. His emotions locked away; his distant, clinical professional mind took over. He knew the high caliber used would cause profound internal damage if it didn't kill her on impact. From eight hundred yards away, he could only watch her slowly die.

No...

An ebb of pain surfaced as he knew Sam's sister, thousands of miles away, had to feel the same way—*so close, and yet so far.* His former adversary, Cougar, who was now wounded, had gotten to Sam pretty fast and seemed to be gentle with her. He scoped her face and her reaction confirmed that Samantha's wounds were mortal. She stayed with she so she wouldn't die alone. She stayed by Samantha's head and neck as lifeblood flowed out of her back.

Burns shifted rapidly out to see whether there were any more possible sniper nests. While yelling at Becky to let him talk, he rapidly found one more with a shooter and spotter, and without much thinking killed them both in rapid succession.

As if watching someone else, he acted yet felt nothing. He just saw targets and one field objective: suppress all enemy movement immediately. As naturally as breathing, he narrowed his focus closer to Sam, and again he controlled his breathing and gave Becky a chance to say goodbye to her sister as he shot two of the ground teams closest to Sam.

He focused back out to take in the entire center of the plaza; he saw that all ground teams were stopped in place; all bystanders were either on the ground or running away, and his contacts, Andersen, Helms and Cougar, were huddled over Samantha's body with guns drawn.

They're protecting her. The thought was analytical and professional. His heart sank.

His scars seemed to ignite, and he felt pressure from a headache forming as he scanned the field of fire and began to reconnect with the world again so he could be with Samantha one last time.

As his breathing returned, he held onto every word that came from Sam's mouth. She asked him to pray in Latin for her and he did. His eyes were welling and his throat was closing.

At least Becky got to say goodbye, too.

He watched Samantha reach out for the cross hanging from the Cougar's neck and held it with first support and then with her own strength as she listened to his prayer. He knew she listened to him all the time when he prayed, and he knew the Latin version of the "Hail Mary" was her favorite. When he was done, her hands fell from the cross and she faded away. He told her he loved her again.

Her words were simple and final, and he would never let them go: "I love you, Alex... I am glad you are here with me, Alex..."

She called his name as she slipped away, holding a stranger's hand.

No! I need you! Please, no!

Lowering his head, Burns never felt such a deep pain, a raw sadness full of pain and void of all other feelings. Face still looking down, he heard a foreign, hollow plea emerge from his mouth.

"Don't leave me, Sam. Please... no." She was gone.

Why did I let her go? Why did I let her go? he kept repeating in his head.

Face down, he remained still.

Maybe if I never move, she'll still be there.

As this irrational thought echoed in his head, his scalp and arms were itching and pulling him back. The mostly cloudy, overcast day had a break in the clouds that allowed some rays of evening sun to pierce through. He had imagined that was the exact moment she must have died. Raising his head to look, he felt the rays of a fading sun hit his face. The sun was warm and he drifted off for a second, praying that Samantha was at peace. He prayed that if there were a heaven, she would be welcomed there.

Why did you take her? Why not me? I deserve it. She's innocent. Becky, David, Emma...why them? They only tried to help me and others? Why...?

He knew she had killed three people in her life. He also knew she was fearful of going to hell for the sin of murder, even though the killings were justified. Burns's train of thought snapped back into the here and now. When he peered back through his scope to see her one last time, he was jolted to see that the woman holding Samantha was looking straight at him through his own scope. Dismayed, he physically pulled back away from the scope.

What the hell?

Angry with himself, it only took him a millisecond more to realize the sun was reflecting off his scope, which in turn was giving his location away. He closed his scope with a cover as he spoke to Becky about next steps. To remain sane and not be consumed with grief, he focused on leaving his position immediately and figuring out the next steps to protect Emma, Becky, and David.

Burns was out of the building in under two minutes. Exactly how he left was a mystery to him since he felt distracted and he wanted to kill those responsible.

Why? was the question that kept repeating.

His arms, where there were fewer scars, were also itching now. He walked a block away from the plaza center and began to think.

Think! Stay focused. Emma, David, Becky. Stay focused for them. Protect them.

Knowing that his contact was shot, he knew they would take her to the nearest hospital.

Where is it?

Burns turned sharply to his right to enter a hotel lobby that cut through a city block to another street where he got lost in the throngs of evening commuters. With sirens fading, he focused on finding the local hospital emergency room that would treat gunshot wounds. As he began to melt again within the mass of people, he had a recurring thought: *I am going to make them all pay.*

Chapter 7

"Ut desint vires, tamen est laudanda voluntas" – *"Although the power is lacking, the will is commendable"* Ovid

The entire string of events—from Davis trying to warn her contact, to the sniper shootings, and everyone with a gun trying to find cover—lasted probably six minutes at the most. They were the longest, most frantic, and now tensely silent six minutes Helms had experienced in a long time. He saw that Andersen had checked Davis's vitals and looked concerned.

"Pulse seems thready, but she's alive. She must be losing blood. Probably just passed out."

Andersen had put his gun down so he could apply pressure on Davis's arm. She had passed out, probably a result of blood loss. He noticed that the ground team's lead agent had holstered his weapon and was attempting to negotiate a "peaceful resolution" while remaining in a crouched position.

Helms had Janeson in his ear; he listened and then said quietly to Andersen, "Extraction on its way."

He wasn't paying much attention to the lead agent. Right now, his two field people were out of a fight; he was covering them both against about twenty very heavily armed agents, and a civilian was dead. The only good news was that they too were pinned down, presumably by Burns, and they weren't going anywhere since they had no cover at all. Helms focused a bit more when the lead agent started quoting jurisdiction and interference with a Foreign Intelligence Agency investigation.

That got his attention: *that fucking Foreign Intelligence Agency again!*

Andersen picked up on it too. Helms shook his head.

Burns is going to make the whole world pay for this.

There was no "If he would retaliate..." It was "How badly and how much will he retaliate?" for his loss.

"You assholes are from the Operations Center? Let me guess, Foreign Intelligence Agency's Operations Center, right?" Andersen blurted out.

Helms was still shaking his head in disbelief when he saw activity behind the small camps of armed agents surrounding him, Davis, and Andersen. A swift, though silent, movement came from the street like water might make, moving around stones in a river. The other team's lead agent put his hand to his ear and also turned around and saw the activity.

With traffic stopped both ways on the street and cars still parked, nearly two dozen FBI agents were now pointing guns at the other federal agents who were stranded and pinned down toward the plaza's center. An additional twenty Boston Police personnel were also well-armed and on the Bureau's side. Helms smiled. He knew Janeson must have mobilized his own team before the bullets started to fly and Gilmore must have called ahead to the local police department about the Bureau needing its assistance.

Nicely done.

Since the Bureau agents clearly identified themselves while the other federal team was not so easily recognized, the officer in charge of the police evidently decided to align with the FBI.

The lead agent was now listening to whoever was talking in his ear as Helms noticed a sole agent from the Bureau walking casually toward the concentrated group in the center. While most of the Operations Center's guns were now pointing toward rooftops where an unknown sniper was thought to be stationed, they knew they were at a major disadvantage—there was no cover and five or more of their own snipers, spotters, and agents were down. And now, there were more guys with guns, in significantly better positions at higher elevation with cover, pointing at them.

Not the way the plan was supposed to go, I bet.

Still, Helms had to strain his eyes to see which *idiot* was walking into an armed situation without cover and a weapon. He eventually figured it out and was completely shocked. He closed his eyes and blinked just to make sure it wasn't an illusion. He suddenly had the thought that maybe he was dead, shot down earlier, and was now living out some hellish atonement since he was now certain that Janeson was completely out of her mind to send Martin.

And what the hell were Gilmore and Johnson doing when this bright idea bubbled to the surface? She must have killed them both to allow this to happen.

As Andersen continued to apply pressure on Davis's arm, he noticed the same very strange event unfolding and looked at Helms with a "What-the-hell?" look. Helms could only shake his head. Violating all known law enforcement safety protocols and standard procedures for negotiating a hostage situation, a sole agent, stripped of weapons and hands raised at chest level, walked toward the center of the shit as if he were heading into a barbeque.

Well, at the very least, this should be interesting. "Always leave them wanting more," Martin would always say.

The sole Bureau agent could be best described as having a stocky build with a light brown complexion and brown eyes with a smiling face. His holster was empty as he walked through the guns, passed right by the other team leader and walked right up to Helms and Andersen. He silently took their guns and held them both pointed down. The leader was about to stand and thought better of it. Helms could easily tell that the lead agent wanted his team to secure Helms and Andersen, but he was stymied about how to do this. As they stood up to assist Davis to her feet and get moving, the FBI agent casually approached the lead Operations Center's agent.

"My name is Martin. I am taking these three with me."

I have my orders," the other leader said. "They are to come in for debriefing with me."

Martin smiled, but his words did not match his seemingly happy demeanor.

That was well done, Helms noted.

"Right now, I have twenty of my guys and twenty of Boston's finest looking at a bunch of armed 'bad guys' who are downwind and have no cover. You may notice you're pinned down, and if you make any sudden moves, there is no telling what will happen next. I now have my shooters in place, but I haven't been able to find the shooter who took your guys out," Martin said while pointing his head at the closest two fallen agents.

He continued unfazed and on-scipt hitting all his marks as he went on: "You see, you boys were so covert in your operation that you didn't clear it with the locals, and they know us well. You? Not so much. There are two news teams taping everything in hopes that two federal agencies and local police will shoot it out like the 'O.K. Corral.' No. You boys screwed up my operation in a colossal way, and I am pissed. While I'm a forgiving man, it ends one of two ways: everyone starts shooting again or they walk out with me."

Martin did not wait for a response as he turned and addressed Andersen and Helms.

Wow... such creative, ingenious bullshit. You'd need wings to stay above this crap he's flinging. How does he stay straight-faced and not get shit on his as he goes along.

If the situation was so God-awful and the stakes so high, Helms would have applauded.

"Gentlemen, will you be so kind as to assist private citizen Davis to the hospital? I will need you two in my office for debriefing."

"Yes, sir!" Helms convincingly responded.

By now, Davis was sitting and semi-conscious. He and Andersen started to assist her; she seemed hesitant to leave the body, but she did with their urging.

"That's... Samantha Littleton," she said.

"I know, Jill. We can't take her. We gotta move," Andersen said.

Helms shifted focus and could see that the other lead agent conceded.

"The body and crime scene stays with us."

"I am only taking the people that can walk out on their own. The rest is yours. Could you please have your boys and girls put their weapons down so no one accidentally discharges a weapon and gets the whole shooting gallery going? Just so you know, I have ambulances up top so you can get your wounded out of here," Martin added as he followed him, Davis, and Andersen up the slight grade to the street.

The lead agent for the Operations Center gave the word and the automatic hardware dropped down.

As Martin approach his own defense perimeter, he gave out a very convincing order.

"Stand down, men. Coming through. Nothing to see here."

Both the Bureau agents and local police lowered their weapons, but they remained behind the cars, just in case.

No one spoke as they walked through the crowd and proceeded up the incline toward their cars.

"Let's saddle up, team," Martin added when Helms and team were in the car.

For the first time in thirteen minutes, all the guns were down and a collective sigh of relief was released. No more shooting. Once in the car, Helms got back on his earpiece to Janeson as Andersen found the first aid bandages to apply to Davis's arm.

He didn't know where to begin.

"Are you out of your mind, Janeson! Did anyone back there question your crazy-ass plan? What were you thinking sending in Martin?"

Helms knew his staff well enough to know what they probably were doing when they heard his voice coming over the speakers back at the control room. He was positive both Gilmore and Johnson simultaneously palmed their faces and closed their eyes as Janeson uncovered her microphone to talk. Helms was positive that Janeson, undoubtedly, would try to explain her decision in a logical fashion.

"Boss, he fits the role perfectly. I have seen his performance, and Gilmore and Johnson thought his acting was quite strong—"

He could hear that Janeson was trying to explain her rational, but he cut her off.

"Janeson, the maneuver was brilliant, well-timed, and well-executed, but pretty high risk in a volatile situation. Next time, please come up with another strategy that doesn't involve an accountant who moonlights in theater. Got it?" he finished.

"Yes, sir," she replied quickly.

Good answer, he thought. *Not defensive or challenging, just acceptance.*

Helms shut off the communication and sat back in his seat. He took a moment to rub his face with both hands to see whether he could get rid of some of the built-up stress in his head. It was quiet and then he realized that his side of the communication revealed to Andersen and Davis that they had just been rescued by an accountant in the Bureau's payroll office who was a part-time actor.

He could see that Davis, now fully conscious, just shook her head in disbelief and leaned back in her seat, too stunned for words. It was all too clear that they had all just bluffed her way out of getting killed. Andersen could only muster one word: "Unbelievable..."

"Hey... Martin is a great accountant and apparently an even better actor," Helms replied. It was brilliant, and he was glad he told Janeson that.

I never would have thought of it. No one in his right mind would have.

~

Thomas Webber slammed his closed fist down on the conference table in Hanscom Air Force Base in Massachusetts as he pushed his chair back to stand up and pace. Rather than be in Alpha's Operations Center in Virginia, he chose to watch the events unfold in Massachusetts, removed from the operational chain of command. Since he knew firsthand what it was like to have a boss breathing down your neck, he wanted his subordinates to be able to do their best work with less stress. His own memories of the events leading up to 9/11 were crystal clear. He knew that if there had not been so much pressure on him back then to "predict" where the terrorists were going to strike, he might have had a chance to do his job. No one ever said it was his fault, but he always felt he had missed something important. Maxwell, Foley, Burns, all of them were able to make a difference. Even though his boss blamed the other agencies for not following up on their intelligence, Webber never could shake the vision of the Twin Towers falling that crisp, fall morning.

Today, though, he was regretting the decision of not leading today's operation with every passing minute. When his own people were held at bay by one shooter and then some cocky FBI agent walked in and took three accessories to murder, conspiracy and probably treason, he couldn't bear to watch it anymore.

"Goddamn it all to hell! It's a simple task!" he said to Ms. Lois Sullivan, an up-and-coming manager and replacement for Denise Cratty.

"We had the intelligence, manpower, surveillance and the entire area secured, and Burns and the Bureau screw everything up! And what the hell was Davis doing?"

Webber was now pacing as Ms. Sullivan remained silently sitting, taking notes.

He stopped suddenly to collect his thoughts.

"Davis, Jillian T. With us for five years, and she decides right now to assist a terrorist escape. I knew she was a weak link! She probably just handed Burns the external drives last May!"

He knew he was venting, but he was so angry he had no other way to express it except to let it all out. As he calmed down and started to pace more slowly in the spacious room, he took the time to clear his head.

These goddamn pants are too tight in the fucking thighs.

While he started to focus on his breathing and to filter out irrelevant thoughts, Webber spoke aloud for both his benefit and his rising star.

"First, Burns disappears for four years and then he returns with a bunch of terrorists to steal classified data critical to national security. Now, the FBI and Davis thinks it's a good idea to try to bring him in from the cold with just three of them and no backup! A golden opportunity to capture him and they piss it away!" His voice was rising again.

He found his heart beating fast again, so he concentrated on his breathing and felt his pulse as he stood still. A full two minutes elapsed before he spoke next.

All right. Time for someone who knows what's at stake to step in.

"Ms. Sullivan," he said in a controlled voice.

"Yes, sir," she promptly responded.

"Contact Operations Center Bravo and have Manager Glenn rally his resources and personnel, seventy percent, to relocate to the field, Boston, Massachusetts."

Boston. Logan Airport. Where they hijacked the planes... I was so close... I just needed more time, he thought.

He shifted his thoughts back to the present with his list.

"We are going to set up a command center here in Massachusetts. Get Alpha's Manager on the deck; they are all coming here. I am not going to let Burns escape."

It was quiet for a moment until Sullivan spoke.

"Sir? What if he's already gone?" she asked.

Webber considered that possibility for a moment as he looked at her attractive, mocha-colored face with strong, brown eyes.

He smiled before he responded.

"No. Burns will stay there until he either comes in for protection or gets even. And because it was Helms and his crew's operation, I am guessing he will be pissed at them. I'm sure he doesn't even know we're involved."

Perfect. Burns's contact is dead, and the Bureau is running the operation. One good thing about keeping this mission off the record, too.

He was still assessing his present situation and next steps when Sullivan asked yet another question. He liked her and thought she had good potential, but her questions and timing could be off-putting.

"Sir? Why is the Bureau and Davis trying to help Burns? It just seems odd."

Good question! How do you explain Stockholm Syndrome when it's another law enforcement agency? he wondered. He still needed a moment to collect his thoughts for a cogent answer.

"I am guessing that Helms and his team don't know what they're dealing with. They see this as an opportunity to 'right a wrong' when it's much bigger than that. We are the only thing between global economic stability and world security; we, as an agency, have made difficult decisions and actions when others have stalled, stopped, and failed."

Webber's mind flashed back to 9/11, and he had to push the images out with great effort so he could refocus.

"So now, even when one of our top assets has gone rogue, has attacked federal agencies and killed one of our own, we need to keep focused on one thing: the retrieval of classified data. His acts alone are treasonous. I'm sure that if Helms knew what data we're talking about, he would be more focused on killing him rather than 'bringing him in.' Because of all this, we need to stay focused on what needs to be done. Burns must be stopped, his team stopped, and the data retrieved. There are no options. No room for error. No mistakes. Just victory."

Webber had lost track of where Sullivan was originally sitting and now found her standing her full six-foot length and smiling.

Well, Ms. Sullivan, we are going to Boston to bring our brethren up to speed on what fire they're playing with and to bring them in the loop of containing this national disaster before it's too late."

Even though he was smiling, he still held the images of burning buildings in his head from years ago.

There was no room for error back then either. And yet, the FBI, CIA... we all failed at the most critical moment.

He shook off the past so he could focus on the future.

"Let's go, Ms. Sullivan. Time to make things right."

They have to understand what's at stake, he thought.

~

Helms and Andersen were just stepping into the control room when Welch caught sight of them.

"Does the word 'Alamo' have any meaning to you?" she asked them both. She did not expect an answer. She was very happy to see that her old friend and former CO had made it out of what appeared to be a 'no-win' scenario.

"I thought that was an urban legend to give Texas a reason to be proud. Their football team is nothing to be proud of," Andersen commented.

"You know, Steve, if we had been killed back there, maybe you wouldn't be running your mouth so much. Not everyone loves 'Boston's Trophy Town,' you know," Helms shot back. It was easy for Welch to see that Helms was still tense in his jaw. She also noticed that Andersen was about to say something but Janeson intercepted, turned and faced Helms as he took command of the control room. Before she could say anything, Helms addressed her first. Welch had the urge to duck and cover, but she was a Marine—*you don't run in the face of danger or worse, a major dress down in front of your peers.* Gilmore filled her in on Martin's occupation with the Bureau and his craft of acting. After she repeatedly asked him whether he was joking, she couldn't get her head around how Janeson could have thought of such a plan, and now she had no idea what would come of that ballsy decision.

"Janeson, I'm still pissed at you, so you need to be quiet for a full five minutes while I talk to your subordinates and find out if you did anything right while I was gone!"

Here we go, Welch thought. *Standard approach: keep the commanding officer last and confront the subordinates first. Classic old school, but still effective.*

Janeson simply nodded. Based on her non-verbal response and her hands folded behind her back, it was clear that this kind of situation, while probably infrequent, had occurred before since her response seemed too well-practiced.

"Johnson! Did you tell Janeson that sending Martin out there was a dumbass idea?" Helms questioned.

"No, Boss... I thought it was a great idea..." he responded.

Confused now, Welch looked squarely at him. *But you told Janeson it was a real bad idea and not to do it.* She was still processing this blatant lie as she watched Helms's eyes narrow in disbelief.

"Really? I thought you were an independent thinker, Johnson?" Helms challenged.

"There is no 'I' in 'team work,' sir," Johnson said in one of the most low key, respectful fashions she had heard from a young person in years.

Welch watched Helms; it was clear his non-verbals conveyed that he did not believe him. Turning his back on Johnson, Helms went to victim number two.

"Right... Gilmore? Did you at least have enough sense to question Janeson's judgment?" he asked.

Welch was beginning to see a pattern and was not shocked at Gilmore's response.

"No, sir... I was about to recommend Martin myself... he is very talented. He says he based his character on how he envisioned what you might have been like back in the day..."

"Shut up, Gilmore," Helms said.

"Yes, sir," was his response.

Welch smiled.

Gilmore and Johnson covering for her. They are a pretty tight team.

The decision she made was creative and outside-the box, but if it failed, it would have been disastrous. But then, the situation Helms and his crew were in seemed genuinely hopeless. She had pulled a rabbit out of a hat.

Helms finally turned back to Janeson since it was now her turn to answer questions. To Welch, it was obvious that Helms knew Johnson and Gilmore were covering for their boss.

"I am assuming that you and you alone were responsible for making that high-risk decision, and these two young men are covering. Am I right?"

Welch waited. The question was clearly not rhetorical; she was wondering why Janeson said nothing. *Insubordination?* Then, Janeson moved her hand from behind her back and looked down at her watch and Helms responded as if he had just remembered something.

It took Welch a minute to realize she was waiting the "full five minutes" Helms had told her earlier.

Wow... she's really concrete. She is going to wait the whole time, Geeze Louis, if I had a platoon like her back in the day...

I know the five minutes is not up; I am shortening the time. Speak," he told Janeson.

Andersen and Welch made eye contact. Welch moved closer for only Andersen to hear her say, "Very literal?"

"You have no idea," Andersen responded quietly.

Welch shifted back to Janeson to hear how she was going to pull another rabbit out of her hat.

"Yes, Boss. Both Gilmore and Johnson were completely against it. I take full responsibility for my action and the actions of my team. I am more than happy to be relieved and be put on administrative leave as—"

Helms interrupted her while closing the distance between them.

"So you can sit this situation out? No way. You are going to see this one through to the end, Missy."

"Missy?" Sounds like Ma, she thought warmly.

Helms started to walk away but then he seemed to have another idea he wanted to add.

"Maybe I might be more forgiving of this matter if you and your team were able to pull together information and ideas of what happened out there... and a way to fix it," he said.

"We're working on that, sir. I should have something for you in ten minutes," she said.

"Get moving. I need to be impressed," Helms warned.

Janeson, Gilmore and Johnson were off to separate parts of the control room, conferring and consulting with various pockets of experts and analysts.

Welch smiled again.

Get information about what happened, she thought. *Of course, they were going to. It's their job.* She had seen this command tactic before. It was evident that Helms was clearly impressed and happy that the three managers demonstrated creativity, problem-solving, and teamwork all while under fire.

He probably wants to buy them a steak and give them commendations.

Welch watched Andersen take a moment to give Janeson some support.

"Take it easy on her, John. She did pull our asses out of the fire back there, and she was able to deescalate a powder keg at the same time."

Helms just smiled and then chuckled to himself. Andersen was clearly wondering what was so funny.

Welch was all over it. She loved Steve, but he was such a stand-up guy that he couldn't see what was really going on.

"He's not going to do anything. He was testing their loyalty to each other to see whether they would support each under pressure. He is building a team through fire."

Turning to Helms, she asked, "I'm guessing you are going to allow them to 'impress you' and that will magically 'soften' the punishment to... let me guess... an additional hour per week for six weeks on the shooting range?" She loved the shooting range.

As a grunt in the corps, being on the gun range was heaven in comparison to physical training. Shame he hadn't been my CO for very long back in the day.

Helms smiled. She could tell he was getting to know her and seemed to like what he was seeing.

"It will be a two solid weeks of advanced residential, leadership camp with a focus on field command for Janeson. It's more of a refresher course for her. For Gilmore and Johnson, it will be a week of basic leadership training and three tours of running their own operations and teams during the third shift... that's for their lying. There has to be discipline in the chain of command."

His smile broadened just a bit more. She figured a guy like him might be close to retiring from public service and was feeling compelled to leave "his" control room in experienced hands. She felt like she was getting to know him again, too.

Welch looked around for a moment. *Where's Davis?*

It must have been obvious she was looking for Davis since Andersen caught the look and answered:

"She's at Boston Medical. Helms forced her there at gunpoint to get treatment, and there is a team to take her home. They will pick her up tomorrow at 9 a.m."

"Oh." Davis didn't strike as the kind of woman to just go to the hospital and stay out of action for very long. She assumed there was more of a story.

Andersen continued, "She didn't take too kindly to Helms saying she had to go there because he didn't have a 'fainting couch' in his office for her. She seemed a bit prickly after being shot."

"I can see how she might feel that way."

It was easy to see that Andersen enjoyed his colleagues very much. She had known him since childhood, so she could tell some of his nuances had meaning. One thing quite evident was that Andersen saw Davis as a younger sister. She knew Andersen had sisters, but they were on the West Coast—Terry was in law enforcement and Darlene, her friend, was a doctor.

Well, Davis doesn't remind me of Darlene, so it has to be Terry, she deduced.

"I wonder why she would object to being called a 'dandy'?" she said.

Shrugging his shoulders, Andersen replied dryly, "Go figure."

With the firefight over and everyone safely "back at the ranch," Welch took a moment to take stock in this task force Andersen had roped her into.

It was a very impressive team of bright and creative individuals. Welch had to admit she had not felt this good in a long time. It was nice to feel that sense of camaraderie again. The last time she had felt it to this degree was Swat Valley, Pakistan.

Nine, R.C., Ice... it was nice to feel something other than sorrow.

Her husband's illness and death had taken a lot of life out of her.

Never sick a day in his life; gets a diagnosis of cancer and is gone in nine months. Just not fair. How many times did I almost get killed? God. I miss Joe.

Welch's thoughts were interrupted by an analyst, Davenport, who was asking for Helms.

"Boss, front desk security reports that there's a 'Thomas Webber,' deputy director of Operations Center, Alpha, Foreign Intelligence Agency... aah... he's 'demanding' to meet with you, sir."

A wave of hatred and fury washed over her. She felt heat rise in her stomach, and the idea of seeing him in public angered her.

You gotta be fucking kidding! Damn it! I can't just kill him here. Too many witnesses.

She felt her fists ball up again, her heart race and her jaw clench. An image of PFC Parks flashed before her eyes, and she had a visceral response to find a combat knife and stab Webber repeatedly in the heart... *that's if that bastard even has a heart,* she bitterly thought. *I'm sorry, Joe... I just hate this bastard so much!*

It must be obvious that she visibly cringed at Webber's name from how Andersen looked at her, although he said nothing for the moment. She knew he would continue to observe her before he asked her anything about it.

There are good reasons why he's good at interrogations.

Welch noticed that Helms was watching her, too, but he also said nothing. Their eyes locked and said volumes.

Yeah... you remember him; Swat Valley. That dick, and his boss, Eric Daniels.

Instead, he turned his attention to the situation as Welch realized that both Andersen and Helms had a bone to pick with Webber for today's cluster.

"Fucking A! Have him escorted down here."

Davenport returned to the call to deliver the message. Once he was off the phone, Helms had another request.

"Davenport, make sure that any conversation occurring in this control room is recorded."

The young man looked suddenly confused.

"Sir... the data here is classified... no recordings are allowed—" he never finished.

Helms brought his fingers to the bridge of his nose to continue rubbing stress from between his eyes as he explained the breach in protocol.

"Davenport... were you not, just about forty minutes ago, one of the guys pointing a gun at this guy's team?" Helms asked.

Yeah, Boss," Davenport answered, not sure where this was going.

"Would it be safe to say that anything this guy says might be important later? And since he can't be trusted, it may be advisable to have a recording of any shenanigans that he might deny later... you know... for leverage," Helms concluded.

The young man's face tilted up as he nodded his head in acknowledgment.

"No worries, sir. Done." Davenport got it.

Helms lesson to you and everyone is "protect the team."

Welch felt more than saw Andersen come up to her side as Helms watched.

"So... you know this guy Webber?" he asked.

Welch had been able to get her autonomic responses and her desire to kill Webber under control so she would at least be able to sound logical when either men asked her this obvious question.

"Yeah... she knows him," Helms answered for her.

Welch took in a breath and continued to give Andersen a little more detail.

"If it's the same guy, yes. He is easy to identify: five foot nothing, bald and last I saw, overweight. He acts like the world and God owe him, and he is God's gift to women. He's a real charmer. You will know for sure, though, when he comes in and starts shooting off his mouth. If he's flanked by an unimaginably attractive young woman, then I'm playing the lottery tonight."

Helms and Andersen were about to question her more when the control room's door opened and a well-dressed, bald, overweight man strode in as if he were entering his favorite restaurant. He was closely trailed by a remarkably attractive, well-tailored young woman of African-American descent. While the gender, age and racial contrast were extreme in and of themselves, it was his short height compared to six feet that nearly made Helms laugh. All eyes stopped to steal a glance at the mismatched couple being escorted into the Bureau's sanctuary.

Well... I have to admit, he knows how to pick pretty women. She has to be a model.

"Oh yeah..." was her only response.

"Let me pay for the lottery ticket, will ya?" Andersen said.

Under different circumstances, she might have found the situation funny.

"Deputy Director Helms? I'm Thomas Webber, deputy director of Operations Center, 'Alpha,' of the Foreign Intelligence Agency in Maryland. May I have a word with you in private? My associate here will be able to take notes as we—"

"Are you joking?" Helms asked. Towering over Webber, Helms's nose was flaring at the sides with the clear expression of wanting to kill Webber. Welch smiled, thinking that he would have to spend time with Webber to imagine killing him.

"Pardon?" Webber looked genuinely surprised. Welch remembered that the last time she had seen that same look was on Webber's asshole boss, Eric Daniels.

Both these guys are just not used to people telling them anything contrary to what they want.

It was Helms's slightly elevated, angry voice that brought Welch back to the present.

"I was running an FBI sanctioned operation with support from local law enforcement, to make contact with a person of interest who was providing us information to retrieve classified data you boys lost a couple of months ago. We had everything covered and contained, and you fucked up everything, including killing our only contact."

Helms was about to elaborate more, but Webber interrupted.

"You had three people to cover an entire city block during the height of civilian congestion. That's not 'running' an operation; that's a lunch date. And your 'contact' was a known terrorist who stole classified data that could jeopardize national security if it's ever leaked. You were about to allow the terrorist to escape, and fortunately my people were there to contain the area and put the terrorist down."

Welch's eyes widened at the entire exchange. Still, she kept her hands to her side and was very happy she was not armed. She marveled at Webber's choice of words—*"put the terrorist down?"* *Like a rabid dog? Is that how you saw her?*

"If you guys weren't there, we would have established contact, gotten the sample data, and then worked out a deal..."

Closing his eyes as he pinched the bridge of his nose, ostensibly to relieve some sinus congestion, Webber interrupted Helms again.

"We don't deal, bargain or negotiate with terrorists. We find them and kill them. My people were there in force. We owned that fire zone, contained the danger, and we were in control of that entire plaza. We kept your incompetence and amateur hour efforts from endangering our nation's interests."

As Webber was speaking, he had directed his comments to the staff rather than to Helms directly. *He still loves his own voice,* Welch mused.

"Really? How many of your guys are dead and injured?" Helms shot back.

"At least their services to their country will be honored. At least they died for something. They know sacrifice," Webber replied vehemently.

"Oh... just like Swat Valley, Pakistan, 2009?" Welch added.

As soon as she opened her mouth, she remembered how Parks said he "just got mad sometimes." Regretting that she said anything, she was pissed that she had jumped into the fight when it wasn't her place. It was Helms's house and operation.

I shouldn't have interfered, one Marine to another.

Webber stopped to peer directly at her. It took a moment but then he remembered with a sickly sweet, fake smile.

Well, Diane... let me remind you that even though you resigned your post, that information is classified."

"And you're an asshole."

The room was still as the enmity each had toward the other became palpable. Her eyes never broke contact with his. Welch knew that everyone in the room must have picked up on the mutual hate. Everyone must have noticed but Janeson. Because of her obvious lack of picking up on nonverbal cues, she managed to defuse the tense situation by walking up to conduct her briefing as if she were walking in on a card match.

"Boss, we have some intelligence that might shed some insight into what we might be dealing with."

Webber broke eye contact with Welch to look at Janeson. Her interruption allowed everyone to take a collective intake of air so as to start breathing again. Except Welch.

I'm still going to kill you someday. Me. Or Nine, or Ice... someone... and I hope I'm there.

Welch seethed as her eyes continued to lock on Webber. And yet, she admired his sociopathic abilities to jump from ostensibly hating someone to being physically attracted to another person, all within milliseconds of each other. It was probably the only time Welch could imagine wishing she had one of Webber's characteristics.

"Hello," Webber said to Janeson. He took a moment to smooth out his tailored, three-piece suit.

Still angry and feeling her blood pressure coming out of her head, Welch found herself with the unusual thought: *Who the hell wears three-piece suits anymore?*

"Hello, sir," Janeson responded.

For all Janeson's oddities, she was physically attractive with her strong, athletic build, sharp facial features, smooth pale skin and very blue piercing eyes. Anyone who could appreciate feminine beauty would want to get to know her. If it weren't for her lack of social skills, she'd be quite the catch.

Suddenly, Welch noticed that Helms stepped in quickly as if he were protecting his daughter from a pedophile. Next, Andersen was putting himself between her and Webber. Johnson, who had been trailing Janeson, also got between Helms and Webber, putting farther distance between Webber and Janeson. In mere seconds, four men wedged themselves between them.

Initially distracted by her boss's unusual gesture of touching her and physically directing her away from Webber, it was evident to Welch that Janeson now regrouped and focused on the new data.

"Go, Janeson. Lay it on me," Helms said. He must have decided to keep Webber there and share information.

Janeson pulled out a tablet, which brought information up on the full screen monitors for all to watch and listen as she went through her briefing.

"Yes, boss. A couple of things: first we did pick up a number of cell transmissions, but it's this cell transmission we believe is between our contact, Ms. Samantha Littleton and Mr. Alexander J. Burns. Initially, each had a code name; Ms. Littleton was called 'Raven' and Mr. Burns was called 'Falcon.' There is a third person called 'Tiny,' but I will come to that later. We got a partial piece and it breaks up in the middle of it, but here it goes."

As the recording played, various pictures and images of both Burns and Littleton appeared on the screens. In the background, there was noise, sirens and people all around. The call sounded painfully clear and drew the attention of all in the room with both distant and close gunshots punctuating parts of the conversation. Through it all, Burns's voice seemed most calm and professional... until the very end:

Burns: Sam... is that a cross hanging... neck?

Littleton: Yes... you can see it?

Burns: Yes...

Littleton: I got it. Alex... Alex... could you pray for me? The short one... do it... please...

Burns: Absolutely, babe. For you, I... the world...

'Ave Maria, gratia plena, Dominus tecum.
Benedicta tu...
et benedictus fructus ventris tui, Jesus.
Sancta Maria, Mater Dei,
...nobis peccatoribus,
nunc et in hora mortis nostrae. Amen.'

I love you..."

Littleton: I love you, Alex... I am glad you are here with me... Alex...

Burns: Don't leave me... please... no.

The room fell quiet as the transmission ended.

Welch could see that Andersen was remembering something that came to him.

"'...now and at the hour of our death...' It's Latin, from the High Mass. It's the 'Hail Mary' in Latin," Andersen said quietly.

Welch thought immediately of Joe as he passed in a hospital bed with all the machines.

She remembered the morphine IV drip while sitting right beside him. He had been out of it for hours. The kids were getting something to eat and on their way back when she felt his warm, firm grip melt away as he slipped from her. Just when she felt her heart couldn't break anymore, it dissolved as his life faded. She didn't want him to leave.

Please don't leave me...

Welch's eyes filled and her nose became suddenly stuffed up. She pushed the feeling and image out of her mind before she started sobbing.

Put your game face on, Damn it! I thought you were a Marine, she thought to herself.

With her mind pushed back into the present, Welch had to admit that the communication seemed all out of character. Burns just didn't seem to be a terrorist. A woman holding onto a cross, a request for last rights and a very soft, consoling voice praying for her in an ancient language. Final goodbyes..."Don't leave me?" It just didn't seem very terrorist-like. Welch said sarcastically out loud what many were thinking:

"Well... it sure sounded pretty 'dangerous.'"

The reply was swift and automatic.

"She was a terrorist and terrorists die, Diane," Webber retorted.

No feeling, no human empathy. Just conviction that he is right and the world is wrong.

Welch felt her blood pressure boil yet again and her hands balled up to strike him.

She was appreciative that Helms took another approach and pressed on with the briefing.

"Go on, Janeson," Helms encouraged.

Janeson did continue, but it was clear to Welch that she was cognitively aware that some emotional discharge was happening.

"Secondly, the transmissions were well within two thousand yards of each other—"

Webber's voice broke out after that piece of news.

"What?!"

Webber was looking at Janeson in disbelief as Helms folded his arms across his chest and Andersen just shook his head.

"Wow... I thought you guys had that place 'locked down.' He was right there? Gee?" Johnson dryly said.

Welch found herself taking pleasure in Webber's shock as she watched him move closer to the monitors to look for himself.

"Yes," Janeson went on calmly. "As you can see, it appears that just as Ms. Littleton

was dying, Ms. Davis must have wondered how Burns saw she was wearing a crucifix necklace. As she looked around, it seems it is about here she sees him."

It was clear to Welch that Helms and Andersen were not surprised by this data.

Davis must have told them about this before she was dragged to the hospital.

That also explained why Helms had sent two teams to canvas an area outside of the plaza. Last report she had heard was that two places seemed likely to be a shooter's perch.

"Shocked, shocked that he would be right there," Andersen pushed.

Welch appreciated the classic movie line and watched Helms smile as Johnson covered his mouth to contain a chuckle.

Wait a minute. Johnson seems kind of young to know Casablanca.

"That's got to be embarrassing," Gilmore uttered maybe a bit too loud from below deck.

As Webber was turning a deep red, Janeson continued with her briefing.

"In regards to the third party cameras—"

Webber finally broke away from the image of Davis trying to look in the distance to see Burns when he turned sharply on Janeson and asked, "What 'third party cameras'?"

Andersen, Helms, and Welch looked at Webber as if he had asked a stupid question as Janeson explained.

"Our team discovered that our own cameras were hacked by a very sophisticated law enforcement agency."

Watching her closely, Welch was impressed that his non-verbals neither confirmed nor denied the report.

"I suspect that the spike and hack is at a more sophisticated level of expertise consistent with an agency such as the Foreign Intelligence Agency than say local law enforcement abilities. Which leads us to our last piece of the other cameras. The signal was picked up by a local laptop and transmitted live to a receiving email account that was already opened when transmission began. The endpoint is a restaurant cafe, Pozzetto, in Paris, France. It apparently recently opened and has Wi-Fi with actual computers available. The person or persons on the other end could easily have been waiting for the transmission and either watched it live, recorded it, or both. While much of the information at that end is unintelligible, a key piece of data was recorded as well as determining that the person named 'Tiny' is more likely Rebecca Littleton."

Welch had to strain her ears to make sure she could hear the conversation that Janeson was saying was key. Welch guessed that the male voice was more likely Burns and the female voice was the victim's sister, Rebecca Littleton.

Littleton: How do we end this? How do we keep Emma and David safe and kill the...

Burns: ...tell you in two hours... Tell David what happened... Andersen in... let him... the 'dead man switch' has been pulled. Tell him 'the flood is coming.' And Becky? Please... don't tell Emma...

The room was unusually silent as everyone tried to fill in the gaps of the communication.

"This is very bad," Helms said with hands firmly placed on his hips.

Andersen spoke next, "I know what he means when he says 'dead man switch,' but what does he mean 'by the flood is coming'?"

Janeson jumped in with her speculation.

"Based on the fact that Mr. Burns witnessed his paramour's death at the hands of a federal agency and that he has five years' worth of classified data, I would guess that the 'flood' is the classified data and that he plans to release it into the world."

"Are we talking Wiki leaks or Snowden leaks?" Gilmore asked

"Worse—we're talking possibly unedited, raw data in multiple formats more likely time stamped and categorized making authenticating easier and easy to identify and possible corroborate and confirm."

"No! He can't do that! That's treason!" Webber protested as he stepped toward Janeson as if she were the one committing the crime. Gilmore and Helms instinctively stepped forward to cover Janeson. Realizing that his posturing might not be a good idea, Webber regrouped pretty quickly, Welch had to admit.

"He can't do that. The information is classified. This could be embarrassing, let alone a breach in national security," he said more calmly.

Welch couldn't stand it anymore. As she turned to face Webber, she felt her skin and face burn with anger and an image of PFC Parks in her arms.

"Webber! Do you think he cares? Last May, he created havoc to attack his old employers and seize your precious classified data to protect his people. That's treason. He tries to work with us and we end up killing the woman he loves. As she is dying, he kills about five or six of your guys in three minutes. Do you think he gives one rat's ass about 'embarrassment' and 'national security?' Do you think he cares about treason? He wants vengeance. It's not treason, Webber. It's Armageddon. And unlike me, he will make sure that you pay."

The emphasis on the last sentence was more for Webber's benefit than hers.

Webber was oddly silent for a change.

Helms closed the gap between Webber and himself to deliver a personal statement in a low tone barely audible to Welch.

"The flood is coming, Mr. Webber. You better build yourself an ark."

Chapter 8

"Fiat justitia, et pereat mundus" – "Let justice be done, though the world perish" Ferdinand

When David Caulfield first got the call from Becky, he could tell that something had gone horribly wrong. She was clearly upset, crying but unnaturally coherent. After the first twenty minutes of shock David experienced, he was able to get out of himself to make sure Emma would be told only after Becky was home safe. Becky told David, "That's exactly what Burns said."

David knew what that meant: Burns was in protection mode, which made him a very dangerous predator. Becky and David conjectured what he would plan next. For him, it was clear because he was positive that Burns would not only make those responsible pay, but he would finalize his, Emma and Becky's safety once and for all.

That's what Samantha would want him to do, David reasoned. *But how?*

David also knew Samantha pretty well, and he knew she was no angel. While capable of doing many things the average person would cringe to do, including killing another human being, she would want justice but not at the expense of her sister's safety. He knew she would want Burns to keep everyone else alive and safe and to kill the bastard who had killed her.

She always had this thing about justice and fair play.

The last hour talking to Becky had been very close to the worst David had ever experienced. While watching his wife be murdered, and almost being killed himself, was at the pinnacle of horrible experiences, the last hour was a close second.

How is Becky staying coherent?

Once he hung up, he went to the laptop and cued the audio that Becky had sent to him of the whole ordeal.

I just can't believe. Not Samantha. She's the toughest of all of us. Even Alex.

David thought he would be prepared for what he heard.

I watched my wife die, he thought.

Within two minutes of the transmission, he fully grasped how ill-prepared he was for the raw heartache and pain he experienced. With images of Samantha dying in his mind's eye, his ears filled with pain, panic and chaos. Then, three of his closest friends were talking as one of them died.

The pain in Alex's voice. 'Becky... I am so sorry!'

David found himself saying the same thing Alex said: "No..."

He slowly put the headphones down and found his heart beating as deep, breathless sobs erupted from his chest and hot tears fell into his hands. He had been depressed for months after May second, and now he knew why. He was afraid someone, anyone of them, would die.

"I'm so sorry, Sam. It was never easy for you... it just doesn't seem fair it was you," he said to no one.

He admired her refusal to submit and survive at all costs. She shared her love of life with her protectiveness of him, Emma, Becky and Alex.

If she didn't make it out alive of the 'four civilians,' who would?

More burning tears fell from his eyes, recalling his special relationship with her. She was more like a daughter than a colleague.

So sorry, Sam, he kept thinking.

David was immersed in thought about how to make sure that Emma and Becky made it out. He had only thought of suicide once and that was to sleep and never wake up when his wife died. But he would have willingly died to have saved Samantha.

I should have insisted that I went. It would have been much better if it were me. I had a life of happiness before. She was just becoming happy. Alex, too. It just isn't fair.

David heard his phone beep, indicating another call. It was most likely Burns. He knew that Burns planned to call Becky right after he talked to him. He knew the conversation would be brief and would most likely set in motion events that would change the world and personally affect him forever.

"Alex?"

Did you hear?" was Burns's only question.

"Yes. I am truly sorry," was all David could muster. His voice was still shaky from his tearful fit.

There was silence. David was used to silence in his clinical work with patients. But for Burns, the logistical, strategist genius, silence was not good. That meant one of two things: either

he was not sure of a plan or the plan was already solidified. And then Burns surprised him with a question.

"David... do you think it's possible for a man to go back to his old ways without losing what he has gained?"

David had to pause. It was an unexpected, existential question.

Are we what we do or are we more than that?

Burns had always impressed David, but his ability to be reflective shortly after Samantha's death was simply remarkable.

I know I couldn't, he thought as he remembered how numb and dead he had felt when Jenny died.

Somehow, because this was the very thing David had been thinking for months, the answer fell right off David's lips.

"I'm not sure, Alex. But I do know this: all we can ask of ourselves is to do our best. When we can forgive, we do. When we can let go, we do. But we are human. Mammals. We have instincts. We protect our loved ones, our children, and those things dear to us. We never fault the tiger when it kills to feed her young. We never blame the lion from fighting back when cornered. As you and I talked about many years ago after you saved my life and my wife was killed, 'There is an appointed time for everything... a time to give birth and a time to die; a time to plant and a time to uproot what is planted...'"

"...a time to kill and a time to heal..." Burns continued.

David could feel the raw emotion in Burns's voice. Those same words they had spoken years ago when he was injured... when he had become blind for life. He knew that when Burns spoke next, they would not just be words; they would be actions.

"Alex, just because we sometimes have to go back to our old ways, it doesn't mean it always has to be that way. What will matter is what you do after. Samantha would want you to be happy. You weren't before, and that's why you changed. She would want you to 'do what you do' and then be who she loved... the guy who prayed for others, the guy who protects a child and friends, a guy who hates injustice. A person who was finally open to his emotions."

There was silence. David could hear Burns's breathing evenly.

"'For what does it profit a man to gain the whole world and forfeit his soul? For what will a man give in exchange for his soul...?'"

"Is that from Mark?"

After some silence, Burns responded.

"I... I don't know... Okay..." Burns said suddenly.

David could hear the subtle switch from reflective to action, from indecisive to decisive.

"Okay... David? I need you to call Andersen and give him a timeline of seven days. Set the 'dead man switch' to start today and tell them it will conclude next week. 'Flood the world.'"

David picked up on the code 'flood the world': time to release a series of classified data that were already marked to turn allies against the U.S., to harden anti-American sentiment and to have the world join forces that would threaten the United States' security.

Treason? Terrorism? Betrayal? Does it matter when they take everything important away from you?

David listened to the instructions that he had practiced probably a hundred times.

"Set it all from the computer in the vault and set it to self-destruct mode. Have the vault go first and the house second. I want to make sure whoever is inside does not make it out. Set it for 'dove' and not for 'hawk.' Repeat, 'dove.'"

David had some relief with the distinction. Even in Burns's state, there was some compassion.

The 'dove' protocol meant that the house's self-destruction would occur under very specific circumstances that involved forced entry from two doors at near the same time and then within three minutes, forced entry into the basement. This was timed out to reflect an assault by a trained team. If the entry to the house and basement did not occur within three minutes, the fire mechanism would not engage and the house would remain standing. If just one door opened rather than two, then the house would not explode. The 'dove' protocol was the 'safest' for some child or innocent person coming in one door and looking around. The probabilities of two people coming in two doors at the same time and then going to the basement within three minutes was pretty low. Not impossible, but not likely.

The 'hawk' protocol was based on forced entry from both doors and a two-minute delay to insure everyone was in the house before the house exploded. Simpler parameters but still requiring two points of entry at the same time.

Burns is back, David thought... *though not completely.*

He confirmed that very thought when he shifted from destruction at all-cost mode to protection of the innocent.

Still, though, David knew he was now stepping over the line.

Once I do this, I will kill people. Not just set them up to be killed by others. I will kill people sent to do a job. They won't be going home to their loved ones. Is that fair? Is that right? Is this what I have become? A therapist who once helped others, now a killer.

Burns's instructions brought David back to the present.

"You and Emma should head to your fallback position. Make plans to be gone no later than mid-afternoon tomorrow. Make sure your neighbors steer clear of the house. Set the terms for two million dollars and four pardons. This part of the mission will conclude in forty-eight hours, so you and Emma have to be secured away. Becky will join you forty-eight hours after that. I will communicate with you next week," Burns concluded.

Suddenly, David felt compelled to say the obvious.

"Becky's going to want to kill whoever did this," David said.

"Yes. I know. I'm not sure she will, but I do need her help."

"I know her, Alex. She watched her sister die just like you. She already lost her brother. She has no family now. If you have an opportunity to let her kill the person responsible, please let her do that."

David could tell by the silence that Burns was surprised.

"Condoning violence, David?"

Ironic. As soon as I set the self-destruct code, I'll be a killer, not just 'condoning' violence.

"Maybe… No. Mental health preservation. She helplessly watched her sister die. She was not able to protect her when Sam was fourteen, and she carried that around with her until you came into the picture. Because of all the things she had to do... lose weight, learn how to fight, shoot, sabotage, and commit mayhem, she changed. It was only after she felt she was in control of her own destiny with Sam, now protected by you, that she was able to let the guilt go over not being there when Sam was a child. If she's not allowed to do something to 'protect' her sister's memory now, she'll never heal. She'll always have unresolved guilt. If that means killing the person who did this... so be it."

My God. What have I become?

"Did you ever think you would be giving advice that justified killing?"

"Never. But then I never thought I would love again or love a child as much as I love Emma. I never thought I would love Samantha. I never thought she would die." David was surprised how rapidly that response flowed from his mouth.

More silence.

"Before she kills anyone, I'll make sure she's ready to pay the price," Burns finally answered.

"Good luck, Alex. Both of you come home."

Acknowledged."

Once David finished his call with Alex, he made sure Emma was still asleep before he went to "the vault." The vault was in reality a basement that had additional insulation and wood to absorb sounds inside. With utilities kept behind a walled partition, the only thing visible in the room's center was a desktop with an array of electronics ranging from laptops to cell phones. The desktop used voice-activated software specifically for David's use. In ten minutes, he would call Andersen, but prior to that he had to set things in motion. Once the CPU was operating and David heard that the system was finally on, he started the voice activation sequence:

"Computer?"

"Password, please," the pleasant voice requested.

"Albatross Kea Islands Emma."

"Accepted."

"Open 'Dove' file and begin program launch."

David hear a few seconds of internal mechanism whirring.

"'Dove' file loaded and program ready to launch. Set parameters, please," the computer requested.

He had done hundreds of practice runs, but he was always nervous. Now, he was surprised by how calm he was.

"Parameters are as follows:

1) Send out a total of seven files; send out 'Dove One' through 'Dove Seven' at eight six-hour intervals within seven days;

2) Start time of 'Dove One' is 0600;

3) Comply with target parameters;

4) Bring standby generator online;

5) Set explosive charges to ignite three minutes after basement door is breached;

6) Set high yield explosive charges to ignite thirty seconds after the first.

Please review parameters."

The computer complied, and David listened attentively.

Final password code to set launch?" the computer asked.

David sat back for a moment and uttered the code: "Flood the world."

It was a code he had never wanted to utter because it meant he would be instrumental in killing people, probably law enforcement, and destabilizing the American government and world economies.

What have I become?

There was a perceptible whirring in the CPU and then the computer issued the final statement: "Dove One launched." And with that, he heard the screen click off and the computer went into sleep mode with a snap. He knew the system was still operating, but it probably looked as if the computer were off.

David sat for a moment more and was struck by an old Latin phrase:

"'Amor animi arbitrio sumitur, non ponitur,'" he said to himself. He thought of Burns losing Samantha. Burns never chose to love her.

How would he stop loving her now that she was gone?

Once done, David removed a number of electronics he would need for their new location. He needed to distract himself for a moment before he made a very important call, a call he had never wanted to make.

~

Steve Andersen was still thinking about Burns's prayer to Samantha Littleton.

No. He's not just a terrorist. He wanted to free his friends. The Hail Mary in Latin? What the hell? I guess if he was Islamic I might feel differently. Is that it? Is it just that I understand his point of view? Is that right?

Andersen remembered his interview with David Caulfield on May second. It didn't take a genius to figure out that all he wanted was to be free from being marked for death and hiding all his life. Not just for him, but for the Littleton sisters, his former patient and a little girl, Emma.

Not exactly "terrorist" qualities. No huge body count. No TV coverage. Just live and let live.

As Janeson was adding some additional information to her briefing, Andersen's attention was drawn away by his phone vibrating in his pocket. As he went to pull it out, he remembered that his phone was affixed to his belt. He carefully pulled out a smart phone that was hot pink and bejeweled with glitter. It was his wife's phone that he had confiscated.

Damn it, Laura, why so much jewelry on a phone, for God's sake?

The call was from Burns.

Andersen snapped his fingers and got everyone's attention that it might be Burns on the line. Helms gave the raised, closed fist signal for silence and then pointed to Gilmore, who was already working his magic to tap into the cell signal for a trace. Janeson was on her tablet, trying to see whether there was still another venue to locate the frequency and source of the call. Once Andersen was sure everything was silent, he put the phone on speaker.

"This is Andersen," he said as casually as possible.

"Lieutenant," the voice responded.

Yes, that therapeutic voice. Not Burns. Caulfield. David Caulfield, he remembered.

David still sounded as soothing over the phone as he had in Interrogation Room 8. A lot of shit had been going down then, but he had been as calm as if he were lying in a summer hammock. Today, though, he sounded tired. *He got the bad news,* Andersen thought.

"David Caulfield?" Andersen asked.

"Yes, Lieutenant, it's David."

Andersen's voice shifted from professional to a softer, collegial voice.

"David... I'm sorry about your friend," he started.

"So am I. Is your agent all right?" David asked. While Andersen was impressed by the genuineness of the question, he was not surprised.

"Yes. She won't be skiing for a while, but she's fine," he responded, trying somehow to lighten a very dark moment that truly promised to get worse.

"That's good," Caulfield responded.

"So, David, what do we do now?"

Andersen could swear that David sounded tired but also muted somehow; the environment around him seemed as if it were soundproof, he thought. There was no background noise, no echoes— almost as if he were talking inside a wall of rugs and his voice was being absorbed.

David's voice picked up in tempo, Andersen noticed, when he

started an outline of things to come.

"Here's what's going to happen. Over the next seven days and nights, a number of significant, classified operations will be conducted by the Foreign Intelligence Agency's Operations Center and released to the world," David said calmly.

"Is that what Burns is going to do?" Andersen pushed back.

Andersen heard a pause as if David were confused.

"I have no idea specifically what Alex will do next. I am telling you what I am going to do. Alex told you in May that if we felt our situation was compromised, we would release this data to the world. Samantha's death more than qualifies as 'compromised.'"

He stopped for a moment, as if to make sure he was clear and then he moved on to the next set of business.

"After the seventh day, we will want two million dollars and..."

Without warning, Webber stepped in as Andersen felt his chest suddenly tighten in response.

"Mr. David Caulfield, this is Thomas Webber, deputy director of Operations Center, Alpha. You are aware we do not negotiate with terrorists." Andersen watched Webber closely to see whether Webber actually expected Caulfield to say, *"What was I thinking? Of course, you won't negotiate. I'll call back later when I have leverage or something. Jesus!"*

Andersen pulled himself from looking at Webber's arrogant smile and began to look at the phone buttons for "mute" without disconnecting the line. It was so wrong on so many levels what Webber did: he interrupted the lead negotiator, called the caller and his dead friend a terrorist, didn't let him finish with the demands and worst of all, identified himself to a very dangerous group of people. Even as Webber continued, Andersen kept looking desperately for the mute button.

"Mr. Webber? Mr. Thomas Webber? Are you the one who killed Ms. Littleton?"

There it is. For the love of God, Webber, shut up! Andersen knew David was obtaining the correct identification of the person responsible for Samantha Littleton's death to make sure his death was confirmed.

He's narrowing the kill shot! Are you that stupid?!

Andersen noticed that Helms had joined him in silently telling Webber to say nothing or tell Caulfield otherwise. Andersen gave up looking for the mute button and began wracking his brain for some lame excuse to get Webber's name off the death list. He was surprised Welch simply closed her eyes as if she were seeing a car accident in progress. He guessed she knew what Webber was going to do next.

In a low voice, mocking David Caulfield's tone and timber, Webber nailed his coffin shut as soon as the words came from his mouth.

"No 'David,' I gave the green light to have a terrorist stopped before she was allowed to get away scot-free. You have no idea whom you are dealing with, do you? If I were you, I would—"

"Are you crazy? Is that your real problem?" Anderson asked quietly.

David's voice climbed a bit in volume, though it was more controlled than Andersen expected as he interrupted Webber:

"Mr. Thomas Webber, thank you for your name, title, and your apparent location. I will make sure to pass that along to Mr. Burns."

It was obvious that David was dismissing Webber, and Andersen could tell Webber was pissed off and would undoubtedly not let the offense go.

"Lieutenant, for seven days and nights, I will release classified files for key governments and media to see. We could get five hundred million dollars from Russia, China, North Korea and the Middle East, but we are asking for two million, so we never have to see each other again. We want four letters of pardon from the president of the United States. These are the terms. Failure to meet the terms will result in continuation of release of classified data until the terms are met. I will flood the world with classified data, and all the lies and secrets will be revealed. It's not going to be pretty."

Andersen truly believed the last part was an understatement of colossal proportions.

David continued with a more level voice:

"Once we receive the money and pardons, we will return two of the three hard drives back to you. The third one will be our insurance."

Webber was about to break in again, but Helms held a threatening finger to his face to lock his mouth down.

Andersen jumped in to retake the negotiation and to keep David on longer for the trace:

"You don't know what Burns is going to do?"

David's voice became as close to agitated as Andersen thought he might ever get. David was calm, but there was clearly an edge.

Losing someone you care about an hour ago, and having the means to hold a country hostage could be stressful... or is there more going on you're not telling me?

"Are you kidding? This is 'Code of Hammurabi' stuff, an 'eye for an eye' thing. You think he is going to let this thing stand? Go unanswered? You killed the woman he loved. Maybe the only woman he loved. You broke a promise, the deal, a covenant. This is Herman Melville's work come alive..."

Webber clearly couldn't take it anymore.

"Caulfield, what are you saying? Give up, and I promise you life in prison rather than execution as a traitor. Maybe minimum security in deference to your disability."

Every set of eyes were looking at Webber in disbelief except for Janeson and Welch; he was sure Janeson was engrossed with getting a location and he was sure his friend was just trying to not throw-up. Anderson not only wanted to throw-up but he wanted to shower after his proximity with Webber.

Oh my God! Did he just say that?

There was silence. It was uncomfortable silence, and for a moment, Andersen had a fantasy that Webber might have gotten through to David somehow with a viable offer to avoid death with imprisonment. The hope was short-lived.

"'...and I'll chase him round Good Hope, and round the Horn, and round the Norway Maelstrom, and round perdition's flames before I give him up.'"

And then the line closed. Helms looked over at Gilmore. It took a moment but then he looked up and shook his head "No."

Helms looked at Janeson, who also shook her head "No."

All was quiet... except for Webber.

"Are you guys really afraid of this poet quoting nut job?" Webber asked with great exasperation and frustration for sure.

Andersen felt the overwhelming urge to kick Webber in the balls. He was sure everyone wanted to. Webber was a unifying force for sure, Andersen thought. *Everyone hates him.* He would have continued this line of thinking, but he heard Janeson say something. Her voice was firm and low, but he was sure that whatever this young woman said next, it was probably going to be right. She had consistently impressed him.

"That was a line from *Moby Dick*."

Janeson looked down to her left as if searching for the exact answer until she found it:

"It's the 'quarter deck' scene when Captain Ahab is talking to Starbuck and is rallying the crew to go kill the great white whale that took his leg. It's all about revenge."

Andersen smiled; *she never disappoints.*

Welch looked at her in awe. Helms put his right hand to his forehead, clearly was baffled at the extent and nature of Janeson's knowledge base.

Helms turned to ask her the obvious question.

"My God, Rachael! How could you possibly know that? I read that book a billion years ago, and I'm positive they don't assign it to students anymore."

Andersen's attention was drawn unexpectedly by Gilmore and Johnson, who were each clearly shaking their heads to her not to reveal her source. But it was evident that she did not understand the harm, and it was a perfectly logical question her boss was asking.

"I saw the play, Boss. Agent Martin played the lead role as Captain Ahab. He said he drew his inspiration from you to get into character."

Helms was speechless as his eyes blinked several times. Andersen had come to interpret this set of behaviors as Helms being dumbfounded but in a pleasant way. There were a number of smiles and smirks.

The positive moment was tainted by Webber's demand for

attention. *Not loved as a child*, Andersen imagined.

Webber started to walk away with his assistant in tow. He turned before exiting and had one more thing to say to Helms and his "merry men."

"Your boss will be hearing from the Secretary of Defense regarding your investigation. You will be ordered to hand over all relevant material, data, and evidence to my agency."

Webber next addressed the entire control room staff as if they were his personal entourage: "Get packing, people. I'll need everything ready for shipping in twelve hours. I may have my people pick up some critical data very early tomorrow morning, so you might want to plan on a late night."

Webber took a phone call as he finally left the room.

Helms was the first to talk.

"Diane? Do his assistants ever talk or are they 'just there' to make him feel 'okay' about himself?"

Andersen saw that Welch was answering the question as if it were legitimate.

"Yup. The last one told me that good things would happen for me and my men if we made it out of the desert alive," she said with deadly seriousness.

Andersen had a sudden appreciation of how dangerous this guy could be.

"You're right, Diane... he's a prick," he commented.

"No. He's a little prick. And he's stupid. Do you think he knows he just put a target on his own head?" Welch asked.

Before Andersen could answer, Helms beat him to it.

"No. He is so narcissistic that he thinks he's untouchable," Helms answered. After a moment, Helms had more to say.

"He's right about one thing, though. We have maybe twelve hours to get as close as we can to finding Burns before the dickhead gets himself killed and the whole world goes up in flames."

Helms addressed the staff as a whole next. With hands on his hips, his voice took on the stereotypical Marine drill instructor's tone, volume, and gravity.

"People. You did an outstanding piece of work today: thoroughness, tenacity, dogged determination, and creative thinking. Whatever this shit that's going to fly will go to everyone on the planet—terrorists, Russia, China. Iran, North Korea, and they're the ones we know about. They don't need any more reasons to want us all dead, and we don't need any more enemies. We have a short time before our investigation is stolen from us, and we need to get something substantial for me to convince the secretary of state, and maybe the president, to allow us to stay on the team to find Burns. Anyone who needs to leave for a prior engagement, you can take off now. Anyone who can stay for the next twenty-four hours, that will be much appreciated."

Looks were exchanged and then various voices were raised with "I can stay," "No worries, boss," and "I hate blind dates, anyway."

Thrown in the mix of the responses was an unidentified voice that called out, "Aye, Starbuck; aye, my hearties..."

Helms said, "Thank you."

Andersen smiled; he could tell Welch was glad to be on the team. *Who wouldn't be?*

"I wish my team were as smart as yours," Andersen commented to Helms.

"Yeah... they are smart. That reminds me..." Helms walked over to Johnson's area and yelled loud enough for others to hear:

"Johnson! Get Martin's ass up here from accounting. He's on the team, too—we're going to need someone to make coffee, get meals, set up cots, and make sure the toilets are plunged... yeah. Martin is the guy to do that."

Oh, boy. Poor guy. "No act of kindness will go unpunished," Andersen thought. *Wait until Davis hears about all of this.*

Chapter 9

"Transit umbra, lux permanent" -- *"Shadow passes, light remains"*
Unknown

Sitting in the back of a clean FBI car, Jillian Davis continued fiddling with her cross and necklace as she had for hours since the shooting. She found herself ruminating about Samantha Littleton's death and her last moments with her. Being in law enforcement and a soldier, seeing death was nothing new to her. Staring out the window, she thought back on how death had changed for her after her mother died. Her mother had been her last living relative, leaving her alone now. Her mother's death was more difficult than she had ever imagined at the time for that very reason.

Well... that's true. She was my mother, after all.

Samantha Littleton was a "contact" and a "domestic terrorist," not a relative or a friend. But the label "terrorist" just didn't fit the dying civilian she had held hours ago, struck down by a government's bullet.

My government, Davis reflected. *No due process; no court. Just executed. What the fuck? She never wanted to be a part of it. She's someone's sister and aunt. She was a civilian, not a soldier. If I didn't know about her would it be different? If she were Muslim would I feel the same way?*

Davis found herself watching the oncoming headlights as a way to focus on something else.

She looked at her watch suddenly. She calculated that she had been released from the hospital half an hour ago and was wondering why it was taking the two agents so long to find her house. As she found herself slipping back to thinking about the firefight, she attempted to focus on anything that might help organize her thoughts since the medication she was on was clouding her thoughts and judgment.

God... the medication. I just can't be goofy this time. Oh, have to watch my mouth.

Davis had begged Andersen and Helms just to apply first aid, give a tetanus shot and antibiotics, in lieu of going to the emergency room. She had truly thought that threatening to withhold spotting Burns as leverage to avoid the hospital was going to work, but it was a no go. In fact, she was genuinely surprised that Helms assigned two of his staff to "Make sure she complies with treatment and then take her home."

She found herself feeling hungry and wanting to lay down. Looking around the backseat, she could see it was wide and leather.

"How you doing back there?" the young agent asked.

"Good... very good," she said a bit more quickly than she wanted.

Nice voice. Kind of cute, she thought. Davis violently shook her head as she remembered the last time she felt this good.

Just shut up, Davis, and don't do anything stupid.

In addition to being tired, she was affected by what the hospital had given her to take the edge off her pacing and reduce pain. The sedative and painkillers were considered light and were often reviled as "nothing" to anyone who ever suffered from panic attacks or addiction. For Davis, though, the medication was relaxing to the point of blunting her reactions, slowing her down and making her feel sleepy, very sleepy. When she woke up from nodding off, she wondered what her peers at the Office of Naval Research and Development or the Operations Center would do if they ever saw her taking a nap. She knew they would have assumed she was dead rather than sleeping.

Still, Davis had to admit, *the pain killers feel good... or are they anti-anxiety medicine... both?*

After five minutes more of trying to figure out what she was on, Davis found herself stumbling out of a car with some assistance from the young agent assigned to watch her. While she was acutely aware that she had a high tolerance for alcohol, which kept her from "acting stupid drunk," as her father used to say, she had no tolerance at all for pharmaceuticals. As she put one step in front of the other, she remembered having her wisdom teeth removed as a teenager and nothing after she took the painkillers. Apparently, she was so high, she shocked her friends and family. To this day, she still had no firsthand recollection of what she did.

Man... I was so messed up. Kinda like now.

For no particular reason, Davis was glad that her front yard was no longer the neighborhood's eyesore since it was now being well-maintained by professionals. Then, her mind wandered and she found herself gazing at the agent who was guiding her up the two stairs to get to her door.

Kinda cute. I bet he's married. Too young? Too young for me or too young to be married.

Davis struggled to focus. Once she was able to produce the keys, the agent unlocked the door and helped her find the lights. Still groggy, she didn't think much of asking the agent to help her undress so she could go to bed.

"All right. The bedroom is over there..." she said and then took a long moment to reorient herself after realizing that her bedroom was toward the right and not the left as she originally pointed.

Positive she had corrected herself, she added, "Can you help me out of these things? I've been in them all day, and I was on the ground and then the hospital. Do you know how germy it is in an emergency room? Everyone sneezing, picking his nose, and stuff..." she rambled. It took her seconds to realize she was struggling to unbutton her blouse after successfully flinging off her jacket.

God, is it hot in here?

Davis remembered she was not alone but also she was sure she was not on a date. Then, she remembered the guy in her house was an FBI agent. She turned to see what he was doing. The look of astonishment was evident on his face. It took her longer than usual for her to figure out that the male agent might have an issue with her undressing and going to her bedroom. Awash with warm heat flooding her face and neck, she started to re-button her blouse. Closing her eyes,

Davis took her time to speak so as to insure she said something coherent and not anything more embarrassing.

"Okay. Could you help me get in my reclining chair in the living room?" It took two attempts to remember which direction to go. He was patient.

I'm so messed up on this shit, she thought.

Davis could still see relief on the young agent's face even though she was dizzy.

"What? Would I be that bad to see naked?" she asked, too seriously to sound sarcastic.

The agent stopped in mid-step as he helped her in the correct direction toward the living room. She realized she had said what she was thinking, rather than keeping it as an internal thought.

Oh hell... just like last time. I say shit that's not supposed to be said, Davis recalled suddenly from years ago.

"I said that out loud, didn't I?" Davis asked. She felt more heat pour out all over her skin, which left her even more dizzy and hot. She wanted to get naked, she was so hot.

"Yes, ma'am," the agent said, picking up his speed so he could leave faster.

As the agent was setting her gently in the chair, Davis decided not to comment on her personal dislike of being called "ma'am."

I think I'll just keep my mouth shut. It'll be safer for everyone that way.

While the weights, heavy bag and mats had been cleared out of the front room, there was still only her chair, flat screen and a couple of tables spread out in the spacious room. She may have been drugged up, but she could easily see that the agent was put off by the room. However, to his credit, he "checked" the house out to make sure no one else was there. She took that moment to make sure her next requests were not lewd. It took great effort, but she was successful in asking the agent whether he would bring her aspirin, water and leftover salad from the refrigerator. Once he gave it to her, he smiled and left the room. A minute after she heard her front door lock, she remembered to say, "Thank you."

Not hearing a response, Davis assumed he left without saying goodbye.

"What? No goodbye? Men," she muttered.

God... I bet he's going to tell everyone what happened. And I'm going to get some serious shit from Andersen.

With great effort and concentration, she took out her semi-automatic gun from her hip and put it on the table.

They shouldn't let me take this, she thought as she made sure her safety was on.

"You're such a dumbass, Davis," she continued to say to herself as she attempted to untie her shoes while keeping up with her rant.

"Hey? I got an idea. Why don't I embarrass myself by asking you to go to bed with me so you can reject me and then tell Helms, Andersen, and the boys about it. Great idea! Stupid, stupid, stupid..."

Davis came up for air, giving up untying her shoes with one hand. With her "good arm," she pulled out one of her bottles of pills that the hospital had given her to relax and hurled them across the room. She vividly remembered her dad telling her all the things she shouldn't have said so many years ago when she was still high from the medication.

"You're right, Dad! Never again!" Davis found the other bottle of medication she had in her pants pocket and tossed that one as well. With both bottles littering the floor underneath the front, bay window, she took a moment to get comfortable in her chair.

That took more effort than it should have, she thought.

With aspirin ingested, and after taking only three bites of her two-day old salad, she decided to sleep the medication off.

This medication shit... it's so disinhibiting it's crazy, were her closing thoughts as she felt sleep coming fast.

With serious effort and force of will, Davis focused her attention on the lamp switch and leaned over to switch it off. As she finally leaned back, she was happy to be alone.

With the day's events, the hospital wait and medication, and just overall fatigue, she found herself slipping right off to sleep.

At first, she couldn't hear anything but her own deep breathing, feeling more relaxed than she had felt in a long time as her mind dosed off until she felt something gently touching her. A rushing wind and ocean smell enveloped her body as she felt gravity pull her toward earth. With outstretched arms, she felt the wind catch her and raise her higher than the white cliffs that rimmed the ocean. In the distance, just below her, she saw her prey gliding in and out of the rocky crevices of the cliffs. *Prey?* Confused, she realized she was not the predator but a dove, returning with a branch for her keeper. Veering away from the coast, she flapped faster as she saw the raven skyrocketing toward her. Eyes darting to her right, a flock of eagles flew past her toward the lone raven. Unable to carry on without knowing what happened, she circled back in a high arch in front of the sun, only to see the raven in hot pursuit with a flock of ravens behind him and all the eagles plummeting toward earth. Startled by the sudden turn of events, she turned into a gyre to pick up speed, flapping furiously. The salt smell and blue ocean filled her senses until the roar of pursuing ravens rushed her. Feeling her heart bursting out of her chest as she feverishly flew, she caught sight of her keeper's boat. The sound of more wings came in from all around, and she felt crowded in the sky. Her breath was nearly gone... almost gone...

Davis felt her body jump as she sharply inhaled for air. As she regained control of her breathing, her hands felt cold and clammy while her face seemed wet from sweating. Breathing normally again and lying back in her chair, she turned toward the window only to see a still, black shadow that seemed perched upon a chair. As her heart skipped several beats, she willed herself to force her eyes wider to adjust faster so she could convince herself that she was not about to be eaten by a huge bird of prey.

No way, she thought. Her breathing and heart began to regulate again.

Davis remained still so her eyes could adjust. The 'bird's' shadow transformed to a human figure sitting in a chair to her right; convinced she was no longer dreaming, her first thought was to find her gun and to feel for the knife she kept in the folds of her chair. She saw that the figure was sitting in one of her kitchen chairs. With the square-built body size of a male, he was sitting two leg-lengths apart with the back of the chair facing her. But the extensions of what she expected would be his hands seemed to be narrow tubes. Quicker than she thought, she leaned forward to flick the light on. Casting a bright light, she could barely make out that it was indeed a man with a hooded sweatshirt that obscured his face. The "tubes" were now recognizably a gun in each hand. The shadow was a man. As he sat unmoving and silent, Davis knew it had to be Burns. As her eyes adjusted, she figured, in light of his loss, he would probably torture her just for fun and then kill her.

So. This is the way it ends. They find me dead in my chair with drugs in my blood system. Just great.

With an unearthly sound of silence, she wondered how one opens a conversation with someone who is armed and has lost a loved one.

My God, he's quiet, she thought. *Quiet enough to move a chair from the kitchen without me even hearing. How long have you been there?*

She looked casually at the clock and was shocked that it was about 5:15 a.m.

What the hell? I just fell asleep.

With dawn breaking, some light came in from the street. Davis decided that if Burns wanted to kill her, he would have done so already. With her eyes fully adjusted, she could see that while her gun was no longer on the nightstand, in its place was an external hard drive, one of the three external drives that Burns took from her last May.

Wow. This is a surprise.

Looking back at Burns, she decided simply to state what was on her mind, rather than trying to figure him out.

"So... this is embarrassing. It looks like you beat me again," Davis said.

His head shifted as if there might be a hint of a smile, but darkness hung around him more than anything. In the dim lamplight and with his hood pulled back, she was able and relieved to see emotions in Burns's eyes. She knew a number of specialists in covert operations and counter terrorism who had the steel, blank look. Burns's "look" was more pain than anything else.

Not necessarily a good thing. The most dangerous animal is a wounded one, she remembered her father telling her.

"You were medicated. Kind of unfair." Looking toward the now cleaned floor, Burns had obviously picked up her medications and replaced them back into their bottles, and put them right next to the hard drive.

Jesus... how long have you've been here?

"You also seemed to be in a deep sleep. You looked like you were dreaming up a storm," he added.

"You have no idea," she immediately responded as if she were talking to a girlfriend over coffee rather than a trained assassin.

Davis suddenly had the embarrassing thought that Burns might have overheard her earlier conversation with the agent. Somehow, that just made her feel ashamed. Her attention shifted downward to Burns's feet. She had to shift her body to see over the side of her chair since her feet were fully raised in her recliner. She applied pressure, but it would require a lot more force and she didn't want to spook Burns.

I think I'll just stay here and look.

Davis saw what appeared to be four lightbulbs until Burns raised his foot and broke one. Now shattered, she could see a transmitter in addition to the bulb's filament.

Unbelievable! I'm still under surveillance. But who...? Daniels!

Next to the external drive was her watch, her favorite military timepiece that had a simple design and job. Similar to the broken bulb, its crystal was fractured, leaving a broken keepsake. Sighing and feeling completely stupid, Davis figured it out.

"My good watch was bugged, too?"

"Yes."

"Damn it. I liked that watch."

"Yes. That's why it's broken. You seem to be a creature of habit. Your chair is facing the doors and window with a clean shot to either entrance. Your gun is loaded with a bullet in the tube, though I was surprised to see that your safety was on rather than off. You take your watch off so it doesn't get caught on anything should you need to get to your gun or other weapons," Burns was saying.

In addition to the house cleaning he had done, Burns had found four bugs in her house and on her person. That meant that he had been there a while. As Davis sat, she casually moved her arm, ostensibly to readjust her injured left arm. She overshot it to see whether she could reach a throwing knife she kept on that side of her chair in the cushion.

"It's not there. I took the knife after the agent left," he said casually.

Fuck! He heard the entire thing, she thought.

"Goddamn it, Burns! You constantly piss me off! How long have you been in my house? Did you move in last month? Shit, you suck!"

Her complaint was out before she knew it, and she suddenly felt a headache explode in the back of her skull.

Clearing her eyes from the sharp pain, she did see Burns smiling. She could at least see he appreciated the professional frustration she was experiencing. Davis guessed he must have had some inkling of what it was like to be completely fooled and duped.

"Sorry... I overheard you giving your address to the hospital billing personnel, and I was able to get here hours before you got home. I knew you were hit and would come here. Not by choice, I'm sure." He said all this while raising his hand toward her almost apologetically.

You have no idea.

Davis found herself amazed yet again.

"So you were at the hospital with FBI and security around and were able to be close enough to get my address? Jesus, Burns. Are you that good or are we that bad?"

"Maybe a little of both," he said, more as a personal reflection than as part of a dialogue.

Davis looked down at the clearly broken transmitter and her broken watch. As she leaned forward to put her watch on as best she could, she realized that if all five transmitters were no longer operational, it would emit feedback that would be readily picked up by whoever was eavesdropping. That meant whoever was listening was probably on the way. Davis urgently looked back up at Burns.

"They're on their way... maybe ten minutes. Fifteen at the most. Two cars for sure; they'll approach from the opposite end of the street."

Raising his hand patiently, Burns clearly was not worried by the incoming danger.

"I know. So there's not much time," he calmly said. "I am prepared for their arrival."

What the hell does that mean? Kill them all? Just one man? Suicide?

Burns continued without explanation, moving on to another subject.

"I want you to take this drive."

Davis was as appreciative that he had returned to that subject as she was truly baffled why he was giving it to her.

"Why? We fucked up and killed your friend."

Burns was still but quickly responded.

"No. You didn't screw up. I saw the video and was there. The bugs here show you were tapped and that was how they figured out our meeting. You and the others were trying to deal in good faith. You tried to help Sam, and you were shot for your efforts. I appreciate that. I also appreciate that you didn't refer to her as a 'terrorist.' She's not. The others are not. You demonstrated good faith, so I am too, and that's why I want you to take the drive to your guys. Not to our former bosses."

It was hard to remember that Burns and she had both once worked for the Foreign Intelligence Agency a lifetime ago.

"Burns... I am sorry... but you got to get out of here..." she was saying as she tried to get out of her chair. The recliner was too high at the feet and her leverage was off. Burns waved her off, indicating she should remain sitting.

"Don't worry about me. I expect them soon enough."

Burns listened for a moment and then he continued.

"I want four letters of pardon signed from the president to give me and my friends immunity. Also, I want two million dollars. One million I want directed to a charity, and the other is for the three surviving civilians. I think you already have their names."

Three? Dr. Caulfield, Samantha's sister... he wants one for the little girl?

"I don't think the little girl will need one," Davis offered.

"Really? I don't want to take that chance. I want one for Emma," he insisted. Burns's ears picked up as if he were hearing something. He continued as he stood up with two semi-automatic guns at the ready. Behind him, on the far side of the room, sat her own gun and knife.

"Classified data will be flowing out at some point this morning. It will continue until I get the money and pardons. In addition to you or anyone you designate, I also want Thomas Webber to be the person to bring them to me. Anyone else and there is no deal."

Oh shit. That name sounds familiar... someone from the agency...

"Is he the guy who fucked up our meeting?" Davis asked.

"Apparently. He was kind enough to take responsibility for killing Sam," Burns responded. More darkness seemed to cloud all around him now.

Is that real or the after-effects of the medication finally wearing off?

Maybe it was just projection since she imagined it was what would happen to her if she were in his shoes. Maybe the morning light was playing tricks.

"Burns... he'll bring his whole team if you want him there," she warned.

"That's okay. I have something I need to give him and my former bosses," he responded without emotion.

Oh, shit... that sure has a double meaning.

As Burns walked toward the door, he continued.

"Is there any one at the Operations Center you can trust?"

Davis had to think before she answered.

Maybe Cratty, she thought. *Last time I heard about her, they were treating her like shit. Maybe Cratty subscribes to the motto, "The enemy of my enemy is my brother."*

"I think so. She stuck her neck out for me, and I owe her one."

Feeling her injured arm ache, she smiled at the irony of her next statement.

"She took a bullet, career-wise, for me, so I'm not sure she would want to again. But I know they're screwing with her. She's also a stand-up kind of gal and doesn't care too much for her boss," Davis said.

"Well... that makes both of us," he replied.

Opening the front door, Burns stood in the passageway a moment longer. He looked back at Davis, and with his foot he moved a computer case into Davis's field of vision.

"I hope she is who you think she is. In this case is a laptop that has a pretty complex program that will immobilize the Operations Center. It is significantly worse and faster than the one that hit you guys last May. If Webber brings his whole team, I may need someone who has access to limit the effectiveness of the Operations Center again. I am assuming you have no access, but maybe your friend might provide you a secured channel to get into its server system. I bet upgrades have been made so access through a secured Internet port will not be possible."

Davis was still before she uttered the next question.

"Are you asking me to assist in attacking my former bosses... a federal crime no less?" Davis didn't feel too bad about it in reality, not after years of service and then dismissal. She had to think about it more.

It could still be considered as treason. No. it is treason, she thought.

As Burns looked at her, she could see his eyes seemingly transition from pain to cold steel. It was the look of a killer.

Well, Davis thought, *I guess I pushed too far. Maybe I just should have told him "Yes" so he would leave and I might live.*

She had a memory of her mother saying, "That mouth of yours is going to get you into some serious trouble one day." She had been shot earlier today. She was positive that he would be swift and not let her suffer.

More than the other bastards who killed his friend.

Instead, Burns responded in a near clinical fashion.

"No. I think you want this to end. I think you know that the presidential pardons, the money, and the one external drive I will keep for insurance is a much better deal than them trying to kill me. I think you know I've limited the level of damage I am capable of doing. I think you and your team want this to end with no collateral damage. I can do that. They will not. If you go with our former bosses, you know how it ends... It does not end well for them. It really won't end well for anyone."

Burns suddenly stopped and shook his shoulders as one would do when about to shoot on a gun range.

"By the way, I took your firing pin out of your gun so when you're asked why you didn't help that will be your answer."

Damn it! Ten steps ahead as always! What the hell?

Burns walked out into the now brightening street. With as much force as Davis could muster, she pushed her legs down, catapulting from the recliner. As her arm throbbed and her headache grew, she moved as fast as she could to retrieve her weapons. As she passed the bay window, she saw Burns suddenly stop and drop to one knee in the middle of the road as two cars rapidly approached from opposite ends. With her own weapons in her hands, she turned at the squeal of braking cars and saw men starting to get out of them. Looking back to the road, she could see that Burns was lying flat on the ground as if he might be giving up.

No way! She was shocked at the idea of his surrendering until she noticed both hands no longer sported guns but some kind of switches.

"Oh shit!" she exclaimed.

A second later, she saw the first fireball explode beside the car that came in from the east. Turning her back and covering her face against the exploding window, she now knew what he had meant when he said he was prepared for their arrival.

Shaking off the glass, she got to her feet—in record time, she thought, considering the circumstances. Right before she got to her door, Davis pulled her safety off her own gun and test-fired into her own floor. There was a click only.

Maybe the throwing knife, she thought.

By the time she was moving again, another massive explosion occurred right outside her house. She dropped to the floor and instinctively covered her eyes again from the glass fragments. Shaking off the second round of explosions, Davis finally made it to her front door, only to see her neighbors' cars engulfed in flames right beside two cars in the road with various agents either moving slowly or not moving at all. As she looked around, Burns was no longer lying in the middle of the street; he was on the other side of the road, casually tossing what she easily identified as a grenade toward the car sitting in front of her house.

"Holy shit!"

She jumped back inside her house. She immediately saw a bright light before she heard the car explode. Uncovering her ears, she didn't even bother looking out the front door at the carnage as she watched the reflections of flames on her hallway walls.

Moving slowly and orienting herself, Davis was still in shock at the amount of destruction that had happened in a matter of sixty seconds.

"Where the hell did he get that ordnance?"

Davis didn't spend too much time assessing how Burns was different from the last time they had fought when he had possessed a gun but refused to use it. Now, looking briefly, she could see no one moving and Burns gone. By 5:30 a.m., her street was littered with dead, wounded federal agents and burning cars. Burns's message was clear.

This is war. No prisoners. No holds barred. Either give me what I want or there will be hell to pay.

As she pulled herself from the mayhem, she dropped her useless gun on her doorstep and made her plan to get to safety as soon as possible.

She knew Burns's level of destruction would be met with the same level or more from their old bosses. Positive that a second wave of agents were en route, she didn't plan on being caught in the middle.

With her throwing knife in hand, she collected the hard drive and laptop case, and ran through her kitchen toward the back of the house. Stopping by the stove warmer, she extracted her spare cell phone and her second gun. While she loved her semi-automatic, her backup piece was the ever reliable .38 caliber revolver.

This will be fine, she thought. She looked out her back porch to make sure no one was there to get the drop on her. She formalized a simple plan: *I gotta get to Helms before they get me.*

Convinced that the back of her house was clear, Davis exited out the back and walked briskly through her neighbors' yards until she was four blocks away. Hearing the sirens rapidly receding as she walked, she felt guilty leaving possibly injured agents back at a crime scene. Still, she had little choice but to make sure the hard drive got into Helms's hands and not her 'former employers.'

At all costs, she thought.

Anyone looking at her might think she was on her way to pick up the commuter rail, though her clothes were wrinkled.

As she approached Main Street, there was more commuter traffic and she felt as if she were blending in a bit more. Fifteen minutes later, she was in a coffee shop on her cell.

Davis could tell Helms was out of breath as if he must have been running.

Where the hell is he running to? Me? she wondered.

"Where the hell are you?" She had come to know that Helms sounded pissed when he was worried about someone or something. He was right to be pissed today.

"Meet me at our favorite morning place. Bring help, now!" was all she said as she hung up and turned off her cell.

The last thing she wanted was her former boss getting to her first. As her head ached and her arm throbbed, she had some regrets about not taking the medication Burns had picked up from the floor. But in light of their effects and what the day was shaping into, it was best she kept away from them, she concluded.

Finally at the coffee shop she sat with her back against the side wall to look out the window. She stayed for five minutes and then exited the shop through the back door. She rounded the side of the building and waited between two buildings, watching the front of the shop. Twenty-five minutes later, she found herself getting nervous and had to remind herself that there might be traffic during commute hours.

Come on guys. Where are you?

She was about to leave and try another site when she saw two blue

SUVs with federal plates show up. Watching closely with her heart in her throat, she tensely waited to see whether it was Helms or "the bad guys." A wave of joy came over her as she watched Helms come out of the driver's seat of the first SUV while Andersen got out of the second one's driver's seat. There was also the familiar face of a woman she had met a couple of days ago; *Welch* was her name, Davis remembered. Three more agents emerged from the vehicles and seemed to stand ground with hands on their holstered guns.

Ugh... Davis thought. *Was that the same guy agent who helped me last night?*

Before leaving cover, she looked at other points on the street to make sure she was not killed once she headed toward the SUVs. Convinced it was safe to move, Davis walked out with the laptop case in her "good" hand, the hard drive under her arm, and her revolver in her waistband. There were times like today when she was glad she slept fully dressed. She was then struck by the thought of what would have happened if the agent who put her in the chair were less of a gentlemen and had put her to bed.

Why the hell do I think of these things in times like this?

Stopping short of entering the coffee shop, Helms saw Davis and immediately talked into his chest. The SUVs suddenly had new drivers; they pulled up beside Davis, giving her cover and blocking the view from the street's other side.

The other agents and Welch jumped back into an SUV while Helms and Andersen continued walking to provide her cover from the street. Once the SUV was beside her, Welch and Helms assisted Davis and her packages into the back seat. Helms jumped in the front passenger side with her and Welch as Andersen got into the first SUV.

As Helms entered and their vehicles sped away, Davis made a sign of silence with her index finger to her lips. When she pulled out the external hard drive first, Welch and Helms's eyes widened. Davis made the sign for pen and paper. After she had it, she wrote "bugged." The rest of the ride back to the FBI office was in silence.

Davis could hear more first responders going in the opposite direction as they drove to Boston. Once there, every part of her body would be investigated. She was glad that an internal cavity search wasn't deemed necessary. As her luck continued, she was able to shower and get a change of clothes.

Davis felt a little better when she felt "clean."

~

Helms never thought of himself as a man who got anxious. Then he thought about it.

Well, there were the times the children were born that I was "worried."

Today, though, he felt as if he now understood the nature of anxiety when first responder reports about the havoc at Davis's home emerged, followed by her urgent call for help.

She's not dead, he kept thinking over and over again. He had known Davis for some time, and she was pretty unflappable for a Navy type. But hearing the urgency in her voice spoke volumes as to the level of danger she was in.

After he got her call and then finished the longest ride to their coffee shop he had ever experienced, he could only relax once she was in the SUV. Once he knew she was safe, Helms found other things to be anxious about such as the local and world news.

By 6 a.m., the local news was abuzz about "explosions" and "fireballs" in the quiet town of Wakefield. But this news was immediately overshadowed by the public's fear that these events were the beginning of another crisis like what had happened back in May.

I wish, Helms thought. *Last May is nothing in comparison to what is to come.*

As news reports gave multiple aerial and local color commentaries, Helms was drawn to an even bigger story breaking on an international scale.

The British newspaper, *The Protector,* had received multiple images of a classified, authentic memorandum documenting a U.S. mission that had occurred five years earlier involving the Prince of Spain and a Saudi millionairess. From the report, the American intelligence community was gravely concerned that the Saudi woman's family might have ties to possible fundamentalists in the Middle East. Unfortunately, the young, handsome Prince of Spain was nonetheless in love with her and they planned to marry. Since the prince was a war hero, well-educated, well-loved, and greatly respected by his countrymen, he held great promise for Spain's strong economic future. His marriage to an influential Saudi Arabian family would assure the future alignment of the two nations.

That was until a tragic car accident had killed both the prince and his fiancée. The official story had always been that the young couple fell victim to anarchists, who were intent on destroying the free world. With their guards' car sabotaged, the couple's car was driven off the road into the rocks along the shore. There had always been conspiracy theories that it was truly Spain's own government or the woman's family, who felt such a relationship with a "foreigner" was disgraceful. Helms remembered he had done follow-up work to see whether any substantive evidence existed for such a claim.

But like all conspiracy theories, there was only speculation and no hard evidence until today. *The Protector* produced startling documents that identified the potential threat to the U.S. and its allies' security if such a union between Spain and the Middle East were allowed. These classified memorandums outlined a series of possible "correcting elements" to "eliminate the danger," and the final specific plan that would simply "remove the variables." The plan itself was laid out in great exactness as were the details of the "crash," the forensic evidence, and the specific name of the anarchist group to be blamed. Helms knew the people of Spain and the rest of the world who read these documents wouldn't just chalk it up to more fiction. Adding to the evidence were mission surveillance images of the prince, who had survived the initial crash and was alive holding his dead fiancée as his own life ebbed out of his body.

My God... we just watched them die, Helms thought. *Nothing good will come of this. Why the hell would they video this?*

He knew that just seeing the images to "confirm the prince's death" would open and strain the U.S. alliance with Spain. While he was sure Spain and the Middle East would readily accept American involvement in an assassination, he was also sure the rest of the world would remain skeptical. In a rare moment of patience, the rest of the world wanted some verification of America's involvement since the story was just too grievous. By 12 p.m., more audio-visual documentation of the same events and a four-page memorandum were broadcast to the world via the Internet. Shaking his head in disbelief, Helms knew that even if the American government were officially to state that the entire production was a fabrication, the authenticity of the footage and corresponding documents could not be ignored by both American allies and old, especially Cold War enemies such as Russia and China.

We caused the car accident with a head of state and then we taped it as he died in front of us. We offered no assistance. We just watched them die. And we're their allies... this is not going to go well at all.

By 1:15 p.m., Helms was briefing with the Directorates of nearly every intelligence agency, the vice-president of the United States, and other West Wing representatives, the secretaries of State and of Defense, the Pentagon, and all branch commanders of the armed forces. Everyone attending this "unofficial" meeting was on heightened alert since a lot of pressure was on everyone as a result of the leaked footage. Time and date stamps confirmed the documents and footage were actual operations conducted by the Foreign Intelligence Agency's Operations Center, which had been breached on May second.

The five dead bodies and three critically injured agents, burned cars, and corresponding damage in the middle of a suburban neighborhood were now last page news as the world discovered an enemy hiding in plain view of the American government. By 2 p.m., the Internet's lead stories were all about "America's Death Teams" and Operations Center's "License to Kill" (and "Kill Again").

You can't make this shit up, he thought.

By 3:15 p.m., Helms had finished yet another briefing with all his superiors in the Bureau, interested parties, and heads of state. He had to review everything from the very beginning, including the first piece of classified data he received, confirming Alexander J. Burns's allegation that he was marked for death by his own government. Helms reviewed how four civilians were caught up in the collateral damage and had been targeted for death as well. He identified these four civilians, who included two sisters, a four- or five-year-old girl, and a blind former therapist of Mr. Burns. He outlined the "Merrimack Valley Crisis" on May second and how there were no civilian deaths or injuries as a direct result of Burns and his team. He next moved on to how he had established a task force to make contact and obtain the very classified data that the Foreign Intelligence Agency had lost and how the operation was compromised by Webber and his team, which resulted in a firefight in the middle of Boston and the death of Helms's contact.

Of Webber's superiors, Chairman Eric I. Daniels was the most verbal in his dissent, claiming it was Helms and his team who had obstructed justice and were involved in the death and injuries of their agents and a former agent's disappearance.

Smiling, Helms had patiently waited until this very moment to present his own hard evidence so as to dispel the Foreign Intelligence Agency's allegation. With eyes locked on Daniels, he first reported that the "former agent," Jillian Davis, had requested and was provided protective custody by the Bureau because she was concerned that her former bosses were going to kill her. In addition, this former agent had confirmed that Burns had given her, in good faith, one of the very external drives that he was trying to give back when at Boston City Plaza. Since Helms's possession of the actual hard drive was a game changer, Daniels's allegation melted away. Halfway through Helms's closing statements, his team had confirmed that Davis's watch had been bugged for surveillance with a known configuration consistent with the Operations Center.

Finally... the truth may get out after all.

For the first time in months, Helms felt as if he were accomplishing something.

When the meeting was over, the Secretary of Defense determined that the Foreign Intelligence Agency had overstepped its authority by interfering with the FBI's investigation, and that the charges of obstruction alleged by the Operations Center were bogus. Helms agreed he would hand over the external hard drive to a "third party," the Central Intelligence Agency, for review. Much to his chagrin, pursuing Burns and obtaining the remaining external drives would be a joint venture with the Operations Center in the lead and Helms and his team in a supportive role. On-screen, Helms respectively objected, but he let it go. Once the link was closed, the retired Marine was as pissed off and foul-mouthed as ever.

So much for feeling like I accomplished something.

In the end, he knew it was political. If the Operations Center cleaned up its mess, the problem would go away, and the agency might even survive. With the Bureau's firm foothold in the case, he guessed that if his team continued to be involved and pulled off more success, the Operations Center might go the way of the dinosaurs and be phased out of existence. It finally hit Helms why he never felt anxious. He always channeled the anxiety into work, which he couldn't do when his children were born.

Work's the cure to anxiety. Thank God.

Chapter 10

"Gladiator in arena consilium caput" – "The gladiator if formulating his plan in the arena" Seneca

Cratty made it to her second shift later than usual, missing both her usual start at 3 p.m. and her manager status briefing. She had taken to coming in as early as 1 p.m., so coming later than usual surprised the first shift manager, Jeffery Glenn, who was pacing the hallways, trying to look busy on his tablet. He was easy to identify from afar, being a tall, blond, handsome young man, with a tour of duty completed in Germany.

Not a real fire zone by any stretch of the imagination.

Slowing her pace, Cratty allowed her longer than usual coat to flow around her, giving the illusion of a long cloak. Smiling at the thought of looking like a dark apparition, she felt her mood fall into darkness as soon as her thoughts went to Chairman Daniels's mandate that she be watched, most likely by Glenn.

Gee, paranoid much?

If he had caught her ten months ago, she might have liked him. But of late, she didn't like anyone, and she had made it clear that she was not interested in anyone, professionally or personally. Still, he continued to surprise her with his continued efforts to be pleasant.

"Missed you at the status meeting today, Denise. You all right?"

Poor thing, she thought. *He seems genuinely concerned.*

Feigning congeniality was difficult, both in attitude and appearance, but she gave it her best shot.

"I had an opportunity to spend more time shooting than I thought I would," she responded. She made no eye contact as she spoke and moved around him to enter the manager's office. With her coat still on, she put her gun in her bin and started to rearrange her personal items for easier access. Hoping he would leave, she continued organizing and reorganizing the same three personal items—gun, knife, and ammunition—in different parts of her spacious bin.

No makeup. No pictures. Just weapons and space... nice, Denise.

He continued to hover above her and looking more uncomfortable than usual. Finally, he began talking to her as he looked at his own feet.

"Well, two things in particular. Deputy Director Webber is pulling eighty percent of resources to Boston and Virginia. Looks like they got a break on Burns."

It was obvious to her that Glenn paused with the full expectation that she would respond in some caustic fashion. While she fought being predictable, the opportunity to voice her anger was too appealing to let go.

"Yes... some break. At least eight dead agents, five critically injured, and the whole world pissed at us for killing the Prince of Spain. Yeah... we are lucky."

Cratty discontinued reassembling her empty bin once it was evident that Glenn was not going to leave. To his credit, he chose to ignore the sarcasm and went on with the real issue he was avoiding.

Clearing his throat, he continued.

"In other words, I'm leaving you with a skeleton crew of ten people for the next seventy-two hours."

Sighing, Cratty didn't even cringe at the numbers as she did the math in her head.

"Ten people out of a fully operational center of forty-five means that real-time support will be non-existent. I'm assuming my assistance will not be required for the Burns affair?"

She could see on his face that he was trying to be diplomatic but opted to be blunt.

"No," was his simple response. He did have more to add.

"I've already broken up the teams into groups, and we leave in thirty minutes. All real-time support to operations are being handled by other agencies and all of ours are paused. Your role back here is in the unlikely case Alpha is down. If you have anyone you want to have stay, let me know."

Not waiting for a response, Glenn started walking away, but then he turned back to finish his thought. "And just so you know, Dillon is looking to speak to you."

Great... just great... Now, that's a surprise.

Cratty shoved her hands deep into her coat pockets. She wondered what the hell Dillon wanted other than for her to tender her resignation.

"Why? She finally going to give up and get out of my shop? If I was smart, I'd do the same thing."

Cratty watched Glenn's face wince and his shoulder slouch as he prepared his reply.

It has to be work for him even to talk to me, Cratty speculated.

"Be nice, Denise. She has improved and seems to be working out. Anyway, she is trying to take initiative so hear her out," was Glenn's advice.

"Hmm," was her only response

Just as before she walked around him but this time to the Operations Center. Keeping her long coat on that obscured her feet, Cratty was cognizant of how the low lighting must have enhanced her pale skin, yet dark ghost-like appearance as she descended stairs into the pit of monitors.

"Dillon. To be fair, I must warn you that I'm particularly prickly today, and my company after hours would be quiet unpleasant. So whatever you've got, it better be something both noteworthy and that makes me smile. And you know it will take an act of God to make me smile," she warned.

Jumping to stand at attention, Dillon was startled by Cratty's appearance.

"Yes, ma'am!" she started and then she slowed down as if to collect her thoughts. Beads of sweat were materializing on her brow.

As she stood motionless with her hands now behind her back, Cratty avoided eye contact with Dillon and instead scanned her peers, who in turn looked away as if they were about to witness a violent response.

They just don't want any part of it. I gotta give Dillon credit for at least dealing with me.

After a moment, it was evident that Dillon collected herself and started her briefing.

"In light of the recent events in Boston, I took the liberty of researching Alexander J. Burns's files, operations, the circumstance of his leaving the Foreign Intelligence Agency, and his MIA status until last May."

Cratty gave the appearance of calm as she continued to stand quietly and wait. Still, there was silence.

Jesus Christ! Do I have to ask every question?

At the mere mention of Burns's name, and Daniels taking most of her people to a mission she was excluded from, she was irritable.

No. Pissed off is more like it, she corrected herself as her hands tightened behind her back.

"Your point, Dillon?" she asked more harshly than she intended.

"Yes... every critical juncture in Burns's career has resulted in a near fundamental change in his behavior. When he was head injured, his kill ratio dropped to one. When he planned and executed the distractions on May second, no civilian injuries or deaths resulted when there could have been a blood bath. Yesterday's shooting of the woman, Samantha Littleton, resulted in another significant change from not killing anyone in five years to killing about eight or more, armed federal officers in a twelve-hour period. Still, he hands over a key piece of leverage, the external drive, because he said he would. He gave it to the woman who went to his friend's aid and was with her when she died—"

Cratty's eyes narrowed. *Looks like Dillon did take initiative.*

She had also seen the tapes and had her own thoughts she was wrestling with since her review of the classified footage.

It looked more like an execution than a justified shooting to me. The woman wasn't even armed. The ground team could have easily stopped her, but they shot her instead. What were they thinking?

"I see you accessed the tapes that Bravo is not supposed to be involved in... a clear breach in protocol," Cratty interrupted.

She knew Dillon's silence was the result of being unsure whether she was going to take this opportunity simply to fire her. Cratty took a different approach.

"Keep going, Dillon. You're showing promise."

She had to admit it was refreshing to be surprised. Cratty interpreted Dillon's continued hesitancy as worry over her boss's changed behavior and maybe the presence of some kind of trap. Again, Cratty was impressed with Dillon's persistence.

"Well, yes... the woman who died I have seen before. She was in two surveillance tapes, once as a brunette and the other time as a redhead. Each time, she was in the middle of a sting operation while Burns was somewhere else making something happen."

Cratty had reviewed those same tapes. Littleton was a brunette when she was at the hospital and a redhead when she pretended to be a police cadet. Dillon returned to her monitor and brought up another image of a woman who was a similar height, weight, and definitely the same body configuration. It was a grainy image from a dashboard camera from some sort of military vehicle Cratty had never seen before in all of her off-the-clock investigations of the Burns case.

How the hell did Dillon find this? Good work.

From the angle, Cratty could see what appeared to be a woman struggling to get up as her car seemed to be on its side off an embankment.

Dillon continued, "This video was taken three months ago from a private security truck transporting military ordnance from the base in Brisbane Falls, New York to a freight train that was heading to Boston for transport oversees. The four soldiers you see here are assisting this woman, who appears to have survived the car accident quite well. It takes about ten minutes, but as you can see, they are able to assist her."

The image was sped up as various attempts first to assist the woman were made and then successful efforts were made to right the woman's car. A few minutes more and an ambulance showed up. An EMT got out of the driver's side and went to the back of his vehicle, ostensibly to take out a medical bag he would need to attend to the woman.

The tape went on for seemingly longer than expected until the EMT appeared briefly again and then went out of view yet again as the soldiers continued to look after the woman.

The woman could be Littleton. And that average looking, nondescript guy has to be Burns, Cratty concluded.

The image then shifted to the soldiers returning to their own vehicles and the transport starting up again. Cratty was impressed with Dillon's research. Additionally, she suddenly felt muscles in the corners of her mouth tugging in an upward direction followed by a genuine emotion of feeling... *happy?*

Distracted by this act of God, she returned her attention back to the briefing.

"When the truck arrives at its destination, all twenty-eight crates are present, but there are six crates that are not intact. Two crates are missing handheld stinger missiles of the MTF-29A type while the other crates are missing two reusable shoulder-launched missiles. As you know, ma'am, both of these missile-systems are 'point, shoot, and forget.' In addition, there are a 'couple' of fragment grenades and a 'few' high-grade explosives with detonators also missing."

Son of a... well... the landscape just changed. Preliminary reports on Burns's attack on the agents at Davis's home indicated he was in possession of both high-yield explosives and a grenade. Damn.

With hands still folded behind her back during the entire briefing, she now crossed her arms over her chest as she thought.

"What makes you think Burns had anything to do with this?"

Dillon's response was immediate. Clearly, she had thought about this for a while, Cratty surmised.

"I think Burns is always planning. He eats, drinks, and sleeps logistics. As a result, he's always thinking ahead and always needs resources and material. The appearance of this same woman, the use of distraction, and the limitation of harm to others seems consistent with Burns's mode of operation. Further, the ambulance shows up with one EMT, not two. I'm no medic, but I always thought there were always two medical specialists—one to attend the patient and one to drive. There was a stolen ambulance reported to the local police, but the ambulance was found two miles away in a garage," she concluded.

Dillon fell silent. Her work was excellent, not flashy, fluffy or over-the-top, but excellent.

Cratty slowly turned away to clear her thoughts, leaving Dillon and all the prying eyes wondering what "The Dark One" would do next.

So... what to do? Bring Glenn and Webber into the fold—give them the data and hope they recognize its value? Let them fuck it up like they did with Littleton? Or do I take initiative like Dillon and find Burns myself?

For the first time in months, she decided it was time for action. With full knowledge that Webber would keep her out of the Burns affair, she decided she was in deep whether or not he wanted. Still though, she was secretly hoping he would do anything to keep her out. More tugging at her mouth emerged as she thought about pissing off Webber.

"Did you come up with this yourself or did you have help?" was Cratty's next question.

Seconds passed before Cratty pulled herself from deep thought and noticed the delay. As she turned back to look directly at Dillon, she was surprised there was still no answer.

Now, was that a difficult question? She waited but nothing still came.

"That's not a rhetorical question, Dillon. Did you have help?"

Cratty could easily see that Dillon had a hard time figuring out her state of mind since Cratty's non-verbals gave nothing away. After all, she had months to perfect her control over her emotions.

Dillon finally gave an answer that was shorter than Cratty expected.

"I did have assistance, ma'am." More seconds passed and it was clear to her that Dillon wanted to protect her peers as Dillon's scalp seemed suddenly to become wet.

For Cratty, it was an easy decision: either identify the people or we let Burns slip through our fingers again. Cratty closed the small gap between her and Dillon and spoke in a low tone.

"You have thirty seconds to identify them... and don't think for one second that 'I'd rather not' will work with me," Cratty demanded. She felt herself getting angry as heat seemed to fly off her body and her eyes peered through Dillon's head.

While Dillon initially hesitated, she reconsidered and relinquished four names.

Cratty stepped away from Dillon and scanned the room. All four women and Dillon were all known to have attitudes as well as difficulty controlling their opinions. At the same time, they were very creative and possessed remarkably high intelligence quotients.

"Sit down, Dillon," was Cratty's only response as she continued her rumination.

She began walking upstairs to the glassed in office that overlooked the entire Operations Center. She absentmindedly took her coat off and stood vacantly looking out for what seemed to be an eternity. She was wearing her standard dark slacks with a matching black blouse, which made her blonde hair, pale skin and blue eyes really stand out.

So many things could go right. So many things could go wrong. And if I do nothing, everything stays the same. And how's that working out for you, Denise?

Cratty's attention shifted when she saw a number of staff below collecting their belongings to relocate either to Boston or Virginia's Operations Center. She made a decision she was sure she was going to regret. But something about what Dillon had said about Burns's behavior was too true.

There is a definable pattern. That makes him a bit more predictable. A bit more human. And if I lost everything like he did and were threatened, I'd take the fight to the enemy. He's going to go on the offensive and Webber thinks he's fighting a defensive campaign... this may be my only shot to capture Burns.

The havoc Burns was wreaking with the classified files he took from her shop was pissing her off, and she wanted to end it once and for all. Not to mention the other little thing called "jeopardizing national security." She was still a law enforcement agent, sworn to protect her country. If that meant she went rogue, she was fine with that; Webber was done with her once Burns was caught or killed.

An additional thought crept into her mind: *If I get to Burns first, it will piss off Webber and Daniels.* That made her smile even more.

Cratty returned to her bin and retrieved her semi-automatic weapon and hip holster. Now armed, she returned to the top of the landing to address the teams before they left as Glenn was on his way upstairs to turn the operations officially over to her. He was surprised when she met him halfway up the stairs.

"Glenn? I will need Dillon and four others to help me run the shop. You can take all of the rest and give Deputy Director Webber my regards."

She could tell Glenn noticed that she was armed. She felt some elation in having a plan and seeing him look nervous.

Are you expecting trouble, Denise?" he asked.

Hey! Do you know me well enough to keep calling me Denise, Jeffery? I don't think so. And I'm armed too.

Wanting to get him out as soon as possible, she focused on her breathing to give the impression of just being herself, tired and unenthusiastic. While technically there was no longer a policy restricting the manager or security from having a sidearm, it was, ironically, part of Daniels's new image for the Operations Center—armed to the end.

"Last time the shit hit the fan, I lost time and material because I was not prepared. That won't happen again. I don't plan to spend time looking for my gun if I don't have to. Anyway, isn't this the new look the chairman is looking for?" she added as she saluted him.

Even though Glenn smiled, it was easy to tell he was trying to convey that he was not nervous.

You would suck at poker, was Cratty's fleeting thought.

Changing the subject quickly, he asked, "What else do you need?"

"I will need five cots, two cases of MREs, and two armed guards at the front door, exterior side. I plan on being locked down when you leave. It will only be the five of us, and the ship will have to run efficiently. The fewer here, the better it will work," Cratty explained.

"Are you digging in for the night?"

"I'm preparing in case the hunt for Burns goes longer than anyone expects. I'm not going to get my bell rung again like last May."

It was probably one of the worst lies she had ever produced. While the logic was way off-base, she was betting that Glenn wanted to get away from her almost as fast as she wanted him to leave. He continued his fake smile and walked away.

Anyway, you made out on the deal. You have an additional five bodies to add to the task force heading to Boston. That will please Webber. It won't help you, but you'll feel better.

With hands behind her back and her sidearm prominently displayed, she descended the stairs to Dillon and caught her before she collected all her things to depart.

Still holding a small travel bag, Dillon stayed at her monitor and waited until Cratty closed the gap within a three-foot personal space distance.

"Here's the deal, Christine," she began in a low, even tone.

"If you want to be on the team that pursues a ghost, you and your friends can leave. If you think you have what it takes for a high-risk, high-gain operation to find Burns, then stay with me. Talk briefly to those who assisted you and they can volunteer or not. No one stays behind unless one hundred percent in. If they value their careers, then it's probably safer to leave. But if you and your team want to be involved in a real hunt, be at your posts in five minutes."

With that, Cratty turned as casually as possible, scanning each woman who had helped Dillon, just to confirm they had all witnessed the entire event. Satisfied that they had, she walked up the stairs where she planned to pace nervously.

I really need their help. There's no way I can do this alone. I wish Davis was here and not shot up.

As her pacing boiled down to her counting the distance from the glass to exterior wall, she decided to do something she hadn't done in some time. Digging deep into the folds of her discarded coat pocket, she found lipstick. Without hesitation or a need for a mirror, she applied it without thinking.

Taking a deep breath, she began her walk back down the stairs to the now cavernous, near-empty sea of monitors where Dillon and the four women waited anxiously.

Christine Dillon, Ana Ramsey, Cindy Belben, Molly Horowitz, and Kelly 'Fitzy' Fitzgerald. Well... so, this is my new crew.

"Last chance to bail," she addressed the group.

No one said anything, but they didn't leave either. Cratty took that as a ringing endorsement.

"All right... Dillon, get Deputy Director Webber or the Operations Center Alpha on the big screen and make sure the recording is working, please."

It was evident by their expressions that the entire group was rethinking its decision now.

"The Dark One" is not only calling Alpha directly; she used the word "please," and is she wearing makeup?

Cratty was still smiling at the imagined dialogue when she heard Dillon's response.

"Yes, ma'am," Dillon said. The rest of her Bravo Team went to monitors close to Dillon.

"Everyone else, find all recent data and history of present events involving Burns, the Boston FBI Regional Office, a former agent of ours, Jillian T. Davis, and a Lieutenant Steve Andersen of the North Reading Police."

Dillon interrupted with her update.

"Deputy Director Webber is on my monitor, ma'am."

Cratty began her rehearsed lines. *Be nice, Denise. You can do it.*

"Director Webber?"

"That's 'Deputy' Director, thanks to you, Cratty," Webber said. He was clearly reading something off-screen and was pissed about something.

In full knowledge of what she had done, Cratty still refrained from smiling while greatly enjoying the dig.

"What is it, Cratty?" he continued.

Any conscious, awake person could easily tell that Webber was not having a good day and looking to kick someone to the curb.

Perfect, she thought. She figured she would be a good target.

"Manager Glenn and his team have redeployed to Boston and Virginia. I presently have five staff in Bravo, and I just want to confirm that you prefer my involvement with the Burns matter be minimal to nonexistent—"

Webber cut her off and was visibly annoyed at her bringing up Burns's name.

"We got the Burns case covered. I prefer you and your team not bother our work here."

"Yes, sir. Just to clarify, is there anything you want us to do, either to assist or support? If we come across some intelligence or have some theories, do you want us to bring them to you, or—" was all she got out before she was cut off. Seemingly at the end of his short line of patience, Webber gave his full focus on-screen to emphasize his point.

Please, be an asshole, I know you can be, and tell me just to stay out so I can have it on the record, she hoped.

"Cratty, can you manage to run Bravo for three days without support?" he asked clearly, getting more annoyed by the second.

"Yes, sir. I just want to let you know that Bravo is here to help should the need—"

Boy. You are pushing it, Cratty.

"Cratty... just follow protocol—you are backup to the mission. We won't need it, but just do your job, stay out of our way, and we'll all get along." And then Webber simply closed the communication.

Cratty smiled. *Today is a great day.*

"Okay... Dillon, switch off internal recording of the Operations Center. We will be running dark."

"Yes, ma'am."

While still basking in the glow of successfully manipulating the deputy director, Cratty had her brief shining moment of glory interrupted by a question about what, she thought, was an obvious ploy.

"Ma'am?" Cratty turned to her left and noticed the question was from Horowitz, a very young Jewish woman from New York, a Cornell graduate in mathematics.

"Yes?" she responded.

"Why are we now running dark?"

178   J.M. Erickson

Cratty was rethinking her whole plan.

If I'm going to be bottled up with this group and a billion questions, I might use my sidearm after all... Okay, Denise... breathe. Find the "nice" Denise Cratty, and be open and considerate.

"We are researching highly sensitive, classified data. If operations are breached, again, I don't want a record of it falling into the wrong hands. I also want it clearly recorded that Deputy Director Webber wants us to stay completely out of his operation. Dillon, make note of that rationale. Thank you."

Cratty started to walk around and then made her plan clear.

Now how did I end up with all women on my team?

"Ladies... I want you to speculate what Burns and his team are going to do next. I want this to be a free flowing discussion where there is no rank or levels. I want creativity and some ideas before I bring our FBI colleagues in on the possibility that Burns might have some more firepower."

Belben, the youngest of the group, who was legendary for drinking everyone under the table, was next with her question.

"Ma'am... shouldn't we keep this in house within our own command structure?"

Aha. And there lies the beauty of my recorded dialogue with Webber.

"Well, yes... but you heard *Deputy* Director Webber... he preferred to have Bravo 'not bother' them in their work," she said with disdain in her voice. Changing tempo and tone, Cratty found herself talking with more emotion and authority than she had expected.

"But you know what? I think Bravo can solve this problem because I was there in May and almost got Burns. Jillian Davis laid hands on Burns and almost got him. You five found a pattern and a connection that Alpha team did not. Burns has changed. He is a man who has loyalties and friends. That makes him human. He feels loss and emotion, and I bet he also wants revenge. Humans make mistakes. I will not let him slip through my fingers again. And there is no small-handed, bald-headed, entitled prick of a guy who's going to tell me not to be involved when it's my job to be involved in my own shop.

Whatever Burns is going to do, it will all be done in twenty-four hours. He wants us to think it will happen in seven days, but that is another distraction, and Webber is too stupid to piece that together. That is why we are moving ahead to solve this... but thank you for clarifying the situation. Are we all in or not?"

Dillon was smiling as Belben's jaw slackened. Horowitz turned to her fellow Cornell graduate, Fitzgerald, and gave a nervous look. It was Ramsey, the short Hispanic woman from Chicago, who spoke next:

"Let's get some!"

"Yes... yes, we will," Cratty responded. She did not think it possible, but she fully experienced both warm feelings and excitation over focusing on something that mattered.

Maybe revenge is a good thing.

Cratty found her seat and shifted closer to her team. Then curious thoughts popped in her head.

Is this how Burns got started? Is this how it all starts? When you know you're right and they're wrong, you plan to prevail at all costs?

"Stay on task," she said to herself.

Chapter II

"Fiat justitia ruat caelum" – "Let justice be done though the heavens fall" Terence

David was feeling the wind on his face as the ferry headed to the mainland. He had come to love Kea, but it was time to go. Still hurting from the loss of his friend, leaving Kea almost took a backseat until he broke the news to Emma.

A couple of hours earlier over breakfast, the conversation with Emma had been far from easy.

"Why do we have to go? I have so many friends here. So do you and Mom. Aunt Sam and Uncle Alex haven't even seen our house. I thought they were coming to visit us here?"

Then came the sniffles and holding back tears. It was times like this that David was glad he was blind because seeing her so upset might be heartbreaking. While not wanting to disappoint her, her safety was more important to him than life itself.

If we're home and they come for us, we might die.

It was a horrible thought.

"Honey, we're going to a new place where we're going to meet Mom so we can see her sooner. Mommy and I also thought that if we moved to a new place, we would be a lot closer to Aunt Sam and Uncle Alex so they could visit more often," he explained. He hated lying.

I do suck at lying.

Even when he was being interrogated by Lieutenant Andersen, he didn't lie so much as he didn't tell him the entire truth.

Emma's voice seemed to lighten up at the prospect of seeing

Becky sooner than later, and being closer to Aunt Sam and Uncle Alex. David had to have a "happy child" for the trip, and that meant letting her have some control.

"So, Emma, I want you first to take the 'gift bag' and run to your friends to let them know we are heading to Italy for a couple of weeks and give each a toy."

"I love that!" she said, jumping up from the table, ready to spring into action. She always loved to give toys to other children.

Slowing her down with both hands on her shoulders and redirecting her back to her chair, he continued.

And after breakfast and then delivering toys, you need to change into your traveling clothes and get your backpack. Fill it with clothes and stuff for teeth and an extra bag for some of your favorite stuffed animals. Okay?"

Will do!" she said as he heard her eating her toast and eggs.

She would be a great soldier.

It only took them an hour to get ready and head to port to make the 7 a.m. ferry ride out. With Emma sipping hot morning cocoa, David took in the sea air as he kept hoping that Burns's assessment would be wrong and that no one would seize the home.

What am I becoming? he kept thinking. *They killed my wife, ruined my first life and then threatened my next life after they killed Samantha... my God. She's gone.*

All the thoughts of what his enemies had done to him still could not quell his fears: *if they breach the house, I will have killed them.*

He had to focus on keeping Emma and Becky safe. At all cost.

Still, if being a murderer takes a piece of you, how does Burns do this? How did Samantha?

In another hour, he expected to be on the mainland. Should anyone looking for them ask questions, the children would let them know they were headed to Italy. In actuality, Becky and he discussed moving to Sao Paulo, Brazil to live since it was a growing urban community, strong in the arts, culture and diversity. Hiding in plain sight would be easy with their blended family. It also offered Emma a great deal of diverse children to be with and a good place to be raised. For Becky and him, it might be a good place to find employment.

Employment in what? was really a big question, but at least it was a start.

He would miss living on Kea. He would miss looking toward the Island of Kos as he did for months in remembrance of Jenny. If he had learned anything in the last several years, it was that survival was based on the ability to adapt. Flexibility would be the key ingredient to keep Emma safe.

~

Becky nodded off into a disturbed sleep. With a start, she awoke and found herself on a flight heading to Logan Airport. Nearly fourteen hours had elapsed since Samantha's death. She knew David and Emma were long gone from Kea and that classified data was flooding the air waves and Internet.

Prior to boarding the plane, Burns called her. He had only one question:

"Do you want to kill the person who killed Sam?"

"Yes," Becky answered without hesitation. She never felt so alone. The specter of her sister was frozen in her head. She never felt so much hate. It was cold and harsh, nothing like she had expected. Not heated fury but cold, removed near frigid isolation of emotions with one focus—kill.

It just keeps replaying in my head. I keep seeing it over and over again... I should have been there...

She just couldn't let Samantha's death go unanswered. And she had to be the one to do it, Becky concluded.

"Are you sure? I can take care of this. You can go and be with Emma and David, and I will make sure I make them pay."

"No... if I was killed, Samantha would make sure she hunted them down herself and killed them. I need to do this for her," she said.

And for the times I wasn't there to protect you when you were a child... Pumpkin. And for Tony.

Becky knew there was no connection, but the feeling was the

same: *I am going to kill those who killed my family.*

"Can you kill? Are you ready for that? Once you've done it, there is no turning back. It changes you—"

"I've already changed. The killed her. They killed me."

"It's different when you pull the trigger. You can't go back."

Frustrated and not wanting to be talked out of it, Becky cut Burns off before he could finish.

"Alex... you were a killer and Samantha's love changed you. Do you think once I am back with Emma and David, I might be healed?"

After a long moment, it was evident to Becky that Burns did not have an answer for that one. It took him a minute.

"Will you be able to forgive yourself? Emma and David will always forgive you."

Good point.

She took her time to answer that as thoughtfully as she could. Guilt did have a way of messing her up. For years she ate herself into near death with food. She hadn't expected Burns to be so reflective.

"If I don't do this, I won't be able to forgive myself," she finally said.

Becky recounted every image from the live video feed of Samantha's death, which made her sick to her stomach and then angry. But again, the anger was cold. The feelings were consistent—she wanted to make them pay. When Burns told her that David had found out the specific person responsible for Samantha's death, she had a powerful emotion of steel determination to crush the life out of him. With a name, that was all possible.

Becky would be at Logan close to 10 a.m. She had already caught some local news that a number of federal agents had been killed in a town called Wakefield. Burns had told her there would be more bloodshed to get the point across. He also said the whole operation would be complete in two days.

"I plan to have this all end," he said.

"Doesn't matter to me," was Becky's response. "Emma has David. He'll keep her safe."

"You're coming back. They need you."

"I'm not coming back until I kill them all."

"No Becky... just one man. Thomas Webber."

Becky took a moment to understand the wisdom of his remark. He was trying to tell her to hate the one man responsible, not the rest of the world.

Maybe Samantha was right about Burns, she thought. *Maybe he is deep.*

~

Burns had been driving around for an access point to a peninsula in Boston Bay for about an hour before he finally found it—an old, deserted fort, circa 1890s, overlooked Boston Bay and its islands. It was isolated at the far end of an island and separated from the mainland by a bridge that was sixth-tenths of a mile long.

On one side of the island were a police shooting range, a water treatment facility, and a shelter for the homeless. On the bridge's far side was an old, concrete fort with bunkers, crawl-ways, tunnels and underground passages that went from one dilapidated building to the next. The only "new" building was an automated lighthouse built in the 1950s that sat on the hill overlooking the expanse of the bay, bridge, and land.

Burns had considered this island as a possible meeting place for the final external drive, but he did not like the lack of escape routes. Now that he was looking to catch another killer and to cause as much damage as possible to his former employers, he needed a place that minimized damage to collateral innocents.

He pondered that thought for a moment: *I don't want to hurt innocent lives.* Maybe he wasn't all gone.

Maybe David's right. Maybe I have to be a predator now.

Now that he had a specific target, he could make "a kill" without widespread destruction to civilians. Happy that he finally had located the gate leading to the island, he had solid ideas of various plans. However, he would need assistance. Part of him hoped Becky would back out at the last minute. He didn't want her to feel guilty about killing another human being. But again, maybe Becky and David were right—if she did nothing that might be worse.

For now, Burns focused on three possible plans—not because it was his nature, but because if he didn't, he would think of Sam. When he thought of Sam no longer being in his life, he felt such sorrow and pain, he just didn't want to go on. Burns had to push it out of his head for now.

Maybe after this mission's done... maybe I can pray again.

It was odd not to pray. Prayer had become such a routine part of his life that its absence was sorely felt. He felt so alone.

~

Andersen thought he would be prepared for more bad news as classified data streamed out. At least the one playing itself was not new to him. Even before the actual release of the news, Andersen had caught Internet rumors that the American government, in particular a clandestine "Operations Center" operated by the "Foreign Intelligence Agency," had been involved in yet another heinous cover-up. There had always been various theories that the terrorist mastermind of multiple American attacks, Oman Sharif Sudani, had not been killed on May 2, 2011, but had, in fact, been captured, co-opted by the United States Government, and was living free somewhere in America. This kind of thinking had always been conjured up as rumor, Muslim propaganda or the usual conspiracy theory of an evil American government.

Similar to the documents about the Prince of Spain's death and its footage, more documents emerged via Internet and then were picked up by all the major networks. This time it was a covert plan to capture Oman Sharif Sudani to gain intelligence on his network. The documents further elaborated that an agent, Alexander J. Burns, had originally planned simply to kill the terrorist and be done with it. However, the report indicated that his helicopter had experienced catastrophic failure, later determined by both foreign and domestic intelligence agencies to be sabotage. Somehow, Burns had lived but was marked for death by his own team, the Operations Center. Since the reports of Sudani's death were fictitious and the American people didn't do well when they were lied to, having Burns alive might be a problem. Again, live footage followed later with inserts of a very much alive and well Sudani being airlifted to a base in Germany, then briefings and Sudani's relocation to the United States, "somewhere in the Northeast."

Well, at least Andersen was no longer burdened with carrying around this classified secret. He thought he might catch a break, but that was short-lived since the next news story hit closer to home than he would've liked. Finally, after all those years of wondering what happened to his good friend Diane Welch, he and the world were going to find out. There were more Internet rumblings, and he was looking forward to seeing the details.

By 8 p.m. that night, every news station was having extended coverage with a focus on the American and Middle East response. By 10:30 p.m., just in time for the 11 p.m. news, more classified data streamed in from the Internet and then followed the now well-traveled route to the major networks. This time it was about one of America's heroes, Warrant Officer Diane Welch, being betrayed by the same clandestine Operations Center.

Even though Andersen knew she had made it out alive, he watched with genuine anxiety since it was about his friend. The report was relatively short: Senior Field Agent T. Webber called in predator air strikes on the location of known terrorists killing all targets. Collateral damage included the town's entire population, primarily women and children, and ground troops Warrant Officer Welch had sent in to extract innocent civilians' prior bombing.

Un-fucking-believable. What bullshit!

The report elaborated on Welch's "resistance to make sacrifices to ensure the deaths of known terrorists." The memorandum went on to state that "Welch's willingness to preserve her own troops and nonessential personal at the expense of having the terrorists escape bordered on treason." The findings of the report clarified that "Welch interfered with the mission based on the misconception that her troops, civilians, and her command were not dispensable. Should she escape the desert, I recommend court-martial." Prior to the signature section was a list of U.S. soldiers killed in action. While the memorandum was short, the graphic, high definition footage of a small hamlet in the Swat Valley, Pakistan was long, uncut, and came from various satellite/predator and mission logs angles, capturing the human carnage of terrorists, plus women, children, and the American soldiers trying to get them out.

At 11:30 p.m., two surviving members of "Pakistan's Alamo" were talking to reporters. While one reporter was shifting blame on Warrant Officer Welch for not coming forward, her former medic took offense:

"Oh yeah... that's a good plan. Just so you know, our own people killed women, children, and our own soldiers for seven terrorists. I'm sure we're all okay with that... Are you guys fucking drunk! She held our nineteen-year-old communications specialist in her arms as he died while Webber and his cronies left us to die. If she were trying to cover up, do you think she would have stayed behind? Why would she have let us all live? For a person trying to cover up, she must really suck at it! Now get that camera out of my face!" Robert Calandra said as he pushed through the crowd.

Daniel Maddox, another soldier under her command, was much more articulate:

"Diane Welch is a Marine. She told you all what happened. She resigned her post as soon as she spoke to every single parent, spouse, and loved one of every soldier killed in that atrocity. As a soldier, she is required to treat classified data as classified. To do otherwise is treason. Instead of committing treason, she resigned her commission even when many asked her to stay. That was the story. None of you guys asked, 'Why?' You just assumed she was some kind of a Roman general. She resigned because she was not going to be part of a machine that kills our own and lies to the American people. We all left. Where were you people then? Why didn't you ask questions then? Why aren't you asking about 'Thomas Webber' and the 'Operations Center?' Why are you asking me now?"

Turning away from the monitors, Andersen was hit with a myriad of feelings ranging from sadness to anger to guilt.

She carried that shit around and couldn't even talk to me about it.

Andersen knew that by midnight the whole world would be on fire. It was easy for him to see how this news would play itself out. Americans were now worried whether anything their government told them was true. Sitting down in a vacated chair, he took stock for a moment. He started to list all the negatives accrued so far from the released, classified data.

Allies around the world were reevaluating their trust in the United States, which had effectively assassinated a "friendly" Head of State, allowed a terrorist to live within its own borders and then killed and covered up friendly fire while punishing the innocent. Enemies of the U.S. were now able to draw support from friends, foes, and those who were once neutral about American intentions. It was the beginning of a new day, and every federal agency was on the hunt for one man— Alexander J. Burns. So were the American people and other world governments. The difference this time was that everyone wanted him alive. Andersen couldn't blame them; he wanted Burns to live, too. Still, he did know of one exception to this rule and he also knew the Foreign Intelligence Agency, and in particular Thomas Webber, still had a "kill order" on Burns's head.

Suddenly, Andersen felt his resolve harden.

"No," Andersen said to himself as he stood unshaven in the middle of the FBI Control Room, "you don't get to kill anyone anymore."

His thoughts went back to his friend Welch. He shook off his anger and went look for Helms.

She carried around a lot of shit. She probably only told Joe, and with him gone... shit.

~

The control room was jammed with people with effectively two shifts occupying one space at the same time. First shift was catching some sleep on cots and in sleeping bags in offices, hallways and some in the control room itself. Diane Welch found herself slowly waking up in Helms's office. While initially she thought she was sleeping in bed with her husband, Joe, she realized that the snoring came from Davis sleeping on the cot beside her. Welch oriented herself to her surroundings and saw that Helms and Andersen were already up and talking low.

God, was it only a day or so ago I was sleeping, wondering what the commute into Boston would be like to get to the FBI by four?

As Welch rubbed the sleep out of her eyes, she looked at Davis; she marveled at how peaceful she looked. She experienced the same feeling she did looking at Davis as she had in the past when looking at her own children now fully grown.

They always look peaceful when they sleep. No matter if they're trained to kill, protect, or serve. They always look innocent when they sleep.

Welch stretched but was motioned to come closer by Helms. She pulled herself of her off the cot and was not surprised that is was more difficult. It had been years since she had slept in such accommodations, and she was looking forward to a real bed. As she walked toward Helms and Andersen, she was cognizant of two things. It was taking her longer than she had hoped for the stiffness to work its way out of her legs and Helms looked grimmer than usual.

"Shit. What did I miss?" she asked. "I'm guessing it's nothing good."

"There's a whole story about the Operations Center screwing you and your team over in the Swat Valley, Pakistan, 2006. I am assuming it's all true," Andersen said.

Shit. They all know.

Welch was still for a moment, weighing the gravity of the leaked data and her personal feelings. She knew that to all observing, it must appear she was recounting all of the events within seconds. While she was aware she had some physical manifestations of post-traumatic stress disorder, its true manifestation was her complete cognitive recall of the last two days of that dreaded mission.

"Yes... that's why there's no love lost between me and that fat, pasty bastard."

That was the best she could think to say at the moment.

Helms shook his head. Andersen spoke next.

"Every service man and woman, in and out of uniform, is going to want a piece of Webber. Right now, if Burns killed him, he might be given a medal."

Welch watched Andersen rub his eyes. She could easily tell he wasn't done.

"Ironic, isn't it? We didn't even know who Burns was last May. And now he has become our "great white whale." If more of this data keeps coming out, Burns and his crew are going to become the modern 'Robin Hood and his Merry Men' and we're all going to look like assholes."

More speculation was about to be made regarding Burns's next move when they were interrupted by the intercom.

"Boss, we are getting a request for a conference from Operations Center Bravo in New York," Janeson said.

Now that was a surprise, Welch thought. It was only after she realized it was "Bravo" and not "Alpha" team that she wondered whether some good news might be at hand.

"On our way," was Helms's quick response.

As all three were leaving, they stopped to wake up Davis. Welch was about to nudge her gently when Andersen pulled her back and Helms got in front. He next gave the signal for them to step back and give Davis space. From above her head toward the back, Helms gently nudged her shoulder saying, "Jillian?"

Davis sprung up like a coiled snake, wide-eyed and her right hand clutching her favorite knife. Then her face grimaced from the pain of her healing, left arm.

"Jeez, Louise! Shit that hurts!" Davis belted out.

Welch was surprised by the violent way Davis awoke.

It was obvious to Welch that Andersen was not surprised one bit by her response to being roused from sleep.

Not so innocent looking now, Welch reconsidered.

"See why I don't let you sleep with your gun," Helms said to Davis.

"Sorry... I'm a bit on edge," Davis explained.

Helms handed her revolver to her as she rubbed the sleep out of her eyes and got her bearings.

"Where are we going?" she asked.

Welch turned and noticed that Davis was now wiping the corners of her mouth as they were walking. It was easy to see that she had drooled as she slept.

Now that's embarrassing.

"Looks like we're not the only ones working late. Operations Center in New York wants a conference," Welch explained as they strode to the control room. If Davis were surprised, she was not showing it. She was again surprised by her lack of response since Andersen had told her of the bad blood between Davis and her ex-employers. Then again, Welch surmised that Davis's training and early years in uniform had trained her not to display surprise. Anything Welch said would not get a rise out of her, especially if it involved Burns and his team.

"You know, Davis, you might want to get checked for sleep apnea. Your snoring is erratic, and I swear you stopped breathing a couple of times. Maybe that's why you are so jittery," Andersen offered.

Davis's head snapped toward Andersen while not losing step.

"I do not snore! And I'm not jittery... just tired," she protested.

"I don't know, Jillian. I think you might want to get that looked at before you ask a federal officer for assistance or something to get into bed. I'm just saying," Andersen retorted blankly.

Welch couldn't understand why Davis's demeanor shifted from annoyance to embarrassment as her face and neck flushed red just outside the control room's door.

It seemed to her that Davis was remembering something and about to respond but then she just shrugged her shoulders.

"You know, if I want this abuse, I just need to talk to Helms," Davis finally said.

It's got to be an inside joke.

As the four entered the control room, more people were asleep in the area than awake. Janeson, Gilmore, and Johnson from the first shift were awake and had commandeered the second shift command.

Janeson was the first to respond to Helms.

"Boss, during a crisis such as this, don't you think it would be appropriate to take a page of Naval etiquette and announce your presence on deck? Something like "Boss on Deck" or something?"

Welch smiled. Janeson was growing on her; there was an innocence about her that she enjoyed immensely.

"I work for a living, Janeson. I'm a Marine. We don't do etiquette. What's the story?" Helms requested.

Janeson slipped back into second-in-command mode.

"There is a Denise Cratty, Manager of Operations Center Bravo in New York, requesting a face-to-face conference."

Welch noticed that Davis seemed to recognize the name.

"Put it on the big screen," he said.

The floor-to-ceiling screen flickered to life, and a high definition image of an attractive blonde, blue-eyed woman, wearing all black with a sidearm prominently attached to her hip, emerged.

Wow, Welch had to admit. *Pretty dramatic outfit.*

"Mr. John Helms, I presume?" the woman said in a low voice.

"Ms. Cratty. It's nice to see you. I only wish hell wasn't raining down on us," Helms said.

"It sure is shit is raining,"

Davis was next to jump in.

"Denise? I must say I personally like your new hairdo and wardrobe. But you never struck me as a 'winter color gal.' But then I never would have expected you to be armed as well in your own Operations Center."

Welch couldn't tell whether Davis's remarks were friendly or adversarial.

Cratty smiled—a faint smile, but Welch could make it out as one.

"Well, in light of the data flooding the Internet, I do expect townsmen with torches yelling, 'Give us the Monster!' to show up at any moment. And they would be pretty much justified with all the shit flowing down stream," Cratty replied.

Hmm. Not much emotion, but she's funny. What's with these ops-center people?

"Good point and apt analogy. It does have that feel," Davis said.

"And Ms. Davis, thank you for your gift. But enough of the small talk. I got some data and want to confer before Burns sets the rest of the world against us."

Welch was confused. She turned and saw confusion on everyone's face but Davis's. *Why was she going outside of her chain of command?*

"I'm surprised you're not conferring with Deputy Director Webber. He seems to be obsessively dedicated to finding Burns, and any help in that regard would be appreciated, I am sure," Andersen said.

If there had been a faint smile prior to the mention of Webber's name, it was now erased and replaced with a scowl.

Seems like Webber has a universal effect of destroying anything pleasant, Welch gathered by the withered smile.

"*Deputy* Director Webber has made it abundantly clear that my services are not required or necessary. I have a staff of five while the remaining thirty-five staff have been redeployed to Boston or Alpha in Virginia. Since I have critical data regarding Burns, and *Deputy* Director Webber is not open to it, I thought I would go on the record as assisting a sister intelligence agency to do its job."

Welch couldn't help but notice that every time Cratty said, "Deputy Director Webber," it was with great vile and contempt.

"'Deputy' director? Webber was demoted? It looks like my leaving was a better choice than your staying," Davis said.

"Yes. But again, enough of the past. I am assuming you have already done a behavioral assessment of Burns since your last interaction with him and the release of classified data?"

"Somewhat. Nothing conclusive. We are lacking data from his record and any other relevant information. Can you help there?" Helms asked.

"Yes. The five people who were left with me have a strong interest in Mr. Burns, and they have compiled a profile that might make sense. Helms, are you recording this?" Cratty asked.

"Yes," was the short answer.

"Please disengage your recording device that is tied to your servers; local recordings are permissible. They can be erased later if necessary."

Now Welch was feeling completely confused; she turned and saw Helms give a puzzled look but then he gave Gilmore the nod to proceed. Once complete, Helms gave Cratty the nod to continue.

Cratty looked off-screen and then a young, tall woman took her place to give a briefing. Even though the woman seemed taller, younger and more athletic, Cratty seemed more imposing.

Welch heard Davis comment off-screen about Cratty's apparent dramatic change.

"Is it me or does Cratty look like she's about to go ballistic... kind of a quiet volcano thing going?" she asked Andersen.

"I gotta tell you, she reminds me of you when we first met. Must be a hostile work environment," he said.

"It was hostile, but it must have gotten worse for her to change that much."

The young woman—Welch thought her name was Dillon—reviewed the tapes she had discovered about the woman, ambulance, and missing ordnance. She reviewed past assignments that led up to Burns's last mission and how high casualties, targeted as collateral, were a source of pride. She also reviewed the treatment strategies and possible effects David Caulfield used that may have significantly altered Burns's personality and how he had accessed feelings, allowing him to form bonds with others. Dillon went on to speculate that the woman in the video was the same woman who had been killed the day before. That Burns's changes in his killing behavior seemed to have been targeted to those he found responsible for her death and a danger to his "crew." That's why he had spared Davis's life and given her the drive and then killed and injured the other agents moments later, just outside Davis's doorstep.

"In conclusion, I am guessing that a loss of his lover, which I'm sure Ms. Littleton was, is the primary reason for his change in behavior," Dillon summarized.

"You think?" was Davis's sarcastic comment.

Dillon was going to respond when, thankfully, Andersen had a real question.

"Does that mean he is going to go on a killing spree?"

"No," was Janeson's response. Dillon looked from her screen and all eyes looked toward Janeson now as a result of the interruption.

"Sorry for interrupting your briefing. With the additional information, I believe Ms. Dillon's assessment is quite accurate. I apologize in advance if you were going to conclude that Burns was not going back to his indiscriminate killing ways for the numbers, but he is now being much more selective," Janeson said.

"Yes. My team concluded that he has not returned to his past state of mind. In fact, his focus on killing specific targets and limiting collateral damage would imply an evolution. He was a killer without a conscious and a focus only on the mission. Now the mission is focused on protecting his dependents and avenging his love. At the same time, he's keeping what promises he sees fit: returning the external disk drive because you did not betray him and attempted to assist Ms. Littleton. He's also keeping his word by his release of classified data, which he said he would do months ago if he were betrayed," Dillon concluded.

"That makes him the most dangerous person on the planet," Cratty interjected.

"That's one hell of a behavioral assessment. Sounds pretty accurate, unfortunately," Welch said.

"I hate it when you're right," Andersen added

"He has the means, skills, and leverage to get the job done. He's injured from a broken heart, and he watched maybe the only woman he has ever loved, and who loved him, die in front of him. We know how this ends. As long as Burns does not have an exact target, he will release as much classified information as he needs to find out who killed her," Cratty continued.

What ever transpired at the control center, whether it was everyone including Welch holding their breath, looking away or dropping their head, it was clearly picked up by Cratty. It didn't take a mind reader for Cratty to infer from her colleagues' non-verbal behaviors, looks, glances, and sudden reflection that Burns may have a target.

Welch could see from Cratty's own non-verbals that she was now pissed off.

"For the love of God! Does Burns already know who he needs to kill?" By now standing up and taking up much of the middle of the screen.

Welch was the first to respond.

"Webber made it crystal clear to David Caulfield that he gave the order that killed Ms. Littleton."

It was hard for her to read Cratty's face to figure out the emotions she might be experiencing. At first, she turned as if to walk up a set of stairs but then she turned back to address the FBI staff.

"Well. Did you inform the Deputy Director of his breach and that his life would be in danger?" Cratty asked.

"Ah... yes," Helms said with a bit of confusion in his tone.

Good. Forewarned is forearmed. Well... I don't think we have any more data to share with you," she said.

The conversation stopped. Cratty looked as if she were done and could have easily signed off. Welch wondered if this Cratty had the same kind of social affliction Janeson had.

Or... maybe she doesn't care. Maybe, she's all right with Burns knowing who should be killed?

Davis asked the question everyone wanted to ask.

"Denise, do you plan to tell Webber of your findings and your suspicion that he might be the target?"

Cratty seemed to look mystified by the question.

"No. Deputy Director Webber has made it clear that he does not want us involved. I have already breached that by contacting you so you could utilize the information. But please feel free to let him know anything that seems relevant."

Cratty was about to cut communication, but Davis stopped her.

"Denise, if I wanted to send a message to Alpha the same way it happened last May, would it still work?"

What the hell are you asking?

Cratty's demeanor became unreadable again. It soon became evident that an entire subtext was about to transpire between Cratty and Davis.

"Ms. Davis... I'm shocked. Shocked that you would ask such a question around protocol," Cratty said.

Shocked? Something about that phrase sounds very familiar.

"That approach would not work at all. We completely changed our protocols so that only faxes via emails will get to servers. Such an attack is made up of science fiction. Anything else I can help you with?"

"Can you speculate where Burns might set up a possible attack?" Welch asked.

Cratty took a moment to consider the question.

"Are you Warrant Officer, Diane Welch, Swat Valley, 2009?"

"Yes."

Sorry for your loss, ma'am, for both your husband and troops," Cratty offered.

Welch felt the pain for a moment, but she was appreciative.

Nice of her to say. She doesn't even really know me and didn't have to say anything.

Then without skipping a beat, Cratty went on:

"Based on my team's profile, we suspect that Burns will find an isolated place where there is little to no chance of possible collateral damage. He will pick a place he has reconnoitered well in advance and has full knowledge of so he has the advantage. I suspect he will minimize distraction and use overwhelming force. And to deviate more from character, he will obtain assistance from someone who is just as vested in killing Webber and as a result just as dangerous as he is. I suspect Littleton's sister will be employed. Finally, it's all going to happen within the next twelve hours. I have my team working on possible sites, and I'm assuming it will happen around Boston... where Samantha was murdered."

Cratty fell silent.

Wow. That was telling. 'Murdered?'

Welch saw that the others were as taken by the last point as much as she was. Cratty called the victim by her first name, and she called it murder. The only thing she didn't give them was the exact address for Webber, so Burns and family could "catch up." Welch was positive that if Cratty could, she would have done just that.

What must it be like to have so many people hate you, Welch thought about Webber.

"Thank you," Helms said.

Cratty continued as she was handed something to read from a young Hispanic woman.

"You have a direct link with me now, and I'll be on station for the next twenty-four hours. We're running dark, but we will respond if Alpha's Operations Center is compromised. At which point all communication switches immediately to Bravo for continuation with the mission. For as long as I am in command of Bravo, the Bureau will be able to access our help. Thank you and have a great day," Cratty said with a smile and then she turned to her communications specialist to cut communication. The screen went dark.

Welch didn't know what to think. When she turned to Helms, he, too, was speechless. No one seemed able to make sense of the interaction. Based on what she could see, Cratty's presentation, demeanor, and overall disposition were radically different from several months ago.

"You know... if she were more like this back in the day, I think I would have found her not only likable, but I would have spent more time getting to know her," Davis offered.

Janeson gave Davis a very puzzled look as she tried to figure out whether there was a double meaning to what Davis was saying.

"Well, it kind of makes sense since both you and Ms. Cratty have similar stereotyped male mannerisms, wardrobe choices, and a high degree of machismo. In light of your recent rebuffed advances of a fellow male agent, one might conclude you would consider other alternatives to your present sexual orientation. Unless, of course, you consider yourself bisexual, at which point you are afforded that flexibility with no need to consider any changes save maybe tactics and techniques," Janeson reported.

Welch felt her mouth slacken. She tried to replay what Janeson said but there was so much information, implications and innuendo that it was hard to do. Welch turned to look at Davis and held her breath as she saw more red in face as humanly possible. It could have been embarrassment or rage, and she didn't want to find out.

Helms's eyes dropped as his hand went to his mouth to suppress either a grimace or a laugh. Welch realized this was the first time she had seen him unable to control his emotion.

Andersen suddenly reported through barely containable suppressed laughter that he had to go to the head.

It was Johnson who saved Janeson from Davis's potential attack.

"Boss, Bravo just sent us a couple of emails for us to get a hold of her and Alpha's main IP address website. She also gave us Deputy Director Webber's email as well."

Davis's attention shifted to Johnson's discovery.

Thank God for Johnson and Gilmore, she thought.

Welch could see that when Davis spoke, it was more out of shock than anything else.

"Cratty just gave us access to Alpha's server system?"

"No, Jillian. Cratty just sent us the email address of her boss, should we need it," Helms corrected. She had to hand it to Helms; his recovery was impressive.

"Janeson, if you could refocus on Cratty's profile on Burns for a moment. Do you agree or have something to add?" Helms asked.

Shifting from her profile of Davis back to Burns, Welch felt like she was still processing data.

"I have to say, boss, that I couldn't have done it better. The analysis make sense." It was quiet for a moment while the control room leadership contemplated.

"Well. I guess we wait for either Caulfield or Burns to call next with a location or we find it ourselves," Andersen said while holding up his wife's cell phone.

"We're going to have to come up with a plan to make sure Webber takes one of us to meet Burns when it all happens. And whoever that person is will be wired for sound so we can be there too," Helms ordered.

"It will be either me or Davis," Welch said. The looks she got compelled her to articulate why.

"He likes young attractive women, and he doesn't want to be threatened. If he picks me, it's because he screwed me once before and thinks I'll not be a threat. If he picks Davis, it's because she is injured and pretty."

That makes sense. Welch knew Webber was a scavenger, although he thought he was a bird of prey.

"Diane, do you think Davis is pretty enough for Webber? He seems to like them very tall and exotic, and, well, Davis has a more 'milking the cows, working the farm' aura to her; not that she's not attractive per se," Andersen offered with his best deadpan expression.

Davis's shoulders slumped while Helms's smile broadened.

Welch felt bad setting Davis up for Andersen to strike.

Chapter 12

"Faber est suae quisque fortunae" – *"Every man is the artisan of his own future" Appius Claudius Caecus*

Andersen knew he wouldn't be able to sleep. Every time he closed his eyes and woke up, there was some "breaking news" that was going to ruin everyone's day.

Actually, it's going to ruin the U.S. Government's day. Burns lights the fuse and the world flames on.

Today was no different—when dawn came, so did more unnerving facts from the stolen classified information.

"Well, that certainly breaks up the monotony of dealing with only one national crisis," Andersen sarcastically said to himself.

The news broke like it always did with rumblings on the Internet; some local news stations in the country picked up the story and then it hit major American news channels. The first story was new but not necessarily alarming, Andersen thought.

The "Supreme Leader" of North Korea, Kim Jong-il's death in 2011 was presented to the world as an ill-timed heart attack. At the time, the void in leadership increased the probability of nuclear war since the new Supreme Leader's resolve had yet to be tested. While the saber rattling continued months after Kim Jong-il's death, his demise undermined the stranglehold that North Korea's military had on its own people. Nonetheless, the Foreign Intelligence Agency intervened in yet another country's government. More memorandums outlining the proposed plan of poisoning the leader, with the method of delivery being a prostitute, all seemed to be the stuff of Cold War espionage.

Except there was follow-up documentation of each stage of the plan and an "after action" report claiming success. Video of the dead leader, covert operatives, and the woman who delivered the poison were now shown all over the world. While initially most Americans and allies did not seem too upset with this revelation, it did galvanize more anti-American sentiment in the Arab world, Iran, and North Korea. He knew this revelation would not go unanswered by the North Koreans, and within two hours they hit the East Coast with artillery shells on South Korean military sites. While damage was superficial, the message was clear: the North Koreans were pissed. Helms found out that NATO was receiving petitions for sanctions and possible removal of the United States from its premier status. These petitions came from various nations, mostly anti-American, but also a couple of historical allies such as France and Spain, and the often more neutral countries, China and Russia.

Unbelievable! The U.S. is thrown out of the U.N.! China and Russia are on the same page! And France and Spain are distancing themselves... great day for the U.S.

News coverage continued pointing to the Operations Center as an agency gone rogue whose actions were effectively turning the world against the United States, thereby threatening national security. He was just beginning to get accustomed to the world hating the U.S. when more news broke that hit closer to home.

As the North Korean story reached its crest, revelations were made that all social media created to date was a government ploy to control people, domestic and abroad. Documentation emerged that the concept, construction, and overall application of the top five social networking engines were all the direct result of the Foreign Intelligence Agency's use of research from the Office of Naval Research and Development. While the remarkably rich and famous inventors were not happy about this new information being revealed, the various memorandums from the Operations Center clarified, "The intent, plan, and successful implementation of social networks will do two things to preserve order: keep U.S. citizens and the world preoccupied with their virtual lives, limiting their interest in political, socioeconomic issues and provide an excellent opportunity to track, obtain evidence and data on those who were deemed a security risk." Andersen had to read the memorandum again to appreciate fully the gravity of these statements.

They're spying on their citizens. My children, wife, me...

Now, this one agency was controlling American lives, in addition to messing with other nations' sovereignty.

Oh, my God! Is there anything this agency hasn't done? Is there no boundary this agency hasn't crossed?

"Nothing good is going to come from this disaster," Andersen said to Welch.

As the day progressed and the icons of social networking were outed as frauds, it was also discovered that a number of corporations, within the computer, financial services and food industries took part in the cover-up to obtain inside market advantages and constant subliminal advertisement opportunities. This advantage provided a number of private investors' unlimited access and influence over consumers without the consumers even knowing it. Anyone inside the fold who wanted to "come clean" and reveal his role in the deception was "terminated by the program"—apparently both figuratively and literally, since in one case a reference was made to a computer company's founder being "terminated" from the program. To the world, his death had appeared to be from natural causes when in actuality he was poisoned.

Again, Andersen sat looking around the control room, ruminating how his world had changed as the worst-case scenario played itself out before the world. With an entire treasure trove of information, the Operations Center could provide information for someone to be held in confinement without due process as a result of the American National Defense Authorization Act of 2012. To keep its secret, the agency would kill its citizens, even heroes. From Andersen's perspective, it was easy to see that once the average American was able to get his or her head around the fact that the government created social networking for control rather than to make money, millions of Americans would feel personally violated.

Andersen slowly sat up and stood silently for a moment as he read the documentation outlining the nightmare.

"You just can't make this shit up," Welch said.

"Yeah... it's not going to take a constitutional lawyer to see how the Sixth Amendment was shattered."

Welch motioned Andersen over to take a look at her list of names in the U.S. and the world of those under "active surveillance." The list seemed endless.

Located farther down in the article were highlights of "a few hundred" who were "terminated from the program." Andersen could see many recognizable names.

Helms joined them briefly as the flood of new allegations filled half of the control room's monitors while the other half were searching for Burns.

"'Cry havoc, and let slip the dogs of war,'" Helms quoted as he shook his head in disgust. Andersen's thinking was on the aftermath of such a huge story.

He knew that once the news was able to "name names" for the targeted, every elected official would be called by constituents who demanded this operation stop and those implicated be brought to justice. Next would come legal actions, individual damages, class actions, and legitimate corporations suing the government for giving other companies unfair business advantages. Once again, fixed and steadfast beliefs were turned on their head.

Corporations indicted in the deception, inventors of social networks are fakes, free enterprise compromised, nothing is sacred.

If today were any indicator for the future, more classified data released would be just as devastating.

And there's still a whole lot of time for more bad news to be released for the noon and evening news, Andersen thought.

"Do you think any of us will survive this?" he asked no one in particular. He was just amazed by how his own belief system about his world was being taken apart piece-by-piece.

"He did say he would 'rain down hell' if we went after him. I guess he wasn't kidding. I've never seen a leak like this before in my life. Not all at once; no one has, I bet," Helms responded.

Andersen knew Helms had seen a lot in his years as a Marine and in the Bureau, so for him to say that meant it was bad, Andersen concluded.

The entire control room team had taken time to find changes of clothing, military meals-ready-to-eat, and food brought in from local stores. Toiletries were in high demand, but Martin had been put in charge of logistics for basic needs, and much to everyone's dismay he did an excellent job.

Maybe Helms should move him out of accounting and have him spend more time in logistics

Andersen hated to admit it, but Janeson's thinking outside-the-box with Martin might have opened new doors for the agent in the Bureau.

That's if any federal agencies are allowed to function after all the damage those damn files released, Andersen considered. Everyone in the control room called the classified data dump, "The Great Flood."

"Helms is right. We're going to need a pretty big ark to get out of this flood," Welch had commented.

Suddenly, Andersen felt his wife's phone vibrating and ringing. He began waving wildly for everyone's attention as Helms gave his classic ear-piercing whistle and the visual cue of raised, closed fist, indicating, "Get to your posts and be silent." In under ten seconds, all staff were silent and in place. Gilmore was ready to run the trace.

Andersen composed himself to sound "calm." *What did that sound like?* he thought.

"Hello," Andersen answered.

"Lieutenant. This is Burns. I will be calling you in three hours to confirm a meet site for Thomas Webber and his team. Once I tell you, he will have sixty minutes to be there. If he's not, it will just get worse," Burns said and then he hung up. The closed lined was loud enough for all to hear.

"Well, that was brief," Davis commented.

Andersen saw Helms look at Gilmore. He shook his head, indicating he had got nothing.

The room fell silent, and for thirty-five plus people, that was a feat.

"Boss? Maybe he was deliberately short because he's really close by. Maybe within ten miles of here. If he is, he would have to terminate the call rapidly before we got a lock," Janeson speculated.

Ahh... Janeson... always trying to figure out puzzles, Andersen mused.

"Could be. It could also be that he's not chatty as a result of seeing his girlfriend killed," Welch countered.

"No. He's a trained operative and logistician. He has more than three dozen missions under his belt and a whole lot of firepower with a target. He's not grieving. He's planning an operation that will avenge Littleton's death and free his crew from charges. I'm guessing he's closer than we all want to believe," Janeson said.

As heads nodded in agreement and silence filled the room, Helms gave a course direction.

"Well then, we still have one simple objective. We need to find the one place where Burns could confine a small task force, kill his prey, and escape without civilian casualties," Helms said.

Andersen had to smile at Helm's deadpan presentation of a critical matter.

Helms looked at the clock and continued.

"And we got three hours not only to find the right place but to be able to move at a moment's notice. Pretty easy, wouldn't you say, team?"

A series of "Yes, boss," "On it, boss," "Gotcha, boss," and one "Aye, mate!" Helms didn't even look to see who made the last comment.

Andersen could see that Helms was on to the next piece of business.

"Janeson, get Webber on the line. I need to let him know about our theories and our thinking as well as the timeline."

"Yes, boss," she answered.

Andersen knew that his expression, along with those of Welch and Davis, expressed surprise at his action, and that surprise was not lost on Helms as he gave his response.

"Come on, people. I'm still a federal agent and so is Webber. While, personally, I don't care much for the man, I still have to uphold my oath and the law."

All were quiet until Janeson gave the word that Webber was on a hard-line on a speaker for all to hear.

Helms took the call and outlined everything about the theories, plans, and the three-hour deadline. Andersen did note that Helms omitted his contact with Cratty and Bravo team.

In a rare instance, Webber seemed to be listening without responding or interrupting. Maybe the news was wearing on him, Andersen wondered.

"Okay. You can have one member on your team on my strike force when we go in," Webber responded.

"I'll go or Andersen. Davis has also volunteered. Also—"

Webber returned to his normal response in cutting Helms off again.

"Well, so much for 'changed behaviors,'" Andersen remarked to Davis.

"I'll take Welch. I've worked with her in the past. I'll send a car for her in ten minutes." And then Webber hung up.

"'Worked together'? That bastard—he uses me and my team like a tool and then kills the majority of us. I'd hate to see what he does to enemies of the state!"

The amount of hate his friend had for Webber was immeasurable.

"Well, we saw that one coming," Davis chimed in. Andersen had noticed that she seemed to be in less pain.

"All right. I want Welch to be wired for sound and visual. Real covert, too. I'm assuming that Webber will scan you, so show him the obvious wires and keep the hidden ones off-line until you are at your destination," Helms ordered.

Welch was still pissed that she had to 'work together' with Webber.

"I'd rather have a hot red poker shoved in my eye," she said.

"For flag and country," Helms said.

Andersen saw his friend smile. He had known Welch so long it was easy for him to tell she would have a smartass thing to say.

"Aye, Admiral," Welch mimicked along with the salute.

"I work for a living, Welch. I'm a Marine. And so are you," Helms shot back.

"Oorah," Welch responded.

~

Davis had been rereading all the released classified data for the past hour and found herself feeling drained and melancholic. While her arms felt significantly better, her guilt was mounting.

I worked for these assholes, she thought. *How could I have been so stupid? I knew there were rumors, but Jesus...*

Davis recalled a number of her own missions; none of them reached the level that was being released. She found that all the released files had one thing in common; they had been signed off on by Chairman Eric Daniels. She knew very little about Daniels since he was a ghost similar to Burns, but Burns was a fairly large cog while Daniels ran the agency.

Both these guys really got around, she was thinking when she was motioned over by Johnson to look at his monitor. Out of habit, Davis glanced at the control room's clock and then at her broken watch. Making a face, she read the clock to get the time and saw that it was a half-hour before noon.

Just in time for more classified data to get on the twelve o'clock news, she thought.

As she approached Johnson, she could tell he was disturbed by something he obviously had read. When she saw "the Centers for Disease Control and Prevention," she said quite loudly, "Oh, this is going to suck."

While Davis was struggling with how things could get worse, she knew that whenever the CDC was involved, it meant something was "biological," possibly affecting millions. She forced herself to read the story, even as guilt and anger rose in her stomach.

The Centers for Disease Control and Prevention had received an unusual strain of H6N3 influenza virus from the Department of Defense. Memorandums traced the source of the virus back to a private corporation that manipulated the virus to be more readily transmittable from poultry to mammals. Once done, the sponsoring government agency, the Operations Center, provided the CDC with both the virus and three potential vaccinations. Davis's eyes narrowed as she reread the preceding paragraph.

Wait a minute... that's a good thing, right? A treatment for influenza?

At first glance, these documents indicated a more benign side of the Operations Center in an attempt to prevent a dangerous disease.

Good news? Something positive? No way, she thought.

Once she viewed the accompanying video that went with the story, it was evident the virus had been first tested on human subjects of Asian descent. The illness's ravages had been meticulously documented as had the failed vaccination attempts. Once the right titration of chemicals yielded the healing vaccination, the surviving subjects were also "terminated" from the program. As horrific as the images were, Davis had to admit that it was not so profoundly shocking to learn the U.S. was involved in infecting people for the sake of science. While it was an ugly part of U.S. history, she knew the Department of Energy had tested the effects of radiation on the mentally ill, and the Tuskegee syphilis experiment on African-Americans had terminated in the early 1970s.

But the true terror of this experiment, other than the obvious on the test subjects, was the memorandum outlining the plan to release the influenza strain within the next year on the countries that consumed the most poultry, fuel, and other limited energy resources.

Davis's back and head shot up in disbelief, and she was overcome with dizziness. Fortunately, Johnson grabbed her arm and guided her to a seat closest to the panel. Rubbing her head and regaining her balance, Davis now understood why Johnson was disturbed—one of the countries named was China.

China? Fuck. This is going to get real bad, real fast. This could be war... a real, shooting war or worse.

At 12:05 p.m., Helms came into the control room to report China had recalled all diplomats and closed its embassy in America. The country's leadership reiterated that either the U.S. Government shut down its black operations or all diplomatic communication would terminate.

Davis tried to refocus on work, but Helms kept bringing in updates when something "significant" broke.

It took thirty-five minutes for him to report that intermediaries were attempting to broker communication between both governments within the United Nations and NATO command before China declared war. When he gave the next update at 1 p.m., the Chinese representatives had apparently walked out of both the U.N. and NATO Command, and were recalled to China. Helms learned that the President had called China's Premier, but the reigning sovereign "declined" the call.

Wow... Davis couldn't tell what amazed her most, that the President's call was refused or Helms's immediate access to the West Wing.

As more news reports started to flood the airwaves, Davis just couldn't believe what she was reading. She remained sitting as she contemplated that for the first time since the Cold War, Russia was in China's corner. Both countries were clear that "America's plan of bio-terrorism will not go unanswered." The U.S., the last superpower on the planet, was on everyone's shit list as reviving empires found a common enemy to unite against. Davis could only guess that the former terrorists' enemies couldn't be happier. Further reports indicated that France, Spain, Germany, and England decided to be "neutral" and would be noncommittal if a shooting war started.

"Looks like our old allies will sit this world war out," Johnson commented.

"Can you blame them," Andersen said.

"Nope. I was just hoping."

Still holding her head in her hands after she reread more detailed horrors of the CDC's flu, Davis pulled herself from the document in disbelief.

"Looks like we're all going to be recalled back to uniform."

Ninety minutes later, Helms came back into the control room, but this time he was sporting a new white shirt and a black tie.

"Okay, people! We are going to have a video conference call from the president in five minutes. Everyone at your posts. If you need to use the head, do it now. And, Janeson, under no circumstance are you to interrupt this conference call. I don't care if Burns is walking through the door; you are not to interrupt."

"Yes, sir!" Janeson replied.

Davis saw that Helms had either forgotten something or reconsidered its importance.

"Actually, Janeson, if Burns does come through the door, please bring it to Davis, Andersen, Gilmore, and Johnson's attention as quietly as possible."

"Thank you for the revision, sir!" Janeson said, genuinely appreciative.

Davis was amazed by Janeson's brilliance, but she was just as fascinated by her level of being concrete and not taking offense to such obvious protocol.

But then, social cues and etiquette were obvious to all but Janeson, Davis reminded herself.

Helms informed everyone a minute before the call that in addition to them, they would also be on with Webber and his team at Hanscom Air Force Base, as well as the corresponding Operations Center, Alpha. Davis groaned at being lumped in with that group.

When Gilmore confirmed the link, all staff were standing at attention as the president of the United States of America addressed them live.

This was Davis's first time meeting the Commander-in-Chief. *I'd wish it were under different circumstances.*

The president was in the Situation Room. He was surrounded by a myriad of uniformed staff and a few civilians. It was obvious that he planned on delivering a very clear message. Two-thirds of the monitors showed the president and his team as the remaining third showed Webber's two teams.

"Ladies and gentlemen, to be blunt, the leaked information from the Operations Center has turned our nation's citizens and allies against us, revived old powers, and has hardened our enemies' resolve. You have three hours to bring this to a close or I will classify the Operations Center as an entity gone rogue and forcefully shut it down. I will appease China and Russia with all classified data that involve them and have the key leadership of the Foreign Intelligence Agency prosecuted."

Webber spoke next. It was strange seeing Diane Welch standing beside him and his personnel, Davis thought. She was none too happy to go spend "quality time," she told Davis, but they both knew that her mission—keeping an eye on Webber—would be critical.

"Mr. President, in five minutes, we will be at the source of these transmissions, and they will be stopped and those responsible captured or killed..."

"I want them alive, Deputy Director. A live traitor is better than a dead patriot," the president interrupted.

"Yes, sir. We are expecting a call momentarily from the terrorist to arrange a meeting."

Davis could see that the president's eyes narrowed, and his voice seemed to be lowering. Davis could also see that he was getting pissed.

How the hell could Webber miss that? she wondered.

The president's voice brought her attention back to the conversation.

"'Terrorist' or the world's new 'Freedom Fighter?' This Alexander Burns needs to be taken alive. I know this runs against policy, but you need to negotiate and insure no more information is leaked..." the president remarked.

"With respect, Mr. President, that is a mistake. This terrorist needs to be brought to justice and made into an example, and being dead is the best message to our enemies," Webber pronounced.

All was eerily silent as the President's mouth opened for a moment and then closed as if he had reconsidered saying something.

Did Webber just interrupt and countermand the Commander-in-Chief? Ah shit... brace yourself.

Davis became suddenly aware of her bowels wanting to move, the same feeling she'd had when she witnessed her best friend disagreeing with their second grade teacher, a nun. She could see Welch close her eyes as if she were waiting for a direct hit from artillery fire. While the president possessed qualities that appealed to the "average guy," he was still the Commander-in-Chief of all Armed Forces and federal agencies. All staff from all agencies seemed to freeze what they were doing and wait for what the president would say next. To Davis, his response was constrained anger.

"Mr. Webber, let me make this perfectly clear. Mr. Burns and his team are not to be harmed. You are to obtain the missing classified data and stop the broadcasts. If you do all that, I will simply shut down the Operations Center. If you fail any of those objectives, I will have no problem hanging you, Daniels, and your superiors out to dry. Am I crystal clear?"

The response was slow from Webber as if he were thinking of another possible response.

Davis's mind jumped to an old poem: *"as idle as a painted ship upon a painted ocean..." For God's sake, answer him...* she thought, looking down at her shoe, just wanting to be anywhere else but there.

"Deputy Director Webber?" the president prodded.

Davis's feeling of wanting to shrink away, so as not to be associated, continued until his answer finally came.

"Yes, sir," Webber responded with little enthusiasm. Without another word, the president terminated the link and Davis felt her breathing start again along with everyone else's in the room. Webber terminated his link next, followed by the Operations Center in Virginia.

With the big screen now dark, an uncomfortable silence remained.

"Sir... I think I need to hit the head," Martin announced.

A burst of nervous laughter broke out. As Davis's lungs filled with air, she saw that Janeson looked surprised as she tried to figure out what was so funny. Helms's smile finally vanished but then he speculated out loud, "What did Webber mean that they were about to shut the broadcast down?"

"I am guessing they found the source of the leaks and sent a team in," Davis responded.

"Jesus. Every time we try to do that shit we miss and that pisses Burns off even more. Anyone else thinks this is going to blow-up in our faces?" Andersen asked.

"Nope; I know it's going to go south and fast," Davis said.

She sighed and went back to monitoring Intel.

"This is going to suck."

Chapter 13

"Dulce bellum inexpertis" – *"War is sweet for those who haven't experienced it"* Pindaros

"These people just don't get it," Webber was saying as soon as he was off-line.

Welch had been with his team for the longest ninety-five minutes she had experienced in a long time, and she was struck by the difference between Webber's team and Helms's. While Helms's team demonstrated spontaneity, creativity and a dedication to serve, Webber's group was quiet, sullen and seemingly married to their monitors to avoid contact with Webber.

My God... they're worlds apart, she thought.

"A country is built on blood and sacrifice. It's never easy to do the right thing. Sometimes, the right thing means forward thinking and closing the distance between us and the enemy."

Webber ranted to no one in particular. Welch knew her role was to "keep her enemy closer" since the closer she stayed with him, the more likely she might be to keep him from screwing everything up. It was the "staying close" part that made her feel nauseous.

Upon arrival, Welch gave up her phone and her obvious surveillance devices and camera. What Webber's merry band of men missed were two deactivated jacket button cameras and listening devices and a blouse device as well. All were turned off to insure their radio frequency was not discovered until she was on the move outside of Webber's secured area. She was allowed to keep her phone on as the link between her and Helms's team that would receive a call from

Burns and Webber. Webber was reluctant about it at first, but his team determined no additional listening devices were attached to the cell phone. It looked like the second-in-command, Jeffery Glenn, seemed to be the brains of the operation and designated to interface with Webber the most.

Lucky him. What did he do in a former life to exact this punishment?

She was amazed by Webber's level of narcissism. *He corrected the president? Major balls,* Welch thought.

"Deputy Director, sir? Operation 'Crusher' is sixty seconds out," Glenn said.

Welch became a little distracted by how handsome the guy was.

"Excellent. Time to turn the tides," he said.

Welch did not like being kept in the dark about the operation, but she figured she would find out soon enough what the mission was, with the expectation that she would most likely not like the outcome.

Nothing good can come from this man.

"We will have a live feed from the field bounced to us from Alpha, sir. Putting it on the main screen now," Glenn said.

A sixty-inch wide monitor held four sections with four different camera mounts of soldiers clearly on some kind of helicopter. Welch could not make out the configuration, except that they were small, fast and very maneuverable. Maybe six men each with significant armament. A blue ocean was passing quickly under them as the transports came in fast and low. Suddenly, there was a rocky beach, sand and then small villages and homes with civilians looking at them. Welch found her pulse racing and palms sweating as she recalled similar chopper rides into hot zones that started just like this, minus the water.

"Can you at least tell me where we are?" she asked.

"Greek island called Kea. I hear it's a nice place and off the beaten trail. It's also the source of the IP address of the broadcasts. Looks like the 'great' Alexander J. Burns got sloppy with his frequency of transmissions," Webber gloated.

Welch may have been new to knowing Burns, but she knew he didn't do "sloppy."

"After all the shit he's pulled off do you think he'd make an armature mistake?"

"Yes. He's good but not great."

Welch looked at him; his obnoxiousness and arrogance was incalculable. It was so obvious that this had to be a distraction or a trap or both. She had to let it go to stay sane and do her job.

"I guess mentioning that carrying out a military operation in Greek airspace is a violation of our agreement with our allies," she mentioned.

Webber simply looked at her and ignored the statement.

"Actually," Welch revised, "it doesn't matter anymore. The whole world is our enemy. Maybe attacking Greece might win us some points with the European Union's financial markets. You might be a hero in this case, Webber."

Welch had to admit that Webber was demonstrating some restraint since he chose to ignore her sarcasm. There was that one redeeming quality her father always said assholes had.

It had to be early evening in Greece since the sun seemed low on the horizon. She knew that such a raid would occur at dawn, but time was not on Webber's side; he couldn't afford more classified data hitting the Internet. Timewise, though, this was too predictable, she thought. Burns was going to call them any minute, and this operation was happening on the other side of the world.

Is it possible that Webber was that lucky or brilliant or was this part of Burns's master plan?

"Webber, I got a real bad feeling about this. Don't you think the timing of your raid and Burns's next call is too much of a coincidence to be random?"

"We have been narrowing our focus with every new broadcast that comes out. The last one gave us an exact pinpoint by a matter of six feet. I don't think that's 'random' but detailed investigative work," Webber defended.

Welch could see that ego was getting in the way of his thinking. She made eye contact with Glenn, who averted his look. She knew Glenn agreed with her, so she tried another tactic.

"I'm not faulting your team's thinking and approach. I was just wondering whether Burns would know the same strategy. I wasn't sure, since he used to be part of your team, whether he might be able to predict this course of action and plan for it,"

She hoped a more conciliatory approach might make an impression.

Welch felt she might get through to Webber if he realized that Burns was not a Middle Eastern trained terrorist or a disgruntled, former federal employee engaged in domestic terrorism. Glenn was listening to the conversation and appeared genuinely worried as if the topic had come up before.

"Sir? It may make sense to abort," Glenn offered. "Maybe a smaller recon team to check things out first," he continued.

Webber didn't answer at first. Instead, he asked for a chair and something to drink as he seemed to ponder his next step.

"No. Jeff, call in to the team leader and tell him to be careful," Webber said.

Welch felt her eyes open wider. She did her best to curb the sarcasm.

"I think they're going to be 'careful,' anyway. May be letting them know what they're dealing with would be better?"

"A disgruntled, sad agent gone rogue? They'll be fine."

"He's a trained covert operative who took out two cars' full of your agents just a couple of hours ago not to mention back at city hall."

"Sir, could I let them know the very high probabilities of it being a trap? I suspect they plan to be careful anyway," Glenn added.

"We already discussed that. They should be prepared for anything," Webber said.

"Sir, this is Burns we're talking about..."

Clearly this discussion had come up before, and it was evident by Webber's response that he was not going back to it.

"Goddamn it, Jeff! He's not God! He's not a legend. He's a fucking terrorist," Webber hissed out.

It took a moment but Webber collected himself as all eyes fell on both men. Welch could feel the silence fill the air like heavy smoke consuming oxygen.

Webber was the first to speak after the meltdown.

"Manager, your concerns are duly noted. I requested you here as my second-in-command in the field to be a support. If I wanted pessimism, negative thinking and failed leadership, I would have had Cratty here instead. Don't make me regret my decision. Crystal?"

Here we go, Welch thought. *Cratty would never be part of this mission, and this guy Glenn is thinking it's a bad idea, too; worse than bad.*

"Yes, sir," Glenn said. He might have said yes but his body language was disagreeable. He returned to his post. Two other agents moved to talk to him in hushed tones.

Webber pointed to his assistant who brought a chair and a can of soda as he became transfixed in front of the monitor. Welch was trying to get the image out of her head of a guy sitting down in front of the television, getting ready to watch a football game. As Glenn and Webber argued, she could see that the operation had started and assault teams had long since landed. They had covered quite a bit of ground and approached a house sitting at the top of a hill.

It's gotta have a great view of the ocean, she thought.

Welch had to strain her ears to understand clearly what was being said. She had forgotten how she had this problem back in the field. Welch suddenly had visions of PFC Parks and the crater-like destruction of the hamlet she and her men used to survive.

Wolves, bears, ravens, and fire, she remembered Nine reporting on Ice's dream so many years ago.

With a strange acrid smell of fuel, burning metal and heavy smoke still in her nose, Welch shook the sensations off and tried to focus on the speaker.

"Team leader to all units: radio silence; hand signals only."

The four camera angles were at first hard to figure out since they were clearly coming from various angles of the home. When their jumbled movements stopped and seemed to be smoother, they were by the front, back and terrace doors. The jittery motion stopped for a moment. Then there was the loud crash of wood and glass as flash-bangs were thrown in the home, followed by loud yells and more jumbled, jittery images. As the cameras panned left and right, there was no sight of people. The home was still lived in, though Spartan might be a good description in regards to furniture. With toys on the floor in a playroom, the home didn't seem to fit the expected "terrorist command center" stereotype. As the various "clear" signs indicated no one was there, one of the men found a door leading to a basement. The tension mounted as the soldiers and agents stacked up on each other, clearly with the plan to break down the door and secure the room below. One camera clearly saw a light on downstairs.

Shit... Welch thought. *No other lights are on except a light in the basement? No... the light was left on in the basement to make sure that whoever saw it would come down,* Welch easily deduced.

Welch withdrew her attention away from the screen to tell Webber her thoughts, but he was glued to the monitor, sipping his drink. As she looked back at the screen, the door was already smashed off its hinges and crashed down a flight of stairs. Again, more jumbling as two of the mission cameras went hurdling down a flight of stairs while the other two sets remained above so as to make sure the perimeter was secured. The noise of the men as they entered the basement was different than expected. To Welch's hearing, it was if the sounds were somehow canceled out.

Muffled almost... Crap!

In an instant, Welch recalled that Andersen, Helms and his team noticed the absence of noise when Caulfield called, indicating that the room he was in might be lined to eliminate sound. Welch's gut was violently turning.

"Webber!" she broke in, but Webber waved her off. She did not give up, though.

"Webber! Get them out of there. They're in the right place, but it has to be a trap!"

As she spoke, the camera angles panned left and right, showing padded walls with insulation, wood and Styrofoam. More than sixty seconds had to pass before all the sudden movements slowed down. In the middle of the well-lit room were a set of servers and a desktop computer that didn't seem to be on.

Welch could see Webber smiling.

Stupid, stupid, stupid! she kept thinking. *This is not good!*

Then, as one mission camera looked back at the doorframe, the person seeing what the camera picked up broke the silence.

"Team Leader, we got a trigger!"

The second camera turned its sights on a small package, twelve-by-twelve inches with wires attached to the servers running across the floor to the wall.

"Bomb!"

In precise fashion, the solders quickly backed out and headed back up the stairs. Pushing the images of her own men racing to escape the bombing in the Swat Valley, Welch was positive they were going to make it until she saw the flash on two of the cameras and explosive sounds through the mission cameras upstairs in the main house. The two cameras in the basement went dead as one camera upstairs picked up only sound while the other seemed to be still working, but the angle was sideways on the floor as if it had fallen. She jumped back reflexively while multiple analysts yanked off their headphones as the sound overloaded their circuits and ears.

More yelling and confusion ensued as the surviving team attempted to regroup and check whether anyone could be rescued.

Webber! Get them out of there!"

Standing still, he looked like he was in shock.

Welch looked for Glenn. Fortunately, Glenn was already responding.

"This is Manager Jeffery Glenn from Field Operation: Crusher team—pull out! I repeat, pull out now!"

Webber snapped out of his trance at the mention of retreat.

"Jeff! I didn't give the order..."

It was the flash of light that got Welch's attention first, followed by another explosion. With all cameras off-line, the room fell silent. Webber looked at the now darkened monitor as Glenn's attention was brought back to his headset. Seconds passed. It felt like hours.

"All right, Alpha. Send us the live feed from Hawk 1 and Hawk 3," was Glenn's response.

As images of a smoking, burning crater emerged where a house once stood, the flight commander's chatter to her other team members came through:

"...I'm guessing the house was rigged to blow... looks like there was a larger secondary explosion in the exterior walls ten or twenty seconds after the interior explosion. Whoever did this set it up for the first one to maim, damage and disorient, and the second one was built to bury anyone inside—"

Welch's mouth felt so dry. She couldn't help but feel sympathy for the soldiers just doing their jobs. She heard Glenn interrupting.

"This is Glenn... hold the perimeter and wait for support. Alpha, coordinate rescue operations and get a forensic and recovery team in there. Glenn, out."

Welch found herself leaning against a counter with a young analyst, who was looking in complete dismay at her monitor.

So young, she thought.

Glenn took off his headpiece and rubbed his hand through his blond hair. All eyes were on him while Webber remained silent. Then her cell phone rang, making her nearly jump out of her skin. Having forgotten it was on, with the tragedy of the attack on Kea so recent, Welch didn't feel real. She opened her phone while still transfixed on Webber, but she didn't say anything.

"Diane?" Helms asked.

It took a moment for her to get her voice back as she tried to bring up saliva for her mouth.

"Ah... yeah, John... what's up?" She was at a loss of words. *The stupidity.*

"Diane, Burns gave us fifty-five minutes to get to Long Island, Boston Bay. We are twenty-five minutes out," Helms said.

Welch looked at Webber and Glenn.

Long Island, Boston Bay, fifty-five minutes and counting."

Webber took a moment, but he seemed back in the game.

"All right, everybody. Time to end this. I want two helicopters ready to go in five minutes. Is the convoy ready?"

"Yes, sir," Glenn responded.

"Let's move people. Welch? Make sure Helms secures the perimeter only. I'm going in. Clear?"

Welch didn't hear anything him said as her attention was drawn to the phone.

"Diane? Burns asked if we found his house yet," he asked.

"Yeah... and he set it to blow up, killing everyone inside."

"Shit... how many?"

Welch could tell he was moving since his breathing had increased.

"I don't know. Maybe twelve..."

"Sixteen," Glenn corrected as he gave her the sign to turn the phone off and directed her to the transport. She hung up on Helms.

Before she left, Helms and she had created a short code: if she hung up the phone with no response, it meant things were going south and Webber was going to fuck it up. If she had said, "Goodbye" or "See you later," or any normal closing remark, it would mean everything was all right.

"So how long are you going to let this go, Glenn?" Welch asked as they followed Webber to the transports.

Glenn did not respond, so she continued while picking up her pace to stay beside him.

"This ends one of two ways. Either Burns wins and the leak stops and he goes back to being a ghost or Webber wins and the world is set on fire by Burns's crew or a dead man switch, or both."

Glenn remained silent. There was no support but no opposition either.

I guess there needs to be more pressure. I guess it will have to get worse than it already is.

~

Davis was sitting in Helms's office away from the control room while he and Andersen were mobile, heading toward Long Island to provide support to Webber. She had to give it to Helms and his team. Based on Cratty's additional information, Janeson, Gilmore and Johnson had narrowed the potential sites down to four, one of which was Long

Island. Of the four potential sites, everyone thought it made the least amount of sense with no visible or easy escape route except maybe by boat. And if Burns took a boat, he would be a very easy target. In light of it being a trapped setting,

Janeson picked and stuck with Long Island anyway, with the rationale that Burns wanted revenge and he needed to make sure his prey came. He must have figured that either he would be able to drive out the way he came or he would be killed. Either way, there was no need to have an exit off the island. Six bottlenecks were along the route once you were on the island, and Janeson bet two weeks salary she was right. When Gilmore suggested that the North Koreans probably had a submarine waiting for Burns off the island, Janeson started her analysis of why that scenario was not likely until Johnson told her Gilmore was joking.

They're just like siblings, she thought. But now Davis was alone.

She was looking at the laptop Burns had given her, and it was on and running. She had already put the flash drive into it, and the program indicated that it was complete, asking the question, "Do you want to run program?" She brought up the Internet and typed in the website to the Operations Center, Alpha address Cratty gave her. As she typed in the email address of Deputy Director T. Webber, she felt guilty for being an accessory to what Burns might be up to.

Helms was mixed on the subject while Andersen was surprisingly all for Burns. She had expected Anderson would be, ever since he got to know Caulfield, and by proxy, got to know Burns.

Maybe a Stockholm Syndrome thing might be going on with Andersen, Davis halfheartedly thought.

Welch removed herself from the decision since she was biased: "Anything that results in Webber's death is all right by me." Then there was Cratty. She was unrecognizable to Davis.

How could someone in just a few short months change so much?

Based on the last communication, it was clear Cratty wouldn't mind if Webber died. Her omission of data was telling. She decided that the best person to ask would be the one not motivated per se by emotions but more by logic. Once again, it was Janeson who seemed to have the best take on it all.

"Since Burns's head injury and recovery years ago," Janeson began, "he has been consistent with loyalty to friends and keeping his word. Even when his paramour is killed, he keeps his word to those who keep it with him. He kills those who strike first and break their word. If we make a deal with Burns, he will keep it. Mr. Webber has demonstrated the opposite behaviors. He is less likely to keep his word."

Devoid of emotion and logical as always.

Davis thought that even though Janeson was attractive, it would be hell to date her. *Boy... I'm thinking of everything to distract me from pushing the button.*

With both website and email inputted, Davis hit "yes" to run program. There was an internal whirring and then an email in fax form was sent. Davis didn't know what to do next.

Should I turn it off? Will it self-destruct?

Davis decided to give it five minutes and then log off. Her concern was that it would be traced and discovered in Helms's office.

That might look bad.

As Davis waited, she pondered whether this was the same thing Littleton and Caulfield had thought when they pressed the button that launched cyber-attacks on the FBI, the Foreign Intelligence Agency, and the rest of the world?

Was it treason for them? A federal crime or self-preservation? What would her rationale be?

Davis liked it better when she didn't think so much. She had become the more "reflective one" as Cratty seemingly became more the "cold machine." As the five minutes elapsed, she was happy to log off the laptop and shut it down.

"I guess the next hour will tell all? Collaborator or hero?" she said to herself.

She stretched her legs and moved her arm more carefully to avoid the shooting pain as she walked back to the control room.

Chapter 14

"Aequam memento rebus in arduis servare mentem" – *"Remember when life's path is steep to keep your mind open"* Horace

Becky had been on the island for close to thirty-six hours. While living in an underground bunker with MREs and weapons galore, she had committed to memory the firing sequence of a stinger missile that Burns described as "point, fire, and forget." Just to cover all the bases, Burns reiterated that the weapon was used on "things that fly."

She was tired, but somehow she was able to sleep underground with rats and bats hanging around. During daylight hours, she practiced her long shot with a .338 caliber sniper rifle that Burns had provided for her. It was different from the one she was comfortable with, but she knew she could make a shot. There was no question that the caliber size would have penetration power to stop a man since the caliber could easily cut through tempered metal. If she had to, she could use it on a reinforced vehicle or a helicopter. Burns had also confirmed distance, location, elevation and wind for the day, time and area he had in mind. Burns was clear—Becky would have to make a shot that was close to seven hundred yards. That was three hundred yards farther than she was used to, and under battlefield circumstances.

She appreciated Burns offering her the next best thing, to be the point person and watch Webber die up close as Burns made the kill shot. She figured it had to be hard for Burns, too. She could tell from his sunken eyes, facial hair growth, and tattered clothes that the loss of Sam weighed on him. For a moment, it looked like he was going to have her be the point person and deprive her from killing Webber herself. But he got an education on where Sam got her stubbornness from. While arguments might have worked with Sam, Becky made it clear that arguing did not work with her. She would either agree or disagree. The only leverage was David and Emma now. If Becky were convinced that killing everyone on the ground would keep them safe, it would be an easy decision for her.

How things have changed. Months ago, the idea of hurting someone was atrocious. Now... I just don't know who I am anymore.

In less than a day, eight hours of work, Becky was able to make her shot at one thousand yards with more moderate winds and dimmer lighting than average. She figured she was officially more dangerous than Burns.

I'm willing to die.

On the day of the final strike, Burns was waiting for his sensor in the Kea house to shut off before he made the call. He told her that he knew the Operations Center had to find the house by the third day and would hit it hard and heavy. The house was rigged to explode, killing everyone inside or at least burying everyone alive.

Hmm. That doesn't bother me. Maybe not being there helps.

After an early morning task of finishing his tire traps of planks with spiked nails being placed in strategically located positions, she saw the light on his sensor finally went out, indicating that the server and desktop were off-line. She looked at him for confirmation. He gave her the nod to get into position as he waited a few minutes before placing the call.

As Becky got in position with an arsenal of weapons and rifle, she could see mounds where the planks were in place at the end of the bridge to bottle up the vehicle. She also knew Burns had a vest of explosives in case everything went to hell. The only thing for her and Burns to do was to wait until their "guests" arrived. The code to Becky to take the shot would be simple: he would use her code name "Tiny" and then ask, "Target?" She would either have him, or if not, she would use a rocket-propelled grenade to take them all out. Burns stated that he hoped she could make the shot since his plan would get more mileage if he could negotiate with Helms or Andersen.

"No pressure," Becky said to herself as she checked to make sure everything was "ready to fire." No safeties on.

Waiting is really the hard part.

~

Welch was trying to make sure she didn't throw up her lunch on the helicopter's deck as it flew fast and low, providing coverage to the convoy of SUVs heading to Long Island. Fortunately, her appetite had been too seriously curtailed by the last forty-eight hours' events she didn't have lunch to throw up.

Maybe that's why I'm feeling nauseous.

The two helicopters were not officially military, but they were well-armed and stocked as if they were. She speculated that they both had to be discontinued Department of Defense prototypes given to the Foreign Intelligence Agency for the Operations Center's missions. As she was able to gulp down more air, she noticed that Webber was attempting to talk on his cell phone. Welch could tell he was having difficulty hearing so he said, "Open it up and send it to me by text."

A moment later, he was looking at the screen of his smartphone and started to laugh as he showed it to Glenn. Glenn gave the "What-does-it-mean?" look and then gestured that she should look at it next. After having it carefully handed back to her, she read the text:

"To the last, I grapple with thee; From Hell's heart, I stab at thee; For hate's sake, I spit my last breath at thee."

Welch read it again. Prior to her leaving for the mission, she had been given, by Janeson, the entire synopsis of *Moby Dick*. Ultimately, it was a story about obsession and vengeance. Janeson had highlighted a number of good speeches, and the one she was reading was one of the better ones.

"Looks like it's another poem from Caulfield," Webber said.

"No. It's from Burns. It's a message to you, Webber. You're Moby Dick, and he plans on killing you," Welch attempted to explain.

Webber laughed.

"I hope he brought more than a harpoon," he laughed again. Once again, it was Glenn who seemed more serious.

"Sir, Ms. Welch is right. He's dangerous. And if she thinks you are marked for death, I recommend you return to base."

Webber took a moment, then feigned surprise.

"You really do care about me," Webber chided and then he went back to looking out the window.

"You're not heading to the zoo," she warned.

"Diane... shut up," he said, sighing as he continued to look out the window.

Welch shook her head in amazement at him and then she noticed one of the tactical officers looking out the side window. He pointed out Helms's convoy of SUVs, along with local police who were now blocking traffic in both directions to allow Webber's convoy immediate access onto the island. As all eyes went out to watch the progression of the Operations Center's convoy onto the island, Welch took that opportunity to turn on her audio-visual devices. All were high definition and in color.

As the convoy turned and headed at top speed toward the connecting bridge, Webber's helicopters were able to see far enough ahead; the pilot reported that he saw a lone man leaning on a motorcycle. She looked and could readily see that the man seemed to be casually waiting for them to arrive at the bridge's very end. The chatter increased as the convoy flanked out and gave some space between vehicles so as not to bunch up and present one big target. Welch could see Glenn was in command of this battlefield and not taking chances. He sent one helicopter up ahead to recon what was happening as he held his command helicopter behind the convoy to provide suppressing fire, should it be necessary. The forward helicopter stayed ahead and seemed to hover slowly to canvass the immediate area behind Burns.

All standard strategy, Welch thought. *Burns would know this. This sucks. We shouldn't be here.*

The convoy finally reached the end of the bridge and flanked out to the left and right with the intent of circling Burns. From her elevated position, she could see a series of tire explosions and plumes of gravel rising as each car seemed to swerve.

Damn it! He's always a step ahead! We're so damn predictable! We're just making it easier for him. Damn it.

Welch hated being on the losing side when simple steps could turn the tide. She figured Burns had anticipated this maneuver and laced the ground with something razor sharp; *probably something "old school"—nails and twelve-foot planks just under the dirt,* she speculated.

In domino effect, each car's front and back tires blew out with the first three SUVs losing all their tires, and a fourth one losing its front, leaving only two SUVs operational; the good news was that since the vehicles were slowing down, they didn't blow out at high speed, so no one was hurt. But Welch could see it was better news for Burns since he had taken out more than fifty percent of the ground vehicles and stalled them in one place, all while just sitting.

Immobilized and he hasn't even fired a shot.

Under different circumstances, Welch thought she would have liked Burns. She knew he had the vehicles right where he wanted them regardless of what an imbecile like Webber might think.

Hmm... with all the cars in one place, a well-placed missile or explosives would take them all out.

She knew that couldn't be the end of the surprises, she thought as her helicopter moved behind the SUVs and descended. She was sure he had more plans in case he needed to take them all out. It was times like these when Welch hoped he had other hobbies besides obsessively planning details.

No. This is personal. He wants to kill Webber and protect the others. I don't know how he's going to do it, but I'm sure he's set on it.

Even as the command helicopter dropped in altitude, much debate continued as the events unfolded. Webber insisted on landing and confronting Burns. The thought of Burns casually leaning on his motorcycle, waiting for him to arrive, had to be infuriating to him.

Against Glenn's advice, the command helicopter landed briefly, allowing Webber, Glenn and Welch to exit. With a line of damaged vehicles and federal agents with their assault rifles trained on him, Burns waited motionless, sitting on his motorcycle as if he were waiting for a date. As her party approached Burns and the din of helicopters receded, she heard seagulls making a loud racket above their heads.

Sea salt air, light breeze, some sun breaking through—it'd be a nice day if I weren't walking into a trap.

Welch looked for an opening to squeeze through the wall of edgy men.

Right when they were about to step beyond the perimeter of agents, Glenn stopped the procession with a waved hand.

"Say again, Alpha?" Glenn requested.

Webber seemed annoyed at first, expecting more of an argument but then he became interested in what was happening. Glenn was asking whomever it was to repeat. Some of the men charged with watching Burns shifted their attention to Glenn as his face blanched, a clear indication that something else was wrong.

"Are you sure?" he asked.

Webber moved in closer as Welch kept an eye on the federal agents, whose attention was now split between Glenn and Burns.

Glenn's expression shifted rapidly from sheet-white to dark red as if he were very angry, frustrated or about to have a stroke. Forcefully closing his link, Welch heard him swear for the first time and then pull himself together to address his boss. His tone was different, Welch noticed, more decisive.

So... had enough? Tired of making the right call but no one listening? Are you finally ready to take command?

"Alpha reports that it needs to shut down everything. A cyber attack came over the server in the form of an email fax that was opened and forwarded to you, sir."

Jesus Christ! Burns!

"I thought we improved safeguards against such an attack? I saw the program that restricts the Trojan horse from—"

"No, Deputy Director," Glenn interrupted. *This is a first,* she thought.

"This attack does not delete programs. It reproduces programs, emails, documents and any memory on a computer's working memory, the hard drives and external drives at an exponential rate. In effect, it multiplies programs and files so fast that RAM is overwhelmed, and it slows the operating system's efficiency so fast that the computer either freezes or crashes. Alpha is off-line, sir. We are walking into a trap."

Glenn looked around as if he were being watched.

More surprises. What else, Burns?

Welch remembered that Burns's new profile included his having backup, and with his lover gone that left only one viable candidate.

And that would be the person who would want us all dead more than Burns, Welch concluded.

"This fucking guy has been two steps ahead of us every time!" Glenn was showing signs of paranoia; *about time,* she thought.

Webber shook his head and walked to Burns without Glenn. While Glenn did not advance, Welch made the decision to follow him with the sole plan to keep her eyes and ears on whatever transpired between Burns and Webber. Hopefully, all the gadgets Janeson and her team had put on her would be working.

Well... here we go. Once more into the breach.

As she slowly advanced, she heard Glenn make a command decision that she knew Webber would not approve. Straining her ears, she heard Glenn call to one of his young lieutenants and give him a direct order: "Ralph, I need you to get Bravo team on standby right now. Alpha is down and we're walking into a trap."

Everyone on the ground had to know that Webber was a buffoon. It didn't take a genius to realize that if Glenn were ordering something, it had to be the right decision.

~

Davis, Janeson, and the control room had been watching and hearing everything from the moment Welch turned on all the devices while in flight over Boston Bay as they were entering the island's gate. Gilmore and Johnson were focusing on external chatter to hear what the Operations Center's team was talking about and to see whether any other third parties were in the air. Janeson agreed with Davis that if someone were helping Burns, that person would remain in radio silence until an order was given. When it was clear that Webber had received a text from the Operations Center, Davis guessed it might have something to do with the cyber "package" sent by Burns via Davis.

Well. You are now officially a collaborator. Nice job.

Davis felt a twinge of guilt, knowing she had something to do with it. She also wanted to be in the field, but that argument lasted a microsecond with everyone. Once the dust cleared from the brief landing and Welch and the others were walking toward the perimeter that surrounded Burns, Davis could hear Helms checking in.

"What's going on?"

Janeson looked at Davis as the "senior officer" to take the lead; Davis shook her head and said quietly, "Your team will listen better to you, Janeson."

Janeson acknowledged this by speaking to Helms.

"Burns has immobilized four of their six cars, so they were unable to surround him and bunched up in a confined space. It looks like Webber got a text from Alpha that might have been sent by Burns. They argued and are now on foot to meet Burns... hold on... Gilmore, pipe this to the boss."

From the cameras' angles, it was not possible to see faces but the sound was crystal clear. The control room clearly caught the last part of one of the ground forces' key leaders telling his boss:

"'...attack does not delete programs. It reproduces programs, emails, documents, and any memory... hard drives and external drives at an exponential rate. In effect, it slows the operating system's efficiency so fast... freeze or crash the entire system. Alpha is off-line, sir. We are walking into a trap.'"

"That's it, Rachael!" Helms said.

"Boss?"

"Call Cratty now. Alpha is off-line, and I bet Webber took her out of the loop so she wouldn't be pulled in even if something happened," he explained.

"On it! Johnson, get Cratty. Gilmore, turn monitoring over to Crepes. I want you to listen closely to outside chatter. If it's going to happen, it will be now. Welch and company are moving toward Burns again."

"Boss?" Johnson called.

Both Helms and Janeson responded at the same time in the affirmative.

Davis had to smile over the confusion of having two bosses.

"Ah... yeah. Cratty is on the main screen left side," Johnson directed. A moment later, Cratty's image appeared. She was dressed and looked identical to twenty-four hours earlier. Her control room was still dark and the same five people seemed to be fixtures, not having moved since last contact.

Wow. Cratty did change. Military hair, clothes, staff rigidly in place, sidearm... Jesus, she thought.

"Manager Cratty. We just got word from our contact on the ground that Deputy Director Webber's tactical team has lost communication with Operations Center, Alpha. Our intelligence indicates that his Operations Center's servers and computer network have been compromised and all communication between the field and base is now severed," Janeson explained without emotion.

"Acknowledge. Please stay on the line. Dillon, locate tactical team under the command of Jeffery Glenn, Boston, Massachusetts... do you have an exact location?" Cratty asked Janeson.

Gilmore jumped in to answer.

"Approximately three miles east of latitude fort-two degrees and eighteen seconds north and longitude is seventy-three degrees and three seconds west."

"Ms. Cratty, I am going to send you the radio frequency of our contact on the ground, who is four feet from Mr. Webber," Janeson offered.

"That would greatly facilitate things. Dillon, impress us all," she replied.

"On it, ma'am," a voice off-screen replied.

Davis was impressed with how both operations teams were working together.

You see. This is the way it's supposed to be.

Ten seconds later, the same voice, Dillon, had a surprise announcement. "Ma'am, I wish I could take credit for this, but the ground team at those coordinates is attempting to contact us. Something interfering with its frequency, maybe some kind of a rogue program affecting electronics both at Alpha and the field. I did get that Mr. Glenn is specifically requesting your assistance and support. To follow-up on your original question, ma'am, I am getting no response from Alpha in Virginia to our calls," she finished.

Looks like Cratty got her team all fired up too.

Davis now regretted that she competed so much with Cratty when they worked together. She had always found Cratty "too girly" for her liking.

"Belben, please note for the record our attempts to make contact with Alpha on our secure line and our subsequent failure to establish communication. Also note, Manager Glenn, reassigned to Alpha, has requested assistance. We are running dark under the assumption that Alpha has been breached. We will maintain communication with the FBI Regional office until we hear from either the Secretary of Defense or State or the president. Oh, and Belben?"

"Yes, ma'am?"

"Make sure the recording is on to insure protocol was followed," Cratty reminded.

"Already done, ma'am," was the response.

Davis picked up on the inference. Last May, none of the recordings were working to confirm that protocol was followed. It was apparent that Cratty was not going to have it happen again.

"Horowitz and Fitzgerald, let's put to work those technical skills you honed at Cornell and find a way to tie in Glenn's line directly with us and our sister agency. Dillon, hand over your search and find out if any other operations were occurring abroad that Alpha was supporting. I am not leaving our people abroad in the lurch."

A chorus of "Yes, ma'am" fired off-screen.

Cratty turned her attention back to Janeson.

"This is going to take a few minutes. Unfortunately, Deputy Director Webber left Bravo out of the loop. Thank you for your assistance, and please hold on." Cratty walked out of view.

Janeson looked puzzled. Davis pointed for her to mute her button, which she did.

"Cratty just threw her boss under the bus for not keeping her in the loop and breaking protocol. If everything blows up, she has an excuse. If it goes well and she saves the day, it will be harder for him to fire her," Davis clarified. Janeson mouthed, "Thank you."

Davis's attention went back to the operation in progress. The movement on the other side of the screen came to a stop, and the cameras had multiple shots of a man in a black-hooded sweatshirt and black military pants, wearing dark sunglasses and leaning on a motorcycle.

Cratty broke in again.

"Could you bounce your surveillance video live to me. Who on your team is broadcasting?"

"Diane Welch, Warrant Office, U.S. Marines, Retired. Images forwarding to you now," Janeson responded.

"No such thing as a 'former' Marine," Cratty commented.

Davis smiled. *Ah... I guess we'll never see the "girly" side of Cratty again. There's a street fighter in all of us.*

Audio broke up a bit as the visual images still showing the torsos of Burns and Webber became less shaky. Davis could easily see the showdown was about to start.

Chapter 15

"Ubi mors ibi spes" – *"Where there is death, there is hope"*

Welch had front row seats to this battle of wills. She would have preferred to be watching it from the comfort of home, maybe on television perhaps. In real life, though, the tension was killing her.

Great. Two pissed off guys about to get into it... just great.

"Mr. Thomas Webber, I presume?" Burns asked casually while leaning on his bike, arms folded over his chest.

She was not surprised that Webber didn't exchange any pleasantries.

"Burns, you're coming with me. I am going to put you in a cell so deep no one is going to find you," Webber sneered. It was easy for anyone to see that he was clearly agitated. Seeing his beloved agency being thrown to the wolves pushed him even more to bring Burns in and secure the drives. If Webber couldn't get the drives at least he had the terrorist captured.

"No, Mr. Webber. That's not going to happen today. At least, not the way you expect," Burns said.

Welch wondered how Burns could be so relaxed.

As Burns unfolded his arms, his oversized sweatshirt opened, revealing he had explosives around his waist that would make a sizable crater. The blast radius would clearly kill anyone within twenty feet. His left hand also revealed that he was holding down a switch. If he let go, the explosives would detonate.

"Great... a dead man's switch. Of course. Everything you do has a 'dead-man' trigger. I really wish I had stayed home today," Welch commented. She was surprised how casual her own voice sounded in light of the sudden shift in power. She was on the losing end.

She only got annoyed when she heard the sounds of semi-automatic gun metal shifting in twenty-plus pairs of hands filled the air.

Oh great... let's start shooting people. Good plan. We'll see who dies first.

Sighing, Welch had her answer... Burns planned on dying and had made peace with it, which explained why he was relaxed.

With a slight drop in the wind and the sounds of birds still crowing, Burns faintly smiled and continued to appear completely relaxed. As he seemed prepared to die, Webber looked confused; he stared first at Burns, then down at the explosives, then at Welch and back to Burns. With eyes darting back and forth, Webber went to his left hip and took out his semi-automatic weapon.

"Enough, Burns! Stop fucking around!" Webber yelled.

Burns did not move. He was stone still. Welch slowly put her hands up in a calming fashion.

"Webber? Remember that the president wants you to bring him in alive. Not dead. The president just wants the transmissions to end. We can do that," Welch said in a low, soothing voice. She had a vivid flashback of trying to convince Webber that the mission could be completed without all the casualties. It was Swat Valley all over again.

"No! Sacrifice, Diane! Sometimes we need to sacrifice!" Webber was now shouting.

"Is that how you justified killing Samantha Littleton? She was bringing you an olive branch and you shot her down," Burns said coolly.

Oh no, Welch thought.

"I shot a terrorist just like I am going to shoot you," Webber said as he pointed his gun squarely on Burns's chest.

Well, that's it. It looks like I am going to see Joe sooner than later. This is going to be hard on the kids. I'm sorry, Joe... I know I was supposed to stay here longer and watch out for them...

"You see, Thomas... you just don't get me. I'm not a terrorist."

What the hell?

Welch was surprised shocked by what Burns was saying. She also saw that it had an effect on Webber, who seemed to listen for a precious moment. With the birds finally moving on as the wind seemed to die down, Burns continued with a fireside chat tone, his hand firmly on the trigger.

"Terrorists have causes and beliefs that they fundamentally believe are right. They feel compelled to force their beliefs onto others, whether or not they like it. Terrorists don't invoke terror to be left alone. They don't have personal interests, per se. And more often than not, they usually don't seek out personal revenge. Terrorists want world economies to falter and governments to crumble under their threat. All I wanted was to be left alone. All David Caulfield wanted was to live in peace with his wife and their children. All Sam and Becky wanted was to be left alone to raise their deceased brother's baby. We all just wanted to be left alone. That's more human than a terrorist, don't you think?" Burns asked.

Webber looked confused for a moment. Maybe he was rethinking his stance. Welch found herself truly wondering what Burns was up to.

This is just too weird? Clarifying the difference between terrorists and his team? Now? There's gotta be something more… this is part of a plan.

The air seemed uncharacteristically still with only the distant sound of surf in the background. Burns, Webber, the men, the whole world seemed to be still. Only the surf and smell of salt could be experienced.

Welch couldn't feel the wind anymore… the wind had stopped.

"Thomas, 'For what shall it profit a man, to gain the whole world, and lose his soul?'" Burns said so softly both Webber and Welch had to lean closer just to hear.

"Enough. Tiny? Target?" Burns said louder.

Oh shit, was Welch's only thought.

Welch figured out what was going to happen next.

That speech… it's theater. It's about keeping your target still, isn't it?

She had been around the best snipers in the world, and she knew the cryptic language to mark a target. She looked at the tree-covered hill behind Burns and continued to feel no wind at all.

Burns tilted his head and replied, "Take him."

Welch broke her gaze with Burns and looked right at Webber as Webber turned to say something to her. She knew she could warn him. For the first time in her life, she hesitated at saving another human being's life when she might be able to. She remembered her orders to her men in the Swat Valley: "Kill Webber."

Welch closed her eyes.

I wonder what Webber's thinking?

A single shot was heard in the distance. By the sound and feel, Welch knew Webber was squarely hit as she felt his blood splatter her and as she heard another shot. When she opened her eyes, she could see he had stumbled backward and fallen on his back with his gun discharge going wide.

The gun shots startled a flock of seagulls that must have been nearby since sounds of yells and flaps filled the air in addition to men behind cars readjusting themselves from a hidden sniper. As Webber hit the ground, Welch moved to his side. She was immediately impressed with the entrance wound. Webber's eyes were closed shut. She knew he was probably dead before he hit the ground since the entry wound was massive. The blood loss, crushed bone, mangled muscles and internal organs completely gutted, the caliber had to be at least .308 0r maybe .338 mil.

Shit... Burns wasn't kidding. He wanted him dead.

If Webber had planned to say anything to her, the opportunity died within seconds of him hitting the ground.

There was shouting behind her as Webber's men trained guns on Burns with Welch right in the line of fire. One of the helicopters was vaulting toward the potential source of the sniper fire. Covered with Webber's blood, she stood up to see the telltale signs of a stinger missile honing in on the approaching helicopter.

Shit... talk about getting help, Welch thought. W*here the hell did he get that ordnance? This is all going south.*

Within seconds, the helicopter was hit, crashing out of control to the ground. Welch turned to Burns, who remained still, unflinching, leaning against his motorcycle as if he were watching a cricket match. Glenn was putting his hands up in the air, waving to the team leaders to hold their fire and listen to their microphones for orders. Somehow the tide had turned.

~

Cratty was still trying to ascertain the correct frequency when Janeson warned her of more chatter outside of their teams. As she continued watching the interaction between Burns and Webber, it was evident to her that Webber's behavior and mental stability were spiraling out of control. She could see Burns was relatively quiet and calm but then he seemed to take offense to his friend and himself being called terrorists. Unexpectedly and completely out of character, Burns began a cogent argument that made sense until he suddenly appeared to be talking to someone else.

Damn it! It's a set-up, she thought immediately.

Eerily, that's when chatter came over her speaker, via the FBI.

"Enough. Tiny? Target?" Burns's voice calmly said.

As if waiting for the other shoe to fall, Cratty and all perfectly heard the answer.

"Target acquired," a female voice replied.

Shit. It's got be Littleton's sister.

"Cratty! We got a shooter. She is targeting Webber," Janeson told Cratty.

"No shit!" Cratty responded as she addressed her team next.

"Team! I need to talk to Glenn now before the world burns up," she ordered.

She knew that once Webber was down, there would be a sixty-second window to keep this incident from turning into a shooting war. Cratty was positive that even if Burns were killed, he and his team would have managed to have all the classified data transmitted. She also knew still worse stuff would come out. That was an unpleasant revelation she had learned through her hearings following the breach.

"Take him," Burns's voice came over two separate speakers. Then, all heard the distant shot followed by another louder one. There was some confusion and shouts as Welch's cameras looked down on Webber lying on the ground.

"Sixty seconds and counting," Cratty said to herself.

The cameras' view switched upward to Webber's men with guns bearing down on Burns and Welch in the line of fire. The image of Webber came back and then it moved upward in time to see a missile hit a helicopter in the tail, causing it to spin out of control.

Suddenly, Cratty's voice was coming over three speakers.

"Goddamn it, people!" Cratty was now standing up.

Dillon broke in next:

"We got a clean line through, ma'am! You're live with Mr. Glenn!"

Thank God! Cratty thought.

"This is Operations Center Bravo. Mr. Jeffery Glenn, please respond. Repeat. This is Denise Cratty of Operations Center Bravo in New York. Please respond now!"

A tense moment followed before the speakers came alive.

"This is Senior Field Agent Glenn in Boston. Bravo, we've lost contact with Alpha and we are in the middle of a firefight that is about to escalate. Do you have rules of engagement? Over," Glenn asked over the shouting and now crashing helicopter.

Cratty controlled her voice and outlined the situation.

"Glenn, we have eyes on you right now. You are to disengage and stand down. Burns has stinger missiles, reusable rocket-propelled grenades and a whole armory of ordnance, and he clearly has help onsite. You don't have a location of his shooter, and you don't have enough firepower to engage your target effectively. All team leaders, you are to disengage and not shoot. Acknowledge." Cratty knew her voice was imperious: not official and not requesting—*it's a direct order.*

"Acknowledge right now!" Cratty demanded.

Damn it people... do it or we're all dead.

"Acknowledged," was his response. It sounded relieved.

There was some chatter and then it was quiet.

Cratty felt her chest relax as if she were holding her breath. Taking in a deep breath, she pushed the adrenaline back down and focused on making her voice soothing.

"Glenn, what is the condition of Deputy Director Webber?" Cratty asked, even though she knew he was dead.

"Webber is dead, Cratty. Burns is still in full view. We could take him," he offered.

Cratty felt her chest tighten abruptly but then she focused on her immediate task of walking Glenn through the minefield.

Welch's voice came over the speaker, and it was evident to Cratty that it dropped several octaves and seemed genuinely concerned with Glenn's idea of taking out Burns.

"Glenn... are you crazy? Burns has enough explosives to create a crater twenty-feet wide. And if he does kill himself, I am guessing China and Russia will be knocking on our door as more shit gets out. Not to mention, the American citizens might think anarchy would be a better form of government than what they've got now."

Cratty was then struck with an idea.

Finally... timing and luck could be on our side.

"Glenn, is that Warrant Officer Denise Welch?" Cratty asked again in full knowledge of the answer.

Yes," was his short answer.

"Jeff, I am going to ask the Warrant Officer to be senior negotiator of the situation. You are to defer to her assessment, and she has command of the field. Bravo has eyes on and will monitor. Have one of your team members make sure that the Bureau's Deputy Director John Helms makes it to your location. Please confirm you understand," Cratty requested.

"Yes, ma'am. Warrant Officer Welch is in command and will lead negotiations. Blue team will be dispatched to make sure Deputy Helms makes it to our location. We will follow her command. Operations Center, Bravo is monitoring," Glenn repeated.

Cratty took a few moments to formulate and carefully articulate her next thoughts because they would have implications for the future.

"One other thing, Glenn. Burns has a mountain of ordnance he stole from one of our private transports. This whole thing is completely clustered with Webber. I would like to have some success with your team in how you assist the Bureau to capture Burns once it became clear to you that Webber's objectivity was compromised. That's in addition to how you retrieved stolen military weapons. That would put a positive spin on this disaster. It's not lost on me that you broke Webber's direct order and contacted Bravo for support. Do you understand?" Cratty asked.

She knew Glenn had to see the writing on the wall. Webber might have been in charge, but she was sure Glenn was probably on record as disagreeing with nearly all of his decisions. But in the end, he was the second-in-command and could have pushed back harder.

"Yes, ma'am. That would be an accurate after-action report," Glenn confirmed.

"Acknowledged. Cratty out." Cratty made a motion to one of her team to mute communication with Glenn.

She then turned to the monitor where she saw the team leader, Janeson, and Davis. She had a curious thought: *How come Davis wasn't in charge of the base of operation. The woman beside her seems significantly younger.*

"All right, Bureau. Make this work. I'll keep eyes on and the dogs of war at bay at my end, but Burns needs to show good faith and bring us both something," Cratty warned.

Suddenly tired, she was about to sit back in her chair and give the impression of steadfast leadership when she heard something she never thought she would hear uttered from Davis's mouth.

"Cratty... nicely done."

"Thank you. See you on the other side... if there's another side to this."

"Amen to that."

~

Welch shook her head in disbelief. She looked over the group of men now in her command and looked over the entire that included Burns sitting casually on the motorcycle, Webber's mangled body and burning wreckage of a down helicopter.

Talk about your no-win scenario. Just like old times, she reminisced.

Her first order was to ground the second helicopter before it got shot down. Next, she redeployed her newly acquired fire teams to secure the perimeter to make sure nothing harmed or killed Burns. Then came the hard part when she turned around and walked back to Burns to find out what was next.

Silent and stoic, Burns remained leaning against his motorcycle, periodically looking at Webber's body and then surveying the fire zone.

"Burns... ah... do you have a first name or do you want me to call you 'Burns'?" Welch asked.

"Burns is fine."

"How do you want this to end?"

Burns took a moment to look at her; she could tell he was assessing whether she could be trusted. It seemed to Welch as if he made his decision pretty fast.

"I want four letters of immunity by the president absolving me and my team of all crimes. One million dollars as reparations for stealing five years of four civilians' lives and the killing of Dr. Caulfield's wife. And another million to go to the orphanage that raised Ms. Samantha Littleton during her early years... she loved that place for the most part..." Burns seemed to drift back to Webber's dead body.

"And what do we get back in return?" Welch asked.

"I'll give you the second external hard drive and end the next wave of classified data to go out. In addition, I'll go into Deputy Director Helms's custody to answer questions."

"What about the third drive?"

"Once I know my crew is safe, the money is in place and I have the pardons in my hands, I'll set things in motion to give you your third drive. If I'm to be taken into custody, fourteen days after my release, I will personally bring you the third and final hard drive for the final exchange. This time, though, there better be no interference or that will piss me off," he warned.

So, this wasn't Burns "pissed off?" I'd hate to see him really angry.

"Honestly, Mr. Burns, I really wouldn't want to see you 'really' pissed," she commented. She did have a question.

"How do I know you'll give us the last hard drive and not make copies?"

"I have always kept my word, and I do plan to keep a few copies of selected classified information. Sorry. I have issues with trust, and I'll need to have insurance for my and my team's safety. Once you have your final drives and I'm sure you'll leave us all alone, we will all disappear. It will be as if we never existed," Burns concluded.

God... I hope so.

Welch looked at him and then she turned around as she heard a vehicle approaching and coming to a sudden stop. She watched to see Helms and Andersen exiting the SUV, carefully surveying the scene and then walking toward her. She waited for Helms and Andersen to come into the fold with Burns before she spoke again.

"Mr. Burns, I am guessing you know John Helms and Steve Andersen?" Welch asked.

Burns smiled.

She thought he had a nice smile. If it wasn't for the scars, death, destruction, treason and setting the world on fire, he might have been a pleasant guy.

"I'm positive they both want a piece of me and my crew, but, yes, I do know them. Both these gentlemen and the woman named Davis have been relentless in tracking me down and retrieving the hard drives," Burns said.

"Ms. Davis, by the way, wants a third round when her arm feels better. Showing up and getting the drop on her in her house has made her next to impossible to be around," Andersen offered.

Welch saw yet another smile. She decided to take advantage of the goodwill. She decided to ask more questions to get everything going.

"Helms? Did your team and Cratty hear the terms and can we get presidential approval?"

"My boss is talking to his boss. Cratty has the Secretaries of State and Defense on the line to confirm it can happen," Helms summed up as he simultaneously took a long look at her, obviously with a question.

"What?" she finally asked.

"Are you hit? Or were you close to Webber when he was hit?" Welch had forgotten that she was sprayed with blood and had to look terrible.

"No... I wasn't hit."

Andersen, who had been listening, handed Welch a handkerchief. As she took it and thanked him, she wondered who carried one of these around anymore.

"A gift from my daughter?" he answered, anticipating the question.

She was surprised that Burns interrupted their exchange.

"Ladies and gentlemen, if we could move this faster. In thirty minutes, I need to get a signal out to stop the next wave of leaks, and my finger is getting tired on this switch."

"So it's safe to say you knew we would find the villa?" Welch asked.

"Yes. It took you longer than I expected."

"You killed sixteen agents there and thirteen the day before," Andersen commented.

Welch knew her glare at Andersen conveyed *"Jesus... Steve. I just put out a fire here."*

"I would have killed the whole world, but Sam and Emma wouldn't want me to do that," Burns said.

Welch was struck that he said his piece without hesitation, but with emotion, more sadness than anger.

An uncomfortable ten minutes elapsed until Glenn approached slowly from behind with an announcement from Cratty.

"Ms. Welch? Manager Cratty reports that the terms are accepted. If Burns hands over the second hard drive and goes into FBI custody, they will move ahead with the pardons and end the "kill orders." Once Mr. Burns answers some questions, he will be released to retrieve the final drive with the caveat that no further classified data be leaked. The money will be wired to his choice of charities, and he and his crew will be allowed to 'live in peace.'"

Helms was apparently listening to his team to obtain authorization for the plan.

"Confirmed. Homeland Security and the Bureau confirm the above plan. We are green to go," he added.

All eyes turned on Burns. Welch truly wondered what was next as she felt herself holding her breath. Burns had remained in nearly the same position he had been in when they arrived. For the first time in an hour, he stood up and started to speak to his support team, still hidden in the background.

"Tiny? Dove?" Burns said.

"Yes... Dove," he repeated. As Burns spoke, he carefully disconnected key wires on his vest and the LED lights slowly dimmed.

"One of my crew is going to come out from behind me. I would be greatly offended if she were shot. She's going to hand me the hard drive and will have to take my bike out, so she can make sure she stops the next wave of classified data to hit the Internet and air waves. If she doesn't get to where she needs to or if she is followed, more newsworthy material will flood the world. You will need to let her go. At which point, I will go in with Mr. Helms and Mr. Andersen. Agreed?"

As always... you have every angle covered.

As senior negotiator, it was Welch's turn to speak for all of them.

"Sounds like a plan. Mr. Glenn, pass that along to all your men. Battlefield situation requires that anyone who takes it upon themselves to interfere will be shot for treason," Welch added.

"Yes, ma'am," Glenn replied and ran back to spread the word.

Looking back at Burns, Welch could easily see a puzzled look on his face, but he didn't say anything.

Smiling at her delivery, Welch was reminded of when her husband and she would take turns being the "bad guy" with one of their children.

"Nice, Diane...'battlefield situation?' Shot for treason?' Did you just add that one for good measure or are you really getting into your role here?" Andersen said, nearly inaudibly.

"Helms, why do you have to bring him with you all the time? You have more class and could do much better," Welch complained.

Helms shrugged.

"Hey, Diane... I brought you into the team," he reminded her.

"Yeah... thanks for that." She said it with sarcasm.

Movement from behind Burns drew Welch's attention until it revealed a young woman clad in all black holding a sniper rifle, a 1997 Lapua, she noticed. She also saw recognition of the respected weapon cross Helms's face. In the right hands and conditions, a good sniper could make a shot from one thousand yards away. Maybe even fifteen hundred yards. The woman looked at Burns and the three in front her; she seemed a bit taken back at the twenty armed agents behind them. She looked pale and haggard.

"I don't like this, Burns," she warned.

"Tiny, no worries. Time for Dove. You need to shut down the next wave of data and get back to your designated rally point for next communication. Leave the weapon, give me the package, and get going. Stay local for the next twelve hours. Get moving," Burns coached in a surprisingly soft, kind voice.

The guy isn't what I expected.

Cautiously, she handed him the external hard drive and continued past Welch to hand Helms her rifle. She got on Burns's motorcycle, revving it up as she put her helmet on. Welch noticed she paused over Webber's body for a moment and then drove off between the wave of agents. Within seconds, she was more than halfway across the bridge.

Welch turned back to see Burns as he watched the young woman drive away.

"Was that Samantha's sister, Rebecca Littleton?" she asked.

Welch noticed Burns pause for a moment.

"Yes... she made that shot from more than 837 yards with light wind in a hostile situation. Five years ago, she couldn't run ten feet without gasping for air and a cigarette. She never held a gun in her life until three years ago. It all went into the shitter when her sister helped me. And now Sam is gone."

The sadness changed to a cold anger.

"If you think I'm dangerous, you don't know Rebecca. For me, I can separate business from personal. For her, it's all personal. We fuck this up, there will be no ends she will go to until she thinks justice is served," Burns warned.

Welch remained silent for a moment and then had to ask the next question:

"So... you're the 'reasonable one'?"

It seemed to Welch that Burns took a moment to embrace the question.

"Funny. You're right. I never thought I would be considered the one person on my team who used restraint. David Caulfield would use restraint, too, I suppose."

"Jesus..." Andersen said.

Just when you thought you caught a lion by the tail and lived, the lion was warning you that there was something worse than him. How far will she go? Will she agree with Burns or just keep the transmissions going?

Welch led Burns to the waiting SUV with Andersen and Helms flanking him on both sides. Without much more drama, it seemed as if the terror were over and now the government had to make peace with its own citizens, allies, and the rest of the world.

Just prior to stepping into the SUV, Burns handed a note to Andersen and seemed to tell him a few things about it before getting in. Andersen brought it to her and looked at the note as Burns entered the SUV. Welch shook her head, and Andersen went to wait in the car as she walked back to Jeff Glenn. She started in a straight line and then weaved to the left for a few steps until she came up the young man.

"Burns thought you might want this," she said, handing Glenn the note.

"What is it?" Glenn naturally asked.

"It's a rough map of where Burns has placed explosives throughout the fort in case he needed to fight a defensive battle. And just so you know, the flanks by the bridge where he disabled your cars—they're sitting on explosives."

"Shit..." Glenn responded.

"Yeah. I know. He also recommends you get a couple of bomb squads out here. Apparently, his accomplice set up a couple more booby-traps of her own and he's not sure where she put them."

Welch finished and was considering running back to the vehicle, but thought that might lack a certain degree of heroism. She did back track her steps to the vehicle.

The last thing she remembered hearing as she entered the SUV was Glenn yelling out a warning: "Guys... you might want to step away from the cars..."

Chapter 16

"Nil sine magno labore" – *"Nothing without great effort"*

Becky was driving pretty fast on Burns's motorcycle as she passed a number of parked FBI and local police cars that waved her on through stopped traffic. Her mind was racing as fast as she was driving. With a finite number of plans to choose from, the one she was least crazy about was the one Burns ultimately chose. Operation Dove meant that Burns had negotiated presidential pardons, money, and their freedom. In exchange, he would turn himself in for debriefing, give the second of three hard drives they stole last May, and stop the classified leaks. The "Dove" was for peace.

She didn't like it because he had to trust that the government would come through on its end.

They don't have a great track record to my liking.

If all went well, Burns would be free to leave, only to return fourteen days later with the final hard drive. The plan was great, if you could trust the enemy. The hardest part of the day was not what she expected. Waiting for him to give the word to kill Webber and shooting down the helicopter was not difficult. Watching him talk to the woman and then having the other two men come in and negotiate while listening passively was the most difficult.

Still, the moments just before she took Webber's life were stressful. All the years of shooting for "fun" had now been with a purpose. Watching her target, standing there pointing a gun at Burns, was not easy. He kept moving.

I could just shoot him now and be done with it, she thought whenever he was perfectly still while in her sights.

The wind had dropped as it now came from the shore, and her arms and back were beginning to hurt from being nearly motionless as she waited for the key word to cue her to shoot.

Shoot at the biggest target... the torso.

Burns was starting some speech, she noticed.

It's only when she saw that Webber was carefully listening and motionless that Becky understood why he was so talkative.

Burns... you fucking genius.

She watched closely with sweat building on her brow as she peered through the scope.

So much power. To kill or not.

After a minute of talking and more waiting, she heard the magic word—"Tiny." That was the code name Samantha had given her last May. Sam used to joke with her and call her names, often referencing her massive girth. It was Samantha's way of being close without getting hurt. "Tiny" was the new name for Becky.

She pulled the trigger before she forgot.

Familiar with the recoil of the Lapua from a prone position, it was strange for her to feel the recoil and see a time delay in hitting the mark. She saw her target fall back violently and hard as his gun discharged to the side.

"Drop the rifle and pick up the missile launcher," she said to herself. Burns had drilled it into her that if a helicopter were in the air and moved toward her, shoot it down. That meant a four-step sequence had to occur: drop the rifle, pick up the missile launcher, point, and shoot.

The kick from the launcher did surprise her since she had no practice at it. The helicopter's explosion took her by complete surprise. She had not known what to expect but the ferocity was overwhelming.

"Oh, my God! How many people did I just kill?" she asked herself.

It was easier to have one target to kill, especially when he killed your sister. It was easy to demonize one person. He was evil. A murderer.

But those guys were doing their job... they didn't kill Samantha.

She remained motionless and was acutely aware that if she had to do more, she couldn't.

I don't think I can do this anymore.

Becky was deep in thought when she finally heard Burns's voice address her with the code name "Dove."

How much time has gone by? she wondered.

She had to clarify with Burns before she revealed her location and handed over the only leverage in her possession. While not thrilled with the plan, she was happy it was not "Phoenix," which would have been to use the rocket-propelled grenades to take out the cars and the negotiation team. Unfortunately, that would mean killing Burns.

Thank God. I don't think I can kill anyone again... how did Samantha do this? How does Burns? she thought to herself as another realization became evident.

Oh, shit. David. He had to set the house to blow up. Shit.

Once the word was given, Becky collected her necessary stuff: cash, credit cards, passport, hard drive, and rifle. As she stood up and descended the hill to meet Burns and company, she was hit with a wave of nausea. Halfway down, she threw up.

Jesus...

Samantha had told her that when she killed three people, each time she threw up. It took her a minute to regroup and talk again.

"Now I know why you threw up," she said to herself.

Guilt? Revulsion? Normal people to kill others...

Becky had always had a hard time understanding how someone she loved could kill another person. She just felt she didn't have it in her. To some degree, watching her baby sister die changed all that. She walked carefully down the hill, afraid she might trip or throw up again. Between Webber and the average number of passengers in the helicopter being at least three, she exceeded her sister's record of kills in numbers and time. And with that horrible thought, she threw up again.

Oh, Pumpkin... I'm sorry I wasn't there, Becky kept thinking.

Killing Webber was not the answer since her biggest regret was not being there for her sister.

As she was about to "break cover," she did a quick inspection of her person to make sure vomit was not all over her. Somehow, she thought the appearance of a sniper should be cool and detached. Instead, she knew she looked sick. Becky smiled for a moment, remembering Samantha had always told her to keep a small makeup kit on her at all times.

"A little bit of lipstick and color can go a long way," she used to say.

Jesus... I'm not prepared, am I?

As she approached Burns from behind, she was struck by the number of federal officers on the ground. The three closest to her looked familiar and somehow not as threatening as the twenty armed agents behind them.

The last bit of communication between her and Burns would be coded for the most part with her telling him something like "I don't like this" or "I don't trust them."

Burns would be reassuring and give her the plan: "Stay local" meant "Get going"; any time said to remain meant "Be long gone before that time." If Burns told her to "disappear" that meant to head back to Bethlehem, New Hampshire to an off-site storage facility they used last May that was still secure.

Get what you need, stay for forty-eight hours, and go across the Canadian border, again.

As Becky got on the bike and took out the helmet in the side bag, she took a moment to breathe. Once she revved the engine and started moving, she looked at Webber's body one more time. The last time she had seen a dead body was when her cousin was killed. Both Webber and her cousin had got what was coming to them, she thought.

Fuck them.

Anger suddenly swelled in her chest as the loss of her sister hit her full-force.

One had killed her sister emotionally, and the other had taken her life when she got some of her emotions back.

She was finally happy, and you all took it away.

Becky couldn't stand the thought anymore of Sam being gone, so she bolted as fast as she could without crashing. Once off the island, she took a number of back streets into Boston rather than the highway. She slowed her pace so she would not get pulled over for speeding. Becky was convinced, by the number of federal agents and police who had locked the island down, that all law enforcement was probably still focused on Burns rather than following her.

Two short blocks away from her destination, Becky dumped her bike, helmet, and some of her exterior dark clothes to a layer of more colorful though subdued clothes. She was able to pull out a full-length sweater that covered her almost entirely so she could walk the short distance necessary without drawing attention.

She had a change of clothes in a locker at the bus depot in Boston where she would dye her hair blonde so she better matched her passport. She had yet another full change of clothes that would be decidedly more feminine—traditional business attire with white blouse, moderate length matching light blue suit, purse, heels, and overnight bag.

Samantha would be so proud. So many changes of clothes, she thought as she smiled at the memory of her sister's knack for changing wardrobe along with personae.

From there, she purchased a bus ticket via credit card in one name, but never planned to use it. Exiting a side entrance of the bus depot, she walked to the nearby Massachusetts Transportation Authority public trains to Logan Airport. Forty minutes later, she purchased a round trip ticket to England with one overnight bag for, ostensibly, a weekend business trip. Burns's direction to her was to remain local for twelve hours, meaning she needed to be as far away as possible within twelve hours. In the time he gave her, that would be Great Britain. The next wave of classified data to go out over the Internet was scheduled for three days from now. Security was a pain in the ass. Fortunately, it was all visual and she had preferred boarding and no gunpowder detectors were in use. She was decidedly lucky.

After four hours elapsed, Becky was looking below as the shore rocks of Boston Bay receded and her airplane climbed into the air. Airborne and on her way to England, she truly wondered whether she was safe.

Did I make it? Did I really make it? They could still order the plane around. They could still have the authorities waiting for me in England.

Once at Heathrow, there would be another change of clothes and then she would make contact with David. Three days after that, she would fly to Brazil. Originally, she had thought about going directly to Brazil but then she had to make sure no one was on her trail. She couldn't afford to lead anyone back to David and Emma's location.

The slow smile, with no editing on Burns's part, indicated he was impressed with her thinking when she discussed her plan. It was the "new normal," of trust no one, get rid of tails, use deception, and make sure you are "safe" before going to a secured area.

Sitting in first class as she looked out over the ocean, she prepared to go to sleep as a "business woman" to blend in better with the other passengers and not to be readily remembered. As she began to fall asleep, her nose itched and she sneezed.

You're kidding me, right?

She was getting a cold. *Made sense*, she thought.

Three days in a bunker underground, on an island with no sleep, and rats and bats for company, made sense she might get sick.

How things change, she thought as she stared out the window, thinking of her sister.

~

Davis was watching as Burns was escorted into the interrogation room at the FBI's main office in Boston. It took an hour to get him safely through the streets of Boston to the office and then into a building before he landed in the interrogation room. She figured that Helms, Andersen, and Welch were not taking any chances that some harm might still come to Burns. The Operations Center in Virginia might be off-line, but that didn't mean there was not another operation to kill Burns still on as backup. Cratty and her Bravo team confirmed no operation was in place, but Davis assumed that Webber would have kept it "off the books." To be safe, Cratty told her she planned to watch the transport via satellite and keep constant contact with Andersen while Helms was in contact with his team in the control room.

Burns had been offered something to drink while he waited as she closely watched him from the observation room. After he entered and took his seat alone, he immediately got up and walked the entire room a number of times to look for weaknesses. Once he spent a full fifteen minutes inspecting the room, he returned to his seat and closed his eyes. Davis could hear a low tone and guessed that Burns had started to recite prayers.

What is this guy? Kills people and protects his friends. Then prays. Who is he?

Not understanding him, she continued to hold vigil as everyone debriefed in the control room. Davis and surveillance records showed Burns sitting in one place for an hour and forty-five minutes, reciting prayers in at least three languages. In an uncharacteristic move, there was a knock at the observation door and Andersen looked in. Davis took the cue and prepared herself for her interview with Burns.

After exiting the observation room into the hall, Davis and Andersen waited a moment, knocked and then opened the interrogation room door.

Burns stood up as Davis entered. Once she sat, Andersen and Burns sat. Davis shook her head in disbelief.

"Always a gentlemen, Mr. Burns," she commented.

"I wasn't always that way. Dr. Caulfield says my head injury and my road to recovery did things he never saw before," Burns explained. He looked around behind him at the mirror and gestured toward it.

"How many people behind there?"

"Probably about half-a-dozen. That includes Diane Welch, John Helms and his immediate command team, and two technicians," Andersen responded.

"Probably a half-dozen behavioral specialists, too. You've changed a lot, Burns," Davis added.

"I sure have. Struck down by missiles, time in the dessert, kindness of strangers and prayers... I don't need to point out the similarities to Saul," Andersen said.

Burns nodded his head to acknowledge he understood.

Andersen spoke again.

"Just for the record, you killed more than twenty federal agents," he said bluntly.

"I was not keeping count," Burns countered quickly.

Then after a moment, Burns collected his thought and spoke again.

"Their agency ordered the death of the only woman I loved. My friends' lives were threatened, including that of a five-year-old girl. I'm not justifying my actions. I killed them to protect my loved ones. To avenge my loved one. It was the first time I have ever been motivated by this... emotion," he responded. It was not lost on Davis that he had to search for the word.

Andersen looked down at his pad of paper for a moment.

"I am sorry for your loss," Andersen said.

"Thank you." More silence.

"Mr. Burns, it would help us all out here to know how this all happened. How you came to know Dr. David Caulfield, the Littleton sisters, and Emma. Why you attacked the Bureau and the Operations Center back in May. How did all of this come about, Mr. Burns?" Andersen asked.

Finally. Some answers. Not some bullshit from a file, but some real answers.

Davis sat with her attention transfixed on Burns; she had waited for this moment for such a long time. She just wanted to understand why everything had happened the way it did. *What was the motivation? Was it simply love and friendship? Why?*

Burns took in the breadth of the questions and seemed to give himself a minute to arrange his thoughts. After a minute more and another deep breath, he began what would eventually be a five-hour dramatic monologue peppered with periodic clarifying questions, two glasses of water, and a bathroom break.

"I think it would be best to start on May 1, 2011. I was Senior Logistics Officer of the Foreign Intelligence Agency's Operations Center, and I shared command with Senior Field Officer Anthony Maxwell. There was disagreement over the purpose of the mission. I wanted the mission to be straightforward and that was to kill a top-tiered enemy of the state..."

He went over everything: his helicopter crash, injuries in the field, and the Red Cross getting him back state-side. He spent time discussing his treatment with Dr. Caulfield, killing the first agent in the garage who was going to kill him, and witnessing Caulfield's wife's murder. Burns elaborated on how he met Samantha and Rebecca Littleton, and their niece, Emma, who was a baby at the time. He discussed in detail his discomfort with his metamorphoses as he gained such emotions as sadness, regret, pain, empathy, sympathy, and finally, love and hate. How his past feelings of apathy and fear seemed to wane into oblivion the longer he was with this group. Burns spoke with pride of how it was Caulfield and Samantha's idea not just to wait to be killed but rather to take the fight to the agency's doorstep; that changed the tide forever for him. No longer was this a mission for policy and country. It was personal; it was about survival and for Emma.

Burns went into detail about their lives in Rhode Island and Massachusetts, how they altered their exercise and eating patterns, how they made money and collected needed clothes, weapons and electronics. Burns tried to gloss over the day they found the Operations Center overlooking the old America's Technological Highway, and how they found a highly skilled field agent they named "Cougar."

Davis's eyes widened at her code name.

Are you shitting me? Am I the butt of everyone's joke on the planet!

"Really? You couldn't come up with something else?"

She turned to look at Andersen and could see his lips thinning to conceal a smile as he underlined the code name repeatedly for emphasis. She looked at the mirror knowing that even now Cratty would be laughing her ass off with this news. Red appeared on her neck and face again remembering how Andersen told her the story, but it was never clear it was her... until now. Now the whole world would know her as "Cougar."

Davis had an irrational thought for just a fleeting second: *Maybe I should just kill Burns and have the world flooded with classified data again... maybe it would be worth it.*

For Burns's part, he did appear genuinely embarrassed.

"It was an accident. A play on words that stuck. Sorry," he said apologetically.

Just great. Sympathy from the world's greatest terrorist and assassin. Just sweet, she thought sarcastically.

Davis simply sighed and ran both her hands through her hair.

"Great. This is what? The third time you screwed me over? Just... just go on, Mr. Burns," was all she could muster.

Burns moved on to how they had found the Auxiliary Control Room and the extensive planning that went into every aspect of the diversions that were put in place: fake bombs in the hospital, the truck in the parking lot filled with dry ice, and a public building near a school—all these events were designed to tie up all first responders within a ten-mile radius. The gasoline fire in the condo development was simply more theater. Caulfield's presence at the police station was to tie up Andersen because the research indicated that he and Diane Welch might see through the diversions and be hot on Burns's trail. Welch was dealing with her husband's dying, so Andersen was the focus.

"Did you have help from your former support team, Jose Perez and Marie Martinez?" Davis asked. She was impressed with how throughout all the events and years they remained off-grid, invisible and untouchable.

"At times. They helped with locating the sites, planning and getting resources. They disappeared before launch. They wanted a head start," he said.

"And now?"

"They're gone. I can find them but I owe them. That's all on them," Burns said. He shrugged his shoulders indicating that there was no more to be said on the subject.

He did go on about the various plans of accessing the external hard drives and some of his miscalculations that if he had known better would have caused him to do things differently. Similar to talking more about Perez and Martinez, he refused to discuss his exit strategies and how his team slipped under a national and international manhunt.

"Trade secret. Sorry. I can imagine if everyone keeps their word I would be happy to outline in detail how we all escaped and remained off grid. Maybe... ten years from now."

Davis had to smile at that one.

Burns talked sparingly about his love affair with Samantha Littleton. She found it hard to look at him as he talked about her, so she averted his eyes, feeling as if she were prying into something very private.

Andersen changed the subject pretty fast as a way of sparing everyone pain, Davis thought. Of great interest was why Burns responded to the first message from Andersen about setting a time and working out a plan to get the drives back.

"I wanted a final solution. I knew I had my former bosses by the balls, but I didn't want that. I wanted them to leave us alone. I hoped that between you and the Bureau, a separate peace could have been brokered and Sam, Becky, David and Emma could be set free. I was willing to come in from the cold so they could be free. It wasn't fair that they should suffer the price of helping someone and be punished for being loyal," Burns explained.

"You would have turned yourself in," Andersen clarified.

"With some backup leverage to insure safety for my crew, yes."

"And your team was okay with this?" Andersen asked.

Burns looked down at the desk and smiled. He was obviously remembering some past discussions.

I bet they were lively ones by that expression, Davis thought.

"No way. David suggested that he bring in all three drives but that we keep copies. His rationale was that he had lost his life, wife and stepchildren, so he had less to lose."

"Why didn't he do it?" Andersen continued.

"Are you kidding me?" Burns asked with more emotion than Davis had seen from him before. It was genuinely an exasperation he demonstrated that required him to explain what he thought was obvious.

"You don't know the Littleton sisters, do you?"

What the hell?

Davis exchanged a look with Andersen and shrugged, indicating that they apparently did not. Burns again rolled his eyes in disbelief and continued with his explanation.

"Yeah. When David offered that suggestion, Becky took him in the next room and ripped him a new one. He was a father to Emma, Becky loved him, he was the 'glue of their family,' and finally, she made it crystal clear that if he did it, she would make sure she killed him first. 'In your sleep' were her exact words. Sam reiterated something similar to me if I were to consider taking David up on his offer."

Burns gave it a moment to let the facts sink in before he continued.

"Let's just say that Becky was clear she loved him, and she would not let me or anyone take him away. Sam made it clear that she wanted her sister to be happy."

Davis had to smile.

An assassin and a trained psychologist were frightened of the girlfriends?

She genuinely regretted not knowing both of these women.

"I hear that," Andersen said with too much empathy.

Surprised that Andersen said that out loud, Davis smiled, knowing that Laura, Andersen's wife, was opinionated, and apparently, to the same degree as the Littleton sisters.

Well, well, well...

Andersen looked at her and Burns, who were looking at him.

As the interrogation was recorded, she felt she now had real leverage.

Finally... a silver lining.

Davis smiled broadened and then refocused on the interview.

"Sorry... this is not about me. Well... why didn't you turn yourself in?" Andersen asked.

Burns was slow to answer and seemed to choose his words with care.

"Two reasons. I loved Sam, and I never wanted to leave her. She loved me, and she would never let me go alone. We would be in separate cells, and I don't like confined spaces, and she likes them less. She would follow me to the end. I couldn't do that to her."

Everyone was quiet.

"Anyway... everyone knew that while Becky might follow through on her threat to kill David, it was clear that Sam would. So, David and I turning ourselves in was simply off the table. Maybe protective custody..."

Davis smiled.

"Strong woman. I knew I liked her," she said.

Burns looked her in the eyes.

Those damn eyes again. They're soft brown now.

"She was a very likeable person when you got beyond her defenses. She had a lot of reasons not to trust people."

After five hours of debriefing, a dinner break was in order. Davis and Andersen had to confer with their colleagues and get an update on what was happening in the world while they were incommunicado.

Burns requested only water as Davis and Andersen exited the room.

With stiff legs and an aching arm, Davis was looking forward to conferring with Helms, Welch, and Andersen. For her, this was a very unusual situation, and the group of people were the most unusual she had ever met. They were about a half-hour into their discussion when Janeson entered the office, holding a large envelope with the White House seal.

"Boss, this was just hand-delivered to me by military courier," Janeson announced.

Helms asked for an update about relevant events both in the field and news that might affect Burns and the world.

Standing on the balls of her feet with hands folded behind her back, Janeson gave a concise update in computer-like fashion without judgment and comments.

How does she do that?

"In regards to the ongoing investigation, both the Bureau and the Operations Center lost track of Rebecca Littleton. While we did discover that a woman fitting her description purchased a ticket for an express trip to Pennsylvania, we determined it was a deception. There is speculation that she is still in the area, but I suspect she is out of the country since Mr. Burns is allowing himself to be debriefed by us for hours, and the need to collect the weapons and defuse bombs is "classic" for him—tie up resources and have his people slip in or out. I would have guessed that she made it into Canada, but the geopolitical landscape changed."

Oh great... now Canada has declared war on us, Davis thought. *What did we do to them?*

"I am guessing if she made it to Canada and its government held her at the border, they would probably not turn her over to us," Andersen joked. After the nervous laughter passed, Janeson continued with her lengthy briefing as if there had been no reaction at all.

Fingering her necklace, Davis figured there were more serious things to come with Canada.

"More than likely not, but I will get to that. All the major news channels, television, radio, blogs, newspaper reports, tweets and all Internet forums are confirming that Mr. Burns was captured by the FBI with the support of the Foreign Intelligence Agency's Operations Center. When asked why the Bureau took lead instead of the Operations Center, Senior Field Agent Jeffery Glenn made the field decision to have a 'more objective sister agency' take the lead because he was concerned about Deputy Director Webber's judgment and stability. Mr. Glenn reported his command decision was supported by Manager Denise Cratty, Bravo Team, who stepped in when Alpha team was breached. Further, with assistance from the Bravo and the Bureau, they were able to locate 'an arsenal of weapons' stolen from the Department of Defense."

"Well some of that fiction is true," Welch offered.

With a wave of his hand, Helms encouraged Janeson to go on.

"The president announced that the Operations Center's missions and black operations be immediately halted, pending review by the Central Intelligence Agency, National Security Agency, and a Bipartisan Commission. Their goal is to review, define or shut down the Operations Center. The president went on to say, 'In light of Diane

Welch's military history, commitment to duty and her country, and her critical role in apprehending Mr. Burns,' he plans on asking you to lead the commission."

Davis watched Welch simply sit still for a moment and shake her head in disbelief.

"Well, that was nicely played. How can you say, 'No' when he has already told the world?" Davis said. She hadn't voted for the guy since he was too liberal, but she had to admit he handled this "snafu" quite well.

"Great..." Welch complained. To Janeson's credit, she was getting notably better in picking up on cues to continue speaking, Davis thought.

"On a national level, it appears that Mr. Burns is considered a folk hero of sorts, more that Snowden and WikiLeaks. The psychology here is the presence of a family versus one sole-analyst and a faceless organization. Already stories are circulating of how he and his 'crew' have been 'relentlessly hunted down' and their lives ruined and 'even a baby was threatened.'"

Pausing, Janeson turned to look at the left ceiling, searching for either the data or the words to continue.

"All this has elevated Mr. Burns from terrorist to... what was it...'an average guy pushed to the limit.'"

"My God... I see a mini-series coming..." Andersen added.

"Yes. On a global scale, North Korea, China, Iran, Russia, Spain and France have offered Mr. Burns and his crew asylum and political immunity for having brought to light America's black-ops center. When the deaths of more than twenty-five agents are brought up, all parties use the counter argument of 'self-defense' and the Operations Center's violation of international and domestic laws, assassinations being the chief crime. In regard to Mr. Burns's crew, there is a huge outpouring of support for 'David and Becky and how they have protected their little girl.' Additionally, the video and last words of Ms. Samantha Littleton being 'shot down in broad daylight' and last rites went viral last night. In other areas, Mr. Burns and his crew have a cult following that includes sovereign nations and figureheads of all sort.

Further, there is a series of individual and class action suits and criminal charges being filed against the U.S. government, specifically the Foreign Intelligence branch."

Now holding on firmly to her cross, Davis felt her chest tightening as the global news seemed to get worse with every word Janeson said. Looking across the table, she saw that Andersen looked suddenly tired as Welch seemed to lean farther back in her chair, rubbing her hands together. Still standing in the same position she had started in, Janeson continued with the global disaster.

"On the political front, China and North Korea are talking an 'alliance' while Russia, Iran, China, Spain, France, Greece and Italy have walked out of the United Nations. On the bright side, England has remained neutral based on a 'common past history.' All the above mentioned countries are requesting U.N. sanctions against the U.S., and Germany, Russia, and Spain have frozen American assets while Greece and China have expelled all American officials. It appears that China is seriously considering restricting all American imports and exports."

For the love of God, Janeson. Please be done, Davis hoped. *Is there anything going right?*

"On the economic front," Janeson continued, "the stock market's losses over the last three days surpass the losses of the 2008-2011 Great Recession. And finally, both Canada and Mexico have significantly increased law enforcement and military personnel along the borders to reduce the increasing number of Americans who reportedly are leaving the country in record numbers."

Davis saw Andersen's jaw slacken as she experienced sharp pains in her injured arm, which now seemed to radiate to her shoulder. If she didn't know she had been shot, she would have bet she was suffering a heart attack. She turned to see that Welch had moved from rubbing her hands to rubbing her head as if she were experiencing a migraine or the beginning of a stroke.

Other than Janeson, Helms seemed to remain unaffected from the report.

Maybe he's just use to how she gives such bad news without emotion or timing to help you digest it all?

"Well... Rachael... thank you for trying to balance out the good and the bad," Helms said.

Noting the sarcasm, which was a feat not lost on Davis, Janeson moved her folded hands from her back to the front as she responded.

"Sorry, boss... there is no 'positive' piece to add with the sole exception of the historically obvious common history America shares with Great Britain. It seems I am not the only one who is not entirely sure whether that was an example of British humor or not," she added.

Janeson nodded her head and turned to leave the room.

Again... a good read on the social cue. Teaming Gilmore, Johnson, and Janeson had been a good idea.

With the envelope in front of Welch, she reached over and carefully opened it as if it were a fragile glass container. Slowly, she extracted a handwritten note on presidential stationery along with five official documents that appeared to be all signed.

Welch read the note but then she must have felt the several pairs of eyes upon her.

"Do I have to ask you to read it?" Davis asked.

Welch cleared her throat to read out loud.

First and foremost, let me express my deepest sympathies for the loss of your husband, Joseph.

Dear Mrs. Welch,

Your commitment to duty and country during such a personal tragedy is nothing short of admirable..."

Davis could see by Welch's short pause that her husband's death was still very raw for her. Welch picked up where she left off after she cleared her throat.

"Secondly, thank you for your assistance in handling the Burns's matter and your continued work to find a solution to a very big problem.

I have signed pardons for the names you and Mr. John Helms requested.

Further, a number of countries have offered Mr. Burns and his compatriots a new home, new life, and safety from our government.

I ask that you strongly encourage Mr. Burns to choose a nation that remains friendly to the United States. As that is now a very short list, England, France, Germany, Portugal and Spain are possible choices. How you handle Burns and his compatriots' safety is your call.

In light of the past few days of ugly revelations made clear by supporting evidence Mr. Burns has made public, it is imperative that included in his and the others' passage to safety is the end of these transmissions and the return of all sensitive, classified data. How you retrieve this data is also your call.

It is unclear whether we as a government will be able to win back the trust of our citizens and our fellow nations, friendly or otherwise. We will need your continued public efforts and those of your colleagues: John Helms, Denise Cratty, Steve Andersen, and former Operations Center Manager Jillian Davis, to press on and demonstrate that one agency and one man does not represent all of us.

Thank you for your commitment to duty, honor, and country."

Taking in a deep breath, Davis took a moment to digest all of it. Still, the hardest part was hearing Welch's timber in her voice change at the mention of her husband's name. That stuck with her throughout her entire reading.

That's gotta be hard, was all she could think.

A weighty silence followed as Davis easily imagined hearing the president's voice saying those very words.

Helms gently took the letter to read it himself.

"Well... looks like the 'Great Diane Lucius Cincinnatus Welch' has returned to duty," Andersen said as he bowed to show respect.

"Can you read his handwriting? He's a lefty, and I know he had to struggle to make it look good, but I wish he had typed it," Helms complained.

"He's a politician. If it's handwritten and difficult to understand, then there is still plausible deniability I bet," Welch explained.

There was a burst of nervous laughter as the letter's seriousness registered.

"Well, guys... I'm happy I'm not the only one who was drafted," Welch offered.

Davis saw Helms become deadly silent. Andersen was the first to ask, "John? What's wrong?"

Helms took a breath and seemed to take time to choose his words.

"Who's going to tell Cratty she's been drafted?"

More silence and then a burst of laughter.

"Let's have Janeson do it? Cratty will kill me," Davis blurted out.

I wonder how Cratty is going to make this one work?

Chapter 17

"Bona fide" – *"Good faith"*

After another thirty minutes of laughter, joking, and speculation of future positions in the "new world order," Andersen returned back to the interrogation room to meet with Burns. Davis tagged along even though Andersen had said she could take a break. He noticed that Davis seemed preoccupied and serious, and he wondered whether the stress of being shot and taking the world back from the brink was wearing on her.

Sitting together with Burns, they showed a copy of the president's letter to him. After seemingly reading the letter without difficulty, Burns confessed that he had seen two other presidents' handwriting before that he considered worse.

Is there anything you haven't seen? Andersen wanted to ask him.

"So. How do you want to do this?" he asked.

Burns thought for a moment before he spoke as if he were remembering some details.

"I need to leave here tomorrow by 7 a.m. During that time, I will stay in contact with you once a day, every day, at 3 p.m. I'll make sure no more data comes from my team, and seven days from tomorrow, I'll return the final hard drive to you. I'll let you know the location. In regard to relocation, I have ideas, but I need to consult with my crew and make sure I'm not being watched."

"Are you going to keep a copy?" Davis asked.

"I'm not sure," he responded.

"That's a little vague, Mr. Burns," Andersen pointed out.

"I know. It's intentional. Have I broken my word to you at any point?" Burns asked.

Damn. Good point. We've been the assholes consistently in that area.

Andersen shook his head "No." *It was true. So far, it had been "the good guys" who broke all the rules and lied.* Sobering thought.

"So, we just open the door and let you walk out and simply follow your lead?" Davis clarified.

Andersen was wondering when she was going to talk. She had become pretty quiet in the last half-hour.

"Yup. If we had done this my way, we would all be resting at our homes... with loved ones," Burns added. Andersen could feel Burns's emotion when he said, "loved ones."

Samantha Littleton. Nearly twenty-five agents. All of them would be alive.

Andersen could see it had an effect on Davis.

Davis, what the hell is wrong with you? he wondered.

Without further words, Andersen and Davis got up to let Burns wait for dinner and let him sleep. As Davis was exiting, she stopped and returned to hand Burns something.

What the hell?

He could see Burns was hesitant at first, but he opened his hand to receive whatever she was giving him. He had to look quickly and then he saw it in full view when Burns let it fall so he, too, could get a good look at it. It was Davis's necklace. It was the same necklace with the same cross that Samantha Littleton held when she died. She stood in front of Burns for a long moment before she spoke.

"I am sorry, Alex," she said and walked out ahead of him. As Andersen said goodnight and headed to the door, he saw Burns hold the necklace tightly.

Jesus. That had meaning.

~

The following day, John Helms and Diane Welch entered the interrogation room to wake him up, but he was already up, sitting on his cot. He had not slept at all and was sure it would next to impossible to do going forward. When they arrived he was still in meditation. He was wearing the necklace and cross Davis had given him. While still not sure why she gave it to him, he accepted that it was the last thing Sam had held.

It's the last thing I have of her. The last thing she touched

Welch offered him breakfast, but he declined.

I don't think I'll ever want to eat again.

Burns knew that Helms and Welch were considered heroes for bringing him in.

It has to be strange for both of them just to let me walk out of their custody.

He respected them both for their courtesy to explain what was going on, especially the part in the president's letter about leaving the next steps up to them.

Pretty broad interpretation, Burns thought. *They're both risk takers.*

Without much fanfare, Welch and Helms walked him to the service elevator, brought him to the ground floor, and gave him his personal belongings.

As light rain fell, Burns looked out, wondering what he was going to do next.

What would Sam do? he wondered.

Distracted by his internal thoughts, Burns said, "So. This is it."

Not expecting an answer, he was surprised that Welch gave him one.

"We're going to do it your way, Burns. I'm telling the president and law enforcement that we have you under constant surveillance and you're cooperating with us. Please don't have them lock us up for treason. I don't look good in orange."

Burns thought she was funny and gave her an immediate offer.

"You can always join my team. We're pretty good in staying ahead of the law,"

"Great... I don't think Leavenworth allows conjugal visits," Helms commented.

Burns watched Welch roll her eyes and ignore the comment. He couldn't help but smile as he zipped up his oversized hooded sweatshirt and fished around in his pockets. He was looking for keys to a bus depot locker.

Burns started to wonder why Welch began fishing in her own pockets until she asked, "I'm sorry. Do you need money?" Helms immediately went for his wallet as well.

Burns smiled and walked away, muttering, "I think I can figure out how to get around without cash. Thank you, and I'll see you in seven days or less."

Burns walked and headed to the corner as the light rain pelted his hood. After he turned, he headed in the opposite direction while making sure his necklace and cross were securely around his neck. *It was the thing she held.* Oddly enough, though, it didn't weigh him down as it hung from his throat. He'd had the irrational thought that it would.

Burns's brain shifted into protection mode, and he decided to change the plan's parameters. Smiling, Burns came up with a plan he knew Samantha would have said was just crazy. "Fortune favors the bold," he said to himself.

~

Burns turned the corner and was gone from Welch's view all the while she wondered whether there was still time for them to change their minds.

This is just crazy. Insane, she kept thinking. In an attempt to distract herself, she asked Helms a question.

"You know. I don't know who is going to take it the worst, Davis or Andersen?" Welch commented as they started back toward the elevator.

"Oh, that's easy. Davis. She never got a shot to see if she could take Burns without him always getting the drop on her," Helms responded. Helms had a good point. In every altercation, Burns always got the upper hand. But Welch had another theory.

"No... Andersen. He had Caulfield in his custody for hours, which was the best chance to pull Burns and his whole crew in. And then he finally gets Burns in his interrogation room, and a couple of hours later, he is gone... just like Caulfield," Welch argued.

Helms pushed the elevator button and turned to look at Welch.

"Are you drunk? There is no way Andersen is going to be more pissed than Davis."

Welch had a vision of her mother saying something to her father. She had to laugh.

"You know, since Davis is Navy and Andersen is Army, it's hard to tell. If either one of them were a Marine... well, the decision would have been easy."

She was pleased that Helms understood, nodding his head in approval.

"Absolutely. If Davis were a Marine, Burns would never have gotten the jump on her. It would have been over on May second," Helms said with conviction while rolling down his long sleeves.

"And if Andersen were a Marine, he would have locked up the whole crew back in May. All done," Welch added while she smoothed out her blouse.

It was quiet for a moment until Helms uttered, "Semper Fi."

"Oorah!" Welch responded.

Chapter 18

"O tempora! O mores!" – "O the times, O the values" Cicero

Not far from the Operations Center's former location, Andros's Diner sat on the main road in Waltham, Massachusetts, close to the intersections of Route 2 and Route 128. It was her first time at the diner while it was one Andersen's favorite small "hole-in-the-wall" for Greek food. So when Burns called a meeting to occur near that particular location, she knew Andersen would pick the diner. Davis was trying to understand why Burns was calling an earlier meeting than planned and at that location. Other than the diner, there were a series of old, abandoned state hospitals in the immediate area. When Helms told her they had let Burns go, it took her a full ten minutes to believe they had let him walk away and not to seem fazed by it. When Andersen asked whether they were worried, Helms said, "No," and that "It's a Marine thing."

What the hell? Still, she noticed relief in Helms's eyes when Andersen got the call to meet earlier.

Burns has an angle. There's always an angle with him.

The meeting was scheduled for 2 p.m. to avoid the crowd, which Andersen confirmed was pretty big at lunchtime.

Maybe he's even eaten here before. Even a hardened field agent like Burns could appreciate the smell of freshly made avgolemono soup and spanakopita prepared by first generation Greeks.

Davis was enjoying the thought until her mind wandered to Cratty. She liked having her own team, so having Cratty join it gave her mixed emotions. While Cratty was instrumental, Burns had never met her before, and she thought her presence might spook him.

As Davis patiently waited, she looked at her new watch on her healing arm and then she caught a glimpse of a slim, dark specter of a woman with an olive khaki jacket, walking quickly toward her. Shaking her head, Davis became acutely worried that Cratty's menacing appearance would make anyone nervous. Making eye contact with Andersen as he fielded a phone call, he shrugged his shoulder and continued with his conversation.

Jesus... talk about melodrama. Couldn't you find any other colors to wear other than black?

While she was sure Burns would expect everyone to be armed, she felt there was no reason to look heavily armed. While her dark outfit did well to conceal, to a trained eye it was easy to see she had a large caliber semi-automatic, a knife, and at least three clips of ammunition. As Cratty removed her sunglasses, her pale skin and blue eyes were prominent as was her sudden complaining that she had to park a half-mile away and was tired. Trying to make small talk as Andersen finished his phone call, Davis asked whether she was tired as a result of "all the weapons you're carrying?" Ignoring the remark, Cratty began adjusting her bra slightly under her blouse, leaving an opening for Davis to make another weapons crack.

All right. Maybe that was further than I had to go.

Standing straight up now from adjusting her holster, Cratty looked Davis in the eye with a lot more attitude than Davis remembered.

"What is your fixation about what I am wearing and concealing? You know you're not my type. You do know that 'No' means 'No,' right?" Cratty said with a sharp grin.

Damn it! How can I respond to that?

"Nice," Davis said. "Just behave when we're in there and let us take the lead. Think you can manage that?"

"Can you?"

Having finished his call, Andersen had been watching the interchange with wonderment and without comment, which surprised Davis to no end. After a minute of reorganizing her thoughts, she clarified that she did not want to scare off Burns.

"It's just that your ensemble is much more ninja-like than

necessary. Couldn't you find something that said, 'Hi! I'm the nice lady who saved you'?" she asked.

"I'm all out. Haven't done laundry in weeks."

"No, I mean really? Just a bit intimidating, don't you think?"

Based on Cratty's widened eyes, it was evident she was surprised by her continued focus on clothes.

"The guy terrorized the planet, Davis. I think he could probably take us three without much of a struggle... when did you start acting so girly? It doesn't become you."

Cratty returned to brushing white lint off her jacket and smoothing out her pants.

Davis couldn't help but respond to how Cratty was obsessing about her wardrobe and appearance.

"Do you need lipstick?"

Cratty looked Davis in the eye and produced her own tube of lipstick.

"No... I got it." Davis could see Cratty went overboard to pucker her lips as she applied the lipstick.

Davis's eyes narrowed, and she was about to say something when Andersen raised both his hands in an attempt to stop the interaction from escalating.

"Ladies, remember, we're all on the same team. It's not a weapons free zone and I'd like to give that impression to Burns, please."

She could see Andersen was nervous about their competitive nature.

"Don't worry about me," Cratty said, donning her sunglasses as she entered the diner.

Hit with the feeling of being twelve years old again, Davis made a face at Cratty as she entered behind her.

"Oh, this is going to be a great time!" Andersen said for her to hear.

Forty-five minutes later, Davis watched Burns approach the booth that held the three of them. Relatively speaking, she knew he would see her and Andersen as "friendly faces," but would wonder who was "the blonde woman clad in dark clothes... with the lipstick."

He didn't look too different than last time she saw him. While he didn't look disheveled, he didn't look great either, she thought. As Burns sat down, he placed a plastic bag on the table next to Davis and Andersen's finished soup bowls.

He's gotta wonder who the blonde having coffee only is.

"I'm surprised Helms and Welch are not here," Burns observed.

Davis knew Burns was aware of who was going to be there.

"Helms is in the control room monitoring every square inch of diner for a two-mile radius with an agent on every corner, and Welch is in Washington having all the naysayers kiss her ass. We do this right, she'll be a senator or something," Davis said.

Davis saw Andersen smile in response. She did enjoy hearing about Andersen's childhood from Welch.

"She struck me as honest," Burns replied.

Andersen cocked his head.

"Is that a joke, Burns? Jokes are not exactly in your profile," Andersen commented.

"Brain injury and treatment will change a man. I know someone if you're interested." Burns reply was not without emotion but there was a serious tone.

Hmm... that's funny. And Andersen is right... it's not part of your profile.

"I'm familiar with Dr. Caulfield's work. I spent some quality time with him in May."

Davis noticed that both men seemed to have a "bonding moment." *Jesus,* Davis thought until she remembered. *Ah yes. Caulfield. Andersen had spent hours with Caulfield before he escaped.*

Davis jumped in and pointed at Cratty.

"Just so you know, this is Denise Cratty, Manager of Operations Center, Bravo; she stepped in at the last minute to give us our shot not to fuck things up again."

"Thank you," Burns said.

"You're welcome," Cratty replied.

A brief silence ensued. Both nodded at the other; Davis was sure they were sizing up each other.

"You see, Davis, I knew these two would hit it off," Andersen commented.

Ignoring him, Davis took the hard drive out of the bag and investigated it, based on what she remembered from the last time she had held one almost a week ago. It was hard for her to hold it with her weak hand, even though it was out of a sling.

She was satisfied and took the lead in the discussions. Andersen seemed absolutely fine as his spinach pie and lamb showed up and he licked his lips in anticipation. Davis was going to take just a bite and then put her pastitsio aside for the time being while Cratty had a refill of coffee.

"You're not eating anything, Ms. Cratty?" Burns asked.

"I'm trying to watch my weight," Cratty said.

Davis put her fork down and had to look at her to see whether that was an actual response or a not-so-veiled crack.

Really? Do we have to do this here? Right now?

Davis became distracted as she saw Burns scratch some old scar tissue on his hands. Glancing back at Cratty before shifting back to the mission, she could swear she saw her smile behind her coffee cup.

I knew that was a crack? I bet no one liked you at school. Probably a teacher's pet who relished in getting people in trouble.

"So how did you come up with this additional part to the plan?" Davis asked Burns before she lost her entire focus.

In addition to getting the external drive earlier, Burns wanted his people to be relocated.

It makes a lot of sense. In addition to followers, there's a large number of Americans who agreed with Webber and think you and your crew should be jailed, or worse.

"I'm a logistics specialist. That's what I do," Burns said cryptically.

Davis smiled. *Maybe that was humor and not a literal statement.*

"Well, just to review, the presidential pardons absolve you and your team of crimes in the United States and its territories, not in foreign nations. Not that you will need pardons there since nearly every country on the planet wants you to work for them."

"Don't worry. I'm not planning to work for any other government again or any freelance either," Burns confirmed.

"Good. As you suggested, we reviewed Spain as a viable place for you and your team to live. Cratty took lead on the analysis and her team reviewed it with us," she reported.

"Just to reiterate, my team will move there permanently. By the coast, preferably," Burns clarified.

"Why?" Cratty asked, even though Davis knew she had already guessed the answer.

"David and Rebecca like the ocean, and Emma will be able to swim there," he said.

Smiling for the first time, Cratty clarified.

"I mean, 'Why relocate in another country?' not 'Why the coast?'"

Davis was surprised to see an actual smirk emerge on Burns's face that made his eyes soften in a way she never expected.

"I know what you meant. It was more of that humor, I'm afraid."

Okay... when did I lose control of this discussion.

Burns didn't skip a beat and went to the truth of the matter.

"I want my team to be safe and not have to look over their shoulders. That excludes the United States. If the Spanish government provides them a place to live with twenty-four-hour security as a result of their being seen as newfound 'national treasures,' I know where they are and that they're safe. You know where they are and can spin it as their being held under 'house arrest' or 'in detainment' in a foreign nation."

"No, Burns. Why won't you stay in Spain with them as well?" Cratty asked.

Davis watched in awe as Burns's smirk evolved into a smile, making creases at the corners of his eyes, which seemed to soften his entire face. At the same time, he absently started to scratch his hands again. Still, there was tension, and even Andersen stopped eating to take note.

So it's not me. He's making his point clear now.

In a calm, low voice, Burns seemed to choose his words with surgical exactness.

"Ms. Cratty. By them being in one place, you have leverage over me. My being somewhere in the world gives me some leverage over you. The field is leveled."

Cratty put down her coffee cup and sat up in the booth as she folded her hands together.

"Not really, Mr. Burns. You probably have copies of classified data that could make their way out into the world again," Cratty countered.

Well... I have to say she's right. Not a bad approach either: "good cop, bad cop."

Davis watched his reaction and knew that Andersen was doing the very same thing.

"Yes. But if you have my family, why would I do that?" Burns asked. Again, it was obvious to Davis that Burns was scratching his hands more and had scratched his head twice. *Nervous tick?* she wondered.

Cratty leaned back in her booth and considered Burns's answer.

"Okay," she finally said.

Davis could tell it wasn't really "Okay." She decided she might as well deal with this now since both Burns and Cratty were quiet.

"No, Steve... I think there is some residual anger between these two," she said. "Did you have issues in another life or something?"

Davis could see that Andersen understood what she was trying to do.

"You might be right there, Davis," Andersen added.

Yup. We're on the same page.

There was a moment of silence until Cratty picked up again.

"Mr. Burns, how would you feel about having, in addition to the Spanish Government's security team, either a private U.S. security team or a U.S. Government detail providing additional security for your family?"

Burns was quiet for a moment. While she was pleased that Cratty had gone there, she was sure it was going to be a deal breaker. Davis and Andersen had reviewed that option with Helms and Welch. It would be a big win if they got it because it would appear that the U.S. Government was keeping tabs on Burns, even if it were by proxy.

"Why?" Burns asked Cratty.

Instead of scratching his hands, Burns had taken to folding them together.

"The U.S. Government is able to have eyes on your team at all times and that's a great spin for us. A U.S. private or government team has a vested interest in nothing going wrong, making sure nothing happens to your family as a way of keeping you at bay. If something does go wrong, there are two governments with resources at our disposal. As U.S. citizens, your family is entitled to our protection if we are there watching them," Cratty concluded.

Davis liked Cratty's approach and thought it was excellent with a guy like Burns—*direct, honest. Refreshing.*

"Do you have anyone in mind?" he asked.

"Yes. Me and five others. All women," Cratty said as she passed Burns a note with their names.

"Dillon, Belben, Ramsey, Horowitz, and Fitzgerald," Burns read out loud.

"They're young, smart, and they were the ones who spent the most time trying to catch up to you," she explained.

"So you are offering me my former employer's cloak of protection?"

"No. I can't speak for the others, but I would resign my post and see if I could get a contract to be assigned to Spain as a private contractor. I hope that Diane Welch and Deputy Director Helms might have some pull in making that happen," she explained.

Time had slowed down for Davis as her jaw slackened; she was recovering while still in disbelief about how Cratty had got on the protection team to go to Spain, and Davis was lucky to work with Helms and Andersen. She had to hand it to Cratty. She was nothing short of brilliant.

No, not just the protection team; Cratty will be chief of the U.S. Security Team. Just brilliant.

Turning back to see whether Burns was buying the idea, she saw he was smiling over the proposal and was now fingering the necklace he wore around his neck. That act suddenly deflated Davis's angry emotions and filled her with sadness.

It was strange seeing her cross on Burns's neck. While she had given him the gold one, she had her mother's white gold necklace with a larger cross.

Funny. He touches it like I do. Kind of a touchstone or something reassuring.

"Okay. I agree to having my team be under U.S. supervision in conjunction with Spanish authorities, as long as it's Cratty and her choice team members. If there's anyone else you want to add, it has to come from both of you as well," Burns concluded as he pointed to Davis and Andersen.

Burns started to get up and was fiddling in his pockets.

Cratty took that moment of distraction to stick her tongue out at Davis.

In response, Davis mouthed the sentence, "You do suck" back at her.

Burns organized himself and started to leave.

You're not twelve, Davis. Get back to business.

"How will we get a hold of you to transport your team?"

"Don't worry. They're in place already," Burns said as he simply walked out of the diner.

Watching, Davis didn't know what to think, but she immediately became worried.

"'They're in place already'?" Cratty asked.

"He does that a lot," Davis responded.

"I know... I hate when Burns says something like that. It's very unsettling," Andersen said.

Davis called in to Helms to give him an update as Cratty called into her Bravo Team to get one as well.

After five minutes of her talking to Helms, he was informed by Gilmore that the posted agents had lost contact with Burns and that satellite surveillance they had borrowed from the CIA had just lost his image and heat signature. Gilmore reported that he looked like he was going to crest Trapelo Road and then he flickered out. Cratty confirmed that's when the Operations Centers, Alpha and Bravo, lost him too.

My God... Burns really is a ghost.

Davis and Andersen finished at the diner, dropped Cratty off at her car, and drove back to North Reading. Meanwhile, Helms called with an answer for Burns's disappearance. Janeson and "her boys" had figured out that the old state hospital had a series of underground tunnels that went from one building of the closed campus to the next.

Burns is still the master of planning, deception and evasion... he's still very dangerous.

~

Andersen was glad to be rid of Cratty. While it was the second time he had seen her and Davis together, it was apparent that whenever they were around each other, they both got competitive. He wondered whether Burns's scratching was a result of their tense interaction. The conversation walking into the North Reading Police Station mirrored the entire ride to Cratty's car and then to his office.

"Well, for someone who gets upset with conflict, it sure doesn't affect your appetite," Davis said to Andersen.

Anger. She always gets angry when she competes.

"You see? If we didn't have Cratty join the meeting like I suggested, you wouldn't be all pissed off now. You say mean things when you get angry, you know. That could explain why you're not married, Jillian."

"Wow. You really went there?"

"I'm just saying that if you're gay, straight, transgender or have any interest with being with someone, a little less competitiveness and hostility would be important."

Andersen had to admit that at six feet, Davis could be imposing, especially when she was angry, but he still enjoyed needling her. Her eyes had narrowed, jaw set and both hands were balled into fists. Before she could respond, one of Andersen's men approached him.

"Lieutenant? You have a couple of visitors. We didn't know what to do with them, so the CO had us put them in your office until you got back," Dempsey reported.

Forgetting about Davis's flushed face, glowering look, and

attempts to respond vehemently to his last remark, Andersen racked his brain trying to figure out who came by.

Who the hell could this be? Andersen wondered. *I've got no appointments.*

Not knowing who it might be, Andersen walked to his office, knowing Davis would follow until she had her say.

God, you're predictable.

If it were someone he did not want to talk, he could use her as an excuse.

When he opened the door, he could have fallen over in surprise. Instead, he stood in place with his hands on his hips and simply said nothing to feel the full visual effect of an unexpected sight. Andersen turned to Davis, whose anger transformed into shock.

Unbelievable! So this is what Burns meant when he said they were already in place.

David Caulfield stood up, turning at the sound of the door opening as Rebecca Littleton stood beside him with Emma peeking out from behind them.

Andersen took it all in as he made a mental checklist of all the demands they had made in exchange for their freedom.

All hard drives; Burns's crew in custody and leverage to keep him in check; Spain's willingness to host them with Cratty and her team watching; and the perfect spin for the papers... a complete win. Well, nearly complete. Burns is still out there, somewhere.

Slowly approaching the family to make sure it was not an illusion, Andersen finally spoke. "Well... speak of the devil and he shall appear."

David stood next to the conference room table and extended a handshake to Andersen. He took his hand firmly and found himself noticing that something was different about him, but he wasn't quite sure what it was. The handshake was strong but his stature, though still muscular was tired.

It's something... something different about him. He looks good, but I think he's looks older for some reason.

"Are you tanned, David?"

"I hate to admit it, but yes." David turned to introduce his wife, Becky, and his daughter, Emma.

Cautiously, Rebecca confirmed remembering Andersen. "We had the pleasure of meeting last week or so... I was not at my best."

She looked significantly better than he remembered—more color in her face, less tense, and presently with blonde hair.

"Yes... you seemed under the weather then, but you look much better," Andersen commented.

So how do you say, "Gee, you look better after killing four people?" He found himself angry and tried to focus on something else.

Still, though, she also didn't look well, like David. *Tired? Guilt? Fatigue?*

Andersen turned to introduce Davis to all three since Davis had actually never met any of them. It had to be weird for her to hear all these stories and not meet the players, he thought. After the usual handshakes, Emma took it upon herself to ask her own questions to Davis.

"Uncle Alex told me you held Aunt Sammy when she died. Did it hurt?" Emma's face scrunched up a bit, anticipating the pain.

Jesus...

Andersen watched Emma and remembered his own little girl's questions about death and pain. He was thrilled he was not asked, remembering how badly he had explained death to his own daughter, resulting in his wife needing to step in and undo the damage. He was impressed with Davis's fielding of the question. For all her training in covert operations and counter-terrorism, she stepped right into the girl's question. Dropping down to her knee so she could be close to eye level, Davis gave the best answer possible, Andersen thought.

"I held your aunt when she passed away, honey. I was there with her and your uncle. We all... prayed together," she said.

Jesus... I always knew you had a mushy heart. I always knew it, Andersen thought. In moments like these, Davis reminded him of his sister at times. *More like Darlene than Terry,* he thought.

How she was keeping her eyes from filling up was beyond him.

Emma shifted rapidly to another subject as many children her age do.

"Uncle Alex showed me the chain you gave him, the one Aunty held? It was pretty. Where did you get it?" she asked.

Andersen noticed that Davis was taking her time with the answer.

"Well... it was a gift from my mother when she died. She went to church all the time, and she gave me two crosses, a gold and a silver one. Well... I wished I could have helped more..."

Oh, Jesus... there's the story. Your mother's cross?

He felt more sadness than he expected, not knowing at the time the significance of this act.

"You did, though! Uncle Alex said you were shot trying to help her... He is so sad, though... So are we. I'm really sad."

Standing as still as possible, so as not to draw attention to himself in case the girl asked him a question, Andersen saw that Davis was finally at a loss for words. *How do you respond to this?*

"I wish I got the bad guy who shot her, honey," Davis said.

"Don't worry! Uncle Alex found the bad guy, and Mom killed him. Uncle Alex told me you all helped get him!" Emma said proudly as she held onto Rebecca.

Andersen found himself very mixed about condoning violence, and at the same time, he respected justice. He was having a hard time justifying the death of federal agents for the death of a loved one. Rebecca looked uncomfortable, but she didn't seem to show any emotion, positive or negative.

But then we took away their lives, forced them into hiding while a federal agency was planning on killing them. Not to mention the murders of Caulfield's wife and Samantha Littleton. And the untold numbers of others killed, all for national security. Maybe Caulfield was right after all—we started it.

"That's right, Emma. This is one of those rare times when we have to hurt someone to protect our family," David explained.

"Yes...'A time to kill, and a time to heal; a time to break down, and a time to build up...'" Emma recited excitedly.

"And what are we doing now?" David asked her.

"We are healing and building up!"

Andersen had a flashback to that very verse back in May when he and David had been in Interrogation Room 8. *So, this is Emma... the little one who was your only weakness,* Andersen remembered. *I can see why you went to great lengths to protect her.*

"Excellent! Now maybe one of Mr. Andersen's men can get you something special from the machine," David offered.

Interrupting, Davis stepped in and took Emma's hand to lead her away with Rebecca close behind.

"Now... why don't me and your mom find something in the machine. I know the best machine in this whole building," she suggested.

"Sounds great to me," Rebecca said.

"Yes!" Emma said eagerly.

Andersen watched as the women left.

Suddenly alone and at a loss what to say, Andersen jumped to a safe subject.

"She is a cutie," he commented.

As David retrieved his chair to sit back down, he smiled.

"Yes. It's a good thing, too. She never puts anything away, which can prove a hazard for me at times. Still though, she's everything to me."

"I can see why."

Taking the chair opposite David, Andersen couldn't help but keep thinking what was different about him.

"Well... just like old times," he said.

David sat back in his chair across from him and seemed to be taking a moment to say something.

"Yes. Minus the deception, cyberattacks, assault on federal employees, destruction of public and private property, theft of classified data and a hundred other charges at a local, state, national and international level," David responded.

Grudgingly, Andersen found himself smiling a bit. Still, he could tell there was something more by the way David folded his hands yet moved his fingers.

David was quiet for a moment and then added, "Just for the record, I felt bad deceiving you."

Andersen wanted to challenge David with, *"You can't just apologize for all that and think we're okay."* Problem was, Andersen found himself understanding David's motivation, and, worse, he was finding it very difficult to disagree with his actions.

"You did this all to protect Emma, didn't you?" Andersen asked.

A darkness seemed to come over him, similar to the last time Andersen likened his actions to domestic terrorism. As David responded, he could also see his darkness subtly change to more sadness than anger.

"Emma, Becky, Sam, and even Alex. My country took one life away from me. Snuffed it out. They weren't going to take another. I just wish Samantha could have made it. She was just becoming happy... Alex too..." David trailed off, looking away toward the office window.

Andersen had often wondered whether if the same thing happened to him, he would be able to do what David did. If the government killed Laura and his three children, would he simply wait to die or take the fight to those responsible?

I just don't know if I could do nothing. I'd have to do something. I can't imagine just sitting back and letting it all go on and not do anything.

"Yes," Andersen replied. As both men sat in silence, Andersen was about to ask a question, but David beat him to it.

"Lieutenant? How many people were killed at my home in Kea?"

So that's why you look like shit. You pushed the button to set the house to explode. Burns couldn't have done it remotely. It would have to be set at the home.

"Sixteen," was Andersen's short answer.

Andersen watched as a myriad of emotions flashed across David Caulfield's face. While still dark, they were more deep and pained than Andersen expected.

"Damn... I know there are no words to convey what I have done..." David started. He choked up, took in a deep breath, and started again.

"There's nothing I can say or possibly do to take back what I've done. I wish I could. It's a line I crossed that I'll never recover from." David simply stopped as he rubbed tears in his eyes.

What else can you say? "Sorry I killed sixteen people just doing their job?"

"I don't know what to tell you, David," was all Andersen could think of.

Silence hung heavily in the air, so Andersen decided to ask his original question.

"So, when you picked the name 'Coleridge' were you consciously aware of the symbolism of 'The Rime of the Ancient Mariner' or was it all coincidence?"

It may have been a distraction, but it was a genuine question Andersen wanted to know. He had reread the dramatic poem after they had met, and he remembered both the symbolism and form.

David finished rubbing his eyes, and his nose seemed to be a little more congested when he next spoke.

"Ironic that you ask a question about a story that is about change and burdens. But to answer the question with a question, have you ever known me to be a person of 'coincidence'?" David replied.

Well... you gotta point there.

"No... not really," Andersen answered.

It was true. Everything Caulfield, Burns, and the Littletons had done was purposeful.

I guess when you're being hunted for years and your only viable solution is to fight back, you either become a predator or die.

Andersen got up and went to his desk to make the necessary calls to secure protection and transportation for his new charges.

"Want some coffee? It's going to be a while. We're going to need to find a safe house, get new documentation, mobilize Cratty and her team to relocate... It's going to be a while."

"It's all right. I've got time," he said.

Andersen heard nothing but sadness in his voice.

It's gotta be difficult being a person who helps people for a living and then to change into someone who kills. Even in defense. It still has to be hard for someone never trained for that.

Andersen started to dial Helms's number.

"Wait till Helms hears about this."

David seemed to come back to the conversation.

"Helms?" he asked.

Andersen realized David never met the man before.

"Let's just say he's the guy who put our team together as a way to bring you in from the cold. It would have worked if Burns's old team didn't jump in to screw things up," he explained as he waited for Helms to pick up.

Andersen found himself still pissed from the mess the Operations Center had made at their first meeting in Boston.

"Yes... they do have a way of screwing up people's lives and walking away," David said reflectively.

That one has meaning, Andersen thought. *Yeah, that sounded like anger.*

"Well, you'll like Helms. He gets pissed when there's an injustice. And right now, he's on a search for the man behind Webber, the man at the top," Andersen offered. He was about to say more but then Helms got on the line.

Andersen did notice a slight smile on David's face; he felt nervous since the smile didn't look pleasant.

What are you planning now?

~

Helms was "surprised" but not "shocked" when Andersen gave him the news of Burns's family showing up at the police station. He did appreciate the irony of David Caulfield "returning to the scene of the crime," so to speak.

Once he was able to reorganize work flow, he had Janeson, Gilmore, Johnson and the new guy, Martin, assist with organizing Cratty's group and at the same time pull Spain in the loop and find temporary accommodations for their guests.

Relieved to get the external drive back, Helms was happy to get Burns and his crew out of the U.S. where so many people saw them as terrorists, particularly one man who, throughout the entire Foreign Intelligence Agency nightmare, had remained a specter, a wraith.

So, Mr. Eric Daniels... where are you in all this shit? Where have you vanished to?

Much to his surprise, Janeson and her team were coming up with precious little on who Daniels was and where he was now. Further, the guy had set up corporate shell after corporate shell, which made finding a money trail next to impossible. While Helms involved the IRS, he was concerned that a man who could do the things Daniels did, creating an empire to carry out those deeds on a global scale, was not the kind simply to give up. It didn't take much convincing to get Welch on board. She was heading to Washington D.C. to head up the investigation of the entire agency.

Okay. If the IRS got Capone, I'm sure they can locate Daniels. There's a whole lot of money missing and untaxed for that matter. The IRS hates untaxed money.

For now, though, he needed to focus on his new charges' safety. At least, he could put his hand on that one.

Epilogue

"Igne natura renovator integra" – *"Through fire, nature is reborn whole"*

Becky was taking a break from baking as she sat on the veranda watching Emma and a friend run around the courtyard. She was glad the sun was setting since it got very hot at noon, when it was the most difficult to get Emma to settle down and stay inside. Sipping cold water and still in her flour-caked apron, she started counting back how many months she had been in their new home. It was easier to think with every passing day.

It's been seventeen or eighteen months, Becky thought, truly impressed with how things had changed since their arrival. Rarely did she smile when she thought of her childhood, being poor and living in the same, rented house for so many years. As a child, she had been sure she would never get out of the town, let alone see places outside of the United States. Kea was the first place, but they were in hiding then. But now, under the watchful eye of two governments, it took a while to get used to living a normal life as an expatriate family in a foreign land.

Living as celebrities in the sun-drenched town of Torrox Costa, Spain was simply over the top. Still, Becky was feeling as if she were now home. The Spanish people had taken them in as "the family who repelled the oppressive, United States Government."

She wished her motivation to expose the U.S. had been all for truth, but it was for self-preservation and vengeance. Feeling a wave of tearfulness, Becky took another sip and watched Emma smiling as she chased another little girl around the well.

As the breeze moved warm air around, she caught Cratty talking to Ramsey and Dillon as they walked to the garage. Now that the sun had truly bleached Cratty's longer hair, Becky had taken to thinking of her as "blonde," which ran contrary to her serious, taciturn disposition. Still, Cratty always walked with purpose, flanked by two women listening intently at the moment. Becky smiled at the thought of just calling her "Blondie" from now on. She knew Cratty was talking to them about their present security updates.

While their home was a series of one large and four smaller structures arranged in a square with the courtyard and walled sections, there was a great degree of privacy but also a great need to cover all entry points. That meant that both Cratty's team and the Spanish team had to work closely together.

There was one good point, though, about being in the biggest compound in a small town. Similar to Kea, strangers stood out. At the same time, the town was filled with friendly natives, which complicated providing a complete blanket of safety.

Turning back to where she first saw Cratty emerge, Horowitz and Fitzgerald waved to her as they walked their perimeter. Smiling and waving back, Becky had come to like these two women in particular. *They're like sisters,* she often thought. *They finish each other's sentences and argue like crazy.* She sighed as she thought of Samantha again. While she had been feeling better, Samantha's death still felt raw and her life unfinished. Becky forced her thoughts to more positive thinking, which brought her to feeling happy for David, who now worked with children as a teacher. While his demeanor and energy had improved because of his new vocation, he was not entirely free from pain. Becky knew his role in killing the assault team on Kea weighed heavily on him. She understood the feeling too well. For her, killing the man who had killed her sister was not gratifying, but it seemed justified to her. For David, he seemed to have no justification, even though she saw it differently.

If we were there, they would have killed us in a heartbeat and not thought anything of it. My little girl would be without parents or worse.
She pushed the dark thoughts out of what *could* have happened.

Still, she could not convince him that it was not his fault. David's commitment to Emma and now other children seemed to ease his guilt. Maybe it was a simple distraction, but it kept him from being depressed. For Emma, the new location meant more children to play with all the time. Both Becky and David had to acclimate Emma to start doing what "normal children" do, such as go to school. Emma's education and religious upbringing were far from normal, requiring her to attend school, classes and even Sunday school. Ever since Samantha's death, Becky became a bit obsessive about Emma's spiritual side. While it took Emma a while to navigate this change, in the end, she blossomed in school.

Looking at her watch, she noted she had ten more minutes before she took the pie out of the oven. Pushing her chair back, she put her feet up on the rail and indulged in a relaxing moment. *It wasn't always like this,* she thought.

As she thought back, her own transition was very difficult. Months ago, the loss of her sister left her feeling empty, sad, and distant from everyone for several months. At times, she would sit in the bathroom, door locked, and not wanting to come out as she wept. It was the only time in her life her appetite completely vanished, leaving her severely underweight. After about nine months, Becky found herself aimlessly wandering the compound like a ghost since Emma and David were both at school. While looking out a window, a very unexpected situation pulled her out of her melancholia.

While three of Cratty's detail were on patrol with the Spanish counterparts, Cratty herself was attempting to show two of her team members how to advance effectively on a target ahead while shooting an automatic assault weapon.

As the compound's courtyard near the back was secluded and enclosed by stone walls, it made for a natural shooting range with life-size targets arranged with varying degrees of visibility. When she first saw the range, her thoughts went back to when she was in hiding in Rhode Island.

How many times did we have to make our own shooting scenarios and layouts?

As Becky peered through the back window, it was easy to see one woman's stride was too long, and she was self-conscious of her footing rather than the target while the other woman's shoulders were too taut.

Jesus. They're too nervous. They need to relax and get comfortable with the weapon first.

As if to reinforce Becky's thoughts, she watched Cratty rubbing her temples and shaking her head as she shouted out her dismay and annoyance.

"Damn it, people! Too much time flying consoles and social media and not enough time on the range. And Dillon! Stop thinking about Jackson! If I knew you were going to be lovesick, I would have left you back in New York!"

The woman called Dillon seemed to smile and say something to Cratty.

From Becky's point of view, it was easy to see that whatever was said provoked Cratty as her eyes widened in disbelief. Closing the distance between them, Cratty jabbed her index finger suddenly toward Dillon's chest and she continued her yelling.

"It's a good thing you got skills, *Christine*, and you're lucky I'm in a good mood! I swear if Jackson doesn't ask you to marry him by next month, I'll make him wish he had."

As Becky walked downstairs, she wondered what Cratty was like in a bad mood.

By the time she covered the distance to talk to Cratty, they were setting up with live ammunition to attempt the drill again. Becky liked Cratty, but she rarely spoke to her. It was the first time she had something to say, and it was in Cratty's field.

I wonder how she's going to take to a civilian giving her advice... granted a civilian trained by Alex Burns with years of my own field experience.

It was a brief two minutes, and much to her surprise, Cratty relayed the advice directly to her team to try again.

They did it worse than before.

"Sorry, Ms. Littleton, but my team seem to be visual learners, and the tall one seems to be distracted. Maybe you could demonstrate," she suggested.

Frustrated that they couldn't replicate her advice, Becky grabbed an unused automatic rifle, ear protection, glasses and set herself up as the targets were reset. Burns's instruction and years of practice came together like breathing, and she hit every target as she methodically advanced. When she finished as all three watched, she had more to add.

"Depending on capacity, you want to be able to use your sidearm as effectively as a rifle. There may be times you need to drop the rifle and get your sidearm out rapidly to ensure your targets are down. Stopping power in the handgun is just as important as it is with a rifle. Grouping is the other key piece, but to reiterate, you need to keep cheek-to-shoulder as you walk and fire. As you already know the largest target, the chest, is the primary focus."

As Becky was talking, she was reloading the weapon with another clip and then she started to look around for a sidearm.

"Take mine. Dillon, set the targets up again and put up three more. Ms. Littleton? Do you want to demonstrate using both?"

Becky smiled as she prepared herself. She was going to demonstrate, anyway.

Two hours vanished as she found herself more animated than she had been in months. Once the session was over she was surprised how sad she felt that the demonstration was over. Cratty pulled her aside and changed her life.

"Ms. Littleton, what I'm about to suggest is unorthodox and not customary practice for security, but let me ask you anyway. Could you give me a hand in some of the instruction in firearms?"

At that time, it was such a simple question, she thought. It did make some sense. Years on the run, training with Burns, practice on her own and actual "field experience" made her a perfect assistant, not expert but a knowledgeable assistant.

"What do you need help in?" she asked.

Cratty shook her head as they both started to walk to the building that held much of the team's ammunition, weapons, and was their place of residency.

"Tons. They need to know and be proficient at evasion and surveillance, use of semi-automatic and fully automatic assault rifles, as well as use of long-range weapons, such as for sniping."

Funny. I killed your boss with the last one, Becky thought. *Though I hear you didn't lose sleep over it. I knew I liked you.*

"Well, what do you think? I thoroughly get it if you don't want to do it," Cratty said.

"I'm sorry. I was distracted. Yes. I would like to do it. But I want to learn stuff too," Becky countered.

Cratty looked askance at her for a moment before answering.

"Sure. What do you want to know? We don't do explosives, rockets or high-tech assault, though." Cratty's response might have been in humor but Becky missed it.

"No. I know a lot about that stuff. More edged weapons and close quarter combat. That's what I want to know," Becky responded in a matter-of-fact fashion.

Cratty's face revealed that her joke about explosives, rockets, and high-tech assault such as cyberattacks, was misplaced since she was obviously good at those things via Burns's tutelage. Becky did note she recovered fast.

"Sure. Sounds like a plan."

Becky smiled and handed Cratty the eye and ear protection for storage as she retreated to her residence side of the compound.

"See you at 0700 for a run if you're up for it," Cratty offered.

Without turning back, Becky gave a wave of her hand and her answer.

"See you then."

She felt a little calmer. A little better back then, just like she felt now. Suddenly, she realized that ten minutes had passed and she had to get the pie out. Standing and stretching her back, she waved at Emma as she blew a kiss to her.

"Things are so much better," Becky said to herself.

~

As David tilted his ears in the dance floor's direction, he found himself feeling happy to hear a lot of children's voices around him. Much to

Emma's chagrin, she did enjoy that she was finally baptized at seven years old, more out of Becky's insistence than choice.

I'm just happy she seems happier, David thought. *Thank God for Cratty and her team.*

Three months prior, he had come home to his favorite meal and a decidedly happier woman. While it had been hard for him, it was very hard for Becky.

Poor thing. She lost her family too. Just like me.

During dinner that night, Becky told David about Cratty's proposal, and while initially he had concerns it was evident she was happier to be doing something. For the last three months, it seemed that she had moved from being a ghost to being part of a family and a team, again.

David drew in the smells of food wafting out from the church's kitchens. He was also happy that today Emma was baptized in the Catholic religion even though she was fundamentally opposed to formal religious training since she would be the only child standing at her own baptism. But it was an opportunity to have a party, for her to wear a white dress, and to have "everyone over." There was some pain for Emma as "Uncle Alex" had to let her know he was too far away and couldn't be there.

Emma is a forgiving soul.

The service was held in the courtyard of the local, Moorish-looking church. The timing was the last Sunday prior to Christmas, which correlated with the annual *Migas Fiesta.* Timing was everything. Since it was a large public event, security was tight with Cratty's team and her Spanish counterparts on full alert.

David found himself tearful at the service. Especially poignant was the moment when prayers were said for the souls of loved ones and Samantha's name was read first. Still, the event was moving and joyous.

While he could drink in the sounds and smells, he truly missed not being able to see Emma in her white gown. He found himself tearing up again.

My God! When did you become such an emotional wreck?

With a myriad of security creating different levels of containment, it was easy for him to tell that the dance floor was now moving as old and new friends began to dance, drink and celebrate. David could hear Becky's laughter from across the floor.

It's nice to hear that laugh again. She must be having a beer at the bar with Cratty, David concluded.

He had been told that Dillon and Ramsey were coordinating the actual details since Cratty was "a guest" at Becky's insistence. *At least she has a friend. It's not Samantha, but it's somebody.*

David felt his hand being pulled as he was grabbed by Emma.

"Let's dance," she said excitedly.

Emma and David's dancing was a long standing ritual that dated back to when she was first able to walk. It was custom to do it every night before bed. Becky very rarely would dance, but he absolutely loved the time with Emma. He knew he was a terrible dancer, but true to form, Emma didn't care. What was different this time, in addition to other families celebrating and live music, was that Emma had her smartphone. Typically, the phone was banned from dinner on. Since it wasn't dinner at home, Emma was not far from her phone when it chimed. David stopped his movements and knew he had successfully given her the expression of "Really?"

"Sorry," she said as she answered the phone.

I thought texting was the only thing those phones did, he thought as he took out a handkerchief to wipe his brow.

"Hello?" Emma said in her maturing voice. Then, a moment later, there was the squeal of a little girl.

"Uncle Alex!" she exclaimed. The music continued playing as Emma and David moved off the dance floor to the far side of the courtyard. From David's calculation, he had to be on the other side from where Becky and Cratty were sitting.

Figures. Just me and no one else to eavesdrop.

David did his best to try to remember everything he heard from his side. *Undoubtedly, Cratty and everyone is going to want a two-hour briefing on what Alex had to say,* he mourned. David patiently listened and mentally logged everything Emma said, ranging from her describing the ceremony and what the priest said to what was more interesting to David.

"You're right, Uncle Alex. That was a beautiful prayer for Aunt Sammy," she responded.

David focused on Emma's voice.

You gotta be kidding me. He heard the ceremony? Unbelievable. That means the place was bugged, and he is either here or was here.

"I know! Mom and Dad found this beautiful cross... yes, it is white gold. Wait a minute? How did you see that? Were you here again?" Emma giggled.

Yeah, Alex? How did you know unless you were right here? How could you hear the prayer in the courtyard where the acoustics are terrible?

David lost track and then refocused on Emma's side of the conversation as it seemed to come to a close.

"I'll definitely look at your pictures, Uncle Alex. I love you so much... I'm happy you were here, too. Love you!" she said.

Then, the conversation ended.

Probably under three minutes. No time for a trace or location via tower or satellite. Perfectly done, as always.

David could hear Emma clicking through her phone, looking at pictures. As he knelt to hold her from behind, he asked her to describe what she saw. From Emma's rapid description, there was an array of shots: pictures of guests, the priest, and parts of the service, Emma in her dress holding her new cross, pictures of him, Becky, Cratty, and "the other girls" on Cratty's team, a few pictures of the other guards "hanging out," and some "mistake" shots of corridors, front and back gate, and "even our house."

David smiled. Another person would have been seriously unnerved, he knew, but this was his way of looking after his family.

Looks like we need serious improvement on our security. There's going to be hell for this.

As David got up, he felt his knees creak a bit and then his own cell phone vibrated in his pocket. He knew who it was, and he knew he probably only had three minutes.

"Honey, could you go show Mum your pictures and let her know Uncle Alex called? I have to take this call," he asked. David felt and found his "emergency phone." It was the very first they had used from when Burns had given it to him to pass along to Samantha as "their lifeline."

So many years ago. A lifetime or so.

Without even saying a greeting, David had to ask the question.

"Do you have any idea how pissed you just made Cratty and Ramsey? You know I have to live with them?" he said in a patient, calm fashion so as not to draw attention to himself.

"They have to get better at timing their rounds and not in such a predictable fashion. To Cratty's credit, her team was the most difficult to circumnavigate. You might as well move to the city and drop the Spanish team. How are you by the way?" Burns asked.

Well, that is a loaded question.

"Pretty good. I love teaching. And now that you've shown up the security details, Cratty will be reinvesting their lives for the next decade to beat you when Emma's Confirmation comes," David surmised.

"Good. I give people reason to live," Burns added. Then there was some silence.

David let the silence sit for a few seconds to see whether he wanted to say something more. He did.

"David. I am going to be gone a while. Could be a couple of months to about a year or so."

David was caught off-guard for a moment.

Why would he just leave us when he showed weaknesses in the security? Then David had another thought: *Is his being close to us putting us in danger?* David had to find out.

"I am guessing it's either for some kind of mission or safety."

"A combination of both. The closer I am to you, the bigger the target you all become," he confirmed.

"Is it your old boss?"

There was a pause before Burns answered.

"If I were him and lost everything, I would be pissed and want either to get it back or to make someone pay. Sound familiar?"

Wow. Talk about role reversals. Now the guy who targeted us is being targeted and is losing everything and is pissed.

"If I'm wrong, I can continue with the life I'm living and continue to piece together more stuff with my new therapist."

Burns's last sentence brought David back to the conversation.

"So how is the therapy going? Any new insights?"

"Yes. Apparently, I've missed cues of people attempting to socialize with me and possibly flirting. My biggest complaint is that she doesn't know how to use silence and likes to answer her own questions. But to her credit, she thinks I have some kind of social phobia or social delays. I may have to give her some clarity to my background," Burns added.

David had to chuckle.

"Yeah... it might be helpful if she had some details to be more useful."

Burns was quiet.

"So, we will see you when?" David asked.

"Possibly a couple of months. But you have this phone if anything happens. Just be on guard. I trust Cratty and her team, but they are not getting much help from the Spanish team and their coverage area is too big for their team. I'm not sure how they can improve it either."

I've never heard such uncertainty in his voice. This has to be big.

Burns continued, "If nothing comes of my fears, then at least I'll get a jump on becoming more 'normal,' whatever that is now. I'm looking forward to spending more time with you."

David took his time to respond.

"Well, Alex, that's why you have family. You take care of business and let us know what we can do to help. We're your family. That's how it usually works."

"Speaking of family," Burns said slowly, "thank you for finding Samantha's final resting place. She never would have believed it if she saw it herself. It's... impressive. More than I ever imagined."

David's smile was bitter sweet recalling his efforts in finding and remotely renovating an abandoned, dilapidated mausoleum in one of the oldest cemeteries near Cumberland Hill, Rhode Island, their happiest time as a family together. David wasn't sure how Burns was going to respond, especially since he took the liberty of purchasing a family plot of four burial chambers together.

"As morbid as it may seem, there are families that buy plots together. It's normal in some customs, even expected," David said.

I hope not to fill them soon, David sadly thought. *Some day but not soon...*

"Yeah... I am trying to learn this 'normal' thing. Thank you... Well, I gotta run. I'll call you in a bit."

"Take care, Alex."

"You too, David. Say hello to Becky for me."

"Will do."

Burns clicked off and David slowly closed the phone.

That might have been more like four minutes rather than three, David guessed.

While he was happy about the prospect of Burns's visiting, he planned to wait to tell Becky and Emma until it was confirmed.

Damn it. Something big is brewing and Alex wants to keep us at arms' length. I'll have to tell Becky, and she can work this out with Denise.

David tried to take a moment to enjoy the music and the occasion. It was his only way to stop thinking about danger everywhere.

Then he heard Denise Cratty approaching while speaking in a low but clearly harsh tone to someone:

"...pictures of entranceways and hallways in and out of the church and courtyard. He has pictures of the residences and weak points. Twenty-eight pictures in all, mostly within twenty feet, and eight shots were from elevated positions with a telephoto-zoom lens from six hundred yards or more. Oh, and in addition, he got a nice picture of your ass, Dillon, while you were looking under someone's car. So, find Ramsey and your counterparts and at least try to find him. The last picture was time-indexed fifteen minutes ago."

David heard a phone click off and then he heard Cratty exhale in disgust.

"Goddamn it," she said under her breath and walked away.

David let his head drop, knowing Cratty was going to be a bear for the next several months.

I knew there would be hell to pay for this.

Becky had clearly followed her and spoke next.

"He's still the master of counter-espionage and surveillance, isn't he?" she casually commented.

David could smell alcohol on her breath as she leaned into him to hold his arm. David felt a small but compact bump under her left arm affixed to her torso.

"Becky? Are you wearing a waist jacket still?" he asked.

He could feel Becky stiffen a little bit, and her response was telling. It was more coy than informational. A dead giveaway that she thought she might have done something wrong.

"Ah... yes," she responded.

"I see. So I take it you are armed? Are we back to concealed weapons again? Is this an indication that you're feeling more like your old self?"

It was quiet for a moment and then he got an unusual response.

"Yes. Do you know I love you?" she asked.

Well, that is one of the most unusual associations I have ever heard.

"Yes. Do you know I love you?"

Becky moved in closer to kiss him gently.

"Yes," David heard her say.

It's a pretty good day.

~

Eric Daniels was taking a moment to appreciate the sunset from his apartment in Houston, Texas. It had been a grueling week, and he was just taking a break from all the legal advice, debriefings and planning he had been subjected to for the last two years. His apartment was a very simple, two-bedroom apartment he had rented nearly thirty years ago when he spent more time in Texas. The area was rundown back then, but in the last ten years, the cheap land and close location to the city had made it a perfect place for renovation and new money. He enjoyed the simplicity of the stainless steel, marble, and hardwood design that made his very simple but functional furniture work well. It would be safe to say that the best description for his home was Spartan with one major exception being his large collection of books. When his apartment was renovated several years ago, he had spent an inordinate amount of money for floor-to-ceiling built-in bookcases on every available wall possible. American history, European literature, classical art, and black-and-white photography, and military strategy books filled his collection. His second bedroom was his office, which he had set up himself with the latest technology for fast processing and artificial intelligence. What he loved most about it was that no one from his public life knew where his home was. With no wife, significant other or children, privacy was possible, but difficult. Ever since his Operations Center had become a private entity, and he was asked to be chairman, this place was his last bastion, his last place to find peace.

And now I have to move, he thought bitterly. He turned away from his view to continue packing his files, tablets, and portable hardware. His chosen profession was all about the safety and security of the United States. He had spent thirty-five years putting together a global organization that protected the interests of his country.

They're giving all the secrets away. They've torn down the last fire wall against terrorism, and now they're all fighting for who will be the master spy agency. Will it be the CIA? Probably the FBI, if Helms has anything to do with it. Unbelievable.

He returned his attention to stripping his hard drive of the second of four desktop computers. A big regret was not transitioning to computer sticks. He was doubtful of them in the past but was wishing he had spent more time investigating and using them.

"Shame I can't take the whole units," he said to himself. He had to make sure that at least his private files were not available for public consumption. Traveling light would be critical.

He was still in the same suit he had worn forty-eight hours ago in the last Senate hearing. With his jacket thrown on the chair and his sleeves rolled up, he had been hard at work collecting key data, supplies, and materiel for his long drive to Canada. If the Bureau figured out where his apartment was, it would probably think he would cross the border into Mexico.

Pretty amateur move. Do they think I've been out of the field so long that I forgot how to throw people off?

Daniels was struggling a bit with the third hard drive as he recounted the injustice of it all.

Sure. The world sees all the stuff about China, Spain, Burns. But do they see the files on Heathrow? Paris? The terrorists' plans to bomb the Golden Gate Bridge and Hoover Dam? Did the Bureau or the CIA thwart those attacks? How many lives saved there? How can they really be pissed off about North Korea? No. Finally the clips of the hard drive released the drive itself. He took a moment to straighten his back and take a drink of bottled water before working on the fourth desktop.

Well, at least I don't have to sit in front of those pompous asshole senators.

Daniels took a moment to run down his task list. He had long since cross-shredded all hard files and had finished packing two tote bags to carry his clothes, computer material and laptop, and some easy food for eating while driving. When the last hard drive was released, he started a new process of putting in new hard drives that had minimal data. The plan would be simple: put the desktops back together and then run an erase software program to give the impression of both sloppiness and the hope for retrieving some data.

"That should keep the their technicians busy for a while. The more time the better."

Daniels entered his master bedroom next and found his casual clothes to wear for his cross-country trek north. Comfort would be critical. Nothing to stand out either.

He took a moment to look at his passport that held his new identity.

"Paul Campbell," he said aloud.

Not bad, he thought. *Though, I could lose some more weight.*

He had been working out much more since the hearings as well as losing weight. He was very pleased to have lost forty pounds in two years and to have regained muscle tone, but all this work was meant for one thing.

"Where are you, Burns?" he asked out loud as he closed his new passport and driver's license. He pulled some more clothes together and began another quick look around for anything he might have missed. As he scanned, he continued his persistence in recalling how everything had fallen apart since Burns had reemerged from the dead and created such hell on May second so many years ago.

You know, I get why Caulfield and the Littleton sisters are pissed off. I get that. I can see that the President, Helms, and Welch are just misguided and shortsighted. I can even understand why Davis and Cratty jumped teams. They suck, but I can see why. But you, Burns? You get fucking religion, and all of a sudden, you're better than all of us and need to get back at us? Over a therapist? Over a hooker? You could have just come in. What were you thinking?

Daniels forced himself to stop thinking about Burns so he could focus on his task of finishing up his cleaning. Every time he thought of what his colleague had done to him, he just got angrier. Daniels put his bags in front of the door and looked back into the private home he'd had for three decades. He was genuinely sad.

I'm going to miss my books.

As he put his hand on the doorknob, he had a pang of sentiment that stalled him from exiting. He worried for a moment because the last time he'd had a sentimental moment, he had allowed Burns to live and get treatment with the hope of him returning to the fold.

No act of kindness will go unpunished, he thought.

Still, Daniels decided to indulge himself; he returned to his bookcase to retrieve one book. It took him just a minute to find the heavy, ancient book. He opened it to a page that had a ribbon bookmark set and read the section.

He smiled at what he read as he calculated the odds of randomly reading this particular passage when he was leaving for another part of his life that he was sure would intersect with Burns.

"I dare damnation. To this point I stand,
That both the worlds, I give to negligence,
Let come what comes; only I'll be revenged..."

He reread the passage again and enjoyed how Shakespeare's *Hamlet* was simply timeless. He closed the book and was glad he had decided to take it with him.

Daniels pulled all his belongings together and marched down the corridor that would take him to the apartment complex's garage.

He had spent months redirecting money and resources from corporate shell to shell so he could have a safety net for this very day that he had hoped would never come. He had more money and securities to live in comfort for many lifetimes. Problem was, every intelligence agency in the world would be looking for him. So instead of simply hiding, he decided to take a page from his old colleague Burns's playbook.

Why run and hide when you can wait, plan, and attack?

Before all of his intelligence sources dried up and all of his official avenues disappeared, he did find Burns's Achilles heel.

Emma in Spain and her half-sister in Boston. Just perfect, he thought as he closed the SUV's door and opened the driver's side.

Daniels took a deep breath while adjusting his mirrors. His plan was simple but had some major flaws. He would have to use all his illegitimate resources to get the job done and get Burns out from hiding. These people were far from reliable, and he didn't like using children for bait, but he was desperate to make things equal.

He started the SUV and began his new journey. His thoughts traveled back at everything he had lost, namely his apartment, his agency, his colleagues, his life, and his respect.

And yet, life seems so much simpler now.

Still his mind felt his anger boil from within.

All was well until you betrayed me, Burns. Thinking of the hundreds of books he had left behind because of Burns, another quote came to mind:

"'*Never can true reconcilement grow where wounds of deadly hate have pierced so deep...*' Milton? ' Paradise Lost?"

Daniels found himself sitting at a red light.

"Where are you, Burns?" he said out loud as he left his former life behind.

~

Welch was rubbing her feet as she sat in her D.C. suite with Thomas "Nine" Williams and Dan "Ice" Maddox. For the last eighteen months, both men had been working with her on the investigation of the Foreign Intelligence Agency. It had been a long day in Washington of reviewing more case files and interviewing more former staff of the now infamous agency. But the key person of interest, Eric I. Daniels, was MIA for a week. Missing a Senate Hearing was nothing to be trifled with, and that's what worried her.

If he blew this off, that means he doesn't care, and that makes him very dangerous.

The only comforting thought was that she knew Helms and Andersen obsessed more than she did and they were looking into a number of leads.

While still rubbing her feet, she watched Nine and Ice pacing the suite like caged panthers looking for anything to eat. She was not surprised that both men were still walking around the suite, looking out the window, with surveillance top of mind. They had done it a dozen times today. A slight increase after hearing how Burns slipped through all the security, Cratty's in particular, last month. She took it as a warning about security that if Burns could do it, so could someone just as determined. Now with the chairman missing, it pushed Welch and her team to make finding him their top priority.

Sitting back in her chair, she heard a familiar rap at the door, and Andersen walked in, much as she expected.

We are both a long way off from our South Boston origins.

Suddenly, Welch remembered she had not told Nine or Ice about Steve Andersen coming by. As expected, both men had their hands on their hips for a quick draw. She felt bad—all three men were startled for different reasons.

"Wow, guys! Same team!" he said, hands raised to show he was unarmed. Both men appeared to relax once they saw it was him... and he was not armed.

Welch shook her head. *I'm positive I told them he was going to knock and come in,* she thought.

"So what's the deal?" she asked as she tried to put her swollen feet back in her shoes.

"About Burns getting by everyone," he started, "Jesus! Cratty and Ramsey are still in the process of ripping someone a new one! Cratty also sent Dillon back to assist Helms's team in finding Daniels," he replied.

Welch shook her head to clarify the issue.

"No, not Burns. What did Helms tell you? Was my intelligence right?" She noticed that Andersen took a moment to answer while he stared at the floor.

Oh, oh. He's delaying and looking away...

She had known him since childhood and that was his "tell" that it was bad news. Deciding to go barefoot, Welch noticed Nine and Ice were now paying attention to the conversation and yet they were looking at all the corners and vantage points at the same time.

"Helms thinks you're right," Andersen said simply. He then decided to articulate a bit more.

"His team has picked up some chatter about something that is going to happen in the summer. He has the 'usual people' working the angles on it, and he and Janeson are positive that your information along with theirs indicates that Eric Daniels plans on getting back at Burns. Finding his apartment in Houston was a gift but nothing yet from the computers there. Apparently, though, there is a treasure trove of data for the behavioral specialists."

Welch shook her head.

"What did they find?"

"Books. Lots of books. Different fields and art. History, literature, art. The guy is complex," he summed up.

Great. Just like Burns—complex. Just great.

Andersen then jumped to the critical point.

"The weakest link or best bait is David, Emma and Becky in Spain, and Emma's half-sister in Boston."

Frowning, Welch found herself opening and closing her fist as she started to pace a bit herself.

"Shit. I hate it when I'm right," Welch said.

The discovery that Emma had a half-sister was based on good old-fashioned detective work. The man who had killed Tony Littleton, Emma's biological father, had another daughter with another woman prior to her birth. When it became evident that Daniels was still "active," all possible scenarios were played out to see how someone like him would strike. For Welch, it was easy—capture the weakest links to lure Burns out. The question for her was a moral dilemma—let Daniels make his move so they could find him, or let the families know the danger and relocate them both.

If it were me, what would I want? She immediately thought of Joe. *What would he say if he were alive?*

"Yeah. I think we need to let Cratty and her team know as well as David and Becky. What do you think?" Andersen asked.

It took her a second of eye contact with her former snipers to answer.

"Absolutely. Will Helms warn the girl's grandfather, John Murphy?" she asked.

"Helms already did. The guy was surprised that we knew about the relationship between his granddaughter and Emma. But he made it clear that he wanted to make sure the kids were protected. I think this guy will be a formidable ally."

Funny. Now I'm looking to the Boston mob for assistance. This is going to be interesting.

Welch took a moment to answer.

"I hope so, Steve. This Daniels guy was the force behind the Foreign Intelligence Agency and the force behind men like Webber. He's the guy who killed my men along with the innocents. He needs to pay. But he is going to be a tough bastard to find, let alone catch."

Andersen remained sitting while Welch continued her pacing out of nervousness and a way to get circulation going in her legs. As Welch stopped in front of the bar for water, Andersen vaulted the next question.

"So when do we tell Burns?" Andersen asked.

She had an easy answer for that.

"We'll tell Cratty and his family tomorrow. We need more data before we call him in. Daniels won't go for Burns directly. He wants more from Burns. But I bet Burns already knows this, and that's why he's stateside and was highly visible in his return. He made it easy for anyone interested to track him."

Andersen's face gave a puzzled expression.

Welch answered the unasked question.

"This guy Daniels not only wants Burns to pay, but he wants him to suffer. He'll go for the weakest link. Burns knows this, and that's why he's making it easier for him to find him and that will keep him away from Emma."

Turning from Andersen, Welch walked toward her two men who stood at attention as she approached and then reached over the table to take a bottle of Scotch and four tumblers to drink.

"Well, men, looks like we have a new mission. Time to find the puppet master behind Webber. Oorah?"

"Oorah!" both men responded.

As she finished pouring the drinks, she handed them out for consumption. Without hesitation, Welch and her men finished their shot in one gulp as Andersen first took a sip and decided to nurse his instead. Shaking her head at Andersen, she smiled as she poured another shot for herself and her men. After all these years of not serving together, Welch still thought of Ice and Nine as "her men."

"Marines... and to think I brought you to the team," Andersen said in disbelief as he carefully took another sip of his drink.

"Come on, Steve. You know us Marines. When we find out we haven't completed the mission, we always go back. We don't like loose ends. And Eric Daniels is one big loose end."

Welch raised her glass to salute.

To those we left behind in the Swat Valley."

All raised their glasses and drank.

As the alcohol's warmth settled in her throat, she put her glass down and stretched her fingers.

"So, was it your dad who convinced you to join the Marines or what?" Andersen asked.

Welch smiled. *Fact is stranger than fiction*, she thought.

"No. It was the nuns. They're the toughest women I know. I knew I couldn't keep a vow of celibacy, so I went for the next best thing."

She watched as Andersen shook his head. Feeling pressed for time and a sudden sense of urgency, she put her glass down and pulled out color-coded files of papers she had under the bar.

"Okay, gentlemen. Let me show you what I would do if I were Daniels," she said. She quickly sifted through a small stack of folders and started handing out the same color files to each of them. There were at least seven different colored sets of folders.

If it weren't for children's lives on the line, I would say it was nice to be back in the field again. We gotta win this one.

Welch heard Andersen take in a deep breath and then release with the question everyone was wondering.

"Where are you, Daniels?"

List of Characters

Alexander J. Burns – aka "**Falcon**." First seen in *Albatross,* Burns survives a helicopter crash while en route to a black-ops mission to kill the terrorist leader, Oman Sharif Sudani. Brain injured, he gets treatment that helps him regain his memory and realizes he is a logistics field operative for the Foreign Intelligence Agency, FIA.

Samantha Littleton – aka "**Raven**." She is the first to find Burns being sedated in the hospital and facilitates his transfer to an outside psychologist who specializes in assisting trauma victims regain their memories.

Dr. David Caulfield – aka "**Samuel Coleridge**." He is the psychologist who treats Burns and helps him regain his memories. He is also the one who convinces his friends to take the fight to the Eric Daniels's organization, the FIA.

Eric I. Daniels – aka "**Eagle**." Mentioned in *Albatross,* first seen in *Raven*, and fully elaborated on in *Eagle,* he is the Chairman of the FIA, a privately held, clandestine, intelligence agency that will work on behalf of the United States government when it aligns with its own interests and objectives.

Becky Littleton – aka "**Tiny**." Introduced in *Albatross* as Samantha's older foster sister as well as Emma Littleton's primary caretaker after her brother, Tony, is killed by the mob. In *Raven*, her lethal skills grow exponentially.

Steve Andersen – Lieutenant, North Reading Police Department, MA, is the first to interview Dr. Caulfield, aka "Samuel Coleridge" in *Albatross*. Additionally, he was on the team of Army Intelligence at Guantanamo that connected the dots to locate Oman Sharif Sudani. He is also best friends with Diane Welch, who grew up in the same South Boston neighborhood.

John Helms – FBI Director, Boston Regional Office, he is the first to detect the diversions and covert plan in *Albatross*, as well as attempting a negotiation for peace with Burns in *Raven*. He was also Diane Welch's CO briefly in Afghanistan.

Diane Welch – Commandant, Massachusetts State Troopers, first at the end of *Albatross* as Steve Andersen's close friend. She is mentioned by Burns as a person of interest, a key player targeted for deceiving if she had been around during the crisis.

Thomas "Steel" Webber – First seen in *Albatross* as the "face" of the FIA and Eric Daniels' top man. He's the director of the agency and was the team leader responsible for keeping Burns sedated and monitored.

Jillian T. Davis – aka **"Cougar."** First seen in *Albatross*, she is an off-duty manager of the FIA's Operations Center who is recruited to courier top secret, external hard drives to a secure location.

Denise Cratty – Introduced in *Albatross*, she is the on-duty manager of the FIA's Operations Center when it is compromised.

Emma Littleton – Introduced as a baby in *Albatross*, she is under the care of Becky Littleton and David Caulfield. Becky's brother, Tony, was Emma's original caretaker before he was killed.

About the Author

In addition to creating the *Birds of Flight* series and the other award-winning science fiction stories, *Future Prometheus* and *Intelligent Design*, Erickson holds a BA in psychology and sociology from Boston College and a master's degree in psychiatric social work from the Simmons School of Social Work. Certified in cognitive behavioral treatment and a post-trauma specialist, he is also a senior instructor of psychology and counseling at Cambridge College, visiting lecturer at Salem State University's School of Social Work and a senior therapist in a clinical group practice in the Merrimack Valley, Massachusetts. To learn more about the author, his writing and future projects, please look at the following websites:

Blog - https://www.jmeindieblog.com
Author's website – https://www.jmericksonindiewriter.com
Publisher's website - https://www.jmericksonindiewriter.net

CPSIA information can be obtained
at www.ICGtesting.com
Printed in the USA
LVOW03s1515230218
567696LV00001B/114/P